SINS OF A KING

SINS Series Book 1

EMMA SLATE

Tabula Rasa Publishing

Prologue

There's a beast inside all of us. Most people never know it's there. It lies dormant, buried deep in the cavern of the psyche.

They are the lucky ones.

But some are born with the beast unfettered, and there's no chaining or muzzling its slathering, snapping jaws.

In them, it reigns.

My once quiet beast has emerged.

It wants blood, desires destruction and vengeance.

For me, there's no going back.

Chapter 1

The hostess looked up from her computer screen, glossy blond hair styled in a trendy side bun I never could've pulled off. The svelte woman looked me over in that quick way that told me she was judging everything about me, but her smile was polite.

I knew she wouldn't find fault in my appearance. My auburn hair fell in lush waves down past my shoulders, and I'd even worn contact lenses instead of my usual tortoiseshell glasses. My black pumps were three inches high, and though my onyx-colored dress was simple, it hugged my form in all the right places.

"May I help you?" she asked with just a hint of snootiness, which was inherently part of the Upper East Side.

"Has Andrew Schaefer checked in yet?" I asked.

"Yes, he checked in fifteen minutes ago. He's already at the table."

I trailed after her, maneuvering through the dimly lit French restaurant, noticing the pristine white tablecloths ironed to perfection, topped with delicate china and flanked by elegant silverware. The quiet hum of conversations was steady, but trailed off as we arrived to a more secluded area in the back of the restaurant. She pointed to my brother who sat at a table in the corner and then left.

Andrew stood as soon as he saw me, face devoid of emotion. I'd learned long ago not to expect any compliments from him.

My brother could be considered handsome; he was average height with a decent build, brown hair, and dark brown eyes. His overall personality left a lot to be desired. It apparently worked for him since he was a trader on Wall Street.

"You're late," he said, not bothering to pull out my chair for me.

"Department meeting ran long."

"I guess I should be glad you managed to change before dinner instead of coming here in work attire."

I let his acerbic, critical tone brush past me. We rarely saw one another despite the fact that we lived in the same city. We had separate lives, and I preferred it that way. So did he.

Usually.

He reached for his cocktail and took a healthy swallow, and before he even finished his drink, he snapped his fingers to gain the waiter's attention. When the server arrived, I shot him an apologetic look, but he was clearly used to attending to all sorts of people because he didn't even appear annoyed.

"I'll have another," Andrew said rudely, lifting his near-empty rocks glass.

"Absolutely," the veteran waiter replied. He glanced at me. "And for you, ma'am?"

"Water's fine, thanks."

"Get a drink," Andrew commanded.

Andrew was in a mood, so I asked for a glass of house red. Alcohol might grease the tension between us. It couldn't hurt.

After the server disappeared, I turned to my brother. "Should we just get on with it? You clearly don't want to be here, and I don't want to be here. Pull out the papers and I'll sign them."

"That's not why I wanted to have dinner."

I frowned. "But the only reason we ever see each other is because of—"

"I know that," Andrew snapped. "But if I told you the real reason why I wanted you here, you wouldn't have come."

He was correct—preservation of my self-esteem was important, so I went out of my way to avoid Andrew. I hated that he'd manipulated me. "So why am I here?"

"Business dinner with a potential client."

"Oh, let me guess; a fat, old Southern gentleman who likes young, pretty things. Which is why you were glad I changed before I came."

"Not Southern. Scottish. Flynn Campbell."

"Great, so now you want me to charm some gruff old Scotsman. I've had a long day, Andrew. I don't have the energy to be charming. So, if you'll excuse me—"

"You can't leave," Andrew said, standing. "Campbell's here."

I held in an annoyed sigh as I rose and turned my attention to the man striding toward us.

He wasn't old. Not in the least. Mid-thirties, if I had to guess. And unlike anyone I'd ever seen.

Flynn Campbell wasn't just tall—he was massive. He made the grown men he was walking past look small. He strode with purpose and confidence. The three-piece charcoal gray bespoke suit molded perfectly to his large form—it was nothing more than a polished veneer, like he deigned to wear it to appease society. His face wasn't classically handsome, but rugged, like the wild beauty of the craggy Highlands. Blue eyes a unique shade of cobalt sat above a sharp nose. His dark hair, almost a bit too long, was styled with product and swept off his face.

I'd never seen a man like him before. He was out of place

5

and time. He would've fit in with the stars from the Golden Age of Hollywood. Flynn Campbell could've held his own against a young Sean Connery or Clint Eastwood.

Campbell's gaze found and dismissed Andrew all in the span of a moment. When Campbell looked at me, my breath caught in my throat and my vision narrowed, shutting out everything except him and his beguiling blue eyes. Andrew introduced me, but it sounded like he was speaking from very far away. Flynn Campbell took my hand in his. He didn't bring it to his mouth, nor did he shake it while continuing to survey me. He just held it in his strong, warm grip.

"Ms. Schaefer." The man's voice *rumbled*. He had a low, intoxicating brogue, which I found pleasing to the ear.

"Please, call me Barrett, Mr. Campbell."

"Flynn," he corrected.

"Flynn," I said, trying out his name. I liked the feel of it on my tongue, like heady scotch.

The return of the waiter with our drinks forced me to break my gaze from Flynn's. I suddenly needed to inhale a deep breath, take a minute, and regain my wits. Flynn helped me with my chair and then took the seat next to me, so I was barricaded on both sides.

"Sir, may I get you a drink?" the waiter asked Flynn.

Without taking his eyes off me, Flynn answered, "Balvenie DoubleWood 17 year. Neat. Thank you."

I smiled without thought.

Flynn's cobalt-blue eyes gleamed. "My drink order amuses you?"

"No. I'm wishing I ordered that instead." My own glass of red wine sat untouched, and I didn't want it anymore. I wanted potent.

"You can share mine," Flynn said, his voice deep and sensual.

The waiter returned almost immediately and set down Flynn's glass of scotch in front of him. Flynn lifted the glass in his large hand, bringing it to his mouth. He savored it a moment before holding the glass out to me. Our fingers brushed as I took it from him. Smooth, elegant flavors lingered on my tongue. I swallowed.

Andrew cleared his throat as if to remind us he was there. It was necessary. I hadn't been able to focus on anything since Flynn Campbell had approached the table. I never believed in instant chemical attraction.

Until now.

My skin felt warm all over, like I was baking from the inside out.

"Your brother told me you're a Scottish historian," Flynn said.

I nodded. "Sixteenth century. Mary Queen of Scots specifically."

"My sister can tell you anything you want to know about Mary's ladies-in-waiting," Andrew interjected.

Flynn shot Andrew a look, and my brother nearly quivered. I frowned.

Was my brother *afraid* of Flynn?

Giving the Scotsman back his glass, I pushed away from the table. In a show of old-world gentlemanly manners, Flynn stood when I did.

"If you'll excuse me for a moment. I need to find the ladies' room."

I didn't have to use the restroom, but I wanted a moment to get myself together. Thankfully, the bathroom was empty, and I was grateful for the privacy. Setting my clutch down on the counter, I forced myself to look in the mirror. My cheeks were flushed, and my heart was thundering in my chest like a herd of wild horses. I washed my clammy hands and dried them before leaving the safety of the bathroom.

As I made my way back to the table, I heard Flynn and Andrew speaking in low voices. Something about their conversation made me pause, so I hid behind a massive potted plant, shamelessly eavesdropping.

"She can help you track your ancestry," Andrew volunteered.

"I already know my ancestry."

"You can find a use for her."

There was a pause. "You didn't mention she was beautiful," Flynn said.

"Does that mean you're willing to—"

"She has no idea why she's here, does she?"

"No, she doesn't. Does that change anything?"

"No. It doesn't," Flynn replied.

"So, do we have a deal?" Andrew asked impatiently.

"Aye. We have a deal."

Chapter 2

I frowned, not understanding the nature of their conversation. Knowing I couldn't keep hiding behind the potted plant, I made my presence known by returning to the table. I looked at my brother whose face was flushed, a picture of guilt.

"What's going on?" I ventured to ask.

"You should sit," Andrew said.

His tone and command made me balk. "What am I really doing here, Andrew? This isn't about helping you woo a new client, is it?"

Andrew's gaze dropped to the white tablecloth, but he wouldn't answer me, so I looked at Flynn Campbell. For some reason, I trusted him to give me an honest answer. His stare was unwavering.

I slowly sank down into my chair. And waited.

Flynn looked at Andrew in disgust. "I'm not doing this with you here. She deserves more. More from you."

Andrew tossed back the last of his drink and stood from the table. "I'm sorry, Barrett," he muttered before he left me alone with Flynn.

"What's going on?" I repeated.

Flynn's face was hard, unyielding. "We're getting out of

here." Standing up, he reached into his trouser pocket for his wallet. He threw down some bills, more than enough to cover the drinks, grabbed my hand, and tugged me out of my seat. He barreled through the restaurant, servers jumping out of his way since it didn't appear as if he was going to stop. I could barely keep up with his long strides, but something told me not to ask him to slow down.

When we got out of the restaurant, Flynn ushered me toward an idling black Rolls-Royce. I swallowed nervously, suddenly aware that Flynn possessed an obscene amount of wealth.

"Get in," he commanded, opening the passenger door for me.

Despite our palpable chemistry, Flynn was a stranger. And I hesitated.

"Barrett," he rumbled.

"I don't even know you," I hissed, mindful of the many pedestrians on the sidewalk. But this was New York, and even if I screamed, I doubted anyone would come to my aid.

Flynn reached up to cup the back of my neck, getting low and close to my face. "Get in," he said again. It was still a command, but his voice had softened, and it made me shiver despite the warmth of the summer night.

I climbed inside the luxurious car and Flynn followed, scooting close, so his trouser-clad leg brushed my black dress. He shut the door and said to the driver, "To The Rex."

"The hotel?" I asked.

Flynn nodded.

"Is that where you're staying while you're in town?"

A glimmer of amusement flashed in his eyes. "I own The Rex."

My head spun with the knowledge that Flynn Campbell owned one of the most elite and expensive hotels in the city.

"You're not a businessman in from Scotland?" I asked with a frown.

"Is that what your brother told you?"

"Well, no. But he let me think you were a potential new client. He asked me to come along because——"

"You're beautiful and you know your Scottish history. He thought that would mean something to me."

I nodded and Flynn barked out a laugh. "Ah, hen, your brother is a manipulative bastard."

Ignoring his statement, I turned my head to look out the window. Manhattan sped by, but I saw none of the glittering excitement that belonged to the city.

"You don't get along with your brother, do you?" he asked.

I shook my head but still refused to look at him.

"Then why did you come to dinner tonight? Why do him such a favor?"

"I don't want to talk about it."

"I do."

I didn't want to tell Flynn I'd fallen for my brother's calculating tricks. "It's none of your business," I bristled.

Another crack of laughter, but he said nothing, and we fell into silence.

The Rex Hotel was on 79th and 5th across from Central Park. Because we were already on the Upper East Side and traffic was surprisingly minimal, it took almost no time to get there.

The car pulled up to the curb and Flynn got out first, offering me a hand. I hesitated only a moment, knowing there was no way out of whatever I had landed in.

Flynn escorted me into his hotel. When we were inside, he pulled me closer, his palm riding the small of my back. I felt the warmth of him through my dress and had to stop myself from moving closer. As we walked through the lobby, my breath caught in the back of my throat. The decor was all dark wood, brass accents, and sensual lighting. Very old world. I was hit with a wave of nostalgia for a time I'd never known.

"Oh." I let out a breath. I looked around before my gaze landed on Flynn.

He stared down at me and waited, his blue eyes intense.

"It's beautiful," I said.

"You've never been here before?"

I shook my head. We passed by the row of elevators, and I almost asked where we were going when Flynn rounded the corner.

"Private elevator," he explained.

The elevator was similar in decor to the lobby, but the floor was a plush red brocade carpet instead of white marble. It should've been cheesy, but it wasn't. Instead, it reeked of class and money. Flynn inserted his key and pushed the PH button. He didn't reach for my hand again, but he stood close enough that his suit jacket brushed my arm.

The doors opened, revealing a vast suite with large glass windows and white walls. The sitting room was complete with a bar and an expensive gray L-shaped couch facing the dark-wood entertainment center, and the kitchen was outfitted with all the newest stainless-steel appliances.

I marveled at the decadence. "Do you live here?"

He nodded, walking toward the bar. Without looking at me, he asked, "Drink?"

"Will I need it?"

"Aye."

Instead of being afraid of the truth, I was suddenly grateful for Flynn's candor.

"Scotch."

I watched a smile flit across his face as he fixed us two glasses of scotch. He stalked toward me like a sleek predator, handing me my drink. We clinked our glasses together.

"*Slàinte mhath*," I murmured and took a healthy swallow.

Flynn's eyes gleamed with something I couldn't discern. Approval, maybe?

He gestured to the couch, and I took a seat. Flynn sat in

the chair that faced me. Leaning forward, he stared into his drink and then finally lifted his gaze to meet mine.

"Your brother has gotten himself into some trouble," he began.

"What kind of trouble?"

"Three hundred thousand dollars' worth of trouble."

I inhaled sharply. "He owes you money?" I guessed.

"Aye."

"How? Were you in business together?"

"No."

"Then I don't understand. How can he owe you so much money?"

"It's not important."

"It's not? It's not like you guys had a friendly bet on a football game. That is some serious cash."

He sighed. "Finish your drink."

"But I don't want—"

"Finish it," he commanded, his voice low.

I did as bid, setting the empty glass down on the table. We'd never gotten around to dinner, and a warm ball of liquor resided deep in my belly.

"Your brother made me an offer," Flynn said. "Your services in lieu of the debt."

I blinked. "Sorry. The scotch must be doing something to my brain. Services?"

His jaw clenched and he nodded.

"What kind of services?" I demanded, suddenly understanding what I'd overheard at the restaurant. "You're not interested in my history knowledge, are you?"

I stood up and began to pace across the living room floor. I whirled on Flynn, who had stood too, but was watching me with an indiscernible look on his face.

"You agreed," I said in realization. "At the restaurant. Andrew asked if you guys had a deal." My eyes narrowed. "What kind of man agrees to that sort of thing?"

In two quick strides, Flynn was in front of me, looming and fierce. "You don't know anything about me."

"So what is this? I work off my brother's debt in the bedroom? Is that what you were hoping? Keep me chained and bound and—"

Flynn gripped my upper arms, dragging me close to him so we were nearly nose-to-nose despite the fact that he was several inches taller than me. "If I wanted a woman, I wouldn't have to pay for it."

"Then what could you possibly want me for?" I asked, still in shock.

Flynn released me, setting me back down on the floor. I nearly stumbled in my heels, but I caught myself.

He gestured to the couch. "Sit down. And I'll explain."

Chapter 3

Flynn went to the bar to refill my glass.

I pinched the bridge of my nose. "I need food if we're going to keep drinking this way."

"What do you want?" Flynn asked, setting my glass down on the coffee table before picking up the receiver of the hotel phone.

"Red meat. Medium rare, please."

A small smile appeared on Flynn's generous lips. He ordered two steaks and baked potatoes. I should've known he was a meat and potatoes guy.

He settled back down in his chair and looked at me. "Tell me about your relationship with your brother. Clearly there's no love lost between you two."

I stiffened. It still burned—Andrew had bartered me like I was an animal to be sold. "Andrew's my half-brother," I said, not bothering to disguise the bitterness I felt. "Same father, different mother. He's a decade older and he was never nice to me. Ever. Even when I was little. Then my parents died in a car accident, and Andrew became my guardian."

"Why?" he asked. "Was there no one else you could've lived with?"

"No one else," I said with a nod. "There was also a stipulation in Dad's will. Andrew had to take care of me, or he wouldn't get his inheritance. Dad's idea of trying to keep the family together. There was money for me to go to college and higher education, so I never really understood why Andrew resented me so much. It's not like he wanted for anything either."

"Why did you come to dinner tonight?" he asked.

"He told me there were some papers I had to sign. Family estate stuff. I wouldn't have come otherwise, and he knew it."

"Family is not always made by blood," Flynn said. "As far as I can tell, that's all you and your brother share."

I took another long drink of the potent amber liquid, wanting it to wash away my anger at Andrew. It was one thing to get himself into trouble—but to barter me? What a selfish prick.

"So," I said, "now you know all about me."

"Hardly," Flynn replied. "But I know enough."

"Will you explain to me what role I have in all of this—if not to be your…what? Sex slave? Mistress?" I laughed. "Mistress. Are they still called that?"

His lips quirked in amusement. "You wouldn't want to be my mistress?"

Tipsy on scotch, I felt bold as I replied, "The idea doesn't repulse me, if that's what you're getting at."

"Then why the big show of being offended by the prospect?"

"Because no one asked me."

"Barrett, do you want to be my mistress?"

"No."

"Why not?"

"Because I don't even know you."

"So you need to know me before you sleep with me?"

"No," I huffed in annoyance. "I'm not a commodity to be traded."

"That was your brother's doing. Not mine."

"Still—"

"I'm not going to argue semantics with you. Nor am I going to coerce you into something you don't want to do."

The elevator doors dinged and opened. Our dinner arrived on a cart, pushed by a male hotel attendant. He quickly set the table in the kitchen and then left.

My stomach rumbled in anticipation, and then I got a whiff of the delicious scent of cooked meat. Flynn helped me with my chair, the heat of him at my back. I had the insane urge to press myself against the wall of his chest and let his hands slide over me.

I set the glass of scotch aside.

Flynn took his seat across the table and placed his white linen napkin in his lap. I picked up my silverware and cut into the steak. It nearly slid apart of its own free will, and I closed my eyes while I savored it.

"Good?" Flynn asked, his voice gruff.

My eyes flew open. He watched me with an unnatural stillness, a look of sheer intensity on his angular face. He was as old-world as his hotel, I realized. A man who didn't belong in the time period he'd been born.

"Good," I rasped.

We ate a few moments in silence but Flynn finally spoke, bringing us back to the matter at hand. "You wanted to know why you're here."

I nodded for him to continue.

"What I'm about to say has to stay between us. Understand?"

I nodded again.

"There's a burlesque club attached to The Rex. Did you know that?"

"No."

"Someone is selling drugs in the club. I know it's an employee, but I haven't been able to discover who."

"Okay, but I don't under——"

"I want you to work in my club."

"As what?" I demanded. "I'm not a dancer."

"Cocktail waitress. It's a simple proposition, Barrett. Help me find out who's selling drugs, your brother's debt is cleared, and then you can go back to your life."

"But I have a job!"

"You'll have to take a leave of absence." He spoke like working for him was already a foregone conclusion.

I sputtered, but he paid no attention as he continued talking.

"Terms are as follows: you work for me for a year or until you find out. Whatever comes first."

"A year! How am I supposed to pay rent, bills?"

Flynn leaned back in his chair and smiled. "Do you know how much my cocktail waitresses make on any given night?"

I shook my head.

"On average, they pull in five hundred dollars."

My head spun. "Five hundred dollars?"

"Aye." He leaned forward. "I need someone undercover more than I need a bed partner, but I intend to make back the money I lost, Barrett. It's your choice how I get it."

"You got me drunk," I murmured, my eyes drooping closed. I tried to keep them open, but they were adamant about shutting.

"Aye," he said, sounding amused.

"Why?"

"Because you looked like you needed it."

"Oh," I breathed, falling onto my side on the expensive, plush, very comfortable couch. "Are my shoes still on my feet?" He laughed softly, and I felt my heels being pulled off.

"I should go home," I said even as I snuggled into the couch pillow.

Flynn tossed a blanket over me, and then his hand stroked my hair. "We're not done talking, Barrett."

"Not tonight, honey. I have a headache," I said and then passed out.

I woke up when light crept through the drapes of the living room windows, my face pressed into a couch pillow, and just a tad hungover. The night before came flooding back, and I remembered I wasn't in my own apartment. My eyes were gritty which meant I had fallen asleep with my contacts in. I had a feeling that last night's makeup was smudged and smeared all over my face and—yep—all over Flynn Campbell's gray couch pillow.

I grimaced, throwing off the blanket and looking around. Flynn was nowhere to be seen, and I wondered if I could sneak out without him knowing. I knew it was childish, but I needed time to think. I'd passed out in my boss's penthouse suite. I shook my head, trying to clear all the confusion—and anger. He wasn't my boss. Was he?

Damn scotch-head.

I stood up and picked up my heels, not even attempting to shove my feet into the tight leather. Before I could make the decision to leave, the bedroom door opened, and Flynn strolled out, his dark hair damp from a shower. He looked perfect and sexy in a pair of black slacks and a blue button-down—and he didn't look hungover at all.

"Good morning," he greeted, his voice low and raspy. Alert.

"Morning," I muttered, suddenly aware that I didn't look my best.

"How are you feeling?"

"Parched," I admitted.

He smiled, and it did something to me. Maybe it was the scotch hangover. I hoped.

Flynn went to the refrigerator, pulled out a bottle of water, and brought it to me. "Breakfast is on the way."

"Oh, thanks but I—"

"We'll have some breakfast." His tone left no room for an argument.

"Okay," I answered weakly. "Mind if I freshen up?"

"Sure. There's a spare toothbrush by the sink."

I raised an eyebrow. "Do this a lot, do you?"

He merely smiled. "I live in a hotel. Spares are easy to come by."

Holding in my grumbling, I set my heels down by the couch and went to Flynn's bedroom. The bed was king-sized with red sheets and charcoal accents. It was all dark-wood furniture and utterly masculine. The bathroom had a glass shower, big enough for two, and a separate tub. I glanced at myself in the mirror and nearly blanched. My mascara had painted rings around my bloodshot hazel eyes, and my auburn hair was a tangled mess.

God, I looked awful.

By the time I washed my face, brushed my teeth, and managed to tame my hair, I was feeling a bit better, but I needed coffee. Breakfast had arrived and Flynn was sitting at the kitchen table, reading the paper and sipping on a glass of orange juice.

"Hi," I said.

He turned his head and smiled. "What would you like? Pancakes? Eggs? I ordered it all."

"I think a waffle—and some coffee, please."

"Have a seat," he said and got up to fix me a plate.

I sank into a chair. Feeling bold and in desperate need of caffeine, I reached across the table and grabbed Flynn's mug. I was sipping on it when Flynn came back with a plate stacked with two waffles.

"Is that my cup?" he asked in amusement.

"It is. Me without coffee is like the world without the sun."

"By all means, then," Flynn said, taking his seat.

We were silent as we ate. It was shockingly comfortable, despite all that I'd learned the night before. In the light of day, my anger at my brother came rushing back.

"Feeling better?" Flynn asked when I pushed away my empty plate.

"I'll live," I replied.

"Glad to hear it. You ready to discuss your job—more in depth?"

"What if I say no," I said. "What if I want nothing to do with this and leave it between you and Andrew?"

"Forget your brother for a moment. Forget he had anything to do with this. I'm asking you for your help. Plain and simple."

"Why can't you hire someone to go undercover for you?"

"Do you ever get a feeling about certain people?" he asked, leaning back in his chair.

"I guess."

"Well, then, believe me when I say I have a feeling about you. It's not just about hiring someone—it's about that someone being able to get close to people. I think you can do it."

What could I say? Flynn believed in me and for some reason, I wanted to help him. But that would mean taking a leave of absence from a job I loved—and there was no guarantee that it would be waiting for me when this mess was figured out. And what if I couldn't find the person selling drugs?

My brother's actions had brought me here. I'd been sucker punched. He wouldn't ever love me the way a brother was supposed to. Flynn had it right when it came to family. Blood didn't make family. Loyalty did, and Andrew had shown me none of that.

Flynn reached for my hand that rested on the table and held it. To my consternation, tears pricked my eyes. Flynn

Campbell had shown me nothing but kindness and understanding. Whatever else brewed between us, I needed to remember this moment.

Once my emotions were under control, Flynn released my hand and asked, "Well? What do you say? Will you help me?"

I nodded. Flynn smiled, a look of relief washing over his face, and then he got down to the business of discussing the intricacies of the job.

"You'll have to come to the club one night this week so you can get a sense of it, the attire, how things work."

"The attire?"

He smiled. "The club is modeled after an old speakeasy. Very 1920s."

I leaned back in my chair. "I get to wear a costume?"

"Excited?"

"I am."

"You sound like you almost want to work in my club," he teased.

Rolling my eyes at him, I smiled. "I wouldn't go that far. So, you'll show me around the club and—"

"Actually, my manager, Lacey, will show you around the club."

I frowned. "Why can't you do it?"

"Because no one, aside from Lacey, can know of our history or why you're working for me. If people see us conversing and acting friendly, they won't trust you."

"Ah, I get it. So in public we have to pretend not to know each other."

"Correct. We'll meet once a week for updates, but it will be discreet and off the premises."

"I feel like I'm in a spy movie."

"This is serious, Barrett."

"I know," I said, sobering.

"A lot is at stake," he said, his voice hardening. "Don't let me down."

Chapter 4

The history department chair—and my boss—had been surprisingly understanding of my vague reasons for leaving. He told me to take all the time I needed and that my research job would be waiting for me whenever I decided to come back. It took me all of five seconds to realize that Flynn had made a call on my behalf. The man had some serious power. It was difficult to remember he was no hero—he had agreed to take me in form of monetary payment. But when he did things like cover me with a blanket, let me sleep on his couch, assured the job I loved would be waiting for me, it made me want to see the softer side of him more often.

The chemistry between us was insane and unlike anything I'd ever experienced. By unspoken agreement, we hadn't discussed it. I couldn't sleep with him. It would confuse the hell out of me, and I had enough to focus on. I needed to find out who was bringing drugs into Flynn's club and then I could get back to my life.

On the night I was shadowing a cocktail waitress, I entered the burlesque club through the street entrance. All the lights were on and I walked through the room, past the long wood bar and stools, toward the back where I was told the dressing room would be. Old-style gas lanterns lined the walls and were casting a bright glow. The tables by the stage were bare, devoid of tablecloths and candles. The club clearly wasn't set up for the night yet.

The dressing room was a large rectangle with full-length mirrors on one wall, opposite the hanging racks of costumes. There were six vanity mirrors, all well-lit with bright, big bulbs and taped names on the glass designating them to the dancers.

"Hello?" I called out.

A twiggy brunette somewhere in her mid to late thirties popped out from behind the clothes. She was already dressed for the evening in a black flapper style gown complete with fringe and headband, her makeup dramatic and flawless.

"Hi," she greeted, holding out her hand. "Barrett? I'm Lacey."

"Nice to meet you."

She studied me for a brief moment before she began riffling through the costumes until she found what she was looking for.

"Here," she said, pulling out a costume. It was all one piece. The top was strapless and red with a sweetheart neckline, a short flouncy black skirt, and the entire ensemble was sequined and sparkly. Matching black elbow length gloves and a small black hat completed the outfit.

"This is gorgeous," I said, taking the hanger from her.

"It is," Lacey said. "Try it on. If it doesn't fit, we'll get it altered. What size shoe do you wear?"

"Seven."

Lacey went to the rack of shoes next to the costumes and found my size. "The heel isn't too high, so they should be comfortable to work in. Comfortable-ish, anyway."

"Thanks." I hid behind the rack of costumes and changed, putting on the stockings and garter belt. Everything seemed to fit, and I stepped out so Lacey could judge me.

"Turn," she said.

I did.

She fiddled with some of the fabric around my middle, tugging here and there, but she nodded. "Looks good. Let's do your hair and makeup, and then you can see the final effect. I'll show you how to do it so you can manage on your own next time."

An hour later, I had on more makeup than I'd ever worn in my life, and my long hair was sleek and tamed into waves and curls, the hat perched at an angle on my head.

"You'll do," Lacey said with a grin.

"I look like a cigar girl." I marveled at my reflection, turning my head from side to side so I could take it all in. My hazel eyes looked big and more green than brown due to the shade of eyeshadow. I blinked, loving that my lacquered lashes wouldn't hit glasses—I'd worn contacts. A smiling red, sinful mouth finished the picture.

"Follow me," Lacey said with a knowing grin of her own. "Let me show you around the club."

We left the changing room and went out onto the floor. The orchestra pit was directly in front of the stage and looked like it could hold at least a fifteen-piece band.

"The Rex has live music every night," she explained. "But we keep it small unless there's a special occasion. A four-piece jazz band is usual, but sometimes we add a piano player to round it out."

The bare tables were set up around the dance floor, ready and waiting for the evening's guests. Three C-shaped booths were directly across from the bar and were farther away from the stage.

"The middle booth is Mr. Campbell's," she explained. "It remains empty unless he visits the club. He comes in a few nights a week to keep an eye on things. His drink is Balvenie DoubleWood 17 year, neat. If you work his section, and he sits in his booth, you bring him a drink without asking. You call him Mr. Campbell, and you don't flirt with him."

"Is that a general rule?" I ventured to ask. "No flirting with the boss?"

The two-inch heels I wore put me at five foot seven, but Lacey was a graceful tower looming over me. All good humor was gone from her face.

"I'm aware of your situation because Mr. Campbell confides in me. I have his trust. You don't. Not yet. You prove to him that you can play the part of a cocktail waitress, befriend the staff, and find out what's going on, you'll have his trust. We all play our parts here, Barrett. Can you play yours?"

I inhaled a shaky breath and nodded.

"Good. I'm about to unload a lot of information on you, so try to keep up."

"Repeat them back to me," Jake, the hot bartender said. He was dressed in a red vest, skinny black tie, and a white button-down, and his face had a few days' worth of stubble. His dark hair was artfully mussed—the whole package worked for him.

Dutifully, I recited the list of wines on the menu, wondering how I was going to do this job. Historical facts stuck in my brain with ease. But this? I was out of my element.

"You're gonna be fine," Jake assured me.

"How do you know?"

Jake leaned over the service station where he'd later set the fancy cocktails the club served. "This is the kind of place where a smile and a little flirting go a long way."

"Are old men going to grope me?" I demanded. "Because I will not work in a place where—"

"No. That's not what I meant. I'm just saying, the people that come here, they come here for a good time. A show, live music, to eat and drink. It's pure entertainment, that's what we sell."

"How long have you worked here?" I asked.

"Five years."

"Long time."

"It's a good place. Mr. Campbell's a good boss. Have you met Mr. Campbell yet?"

I shook my head, feeling a twinge of guilt for lying. "Lacey hired me. What's Mr. Campbell like?" It was easy to pretend I was curious about him because I *was* curious.

"Intense. Sees everything. Fair. Pays well. Popular with the ladies."

I rolled my eyes. "What about you? Are you popular with the ladies?"

"Is that your way of asking me out?"

"Are coworkers even allowed to date or is there a no fraternization policy?" I should've asked Lacey, but I hadn't been thinking about it. Jake might be a way in, but could I really sleep with someone for an exchange of information over pillow talk?

I needed to lay off the mob shows.

Jake grinned. "I'm engaged."

"So this conversation is a moot point, huh?"

"Guess so."

"Well, I hope I get to meet your fiancée."

"Let me introduce her," he said. "Alia!"

I looked to the entrance and watched a tall gorgeous woman of Asian descent stroll toward us. She leaned across the bar and pecked Jake on the lips and then gazed at me.

"This is Barrett. She's the new waitress. Barrett, my fiancée and the best burlesque dancer at The Rex, Alia."

"You're biased," Alia said. "But he's right. I am the best."

I laughed. "Nice to meet you."

"And you. First night, huh?"

"Yeah, I'm just getting the lay of the land."

"Well, you already look the part. Why don't you come

27

hang out with us in the changing room? Meet some of the others that are working tonight."

My smile was genuine. "I'd like that."

"Here's your drink, Mr. Campbell," Chelsea simpered with an obscene amount of respect.

It took all of my willpower not to roll my eyes. I'd been following Chelsea all evening, learning the flow of the club. She was sweet, young, and a flirt. It worked for her since she'd already made a little over two hundred dollars, and it wasn't even close to midnight yet.

"Thank you, Chelsea," Flynn said, his brogue downright sinful. Maybe it was the atmosphere, maybe it was just him. Either way, it sent a delightful shiver up and down my spine.

Flynn looked at me. "Ah, you must be the new waitress."

"Barrett," I introduced, offering my hand, feeling stupid that we had to pretend not to know one another.

He shook my hand and dropped it far too quickly. "Welcome to The Rex." He turned his attention back to the stage, clearly dismissing us.

For some reason it irked. But there was no time to worry about it because Chelsea was moving away toward another table, and I had to go with her. I forced myself not to look behind me to see if he stared after me. I shouldn't care. But I'd seen the raw hunger on his face when we'd met. I'd take it any day over the mask of indifference—even if it scared the hell out of me.

"See? Not much to it," Chelsea said, a little after midnight as she counted her tips. Because she was the early shift, she got to leave sooner. The others would have to stay closer to two.

"How many nights a week do you work?" I asked her.

"Three. Sometimes four."

"You must pull in a good amount," I said.

She nodded. "I would work more, but I'm also taking a full class load."

"How do you stay awake?" I wondered.

"Coffee," she said with a smile. "Lots and lots of coffee."

"Is the staff close?" Though I'd hung out in the dressing room and met people, it seemed the dancers stuck with the dancers and the cocktail waitresses stuck with the cocktail waitresses.

"Close enough."

"Hmmm. Do the cocktail waitresses ever dance?"

"Nope. Cocktail waitresses bring the drinks. The dancers dance."

"Shame, I think it would be fun. To dance."

"Eh, it is the way it is," Chelsea said, completely disregarding me. "See ya tomorrow."

Chapter 5

My cell phone rang, jarring me out of a sound sleep. Grumbling, I rolled over, trying to find the odious device. Barely cracking my eyelids, I answered the phone and growled, "Hello?"

"Were you asleep?" came Flynn's deep voice.

"Yes."

"It's noon."

All week my hours at the club had been closing shifts, meaning I didn't get home until close to three a.m. I wasn't used to being on my feet, in heels, and my body was taking a severe beating.

"Today is my day off. Why are you bugging me?" I demanded. The man had been into the club a handful of times while I'd been working and had ignored me except for a few polite hellos.

Flynn let out a soft chuckle. "I wanted to buy you lunch."

"I'm busy."

"I also wanted to hear about your first week of work."

"I'm still busy."

He chuckled again. "I'm downstairs."

"Are you sitting in your car?"

"No, I'm waiting to be buzzed in."

"You're not going to give up, are you?"

"No."

I hung up on him. Sighing, I stumbled to the buzzer. I looked around my prewar apartment and realized there was no hope for it. It was cluttered and a bit messy. Clothes littered the short hallway, the sink was full of dishes, and there were far too many Chinese takeout containers in the garbage.

The aroma of warm coffee swirled in the air as a knock sounded at my door.

"Who is it?" I asked.

"Sean Connery."

I smiled at Flynn's flirty, teasing mood. I opened the door and gestured for him to come in, trying to be inconspicuous about checking him out. Jeans and a plain white T-shirt—though knowing Flynn—the tee was probably custom made and very expensive.

"You're looking casual," I said by way of greeting.

"So are you." His eyes drifted down my body, heating with each inch.

Whoops.

I was in a gray V-neck that barely covered the tops of my thighs. No pants.

"Help yourself to some coffee," I muttered, feeling my face heat as I staggered in the direction of my bedroom. After I pulled on a pair of pajama shorts, I came back to the kitchen. Flynn had made himself comfortable at the tiny table that sat only two, a cup of coffee in front of him.

"I like how you look in the morning," he said with a smile.

"What? Glasses, tangled hair, and morning breath?"

"I meant you in a threadbare shirt and no bra."

I poured myself a cup of black coffee, sat down across from him, and purposefully crossed my arms over my chest. "A boss shouldn't mention his employee's lack of bra."

"I'm not your boss."

"What are you?"

"I'm not sure there's a word for it." He took a sip of coffee. "This is terrible."

"Well, you don't have to drink it," I pointed out. "And I like it. Besides, you're spoiled—living in a hotel."

He shrugged and looked around. "My suite is larger than your apartment."

"Thanks for the judgment," I snapped.

"No judgment. Just an observation."

We sat in silence for a moment while I managed to chug down some coffee. Then he said, "Are you happy? Here?"

"Yeah, I'm happy here."

He nodded thoughtfully.

"What's it like living in a hotel?" I asked.

"You feel like you're always traveling. But at least my sheets are ironed." He smiled, but it looked a little sad.

"Why don't you get an apartment?"

"I spend so much time at the hotel it doesn't make sense. Are you hungry? I wasn't lying about taking you to lunch."

When was the last time this man had had a home-cooked meal? I stood up. "If we go out, there's a chance someone from The Rex will see us. Let's stay here and I'll cook."

"You cook?"

I smiled at him on my way to the refrigerator. "You like ham?"

Flynn polished off the last bite of his *Croque Monsieur* and grinned, looking boyish. I was becoming acquainted with his smiles, and this was a new one.

I liked it.

"Happy?" I asked with a smile of my own.

"Happy." He wiped his mouth with a paper napkin. "Ready to talk business?"

"Yeah. Did you know there's a huge divide between the dancers and the cocktail waitresses?"

He raised his eyebrows. "Huge divide?"

I nodded. "Not that they don't get along, but they don't hang out with each other. Each group kind of keeps to themselves."

"That's a problem because…"

"Because it means as a cocktail waitress, I won't have the friendship of the dancers. Which in turn means—"

"They won't be open or confide in you."

"Exactly."

"And you noticed this after only a week of work?"

"I'm an outsider," I said, "I came into a situation not knowing what to expect. I paid attention."

"Aye, you did. Any ideas on how to bridge the gap?"

"I think the burlesque dancers should teach the cocktail waitresses how to dance. And if you can involve alcohol, well, I think some girl bonding just might happen."

He laughed. "Not a bad idea. Only, if all of you are drunk and dancing together, who will be working in the club?"

I shook my head and grinned ruefully. "Point taken. Okay, maybe instead, one night after work we could have a giant slumber party in one of The Rex's hotel suites—complete with alcohol I was talking about. And then in the morning we order room service."

"I'll think about it."

"Is that your way of saying you'll arrange it?"

"It means I want some time to think about it."

"No Lacey."

"Why not?"

"Because you can't loosen up around your boss. She has to stay far away from girl bonding."

"I like the idea," he admitted. "But I want to give it a few weeks. Maybe even a month."

"Why? Bonding should happen as soon as possible."

"You're still new. That's enough of a change for the moment. Once they're used to you, we'll probably go ahead with it."

"I'll start researching trust exercises," I quipped.

"It's not so bad, is it?"

"What?"

"Working for me."

I frowned in thought. "What would have happened? If I'd refused to help, and you were left with a monstrous debt?"

"What would've happened to you—or Andrew?"

"Me."

"Nothing."

I raised an eyebrow. "Nothing? Really? So I could've said no to you?"

"Of course."

Before I could feel relief unfurl in my belly, his next words shattered any illusions I had about him being soft and gentle.

"Andrew would've paid. One way or another, but not through you. He incurred the debt, I would've settled it with him. But you working for me, helping me, is a much better option, don't you think?"

I dropped my gaze to the table, not wanting to see the steely reserve in his eyes. "Yeah, I think so. You would've hurt him, wouldn't you?"

"Barrett, look at me. If you're going to ask me a question like that, look at me so you can see my answer."

Sighing, I managed to lift my gaze to his.

"With me, debts always get settled."

I nodded in understanding.

"I've got a question for you. Why did you take on your brother's debt?" he asked.

"I don't know."

"Yes, you do."

I hated that he wouldn't let me get away without

answering him. I blew out a breath of air. "Misplaced loyalty, I guess."

"It goes deeper."

"Does nothing get by you?" I demanded.

He didn't smile, only waited.

"I decided that if I did this for Andrew, I wouldn't feel guilty about cutting ties. Forever."

"I thought you were going to say something completely different."

I cocked my head to the side. "What? You thought that if I did this for Andrew, all his resentment would suddenly disappear, and we could have the relationship I'd always hoped to have with my brother?"

"Maybe. People have a hard time cutting off their family —even if they're toxic."

"Are you close to your family?"

I'd seen the blank cold mask on Flynn's face before. But nothing could've prepared me for the bitterness in his eyes and voice when he said, "I don't talk about my family."

I woke up early the next morning, since I'd gone to bed at a reasonable hour the night before. As I was about to make coffee, my door buzzer sounded. A few minutes later, I was opening a box of gourmet coffee. Shaking my head, I let out a sigh.

I brewed a pot and then took a selfie with my cup and sent it to Flynn.

Over the next few weeks, my life seemed to iron out into a routine. I worked four nights a week at the club. Mornings after my shifts were lazy, but on my days off, I went for jogs in Central Park. Summer was bountiful and bustling, and I tried to get outside as much as possible before the weather turned.

The exercise cleared my head, but Flynn was rarely far from my thoughts.

Flynn came to my apartment on Fridays at noon, and while I gave him a rundown of his club, I cooked for him. The conversation always stepped away from business, but I tried to keep our time together light. I didn't ask him in-depth questions about his life, but the same couldn't be said for him. He wanted to know everything and anything about me.

It was almost like we were dating. Only we weren't, because while he was getting to know me, he only revealed slivers of himself. And he never tried to kiss me or touch me when he came over to my apartment. He'd drawn the line and was very adamant about not stepping over it. It was driving me insane. I'd never wanted a man more, and I was sure the bastard knew it. The sexual tension between us was on a simmer, and I wondered what it would take to bring it to a boil.

Saturday nights at the club were always busy, but tonight was a different beast. Tension thrummed along my skin, so thick it was palpable. I moved slowly through the crowd. The four businessmen at a table in my section were growing rowdier by the second, impatiently snapping their fingers to get my attention

"How we doin', gents?" I asked with a wide insincere smile. "Ready for another round?"

"Yeah, another round," the ringleader said. He was middle-aged but still had all his hair. Apparently that made him fearless. "And I wouldn't say no to your phone number."

His friends laughed like baboons. My smile remained in place, but it tightened. "I'm flattered," I lied. "But I've got a boyfriend."

"Come on, sugar," he nearly whined. "He doesn't have to know. I can show you a good time."

And then his hand settled on my ass. His friends continued to laugh. Before I even had a chance to move, Flynn was next to me, removing the man's hand for him. Only he didn't drop it. Instead, he bent the man's fingers back, making him yelp in surprised pain.

"The Rex isn't that kind of place." Flynn growled, looming like a dark avenging shadow. His face was menacing with rage, and I was glad it wasn't directed at me.

The man's friends had gone silent, their glassy eyes clearing just a bit.

"Apologize to the lady," Flynn commanded. The man paused, causing Flynn to yank back his fingers. "Apologize. Or I start breaking things."

My heart began to hammer in my ears, and I waited.

"I'm sorry," the man wheezed out, "I'm sorry I put my hands on you."

Flynn tightened his grip one final time before releasing the inebriated guest. "Get out. You and your friends."

The group of men didn't argue and all but scurried from the busy club. Flynn's gaze followed them until he was sure they were gone.

"Are you okay?" he asked, voice trembling with ire.

"Fine. Thank you."

With a clipped nod, he turned and strode away from me.

"What the hell was that about?" Chelsea demanded, coming to my side, carrying an empty tray.

"You saw that?"

"Uh, yeah."

"A guest touched my ass. Mr. Campbell was…handling it."

Chelsea looked at me, brown eyes speculative. "The last guest to touch my ass was thrown out by security."

"What are you saying?"

"I'm saying that Mr. Campbell usually lets his security team handle issues. He doesn't get involved. Until now."

"Huh," I said, finally turning away so she wouldn't see my cheeks blush despite the dim lighting.

"Huh, indeed. Bossman has the hots for you."

"No," I vehemently denied.

"And you clearly have the hots for him, too."

"Chelsea," I hissed.

She smiled, sauntering away.

Damn it.

Chapter 6

I finished my shift and then left. Or tried to. When I was near the exit, a brutish man in a suit resembling an aging line-backer caught my elbow and said, "Mr. Campbell would like to see you."

Nodding, I let the man lead me into the lobby of The Rex to the private elevator. "Brad Shapiro," he said, holding out his hand. "Head of security."

"Barrett Schaefer." I dropped my hand, and the elevator began its ascent.

"I know," came Brad's reply.

"Oh, right. Head of security thing."

He didn't reply, but he shot me a smile that rearranged the features of his face and made him seem approachable and less scary.

The doors of the elevator opened, and I stepped out into Flynn's penthouse living room. He was standing by the open drapes, staring at the tree-lined park. He didn't acknowledge I was there, so I was able to take a moment and study him. The elevator doors chimed, signaling that Brad had left.

When we stood in silence with no hint that Flynn was going to speak, I ventured out, "You wanted to see me?"

Flynn turned. I hadn't known what to expect—anger, coldness. Not hunger. Raw, naked, unabashed hunger. He stalked toward me and cradled my face in his large hands.

I looked up at him and my purse slipped from my finger to hit the floor with a gentle thud. My eyes widened, and a slight sound escaped me—nothing more than a quick inhalation.

His gaze searched my face, and then his lips met mine. Possessive. Heat.

His tongue invaded my mouth. I opened to him, and his hands dropped from my face and slid down the length of my body, pulling me into him. I was pressed up against the wall of his chest, my stomach fluttery.

Abruptly, he tore his lips from mine and took a step back. We both were breathing hard, and the last thing I wanted was distance. I tried to go to him, but he held up a hand.

"I'm sorry," he rasped.

"For what?"

"For kissing you. That's not why I called you up here."

My thoughts pinged around in my head as I tried to clear the wave of lust still surging through my veins. I attempted to focus on his face, but my eyes dipped to his taut body. What would it feel like to have my hands on the bare skin of his back while he moved inside me?

I swallowed.

"So why did you call me up here?" I demanded.

"I don't remember anymore."

"What are we doing?" I whispered.

"I lost my head. In the club." His jaw clenched. "I saw a man put his hand on you, and before I knew it, I was out of the booth and—"

"And ready to break a few fingers?"

"Did that scare you? Did *I* scare you?"

I thought for a moment before shaking my head. "No, I don't think so. I was scared—for that guy. You would've hurt him. For me."

"Aye."

The finality of that word had me sucking in a breath. "Chelsea saw and said that when stuff like this happens, it's usually security that escorts them out, not the owner of the club."

"I was closer."

"Flynn," I murmured.

"Don't," he said harshly. "Don't say my name. And don't say it in that breathy voice or look at me with those doe eyes."

"Why?" I asked, taking a small step closer to him like I would toward a frightened, feral animal. The similarities weren't lost on me. Flynn looked cagey, wary.

"You know why," he stated.

"No. I don't."

"I want you when we're free and clear of this."

"Why? Why wait? If I'm offering—"

"You're not offering. You think you are, but what happens after we sleep together? Tell me you won't find a way to blame me for what happens between us."

I frowned. "I wouldn't do that."

Would I?

"I want you. You know I do. But not like this. Not because your brother originally brought us together." His eyes went hard with lust. "I want you when it's just us and none of this club business is in the way."

At a loss for words, I picked up my bag. Trying to regain as much dignity as I could, I haughtily tossed my hair over my shoulder. "Guess I'll be going then."

Without a backward glance, I left Flynn in his penthouse suite.

On Sunday, I sat in my apartment, brooding about Flynn, our kiss, and the fact that I wanted more. I wanted more with a man whom I really didn't know. He had nearly broken a man's fingers just for touching me.

Over the top? Definitely. Did I find it hot? Definitely.

Flynn claimed. In everything he did.

Worst of all, he knew me because everything he had said was true. I would've found a way to blame him after I slept with him. How did he do it? How did he know me, but I didn't know him?

I was such a stupid fool.

While I was lamenting the state of my mind—and my life—my cell phone rang. I smiled when I saw the name across the screen. "Does this mean what I think it means?"

"I'm back in New York," my best friend confirmed.

"When do I get to see you?"

"What are you doing right now?"

"Stewing."

"Stewing? Like you're making stew?"

I snorted. "No, like, I'm overthinking."

"Why are you overthinking?"

"Can we do this in person?" I asked.

"Hell yes. You wanna come here?"

"Is John there? I don't want to put him out if he is," I said, mentioning Ash's fiancé.

There was a pause. "We have a lot to talk about."

I glanced at the clock. It was just past two. "How many bottles of wine do we need?"

"I have one here. Grab another. Just in case."

Ashby Rhodes lived on Park and 88th in a building that had been in her family for two generations. Ash came from old money. We met freshman year at Columbia and despite our differences in backgrounds, we'd been best friends ever since.

After stopping off at a liquor store, I arrived at her place.

"Hey, Tony," I greeted the doorman who'd known me forever.

"Ms. Schaefer, good to see you. How's the job at Columbia treating you? Are you department chair yet?"

"How many times do I have to tell you to call me Barrett?" I demanded with a smile, deflecting the conversation about the job I no longer had.

Tony chuckled. "I'm old school."

I rode the elevator and then stepped out onto Ash's floor. I walked down the quiet hallway and knocked on her door. She opened it, looking immaculate in skinny designer jeans and a slouchy comfortable sweater. Wheat blond hair pulled up into a ponytail showed off her high cheekbones and the subtle bronze tint to her skin. She clearly had been sunning herself in Monaco. Knowing Ash, she'd gone topless and had no tan lines.

Ash blinked at me. "Something's different." She waved me inside, and we stood in the foyer while she continued to survey me.

"No glasses," I said.

"Right. Contacts?"

I nodded.

"You hardly ever wear contacts." She took the wine from me, and we went into the spacious kitchen. She set the bottle on the granite island and opened a drawer, searching for a corkscrew.

"Eh, I've been trying something new the last few weeks. Where's John?" I asked.

"Will you get out the wine glasses?"

I retrieved the wine glasses from the designated cabinet and set them down in front of her.

"Cheese?" she asked.

"Sure."

We took our glasses of wine and cheese platter to the living room. Making ourselves comfortable on a plush white couch—something only a person with an excessive amount of wealth would buy—I turned to her.

"You first," I said.

"John and I broke up."

"What?"

"John and I broke up," she said again, far too calmly.

"But, why?" I sputtered. "You went to Monaco to visit his grandparents. You guys were engaged—"

"I'm not ready to talk about it. Not yet," Ash said, a frown marring her gorgeous face. Her blue eyes were troubled but pled with me not to push her.

"Okay," I said slowly, taking a small sip of my wine.

"Your turn. What have I missed?"

I blew out a breath of air. "Where should I start?" She waited while I gathered my thoughts. "So, my brother…"

I told her everything from Andrew's debt to working it off in The Rex Burlesque Club, but I left out the part about the drugs.

"Are you kidding me?" she finally managed to ask, closing her gaping mouth.

I shook my head. "Nope."

"Wait, are you talking about Flynn Campbell's club?"

"Yeah. Do you know him?"

She shook her head. "We've never met. But I've heard of him."

I didn't like her cryptic tone. "Spit it out, Ash. What do you know?"

"You said Andrew owed Flynn three hundred thousand dollars. Did either of them tell you how he came to owe that kind of money?"

"No. Flynn just said that Andrew owed him the money. I assumed it was a bad investment or something."

Ash tapped the rim of her wine glass, her face thoughtful. "I'm going to tell you something, but you have to promise me you won't freak out, drop your wine, and spill it all over my couch."

"You're scaring me."

She paused a moment and then, "Flynn Campbell runs an illegal casino and brothel."

It felt like I'd been punched in the throat. "What? How do you know that?"

"It's well known in my social circle. Jack's been—to the casino, anyway. I have no idea about the brothel, and I don't want to know."

"Your brother?" I murmured. "Your brother has been to the casino?"

She nodded, looking wary as she watched me.

"So you're saying my brother owes Flynn money because... Oh God. It has to be the casino, right?"

"I—"

"But, how?" I cut her off. "How can Flynn get away with a casino and a brothel?"

"I imagine he has a few dirty politicians and cops in his back pocket. I wouldn't be surprised if the dirty politicians and cops have been to the casino and brothel. You know, like a gesture of goodwill."

I threw back the rest of my wine and immediately refilled my glass. Probably not the smartest idea in the world, but I was having trouble coping.

"So, why did you follow through with it?" Ash went on.

"Huh?"

"Why did you let Andrew all but trade you like a baseball card? You gave up a job you loved for a brother who has treated you badly your entire life. Why? Why did you do it? And why aren't you more irate about it?"

"I was irate. In the moment, I guess. I tried not to think too much about it. And I didn't do it for Andrew," I said. "I did it for Flynn. And for myself."

"Explain."

"Flynn and I have our own deal," I said evasively. "I can't get into it, but there's nothing sexual about it. He didn't exploit me. As for Andrew... I figured if I did this, bailed him out, then I wouldn't feel bad about never giving him anything ever again, for not feeling bad that there's this emotional distance between us. He may be my family, but he's dead to me, Ash. He's never loved me the way a brother should. And yet…"

"And yet you feel like you owe him something. For at least being there when your parents died."

I shrugged. "I know it doesn't make sense. But, yeah. If I got him out of this, I figured I could cut him out of my life and not feel guilty about it."

"It makes sense. In a strange sort of way."

I drank some more wine.

A brothel and a casino.

Holy shit!

Chapter 7

When I left Ash's apartment a few hours later, I was still revved up—and a little tipsy. I wanted to speak to Flynn, but when I called his cell, it rolled to voicemail. In my hyper state of anger, I stomped all the way to The Rex Hotel.

"Good evening. How may I help you?" the concierge greeted.

"I'm looking for Mr. Campbell."

"He's in a meeting at the moment," she said.

I smiled, but it must have come out feral because she flinched. "Please call him."

"Oh, but—"

"Call. Him." I didn't raise my voice. Showing anger loudly didn't prove anything, except that I wasn't in control of my emotions.

She hesitated only a moment before picking up the desk phone and dialing. "I'm sorry, Mr. Campbell," she apologized, "There's someone who—"

I leaned over the desk and snatched the phone from her hand. She squeaked in protest but otherwise did nothing. Putting the phone to my ear, I said, "We need to talk. Now."

"Barrett. I'm in the middle of an important business meeting," he said. "Can I call you when I'm finished?"

"I just found out about some of your business ventures."

Flynn paused and then, "My suite. Five minutes."

He hung up, and I handed the phone back to the desk agent. "Thank you."

"You're welcome," she murmured.

Anger thumped in my blood as a bellhop took me up to Flynn's suite in the private elevator. I paced back and forth across the living room carpet while I waited for him to show up. I was ready for a fight. Physical or otherwise. The elevator doors opened and Flynn stepped out.

My stomach dropped—he was so damn rugged and masculine. It only pissed me off more. I hated that I wanted him. I hated that I couldn't trust him.

His eyes, cobalt blue and fierce, searched my face. He stood in front of me and waited.

"You own a brothel and a casino?"

"Aye," he said. No hesitation. "How'd you find out?"

"Doesn't matter, does it? *You* didn't tell me."

"It wasn't for you to know."

My eyes narrowed. "My brother traded me to pay his fucking debt. And I think I have a pretty good idea how he got that debt!"

"Casino. It was in the casino."

"That hardly matters at this point."

"Are you mad because I didn't tell you, or are you mad because I own illegal enterprises?"

"I'm mad because you didn't tell me."

"Really?" he asked in that slow way that signified he didn't believe me.

"I *don't* care—I'm not a fucking prude! I've been to Vegas. I've gambled. And if women want to sell their bodies, as long as they're safe and protected, then I'm good with that. I wouldn't want to do it, but I'd never stop those that do. And if men want to pay for it that's for them to decide."

"That's all well and good, Barrett. But you're forgetting something. It's all illegal."

"Why do it then?"

"I like the danger."

I stared at him, but he gave nothing away. I shook my head. "Nope. I don't buy it."

"Don't buy it?" he repeated, his face slackening with astonishment. "What do you mean _you don't buy it?_"

"Exactly that! You like danger? What kind of bullshit line is that?"

His jaw clenched. "Careful, Barrett."

I crossed my arms over my chest in a pugnacious gesture. "Careful? You're nothing but careful, aren't you, Flynn? Can't let feelings or emotions get in the way. Wouldn't want you to get the wrong idea and have you think you could ever trust me."

I was being irrational. I knew it. But still…the more closed off he was, the more I wanted to chip away to get to the heart of him. I was worried he was already close to the heart of me.

"It's not easy for me to trust people, and there are just some things I can't tell you," he replied.

I studied him. "We're not talking about the casino and brothel anymore, are we?"

He shook his head.

"Do you think you'll ever trust me?"

"I do trust you."

"You do?"

"Aye. I'm trusting you to find out who's selling drugs in my club."

"That's different and you know it."

It wasn't supposed to be like this. I wasn't supposed to care about him. I wasn't supposed to pine for _him_.

"What is it you want from me?" he asked, exasperation finally creeping into his voice.

I couldn't even hide my look of disappointment. "Nothing, Flynn. I don't want anything from you."

A night working in the busy club was exactly what I needed to keep my mind off Flynn and the stalemate fight we'd had a few days ago. I plastered on a smile and moved through the crowd, taking drink orders and dropping them off. Around ten that evening, a stacked, gorgeous blonde perched her perfect ass in Flynn's otherwise empty booth. I frowned. I'd never seen Flynn sit with a guest in his booth—this woman was incredibly ballsy.

I went up to the service bar where Jake was busy shaking a cocktail for Chelsea's ticket. "There's someone in Mr. Campbell's booth."

"Describe her," he said.

"Blonde. Tall. Big breasts. I thought only Mr. Campbell sat in that booth."

He shrugged. "It's probably Lana."

"Lana?"

"Mr. Campbell's girlfriend."

I gripped the edge of the bar, suddenly feeling lightheaded.

The nerve of that guy! Did fidelity not mean a damn thing to him?

"Might want to mention her to Lacey," Jake continued. "But in the meantime, I'd go over there and get her a drink. She's not a very patient individual."

Silently cursing Flynn Campbell and the fact that I was working the section with his booth, I maneuvered my way through the throng of people. Lana sat by herself, looking smug and regal.

"Good evening, ma'am," I said to her.

She turned her head, looking me up and down through the sweep of her long lashes. "You're new."

"Yes."

Flynn's girlfriend must come to the club enough to recognize a change in staff. Bitterness and bile churned in my stomach.

"I'll have a vodka gimlet. Up. And Flynn will have his usual."

My smile remained in place. "Mr. Campbell is joining you?"

"Yes."

"Fantastic," I chirped. "Be right back with your drinks."

My steps were heavy as I made my way toward the bar. I waited for Jake to make my drinks and then approached the booth again. I nearly stumbled when I saw Flynn in the middle of a heated discussion with Lana. The woman grabbed the lapels of his suit, but he shrugged her off, his face an angry picture. Lana's gestures and body language were all supplication, but Flynn wasn't giving an inch. He said something and pointed to the door. Lana pouted. Flynn waited. She grabbed her clutch and left.

I moved forward, careful not to spill the drinks. I slid past Flynn and set them down on the table. "Your friend ordered these while she waited for you."

"She's not my friend."

"Your girlfriend," I corrected.

"She's not that either."

"None of my business," I said, finally making myself look him in the eyes.

"Barrett—"

"I have to get back to work." I attempted to turn away from him, but he placed a hand on my arm. I glanced down at it like I wondered how it had gotten there. He slowly removed it as if he didn't want to.

By the end of my shift, all I desired was a glass of wine and my pajamas, but Chelsea had other ideas. "Come on," she said. "We're going to grab a slice."

"We are?" I asked.

"Yup. My morning class was canceled. Professor has a meeting with the Dean or something, so I finally can enjoy my night and then sleep in tomorrow. Grab your stuff, let's go."

I looked at Lacey. She nodded, letting me know she'd tell Flynn. I hated that I had to report to either of them, but at least I was free to go.

When I was nibbling on a slice of pepperoni, she asked, "So, are you going to stop lying to me?"

"Lying? About what?"

She gave me a look. "About what's really going on between you and Mr. Campbell?"

"Nothing. He has a girlfriend. She came in tonight."

"And left pretty quickly. Every time I see you and Mr. Campbell together, it's like you guys can't stop eye-fucking each other. Unless of course, you're pretending to ignore one another."

The rational side of my brain told me it was dangerous for Chelsea to be noticing anything when it came to my interactions with Flynn. The emotional side, however, was infinitely glad that Flynn seemed as torn up about me as I was about him.

"Nothing's going on," I denied.

"But you want there to be."

"I won't be the girl who sleeps with her boss. Too much unequal power, ya know?" It was an easy excuse, but maybe Flynn was right—sleeping together while I worked for him would only complicate things, befuddle the mind.

"I respect that," Chelsea said.

"What about you? Any guy on the horizon?"

"Nah, I don't have the time. I can't wait for winter break. I might catch more than five hours of sleep at a time."

"Jeez. That's crazy."

"Yeah. NYU, though. It's expensive. Have to work."

We finished our pizza and took our sodas for the walk.

"Where do you live?" I asked her.

"Brooklyn. You?"

"Just a couple of blocks from here. Over on York."

"Nice. Makes your commute to work easy."

I smiled. "Yeah. Easiest thing about the job."

She laughed. "See you later." She gave me a quick hug goodbye, and we parted ways. When I got home, I slipped into my pajamas, no longer wanting a glass of wine—the pizza had been a decent emotional Band-Aid.

But when I climbed into bed, alone, I hated how empty it felt.

My apartment buzzer woke me up. Rolling over, I expected to see sunshine. Instead, all I saw was dark sky. In confusion, I thought I had dreamt it, but as I was getting comfortable and settling down, the buzzer went off again.

"What the hell?" I muttered, flinging the covers off me and heading to the front door. I pressed the intercom button. "Who's there?"

"It's me," came Flynn's husky voice.

"What are you doing here?"

"Let me up."

"No."

"Barrett," he growled.

"It's the middle of the night!"

"No, it's only a little past two."

"You could've called if you had something to say."

"You wouldn't have answered my phone call."

"I meant tomorrow. You could've called tomorrow at a reasonable hour."

"Still wasn't sure you would've answered. Please let me in."

Debating for a split second, I decided to buzz him up. The man was relentless, and at this rate, I'd never get back to sleep. I waited for the knock on the door and then opened it. Before I could get a word out, Flynn stalked toward me, took me into his arms and kissed the breath out of me. His tongue tangled with mine, and I tried to move closer, despite my sleep-hazed brain. My hands wove their way into his dark hair, and I relished his stubbly, raspy jaw against my skin.

"Wait," I said against his lips.

"No. I don't want to wait anymore."

It took all of my resolve to place a hand on his chest to push him away. It was a damn fine chest, and I wanted to see it without a shirt.

No. Focus.

"What are you doing here?" I asked him again, trying to regain my breath.

"Seriously?"

"You can't do this," I stated. "You can't decide all of a sudden that you want me and show up here in the middle of the night—"

"It's two. Hardly the middle of the night."

"So you already said. That's not even the point. And as far as I know, you have a girlfriend."

"I told you, Lana isn't my girlfriend."

"That's not how it looked."

"You should know by now that appearances can be deceiving."

Well, he had me there.

"Lana and I dated for a few months. I broke up with her three months ago because she started hinting at a deeper commitment."

"Hinting?" I asked in disbelief.

"Fine. She was obvious about wanting to marry me. I caught her poking holes in condoms. That's when I ended it."

"Oh God!" I said, completely and sincerely horrified. "I can't believe women actually do that!"

"Yeah, well, you're different."

His voice and gaze were warm. I tried not to be swayed by him.

"No," I said.

"No?"

"Not like this."

"Like what?"

"Middle of the night sexcapades. Sleeping together in secret while I work for you in your club. I can't be that girl."

"Barrett," he said sadly. "We can't—any other way—"

"I know," I said. "I know we can't be out in the open about whatever this could've turned into. But we both agree that finding out who's selling drugs in your club is the most important thing. Right?"

"Right," he agreed. "But—"

"I'm not your personal yo-yo. One minute you're all over me, the next you're pushing me away. It's not fair."

He sighed. "You're right. You deserve better. And I can't give it to you."

Chapter 8

I stretched my legs out on the white carpet of the very luxurious Rex suite, my back pressed against the base of the couch. Chelsea sat across from me. Alia and the other burlesque dancers sat around the coffee table, eating junk food, drinking and talking. Those that were closing the club would come up later and join in. Hopefully, the rest of us wouldn't be too drunk or tired to welcome them.

"Truth or dare," Alia asked me as she reached for another Oreo.

"Truth," I said.

"Highest number of orgasms in a sexual experience."

"You're shameless, you know that?" I asked in exasperation. "All your questions have to do with sex."

Alia shrugged. "It's the only thing that's interesting."

"I'll drink to that," Shawna, a curvy brunette who looked like Natalie Wood in *Gypsy*, said.

"Single sexual experience," I repeated. "Does that include all-nighters?"

Another dancer snorted. "All-nighters? I've never met a man that can go more than once."

"To be fair, I can't go more than once. I fall asleep as soon as it's over," Chelsea admitted.

Alia kept her gaze on me. "One experience."

"Ohhh, I see what you're asking. You're wanting to know if I have multiple orgasms."

"No, that's not what I meant. Like foreplay to the deed. How many?"

"One."

"One?" Alia asked like she didn't understand. "Were they doing it right?"

We busted out laughing. We were drunk and high on sugar, and I doubted we'd sleep until dawn. Not that I cared, because tonight I was going to do some amateur sleuthing.

"Okay, new game," I said. "'Never Have I Ever.'"

"I love that game!" Renee exclaimed. She was another cocktail waitress and the only one of us who was married with a kid.

The questions started off with a bang. Never have I ever kissed another woman. Never have I ever had a threesome. When question time came around to me I said, "Never have I ever smoked weed."

A few people drank.

The questions went around again and then came back to me. "Never have I ever skinny-dipped."

"You haven't?" Shawna asked. "You're a total prude."

"Why? Because I haven't swam naked? Maybe I've never dated anyone that made me want to do that."

"That's just sad," Renee said with a shake of her head.

"Okay," I grumbled. "I'm bored with this game. Let's do something else."

"Like what?" Alia asked.

I scrambled up from my seat. "Who's got a good music selection?"

"I do!" Shawna volunteered, whipping out her phone. She

scrolled through her playlists and then looked at me in triumph. "How about my eighties mix?"

"Perfect!"

She synced her phone to the sound system, and before I knew it, we were having a full-out dance party. We danced until we were sweaty, and then we collapsed onto the floor and couch. The closers of the club finally joined us, but they trudged in looking weary and exhausted.

I wasn't good for much longer.

"Now that we're all here," Alia said. "I can share the gossip."

"Gossip?" Renee perked up.

When Alia was sure she had twelve pairs of eyes on her, she revealed, "Mr. Campbell broke up with his girlfriend."

There was a smattering of conversation and surprise. "How do you know?" Shawna asked.

"Jake saw them going at it the other night. He said Mr. Campbell looked really angry that Lana showed up." Alia's gaze found mine. "What did you see? You were working his section that night."

Everyone looked at me, waiting for me to speak. "I didn't see much more than Jake—they argued and then she left."

"That's it? You didn't hear what they said to each other?" Renee asked.

"Nope," I said truthfully.

"Damn it!" Alia cursed. "I wanted the full deets."

"I don't think Mr. Campbell would appreciate us discussing him," I said, wanting to steer the conversation away from Flynn. Unfortunately, my words had the opposite effect.

"I've noticed him checking you out," Renee commented.

I rolled my eyes. "Oh, please."

"That's what I told her," Chelsea said. "Not like he's subtle about it. His eyes are always on your ass."

"Who wants more chocolate?" I asked, holding out a bag of candy.

"You're blushing," Alia taunted.

"Am not."

"You are!" Shawna agreed.

"Okay, you guys are terrible friends."

Chelsea shook her head. "Nope. We're awesome friends."

A pang of guilt went through me. One of them was the reason Flynn had drugs in his club. I was going to have to be a nark. And it sucked.

Flynn and I were in the corner of an expensive restaurant having our weekly meeting. We came separately, and we'd leave separately when the time came. After what had occurred the other night in my apartment, we both agreed a public setting might be better for our future get-togethers—even if there was a possibility someone from the hotel saw us. If it came to that, I'd prefer to lie about why I was having lunch with Flynn rather than be forced to endure his sensual presence in my tiny apartment. I only had so much willpower.

"Any new thoughts on the matter? Now that you've gotten drunk with the girls?" he asked, taking a sip of his black coffee.

"I don't know. I have my suspicions, but nothing concrete. Have you done background checks?"

He gave me a look.

"Okay, stupid question." I'd been tossing a thought around for a while, but I wasn't sure I wanted to say anything.

"What is it?" he asked.

I sighed. There was no point in hiding anything from Flynn. "There's something about Chelsea."

"Yes?"

"I dunno. She talks about how busy she is, how expensive her tuition is, and I know we make really good money at The Rex, but I wonder if it's enough."

He nodded. "Astute. Always listen to your intuition."

"Good advice. Anyway. I'll keep my eyes and ears open, but you should do whatever it is you do."

"You look upset."

"I like them—the girls. I just hate that I have to betray one of them."

He didn't reply right away. Setting his coffee cup down in its saucer, he finally said, "It would be easy if it was black and white. But you have to remember that one person is hurting the greater good. This is my club, my hotel, my livelihood."

"I know. I just never thought I'd feel this conflicted about…everything. But I guess that's the way it has to be." I bit my lip. "They're giving me a hard time—the girls."

"About what? Are they not treating you well? Does Lacey need to have a word with them?"

"No. Nothing like that. Just, well, they seem to be aware that there's something between us."

"How? What did you say at girls' night?"

I raised my eyebrows. "Me? You think this is because of me?"

"Isn't it?"

I let out a laugh. "You arrogant bastard," I said without any heat. "They told me you look at my ass every chance you get. If anyone should be accused of being a shitty actor, it's you."

His eyes sparkled with humor. "I'll try to keep my eyes off of your arse—when you're working."

"Thanks," I said dryly. "I'd appreciate that."

Flynn signaled to the waiter for our check, and I busied myself by gathering my belongings.

"Barrett?"

I looked up and grinned. "Jack!"

Where Ash was blond, her brother had inherited their father's looks with dark hair and intelligent brown eyes. Jack was average height, yet like all powerful lawyers, he knew how to command the space around him and appeared much taller.

I got out of the booth and hugged him.

"How you doing, Imp?" he asked.

"Can you not, with the nickname?"

"It reminds me of a simpler time," he teased, his gaze straying to Flynn who had risen from his seat. "Jack Rhodes."

Flynn clasped Jack's outstretched hand. "Flynn Campbell."

Jack raised his eyebrows, glanced at me and then back at Flynn. "Owner of The Rex."

"Aye," Flynn said, his brogue thickening.

The two men continued to exchange a look, and then Jack all but dismissed Flynn and turned his attention to me. "Have you seen Ash since she's been back?"

"Uh, yeah."

"Do you have any idea what's going on with her? She's avoiding my calls."

I shook my head, refusing to divulge what I knew about Ash. "I'll pass along that you're worried about her."

"Do that," he said. With a final hug he left, but not before throwing a measuring look at Flynn.

While we'd had our interlude with Jack, the waiter had dropped off the check. Flynn put down a few bills and then handed it to him with a smile and a thanks.

"So," he said to me.

"So."

"Who's Ash?"

"Ashby Rhodes. My best friend and Jack's sister."

He nodded thoughtfully. "He's protective of you."

"I guess. A little. I've been friends with Ash since we were eighteen. Jack still sees me as the best friend of his younger sister in need of protecting."

"No, he doesn't."

"Huh?"

"He was not looking at you like a little sister. Trust me."

I blinked. "But it's Jack. And our ten-year relationship has been nothing but platonic."

"Doesn't mean he wants it to be."

Chapter 9

"I can't believe I've never been here before," Ash said as she sat down on a barstool. Her gaze roamed the room, taking in everything. "It's like a set from *Boardwalk Empire*."

"Love that show," Jake said with a huge grin. He looked at me. "What are you doing here on your night off?"

"Wanted to show my best friend the digs. Jake, Ash. Ash, Jake."

They shook hands. "So, ladies, what are you having this evening?"

"Two Manhattans, please," I said to him.

"Coming right up," Jake said, reaching for a cocktail shaker.

After he set our two cocktails in front of us, I said to Ash, "Let's go find a table near the stage and watch the performances." I looked at Jake. "Is Alia dancing tonight?"

"She is." His smile widened, and a dopey look crossed his face.

"What was that about?" Ash asked as we sat down at a free table.

"Jake and Alia are engaged."

Ash's mouth flattened, and she dropped her gaze into her

drink. I'd said the E-word, and now she looked uncomfortable.

"Okay. You need to tell me what happened between you and John."

"I don't want to ta—"

"Talk about it, I know. But you're not talking to me and you're ignoring your brother's calls."

"How—"

"Because I ran into him the other day. Which also leads me to believe you're ignoring your parents' calls. Just tell me what happened."

Ash absently touched her bare ring finger. "I cheated on him."

"Oh," I said, almost involuntarily, the air leaving my lungs. She looked tortured and tormented before she quickly buried her emotions. I made it my goal to distract her and change the subject.

"Jake makes a good Manhattan, doesn't he?"

Ash's smile was small, but it was there. She nodded, obviously grateful for moving past the moment. "Very good."

The music shifted signaling a performance was about to begin. Shawna pranced onto stage, all curves, wearing red sequins and feathers. When she finished her routine, she blew a kiss to the audience. People cheered and clapped, excitement pulsing through the club.

Ash said, "She's really good."

"Yeah. All the dancers are really good."

Shawna, still in costume, came out into the audience. She worked the crowd, flirting and laughing. But when she saw me, her smile became genuine.

"So, tell me, how amazing was I?"

"So amazing!" I told her. "Sit with us." I introduced Ash, and they began to exchange friendly chit-chat.

"Does Bossman know you're here?" Shawna found a lone

64

chair and pulled it up to our table. She boldly took my drink and downed half of it.

"I don't know. Is he even here?"

"Of course he's here. He's in his booth. He came in about thirty minutes ago."

"Oh look, Alia is taking the stage," I said, purposefully ignoring Shawna's probing eyes. Ash raised her eyebrows, but I subtly shook my head.

My worlds were converging, and I was playing so many roles, it was difficult to remember who I was supposed to be at any given time.

The audience's reaction to Shawna was nothing compared to how they felt about Alia. She had them eating out the palm of her hand. Some performers just had a presence that was intuitive and natural—it couldn't be taught. Alia had the *it* factor.

"Can any of you sing?" I asked Shawna.

She looked at me. "A few of us, I guess. I can sing okay. Why? What are you thinking about?"

"I'm gonna pitch an idea to Bossman," I said with a grin, glad to have found a legitimate reason to talk to Flynn. I got up, grabbed my near empty martini glass, and walked toward Flynn's booth.

He sat with his usual drink in front of him, his dark hair effortlessly styled. It was dim in the club; his three-piece-suit looked black, but I knew it was gray. He glanced up when I stopped at his table.

"Good evening," he said. "Are you and your friend enjoying the show?"

"You saw us?"

He raised an eyebrow.

I smiled. "Yes, we're enjoying the show."

"So, are you dropping by my table as an employee saying hello to her boss?"

"Yes. But also, I wanted to pitch an idea to you."

"Should we go somewhere private?" he flirted, his eyes glittering with banked desire.

"No. Are you going to ask me to sit down?"

"Barrett, sit down."

I went around to the other side of the booth and slid in next to him. Not too close so people would think anything of it, but not too far that I had to yell to be heard.

"Need another drink?" he asked with a look at my near empty glass.

"Please."

"And what are Shawna and Ash drinking?"

"How did you know I was here with Ash?"

He grinned. "I have ways."

"Of course you do. Shawna shared my Manhattan and Ash had her own. Why? Are you gonna send them a round?"

"Maybe."

"Are you trying to make every woman fall in love with you?"

"Ah, if only I had that power," he said with a grin.

"The feigned humility freaks me out."

"Sorry, I'll stop."

After we ordered drinks from a sever, I said, "So, have you ever thought about having more than just burlesque?"

"What do you mean?"

"I mean what about singers? You could give a little more variety to the performances. Maybe even do vaudeville style vignettes."

"It's a good idea. I'll think about it."

"Yeah?" I asked in excitement.

"You have any more good ideas?"

"Not at the moment."

"Well, when you think of more, let me know."

"I will," I promised.

Sitting in Flynn's booth, not being able to touch him, was killing me. But there were eyes watching.

"I should head back to my table," I said with obvious reluctance.

"Probably," he agreed.

I sighed and unenthusiastically stood up. As I made my way back toward Ash, I heard a shout, followed by Alia's scream. I watched as someone pulled her down into the fray of the audience.

Security monitoring the club rushed to her aid, extracting Alia from the turmoil. She was sobbing and holding her face while a burly security guard escorted her out of the club to the lobby. The four-piece band had gone silent and patrons were shouting and screaming. Two security guards hauled a tall, muscular man by the arms into the club's office. Flynn zoomed past me. Before I could think about what I was doing or who would see me, I followed him, shutting the office door behind me. The security team threw the man into a chair. No small feat considering his size. Brad Shapiro, Flynn's head of security, stood with his arms crossed over his bulging chest. He looked like he could tear a man's arms from his body. I was surrounded by giants.

Flynn, cold with fury, loomed. "What's your name? Look at me, bastard."

"Simon Lewis," the man mumbled, lifting his head, showing glassy eyes.

"He's on something," Brad said.

Flynn muttered a curse and then gestured with his chin. A security officer went to the computer and typed something on the keyboard. A moment later, Simon's photo and information appeared on screen.

"What are you on?" Flynn demanded.

Simon shrugged, and then his eyes rolled back into his head. He slumped into the chair and started seizing.

"Someone has to call an ambulance," I said, my voice rising in panic.

"No!" Flynn barked.

"He could be—"

"No one can know," Brad clipped.

I didn't suggest it again, but I had no idea what to do, feeling utterly useless as I watched everything unfold. Simon stopped seizing, and his limbs stilled. He was breathing, but it was shallow.

"Get Jordan to handle this," Flynn demanded to Brad. "Then find out how Alia is and call me." Flynn looked at me and commanded, "Wipe that look off of your face. Smile."

Obediently, a smile flashed across my mouth. Flynn opened the office door and went out first. The band was still silent and patrons looked at us, hoping to discern the truth.

Flynn plastered on a grin and said, "Don't worry every-one. Our guest had a little too much to drink, and we're letting him sleep it off. Please go back to enjoying your evening." He signaled to the bandleader who started playing a lively number, and the guests milled back to their seats.

He gestured to me, and we walked to the bar. Lacey was manning it—Jake must have left to be with Alia. "Send everyone a free drink," Flynn said to her.

"I'll help," I volunteered.

"Lacey can handle it. You're not working tonight." He grabbed my hand and pulled me out of the club and into the hotel lobby.

"I can't just leave. What about Ash? I ditched her in the club—"

Without appearing as though he'd heard me, he took out his cell phone and pressed a button. He put the phone to his ear. "Barrett's friend is still in the club. Escort her to the lobby and wait for my call."

Flynn hung up and then dragged me across the floor to the private elevator. We rode in silence.

Flynn was terrifying, but I felt a thrill of desire. Fear, too. But desire first and foremost. When the elevator doors opened, he held them and let me step out. I slowly walked past him into the living room and plopped down onto the couch.

He went to the bar and poured two glasses of scotch, bringing me one, and sitting so close that his pants brushed against my bare thigh. Bare, because my emerald colored dress was slowly riding up.

"What happens now?" I asked faintly, clutching my glass and trying to tug down my dress.

"Brad will take care of it with the help of someone who is good at cleaning up messes. No one will know the truth."

"Does this happen often? Stupid question. Of course it does. Why else would you have a man who *cleans up*?" I finally took a sip of whisky. "I didn't expect this. Naïve of me, probably."

"People are monitored. People who look suspicious are watched. He didn't have anything on him."

"You think someone slipped it to him?" I asked.

He nodded.

"Someone who worked tonight?"

"Yes." Flynn's cell phone rang. He took it out of his pocket and answered it. "What is it? Okay. Thanks." He clicked off. "A doctor is with Alia now. The guy clipped her cheek, so it's a bit swollen. Otherwise she's fine—physically. She'll stay at the hotel tonight." He slammed back his scotch, and I did the same.

"I can't believe I just left Ash in the club with Shawna." I put my head in my hands. "Everything happened so fast, I didn't even think—"

"No, I'm glad you followed me. I needed you to see."

The adrenaline poured out of me, causing my limbs to feel achy and tired. A slight headache was forming at my temples and I suddenly wanted to be curled up in bed. "I need to get Ash and then get out of here."

"Stay here tonight."

"What?"

"Not here in my suite," he said. "I mean the hotel. You and Ash."

"That's ridiculous. We can just go home."

"Please, Barrett. Let me do this for you."

His tone was earnest, and I realized something about Flynn. He hated being out of control, of not knowing information. Though most people were like that, some dealt with it better than others.

I smiled tremulously. "Let me talk to Ash, but I think I know what she's going to say."

He grinned. "If she gives you any lip about wanting to leave, just tell her breakfast room service comes with mimosas."

Chapter 10

"I'm starting to feel like a kept woman," I said to Ash the next morning. We were wearing matching hotel robes, lounging on the couch after finishing our room service breakfast plates.

"Except that you're not even sleeping with him," Ash pointed out.

"But I want to be."

"Despite the fact that he owns an illegal casino and brothel? We never really talked about that."

"It doesn't bother me."

"Yeah, with a face and body like that, I don't blame you for not caring."

Ash had gotten a good look at Flynn when he'd shown us to the luxury suite the night before. She'd observed his overly solicitous behavior where I was concerned and made no qualms about liking that he was a man who took charge of things.

"I do care," I protested. "I mean, I know I'm supposed to care because of the illegal thing, and that means he probably pays people off—"

"Not probably. He does."

"Okay. So he does. But"—I shrugged—"I don't know."

"He made a deal to take you in lieu of three hundred thousand dollars," she pointed out. "And from the sound of it, he was perfectly happy to take payment in form of…" She gestured to my lap.

I rolled my eyes. "But he didn't. If I tell you something, you have to swear to me you won't blab it to anyone."

"I promise."

I stared hard at her.

"I promise," she said again.

"Someone is bringing drugs into Flynn's club. Our deal, independent of my brother, was that I'd help him figure out who it is."

"So working in his club is just a cover."

"Yes."

"So you had no intention of ever trading sex for money?"

"Way to break it down, Ash," I said with amusement. "I thought about it. Briefly. But I couldn't do it."

She smiled, but it quickly died. "I know you, though. If you get involved with a man who lives in a gray area, makes up his own rules, and has the money to do whatever he wants, that will rub off on you."

"Are you saying I'm corruptible?"

"I'm saying you didn't grow up with wealth. It changes how people see the world. It will taint you."

"Oh, not the *poor rich girl* speech!"

"That's not what this is and you know it."

I sighed. "I know."

"Be careful. That's all I'm saying."

"I will."

You couldn't be careful when you were falling for someone. It was all or nothing. But because Ash was my best friend, she pretended to believe me even though she knew I was lying to her.

~

The back of summer broke, and a slight chill took over the city. It felt good breathing in the crisp air as I pounded the walkways in Central Park. I still wasn't any closer to being a night owl, but my body was slowly acclimating to my new routine. Though I missed my academic job and getting lost in history, I was glad to be working in the club. I'd always enjoyed puzzles and discovering who was behind bringing drugs into The Rex was a puzzle of epic proportions.

I slowed my pace to cool down as I left the park and jogged home. As I rounded the corner of my street, I saw Andrew approaching my apartment building. I hadn't heard from him in nearly two months, not since he'd coldly traded me like a commodity on the stock market.

I halted.

He turned and saw me.

We stared at each other, like two wild animals in the jungle, waiting to see which one would pounce first. I approached slowly, hesitantly. Though my heart was pounding, I managed to school my face into a blank mask of indifference.

"Barrett," he said finally when I was standing in front of him.

"What are you doing here?"

The cool air dried my sweat-dampened temples, and I shivered. My brother noticed and asked gruffly, "Do you want to go inside?"

"You mean do I want to invite you up to my home? No. Whatever you have to say you can say it down here."

"On the street? We have no privacy."

I shrugged and made a move to go around him, but he stepped in front of me. "What?" I demanded, suddenly angry. "What do you want?"

"Are you okay? Is Campbell—"

"Now? You're doing the concerned brother thing now? Go to hell!"

His face registered shock. I'd never really lost my temper with him before. I'd always been supplicating and pleading, trying to bring us closer, but I never understood why he loathed me so much.

I shoved past him, eager to get inside and shut him out. Shut everything out.

"Barrett!" he called after me.

"We're not family, Andrew. You used me to pay a debt. You don't get to show up here and expect anything from me. We're done. Don't contact me. Ever again."

~

"Can you tell?" Alia asked, turning her face to the side to show me her cheek.

"No," I said truthfully.

She breathed a sigh of relief. "Good. I've been icing it for two days. It still hurts a bit."

"That guy really whacked you, huh?" I looked in the vanity mirror and reached for my eyeshadow.

Alia tested her curling iron as she nodded. "Yeah, it was really scary. And it happened so fast."

"Anything like this happen before?"

She shook her head. "Nope. I mean, there are times when the crowd gets kind of rowdy, but I've never had someone yank me down from the stage. Do you know what happened to him? The guy?"

"I don't," I admitted. I hadn't thought about much of anything since Andrew had popped up at my apartment earlier that day.

"You ever feel like life is just putting out fire after fire?" She wrapped a strand of hair around her curling iron, her dark eyes finding mine.

"Starting to," I said with a laugh.

"What are you thinking about?" Alia asked.

"Choices. The ones we make, the ones we don't. Where we wind up. Who we love."

"Oh, you're one of those deep-thinkers, aren't you?" she teased.

I chuckled.

"Why did you come to work here?"

"I've already answered that," I evaded.

"Uh, no you haven't."

"Huh, I swore I already told everyone why I was here."

She looked at me and waited, and there was no getting out of it. I sighed. "Just wanted to try something new."

"What did you do before?"

"I worked in the history department at Columbia."

"Scholar, huh?"

"Something like that."

"If you want to try something new, you should think about performing."

"Performing what?"

"Burlesque." She smiled. "It's super fun."

"No. I'd be too nervous," I said automatically. But that didn't really feel true. A part of me was intrigued, this new part of me I was discovering ever since I'd been thrown into Flynn Campbell's orbit.

"What if," she began, "I taught you. In private. No one will know until you're comfortable and ready to perform in public."

"Why? Why would you do that?"

"Because I think you'd be good at it. Give it a shot."

I smiled. "Okay. Thanks."

Lacey walked into the dressing room, looking sharp and assessing. "Staff meeting in twenty minutes."

"About what?" Alia demanded.

"About things," Lacey said.

"That explains nothing," Alia said to me.

I shrugged. "All will be revealed in twenty minutes, I guess."

We finished our hair and makeup, but waited to change into our costumes until after the meeting. Heading out of the dressing room, we chatted with the other dancers and cocktail waitresses including those that weren't working that night but had come for the meeting. We sat down at a cluster of tables and waited for Lacey to speak.

"Where's Chelsea?" she asked.

I shook my head. "I haven't seen her."

Lacey frowned. "She's supposed to work tonight. Has anyone spoken to her?"

All of us shook our heads.

"I'll give her a call after," Lacey said. "So, the reason for this meeting is because I want to discuss what happened the other night in the club when Alia was pulled off the stage by a man in the audience."

There were whispers of shock from those that hadn't been to witness it first hand. I kept my eyes on Lacey who was composed and steadfast. She waited for the murmurs to die down before she went on. "The man was high. We're not sure if he brought drugs into the club or if someone gave them to him while he was here. I'm asking you to please be on your guard and keep your eyes open."

"If we see something suspicious, we should tell you, yeah?" Shawna voiced.

"Exactly. Okay, everyone, that's it. Thanks for listening."

"Quickest staff meeting ever," Renee said as she headed back to the dressing room with Alia.

"Lacey, can I talk to you a second?" I asked, getting up out of my chair.

"Sure," she said.

I gestured to the corner of the club where we could have a modicum of privacy. "What happened to him? The guy on drugs?"

Lacey paused before saying, "You didn't ask Flynn?"

I shook my head.

"He died. Seizure."

"Oh." I frowned. "How is that not public knowledge? Wasn't there an autopsy? Surely—"

"You should know by now that Flynn has the resources to keep things quiet."

"Right," I said, remembering that Flynn had mentioned a man named Jordan who cleaned up messes. "Did he—say anything? Before he died?"

"You mean, did he tell anyone who gave him the drugs?" She shook her head. "No. He didn't say anything."

"Okay."

"If anyone asks you what happened that night, and people will because they saw you follow Flynn into the club office, you have to tell them the guy is fine."

"I have to lie," I said flatly. "What else is new?"

Chapter 11

On my next weekday off, I called to make an appointment with Jack Rhodes. His secretary claimed he didn't have the time to see me last minute. I hung up in annoyance. Jack called me back within the hour to tell me he'd rearranged his schedule and to come by.

Ash's older brother always had a soft, fond spot for me and treated me with the same casual affection he always showed Ash. Sometimes it made me lament the fact that my own brother was cold and resentful. Other times, I felt incredibly lucky that I had someone like Jack to count on.

I dressed in a black pencil skirt, crisp white shirt, and kitten heels. I left my hair loose and put in my contacts instead of wearing glasses. I was a mix of my old and new self and it felt good. Strange, but good.

At two in the afternoon, I walked into Miller, Banks, and Rhodes and checked in with Jack's middle-aged, beige-wearing secretary. In a perfectly tailored black power suit and tie, Jack came out of his office, a big grin on his affable face.

"Barrett," he greeted me affectionately, wrapping me in a sincere hug.

I pulled back and frowned at him.

"What?" he demanded.

"You didn't call me Imp. I find that odd."

"You asked me not to call you that the last time I saw you." Jack ushered me into his office, gesturing to the chair across from his large walnut desk. "Can I get you something to drink? Coffee? Water?"

"No, thanks."

"So," he said, taking a seat in his office chair. "What brings you to my humble office?"

As a name partner in a prestigious Manhattan firm, there was nothing humble about his office, which had a beautiful view of the city. Not to mention the twenty-five grands' worth of furniture. He was a Rhodes, through and through. He had expensive taste—that was for sure.

"Ah, I don't know where to begin," I said truthfully. "Andrew got himself into some trouble in one of Flynn's establishments."

"Establishments?"

"Don't play dumb," I said. "You know he owns a brothel and a casino."

Jack's jaw clenched, and he nodded.

"I don't care what you do. Honestly. None of my business."

"Andrew got himself into trouble, you said?" Jack asked, staying focused.

"Yeah. He lost three hundred thousand dollars in the casino and then offered me in lieu of his debt."

"*Offered* you? You better explain and explain fast because I have an idea of what I think this is and I—"

"I left my job two months ago to work for Flynn."

"Are you having sex with Campbell to wipe a debt clean?" he asked bluntly. "Because if that's the case then I'll lend you the money and we'll fucking sue the hell out of—"

"It's not like that," I assured him. "I promise. I'm working

in his club as a cocktail waitress, and Flynn has been nothing
but honorable."

I could tell Jack didn't believe me, but he held his tongue.

"I didn't come here to discuss my arrangement—I need
your help with something. And I need you to be discreet."

"I am nothing if not discreet," Jack promised. "What is it
you need?"

Alia handed me a bottle of water as I tried to catch my
breath. We were in the living room of her loft apartment in
Queens, and she was teaching me a basic burlesque routine.
Dancing was nothing like running, and it used different
muscles, but Alia had been right. I did enjoy it.

"Chelsea didn't show up last night for her shift," Alia said.

"Really?" I asked. "Did she call?"

Alia shook her head. "Nope."

I took a drink of water while I thought about what that
meant. It was pretty coincidental that someone had died in
the club from a drug overdose, and then Chelsea had disappeared. For all I knew, it was a sign of guilt.

"Has anyone heard from her?" I asked.

"I don't think so. Lacey called her the night of the staff
meeting and left a voicemail, but Chelsea never called back
and she didn't come in for her shift. She didn't show up for
her next shift either. It's really unlike her. I'm kind of
worried."

"How well do you know her?" I asked.

Alia shrugged. "I know her as well as any of us know each
other."

"What's that mean?"

"It means that some of us are only work friends and some
of us actually see each other outside the club. Chelsea was
always reliable—on time and everything. She rarely called out.

I know she's in school, and when she's not at work, she's studying. But we've never hung out. Not until we had that sleepover at the hotel."

"That was fun," I said.

"Yeah, it was. It was your idea, wasn't it?"

"My idea?"

"Don't play dumb. Ever since you started working at the club, things have been changing. For the better," she said, "but still changing."

"I pitched Flynn an idea—instead of just having dancers perform, I suggested singers who would keep in the theme with the 1920s."

"Flynn?"

Oh, crap. I'd totally slipped up.

"There's something going on between you and our boss, isn't there?" she asked gently, not at all like she was prying or judging.

"I can't talk about this with you."

"Why not?"

"Because you're engaged to Jake, so there's a good chance you'll tell him, and we all work together. I can't have my private life all over the club."

"I get everything you're saying," she began, "but I need to point something out to you. Every time you both are in the same room together, everyone can tell something is going on between you two."

My eyes widened. "Are people talking?"

Alia nodded. "Talking, speculating, drawing their own conclusions."

"What are they saying?"

"Most people think you're just a piece of ass."

"But you don't," I guessed.

She shrugged. "His eyes follow you. Everywhere you go. But not just in this *I have to get into her pants* kind of way."

"What kind of way?" I whispered.

"Like he's under a spell and he's compelled to watch you."

"Do you really think Flynn Campbell is the kind of man that would…I don't know, let a woman in?"

Alia looked thoughtful. "He laughs now. He never used to laugh."

It wasn't enough. I knew next to nothing about the mysterious man. He never opened up, never shared. That wasn't the kind of partner I hoped for. It wasn't the kind of partner I could build a future with.

I scrambled up from the couch and set my water aside. "Can we go through the routine again? I think I almost have it."

A few nights later, I met Ash for dinner at our favorite Italian place. The weather was perfect for a glass of red wine and a bowl of pasta. Autumn in New York was magical—the leaves changed and so did the wardrobes. It was all slouchy sweaters and corduroy. Food became all about warmth and comfort.

"Another glass of wine?" Ash asked, gesturing to both our empty glasses.

I shook my head. "Nah, I've got rehearsal tomorrow. I don't want to be hungover."

She smiled at the waiter and ordered another glass for herself. "So, are you liking the dancing?"

"Yeah, Alia is a good teacher."

"Have you told Flynn you're learning how to dance?"

"No. Not yet."

The waiter brought Ash her glass of wine and then asked if he could clear our dinner plates. I sat back as I waited for him to leave, observing Ash and noting her unusual melancholy mood. It took a lot to bring Ash down, and I gathered she was still dealing with the repercussions of her actions and the end of her engagement. I decided to distract her.

"So, Andrew showed up outside my apartment the other day."

Her eyes widened. "You're serious? Why didn't you tell me sooner?"

"I just couldn't think about it. Because every time I think about it, I get mad at Andrew, but I don't just get mad at him —I get mad at myself."

"Why?"

"For the way I let him treat me all those years. The emotional distance—"

"Abuse," she corrected. "It was emotional abuse."

"Yeah," I agreed. "It was. And I let it happen."

"You were a kid when your parents died. The one person who was supposed to offer you comfort and security wasn't fit to be in your life. I know you think you could've done something, but that kind of conditioning is hard to break. Even as an adult. Even as a smart, capable, hardworking, emotionally sensitive adult, it takes time to get over the kind of shit Andrew put you through."

"I'm worried that I think of Flynn as some sort of…savior. Like he all but rescued me from my evil brother and didn't take advantage of me. But I don't know anything about Flynn. Nothing personal because he doesn't share—and I know I have no right to expect him to share because that's not what we're—"

Ash thrust her glass of wine at me. I took it and drank half of it.

"You think too much," Ash said.

"You're right. And what I *do* know about Flynn is that he's not a long-term commitment kind of guy."

"How do you know that?"

"Did you not hear the part about him not opening up?"

Ash leaned over the table and whispered, "Seriously? The man owns an illegal casino and brothel, and you wonder why he's not a Chatty Kathy? I love you, but you're being a little irrational."

I glowered at her, hating that she made a valid point. The tension diffused when the waiter came back and brought us dessert menus.

"Want to split something?" she asked.

"Nothing chocolate."

"Yes, I know. You hate chocolate. I remember."

"What happened with John?" I blurted out.

Ash slowly lowered the dessert menu and stared at me. "We weren't discussing me. We were discussing you."

"Your three-year relationship just ended, and you haven't told me why."

"I did tell you why—because I cheated on him. The apple tart with vanilla ice cream looks good."

"Ash, come on. Why did you cheat?"

"Because I didn't want to marry him."

"Then why not just tell him that? Why did you—"

"The apple tart," she interrupted. "You want to share it or not?"

That was it. Ash was done talking about it. For now.

I sighed. "Whatever you want."

Chapter 12

A few days later, I stepped out of my apartment building and recognized the black Rolls-Royce idling at the curb. It was hard to miss considering the car was a sign of supreme wealth and luxury. It was not an average, run-of-the-mill vehicle. The window rolled down to reveal Flynn's angular, rugged face.

"Barrett," he said.

"Hello."

"Get in."

"Why? Today's not our day for a meeting."

He smiled. "Get in and I'll explain," he urged, opening the passenger door and then sliding over to make room for me. I got in next to him. He was still smiling, his eyes warm.

"What's that look for?" I demanded.

His answer was to lean over and kiss my lips, his arms going around me, caging me in. I sighed against his mouth, pressing into him. His fingers skimmed along my jaw, leaving tingles in their wake. He pulled back but didn't let me go as he looked down at me.

"I wanted to give you a proper hello," he said.

"But I thought we agreed—"

"I'm tired of waiting, Barrett."

"And I told you I won't be your dirty secret. And I hate the back and forth, you being hot then cold."

"I plan to change that," he stated.

I shivered at the promise in his voice.

The car came to a stop and Flynn got out, lending me a hand. I stood on the sidewalk and looked around. We were outside an Upper East Side dress boutique, and I glanced at Flynn, waiting for him to explain. He said nothing as he pulled me inside.

A saleswoman in a black silk wrap dress and red pumps clacked her way toward us, her smile polite, her eyes taking in Flynn's expensive suit. I wouldn't have been surprised if her pupils turned into little dollar signs.

"Hello, sir," she greeted. "How may I help you?"

"Hello." Flynn smiled, turning on the charm. "We need a dress suitable to attend the opera and heels to go with it."

"Undergarments?" she asked, clearly knowing her way around expensive retail.

"Yes."

"Very good, sir." The woman finally looked at me and eyed me like a mannequin. After a moment, she nodded and flitted away.

"Opera? Are you taking me to the opera?" I asked.

"No."

"Then why—"

He leaned in, his warm lips brushing my ear as he whispered, "I'm showing you the casino, but I couldn't really say that in front of a stranger."

I quivered with desire. "Why? People will see us together."

"Exactly."

"That will change everything."

"Maybe."

"Care to enlighten me on your thought process?"

"No."

The saleswoman returned and said, "If you'll follow me,

I'll show you to the dressing room. I've hung up three different choices for you."

We trailed after the woman to the back of the boutique and the last changing room. "Please let me know if you need anything." She disappeared, leaving us alone.

"This feels too much like *Pretty Woman*," I muttered as I went into the dressing room. I turned to close the door and let out a gasp. Flynn had followed me inside.

"What are you doing in here?"

His eyes weren't on me; they were on the three dresses hanging along the back wall. All of them were floor length, but he bypassed the emerald green and navy dresses and went immediately for the black, strapless sheath.

"This one," he said, picking it up and handing it to me.

"You don't get a say," I quipped.

"Aye, I do," he teased. "Show it to me when you're ready."

He gave me a quick peck on the lips and then ducked out.

I stripped out of my clothes and shimmied into the sheath dress. Zipping up the side zipper, I adjusted the bodice and then looked in the mirror.

Oh. No. It showed off a lot of cleavage, way more than I was comfortable with.

"Barrett? Are you dressed?" Flynn called.

"Uh, yeah. I guess."

"Let me in. I want to see."

"No, I don't think——"

"Please?"

"Have you ever said that word?" I asked.

"I can't remember the last time I said it."

With a labored sigh, I opened the dressing room door.

He froze, his gaze perusing me, eyes lingering on the swell of my breasts. "You're gorgeous."

"Stop looking at me like that," I commanded.

"Why?"

"Because."

He let out a low chuckle, and it took all of my willpower not to launch myself into his arms. "I told you that was the dress."

I slipped back into the dressing room and put on my street clothes, feeling some of the magic disappear. Total Cinderella complex.

Picking up the dress and matching shoes, I headed out of the dressing room toward the cash register. I knew Flynn was going to pay for everything. I could accept moderate gifts without a problem, but letting him pay for my clothing, pay for my undergarments… It was too much. Wasn't it? Or was it just generous of him?

Handing off the dress and shoes to the saleswoman, I turned to look at Flynn. He raised an eyebrow. The saleswoman wrapped our purchases, and with a smile told us to come again. Flynn took the boutique bags, and we walked outside to the waiting Rolls.

"You're not going to fight me about buying you a dress?" he asked when we were driving away from the boutique.

I snorted with laughter. "Would there be a point?"

"No," he said with a grin. "There wouldn't be."

"Thank you," I said. "The dress is beautiful."

"Not as beautiful as the woman, but it'll do."

I warmed from his compliment and was downright giddy when he reached across the seat and grabbed my hand. I looked out the window, trying to keep my heart rate under control. Ten minutes later, the car stopped again.

"Where are we now?" I demanded.

"Salon," Flynn said.

"No," I stated. "I draw the line at a professional doing my hair."

"Why?"

"Because there are levels of being a kept woman."

"You're not a kept woman."

"You're dressing me in pretty clothes."

"One outfit. And frankly if you were a kept woman, we'd be——"

"No. Salon."

"There's nothing wrong with enjoying my money, Barrett."

I refused to retract and finally Flynn relented. "Fine. You can get ready in a private suite at the hotel with your own makeup and your own hair styling products. Is that all right with you?"

"I suppose," I said, hiding a smile.

"Barrett?"

"Yeah?"

His stare was blue and piercing. "Do you like to gamble?"

Flynn's arm snaked around my waist as he escorted me through his secret casino. He wore his standard three-piece gray suit, and when I caught our reflection in one of the casino's many mirrors, I thought about how good we looked together.

The casino wasn't at all like the club or hotel; it was its own entity, decorated in gold accents and gleaming wood. Craps, poker, blackjack, and roulette were the games of choice, and I noticed immediately that it was a predominately male crowd. The women that were there were either cocktail waitresses or companions.

"Can I ask you a question?" I leaned closer so we wouldn't be overheard

Flynn inclined his chin and waited for me to speak. "Why are your establishments geared toward men and not women?"

In his free hand, Flynn carried a glass of scotch. He brought it to his lips and took a sip before he answered. "Men are visual creatures. And they like beautiful women, and they like to drink and gamble. It's easy to cater to them because they have no problem giving into their baser instincts."

"And women don't give into their baser instincts?"

"Do you? Give in to your baser instincts? Think about the night we first met. You wanted to sleep with me then."

"Arrogant statement," I groused.

"Yes or no?"

"Yes," I admitted.

"But you didn't go through with it? Why?"

"Because of my brother and the trading me for—"

"See what I mean? A man wouldn't have cared. A man would've gone for it."

"You didn't," I pointed out.

"I don't take advantage of women. If we'd had sex then, with all that stuff between us, you would've woken up in the morning and felt regret."

"And men don't feel regret?"

"Not saying that. Just saying that men can have sex without emotion a lot easier than women." He looked at me. "If we'd met under normal circumstances, would you have gone home with me the night we met just because you wanted to, or would you have waited because you think that's what you're supposed to do? What society tells you you're supposed to do?"

I sighed. "I see your point."

"I'm glad you do. Even though I own a brothel, my employees are protected and have a choice. I don't exploit them."

"I never said you did."

"You don't think sex for money is a form of exploitation?"

"It is only if the women don't have a choice in the matter. And as you said that's not how you run your business."

Sex for power was something I'd never been able to pull off. I just wasn't wired that way, but some women were, and good for them.

I took his glass from him and threw back the rest of his drink. He looked at me in amusement and handed off the empty glass to a passing cocktail waitress.

"You surprise me. All the time," he said with a soft smile.

"Why? Because I'm not arguing with you? I don't fight for the sake of fighting."

"So you don't think I'm a misogynistic arsehole?"

"Are you?"

He sighed. "Do you ever answer a question with a straight answer?"

"Do you?" I fired back.

Flynn laughed, causing other people to stare at us. "Do you want another drink or do you want to gamble?"

"Take me to the blackjack table."

"As you wish."

An hour later, I was winning at the tables when Flynn got a phone call. He glanced at the screen and said, "Sorry, but I have to take this."

I waved him away and went back to gambling. Flynn left my side and someone else took his spot. Turning my head, I looked at the newcomer. It was Brad Shapiro, Flynn's head of security, and he was watching me with a steady gaze.

"Hello," I said.

He inclined his head in greeting but otherwise remained quiet. Even though I went back to focusing on the game, I knew Brad kept his eyes trained on me. Maybe it was because Flynn didn't want to leave me alone in the casino, but it felt like something more than just protection. It felt like possessiveness, too, like Flynn wanted to make sure of my whereabouts at all times.

"Where's Flynn?" I asked Brad after a moment.

"Dealing with business."

"So what am I supposed to do until he gets back?"

Brad gestured to the rest of the casino. "If you're sick of blackjack, you can always play poker. Or craps or roulette."

"Do you think he's going to be a while dealing with business?"

"It's a safe bet."

"No pun intended?" I said with a wry grin. "You don't have to keep me company."

"Yes, I do. Boss's orders."

I sighed. "Do you know have any idea when he'll be finished?"

"Not a clue."

"Can I go home?"

He blinked and then frowned. "But you're winning."

"Yeah, I know, but I was having fun and now Flynn's gone and stuck me with a babysitter. That puts a damper on the evening."

Brad's severe face softened as he smiled. "Flynn was right."

"About what?"

"You're funny."

Flynn talked about me? I liked that. I liked that *a lot.*

Chapter 13

I lifted the kitchen window to let in some fresh air. My land-lord had prematurely turned on the heat, and it was stifling and humid in the apartment.

"Sure I can't get you something to drink," I called to Jack.

"Water, I guess. It's freakin' hot in here," Jack answered.

I laughed and brought him a cold bottle of water. He sat on my couch, looking completely at ease, despite our subject of discussion.

"Campbell did a background check on you," Jack said.

I took a seat next to him and tucked my feet underneath me. "Doesn't surprise me."

"No? Did he tell you he was going to do that?"

"No. But knowing Flynn…it's not so shocking. Andrew was the only skeleton in my closet, but Flynn already knew about him. Obviously."

"I did what you asked and looked into him, but I couldn't find anything."

"What do you mean?"

"I mean, everything is locked up tight. I couldn't find out a damn thing about him. It's like he doesn't exist."

Ripples of unease swept down my spine. "I don't like that."

"Yeah, I agree. I can hire someone—to dig into his past, but it will take some time to get results."

Flynn wasn't just a mystery, but a man who went out of his way to conceal his identity. Why? What was he hiding? What didn't he want anyone to know?

"Barrett, you okay?" Jack asked.

"I don't know."

"Ash finally called me back," he said, changing the subject. "She told me she broke up with John."

"Oh, good."

"Do you know why?"

"Sort of."

"What does that mean?"

"It means, I know the excuse she gave me, but I think it runs deeper," I said.

"And what excuse did she give you? She didn't tell me anything."

"That's all I can say about it then. It's for Ash to tell—when she's ready."

"My parents are not happy."

"Yeah, I can imagine."

John came from old money. Marrying him would've pleased her parents. Maybe she hadn't really loved him after all, and that's why she had cheated on him. I knew it wasn't as simple as that, but only Ash could enlighten us.

"I think I'm ready for a real drink," Jack said.

"There's a bottle of rye. Help yourself."

While Jack rooted around in my kitchen, the shrill sound of the buzzer filled my tiny apartment. I hopped up and pressed the intercom button. "Hello?"

"It's me."

His sensual brogue wasn't diminished in the slightest by the old, crackling speaker. His voice had desire licking along my nerves, but it came with a bout of anger, too. I hadn't seen Flynn in the three days since he'd abandoned me in his casino in the name of business. Not even a text or phone call to apologize for never returning. I understood that things in life came up, but to go completely silent? It was rude. And I'd had nothing but time to stew over his absence.

"I have company," I said, trying not to snap. I didn't want to be a shrew, yet I didn't want him to think he could just show up and I would be there waiting for him.

"If it's Ash, I'd like to come up and say hello."

"Not Ash."

There was a pause on the other end of the intercom and then, "Is it her brother?"

"Yes."

Another pause. "I still want to come up."

"I don't think that's a good idea."

"Can we not have this conversation while I'm outside and you're in your apartment?"

"You can't just show up here and expect me to be available—"

"What's going on?" Jack asked from somewhere behind me.

I released the intercom button and turned to him. "That was Flynn."

"He comes to your apartment."

"Yes."

"What's going on between you two?"

"I don't know," I said truthfully. We were in some kind of gray area where the rules changed on a daily basis. I couldn't keep up, and it was exhausting.

"You should let him in. I'll go," Jack said, setting his glass of rye on the coffee table.

"No. Please stay."

"I don't think that would be good. For any of us." He

came to me and briefly kissed my cheek. "I'll keep you posted about what my guy finds. Okay?"

I nodded and was getting ready to see him to the door when there was a knock. "I didn't buzz him in."

"Well, someone did," Jack said, shrugging on his light jacket.

"No hope for it then." I opened the door and caught my breath. I didn't think I'd ever get tired of seeing Flynn fill out a doorway. It was like he occupied all the empty space.

His intense eyes slid from me and glanced at Jack. Reaching out his hand, he said, "Jack. Good to see you again."

With a look of astonishment, Jack clasped Flynn's hand. "You too. If you'll excuse me, I've got somewhere to be." He smiled in my direction, and then was gone.

"You're upset," Flynn said as I closed the door.

"I have no right to be, do I?"

"But you are."

"We're not a couple. You don't owe me an explanation. But you do owe me some common courtesy."

"You're right." He sighed. "I'm sorry. The night I was with you, I got a call about Chelsea. She's missing."

Icy fear balled in my stomach. "Missing?"

He nodded. "She's the one who's been bringing drugs into the club. I still don't have any idea who put her up to it, though. And now she's disappeared. Brad and my men were trying to find her trail, but it's gone cold."

"You couldn't shoot me a text to tell me this? You had to ignore me completely?"

"You're right. I didn't handle it well." He raked a hand through his hair. "I'm not used to having to answer to a woman."

I raised an eyebrow.

"What I mean to say is that I'm not used to having a woman I want to answer to."

He took a step closer, but he left it up to me to cross the emotional and physical distance between us. I didn't question what was happening, I just went with what I was feeling. And I was feeling scared and in need of assurance.

I pressed my face against his chest, breathing in and closing my eyes. His hands went to my head, stroking my hair, holding me close.

Where was Chelsea? Was she hurt? Was she going to hurt us? "What do we do, Flynn?" I whispered.

"I don't have a fucking idea."

We spent the night in my bed, but all we did was talk. For the first time since I met him, I felt like he was trying to open up to me. Worry for Chelsea weighed heavily on the both of us.

"The longer she's missing, the greater chance she's…" he trailed off.

"Yeah, I know." It made me sick to think about. "Any leads on who she's working with?"

"Not at the moment. Three days of brainstorming and following dead-ends. I hate being out of control."

He pulled me into his arms, and I must have dozed because the next thing I knew, it was dawn and Flynn was kissing me goodbye. I rolled over and went back to sleep. When I woke up a few hours later, my mind was on Chelsea and all the variables of unknown. Nothing cleared my head like a run, so I dragged my butt out of bed and threw on some exercise clothes.

I did a warm-up jog on my way to Central Park, feeling my hamstrings stretch and my lungs expand. It was early on a weekday, so I had most of the pathway to myself. After a while, I had a good rhythm. I never ran with ear buds because I liked to be aware of my surroundings, and most of the time the park was congested with bike and foot traffic. It would be so easy to get run over.

I heard the steady sound of running footsteps behind me and moved to the right to share the path. The runner didn't pass me and instead sidled close.

Too close.

Turning my head ever so slightly, I let out a gasp when I saw who was next to me.

Chelsea was dressed in black running clothes and a baseball hat.

"Where have you been?" I asked. "Everyone is worried about you."

"I'm fine."

"Obviously."

"Keep running," she said. She didn't sound at all like her usual self. Not as the young woman I'd come to know.

"What's going on?" I demanded.

"I'm here to warn you."

"Warn me?"

"Whatever you've got going with Flynn Campbell, shut it down now. Quit his club, find another job, break up with him. Just get out."

"What? Why would I do that?"

"I can't tell you. But I like you, Barrett. I think you're a good person. If you stay close to Campbell, you'll get hurt."

It wasn't a threat—that wasn't the tone of Chelsea's message.

"Heed my advice," Chelsea said before sprinting away from me and disappearing around the bend.

Any peace or clarity I'd hoped to achieve on my run was quickly dashed.

"What do you mean he's not here?" I demanded.

The concierge behind the hotel desk shot me a sympathetic but helpless look. "I'm very sorry——"

"Where is he?"

"I'm not at liberty to say."

I smacked my hand on the counter, causing her to flinch and others in the lobby to look at me. "This is important."

"I'm sure it is," the concierge said with a strained smile. "I can call Mr. Campbell's cell phone and leave a voicemail——"

"I can do that myself!" I snapped.

"Barrett," Brad called as he strolled across the marble floors of the lobby. His eyes raked over me, his gaze taking everything in from my lopsided ponytail to my running clothes. "What's going on?"

"This woman just informed me that Flynn isn't here and won't tell me where he is."

"Why don't you come with me," Brad urged, grasping me by the arm, not taking no for an answer. He all but dragged me to his private office. Monitors were mounted on the wall, all depicting various parts of the hotel. He had his eye on everything.

Closing the door, he gestured for me to take a seat in the chair across from his desk. Adrenaline still coursed through me, but it was ebbing, just a bit. Brad perched on the edge of the desk instead of taking a seat in his chair.

He stared down at me and said, "Care to tell me why you were about to make a scene out there?"

"Where's Flynn?"

"Business trip out of town," he replied casually.

I raised my eyebrows. Flynn had left my bed just that morning, and now he was gone. Again. And he hadn't told me. Again.

Fool. I was a raging fool. When would I realize that actions spoke louder than words? He could say he wanted to check in with me, but when it came down to it, he didn't.

"Does this have to do with Chelsea?" I asked.

"No. Something else unrelated. Are you okay?"

"Fine," I stated.

"You don't look fine."

"Just a little surprised that he left town and didn't tell me, that's all."

"He'll be back in a few days."

I nodded absently. Good. It would give me some time to sort out my feelings and sit on the news of Chelsea warning me away. Maybe it would give Jack time to find out more about Flynn's past because, at the moment, I really hated feeling like he held all the cards. But I had to find a way to compartmentalize and divorce myself from my emotions.

"You can always call him, you know. Leave him a message," Brad suggested. "I'm sure he would be glad to hear from you."

"Is that—are you reassuring me?"

He sighed. "I'm not good at this."

"Good at what?"

"The comfort and reassurance thing. If that's what you're looking for, then you should talk to Lacey."

"I don't want to talk to anyone about anything."

"Fine. But whatever's going on with you, having a tantrum in the middle of the lobby is not the way to deal with it. If Flynn were here, he'd tell you that himself."

"So you're Flynn's spokesman?"

Brad's eyes glittered and his jaw clenched. "I've worked with him for a decade. I've been with him every step while he built this hotel. I've been with him through girlfriends who inevitably became ex-girlfriends. He's a good man, and I consider him one of my closest friends. He doesn't have a lot of people he can trust, Barrett. And because he's wealthy and powerful, people always want something from him."

He stared at me, debating what he was going to say next. "I'm afraid you're going to want something from him, and because he's different with you, he'll give it to you, and then you're going to ruin him."

"Why do you think I'd ruin him?"

"Because men always try to live up to a woman's expectations and then inevitably fail."

Was that what I was doing? Asking Flynn to be someone he wasn't? All I wanted was the common courtesy of a text. I didn't need to be coddled or entertained. I just wanted to be more than an afterthought. I didn't like feeling left out or left behind.

Brad pinned me with his unwavering stare. "The more you learn about him, the deeper you realize this goes, you'll want out. But Barrett, you can't take parts of a man—you either take all or nothing. So you have to make a choice."

I felt dizzy from Brad's words. "A choice?"

"It's simple, really. Are you in or are you out?"

Chapter 14

I set the last dish in the drying rack, removed my rubber gloves, and went to answer the intercom buzzer. It was a flower deliveryman carting the most beautiful red tulips I had ever seen. Thanking him, I took the bouquet and set it on the coffee table. I opened the card. It was from Flynn and all it said was, "Miss you."

I pressed the card to my lips, deep in thought. I'd gotten a text a couple of days ago, after I'd spoken with Brad. Flynn's message hadn't been very forthcoming, but he'd said he'd be back in a few days. So far that had been our only communication. I assumed Brad had told Flynn to communicate with me, just so there wouldn't be another melt down in the middle of the lobby.

The flowers were a nice touch and the universal sign of an apology. Was I going to let it go? It didn't behoove me to hold onto my hurt.

Before I could think too hard about it, I picked up my phone and called him. It went to voicemail and even hearing his gravelly, deep, Scottish-tinged voice in a recording did something to me. I left a stuttering message and thanked him for the flowers. And then I took it one step further and told him I missed him, too.

I didn't care how we had come to know one another, and I didn't care that he owned a brothel and a casino. It was as simple as wanting him and as soon as he came back, I'd tell him.

My intercom buzzed again, and I frowned in confusion. Only Flynn showed up unannounced, and I highly doubted it was him.

"Hello?"

"Hi, it's Lacey."

"Oh, hi."

"Can I come up?"

"Um, sure."

I buzzed her in and tried to wipe the look of puzzlement from my face before she showed up at my door. It was odd, seeing her outside the club and in street clothes. Her brown hair hung just past her shoulders and had a slight wave to it. Her makeup was light, and she looked amazing in her dark skinny jeans, calfskin boots, and cream fisherman sweater.

"I know I showed up unannounced," she began, holding up a shopping bag. "So I brought supplies."

I peeked into the bag. "Vodka? And olives?"

Lacey grinned. "Martinis."

Waving her inside, I closed the door behind her. "Not that I'm not grateful for the liquor, but what are you doing here?"

"Beautiful tulips," she said instead of answering. She gazed around, taking in my home. She nodded like she understood something.

"They are."

"Flynn has good taste," she said, heading into the kitchen.

"He does."

I knew we weren't really talking about flowers.

"So, Alia told me she's been helping you learn a dance

routine." She began to unpack her ingredients from the bag and opened a jar of olives.

I went to the freezer and pulled out a tray of ice and handed it to her. Lacey cracked it and dropped a few cubes into the waiting martini shaker.

"Yeah, I'm having fun. She's a good teacher."

"You think you might be ready to perform?" she asked.

"Do you think that's a good idea?"

Lacey smiled and shook the martini shaker. "I pitched the idea to Flynn already. He totally approves."

"He does?"

"He's pretty excited to see it, actually, but he wondered why you didn't tell him yourself."

"I was waiting—until I was sure I wanted to dance in public."

"Have you talked to him?" she asked, handing me a martini.

"Not recently. Not since he left. Again." I took a sip of my drink. It was cold and salty and perfect.

"Brad mentioned you stopped by the hotel the other day."

"Ah," I said. "This martini is designed to get me to spill my guts."

"Only if you want to. Can we move to the couch?"

We took our drinks and settled into more comfortable seats. I stared at the greenish tinted vodka when I said, "I appreciate that you're willing to lend an ear, but there are some things I should say to Flynn first." Like my run-in with Chelsea at Central Park and my tumultuous feelings for him.

"I respect that."

"Can we just sit here in silence and drink our martinis?"

Lacey smiled in understanding. "Can I do it while staring at your tulips? They really are gorgeous."

~

"Are you okay?" Alia asked. "You look like you're going to throw up."

"Not helping," I wheezed, trying to calm my racing heart and sweaty palms. I had a wicked case of stage fright.

"Once that spotlight hits you, you won't even know there's an audience. Besides, you've rehearsed out the wazoo—you're completely ready for this. And Mr. Campbell isn't even going to be in the audience tonight."

"Thank God," I muttered. One good thing about Flynn still being on his business trip was that he wouldn't see me vomit all over the stage. Though Flynn was on board with me performing, I wasn't sure I wanted him to watch. What if I was terrible?

Alia and I stood in the wings of the stage and I swore everyone could hear my heart running a seven-minute mile while I waited for Lacey to introduce me.

"Ladies and Gentleman," Lacey began, "it gives me great pleasure to present to you a new performer this evening. Without further ado, please put your hands together for the musical stylings of Miss Brandy Alexander!"

There was a smattering of polite applause as the lights dimmed—it was my cue to take center stage. When the lights came up in a spotlight, the piano began its introduction. I thought I would forget my lines, but I recovered and sang out in a seductive voice.

Adrenaline overpowered the fear. I removed the pearl strand and tossed them to a random guy in the audience who howled in excitement as I sung "Take Back Your Mink" from *Guys and Dolls*. With each correlating piece of clothing I mentioned, I took it off until I was in nothing but a satin pearl-colored 1920s teddy, garters, and stockings.

The crowd whistled and clapped in appreciation as I strutted and sang the last of the song. Scooping up my pile of garments, I blew a kiss to the audience and then headed off stage. Once in the safety of the wings, the other dancers hounded me.

"I was okay?" I asked breathlessly. I had to remember this feeling. Though it had been terrifying, I faced a fear and let go. I felt alive.

"Okay?" Shawna smirked. "Are you kidding? You were awesome!"

"Tonight we're drinking champagne," Alia remarked. "We have to celebrate."

"Brandy Alexander?" I asked Alia with an eye roll. "Whose idea was that? Yours or Lacey's?"

"I take full credit for your stage name." She shrugged and grinned. "Classy with a hint of slutty."

Shawna and I laughed.

"Ladies and Gentleman," Lacey said into the microphone, "we hope you had a wonderful time here at Rex Burlesque. That concludes our show for the evening."

"Guess I better get dressed," I said.

"Put your costume back on," Alia said. "And we'll go out and work the crowd."

"Work the crowd? You guys don't normally do that."

"We'll stay in character," Alia said. "It'll be fun."

Fun. I liked the sound of that. "All right. Someone help me back into this dress. I'll work the crowd but not in lingerie." I needed to find Lacey and thank her for her amazing costume skills since she'd been the one to outfit me.

Five minutes later, the other dancers and I walked out onto the club floor. Whistles and applause greeted us.

"Looking for these?" A hand held up my strand of faux pearls.

Through the sweep of my lashes, I looked up at the man I had tossed my necklace to and grinned. "Maybe."

"May I?" he asked. At my nod he settled the necklace around my neck.

"Thank you." He was attractive, tall with dark hair, and he

looked good in a suit. But not as good as Flynn. No one looked as good as Flynn in a suit.

"Buy you a drink?" he asked.

Before I could answer, Alia and Shawna joined us and Alia handed me a flute of champagne. "Cheers," Alia said, clinking our flutes together.

"Guess you don't need a drink after all," the dark stranger said.

"Guess, I don't."

"But you do," Shawna told him.

"I do. Excuse me, I'll go get one." He leaned in close to my ear and whispered, "Don't move, I'll be right back, okay?"

I nodded, and he headed toward Jake and cocktail central.

"Oh my God," Shawna breathed. "Who's the guy? He's hot."

"No idea," I answered, taking a sip of champagne. "I tossed my necklace at him." I fingered my strand and looked for the guy in the crowd.

"Well, I think you should go for it," Alia said.

"Yeah, I don't think so."

"Why not?" Shawna asked. "It's not like you have a boyfriend."

I shrugged but didn't reply.

Shawna sighed all dreamy. "If you don't want him, can I have him?"

The dark stranger returned and smiled at me. "So where were we? Oh yeah, you were going to tell me your name."

I laughed. "Barrett."

"I'm Eric."

A person bumped into me, causing me to domino into my new companion, dousing us both in champagne.

"Crap," I muttered. "I'm sorry."

"It's okay, it's not your fault." Eric shot a glare at the drunken guy who was gently being coerced to the front door by security. "You spilled your drink."

"I'll get another," I said, attempting to move away toward the bar, "and I'll get us a couple of napkins."

"No," Eric said. "I'll go. One glass of champagne coming right up. And some napkins."

"How about a scotch?" I asked. "I really don't like champagne that much."

"Whatever you want." He left with a wink.

"He's nice," Shawna said. "I wish I could meet a nice guy."

"You can," Alia said.

"I always pick the wrong ones. Eric," she sniggered. "Like Prince Eric from *The Little Mermaid.*"

I saw Eric work his way through the crowd, coming toward me. "Let's cheers again," he said, handing me a glass of scotch.

"Here, here," Alia said.

As we sipped our drinks, Eric engaged me in conversation, but my eyes wandered around the club. I kept hoping Flynn would randomly show up, and we could spend the rest of the evening flirting and talking and moving forward in our strange relationship. I wanted him despite our circumstances, despite his mysteriousness, despite him basically being my boss.

"You okay?" Eric asked, rotating his body away from Alia and Shawna just slightly, so I was forced to turn with him.

"Hmmm? Oh, fine."

"You seem a little distracted."

"Sorry."

"I really enjoyed your performance," he said.

"Thanks, it was my first time."

"Couldn't tell. You have nerves of steel."

I laughed, feeling warmth in my cheeks, my head a bit fuzzy.

"What song did you sing?" he asked.

"'Take Back Your Mink' from *Guys and Dolls.*" I swallowed,

my mouth suddenly dry. "I'm a little hot." Frowning, I fanned my face with my hand.

"Want to get some air?" he asked.

"Yes, please."

I stumbled toward the exit, and Eric's hand whipped out to steady me. My stomach rolled, and my throat constricted. I swallowed a few times, but my mouth was dry and I had a hard time focusing. My vision flickered in and out, like someone had installed a strobe light behind my eyes.

"Something's wrong…" I slurred as cool autumn air hit my face.

Eric's arm went around me as he dragged me toward the curb. Cabs whizzed by in a blur of yellow and shadows.

"I can't seem to…" My eyes closed, my knees buckled, and everything went dark.

Chapter 15

I woke up with a pounding headache. Turning my head, I groaned, my cheek pressed to a soft, satiny pillow. Opening my eyes, I rolled onto my back and slowly sat up, taking in my surroundings.

I was in a Rex Hotel suite, but I had no recollection of how I'd gotten there.

Attempting to climb out of the king-sized bed proved difficult. I was weak and shaky, and a hint of nausea churned in my stomach. Forcing myself to get up, my toes sank into the plush white carpet. I headed to the bathroom to splash some cold water on my face. There was an unusual taste in my mouth—like chalk, cotton, and something sour. I cupped my hands under the faucet and drank a few handfuls before grabbing the tube of toothpaste and spare toothbrush.

Masculine products littered the sink counter—aftershave, a razor, shaving cream. I was starting to put the pieces together; someone must've brought me to Flynn's penthouse suite. My fear began to fracture as I realized I was in a safe place. Feeling marginally restored but still brain fuzzy, I walked into the living room and stopped in surprise.

Flynn was on his cell phone, pacing back and forth. He

was dressed in slacks, his shirtsleeves rolled up to reveal strong forearms. The man looked ruffled, and that wasn't a word I would have ever associated with him.

"I don't care, Brad, find out—" His eyes met mine, and they were glacial. "Take care of it," he snapped before ending the call. He stalked toward me. "How are you feeling?"

"Okay," I said, my voice sounding weak and confused. "You're not supposed to be here—you're supposed to be on a business trip."

"I left early. I arrived late last night."

"Oh," I said. "What—what happened? How did I get here?"

Flynn stood close enough to me so that his shirt touched mine. I realized I was wearing a man's white undershirt and my nipples were jutting out and visible through the thin fabric. I crossed my arms over my chest in order to conceal my reaction to him. I physically felt terrible, and I was confused, and yet my body still wanted him.

Flynn was staring at me with a dark, impenetrable blue gaze.

"You don't remember?" Flynn asked softly.

"I performed burlesque, the girls and I worked the crowd, and then nothing."

"Someone drugged you, Barrett."

"Drugged?" My head snapped back. The truth fought through the cloudy memories of last night. "But how did I get up *here*? To your suite?"

"The girls saw you leaving with a stranger. Jake went after you and saw a guy trying to get you into a cab. Then you blacked out. Jake carried you inside and had Brad call me. I was already back in the city, but I had Brad bring you up here immediately."

If Jake and the girls hadn't been watching out for me…

My eyes widened. "I'm wearing your shirt, aren't I?"

He nodded slowly.

"Did you—was it you who undressed me?"

Another slow nod. Flynn's hand moved up my arms to my neck and then cradled my face. Heat suffused my face.

"You scared the shit out of me, Barrett."

My tongue darted out to touch my suddenly dry lips. His hands tightened ever so slightly as his thumbs stroked my jaw.

My hands grabbed the front of Flynn's shirt, and I hauled him to me, our mouths mere centimeters apart. "Kiss me," I whispered, taunting, daring.

He growled. Animal.

One of his hands left my face to cup a breast through my shirt. He grazed his thumb over my nipple, and it hardened immediately.

"Your body wants more than a kiss, aye?" he murmured, his voice thick with desire. I shivered as his lips finally met mine, his mouth insistent but soft. He dragged me close, his hand skimming down the curve of my back.

I pressed into his body, feeling the hard length of him through his trousers. I wanted him, and I was done denying him. Done denying myself.

I clawed at his shirt, tearing at it, wanting—needing—to feel his skin. Our breaths were ragged, and when his possessive hand skated up my body to grip my hip, I cried out, wanting more. Wanting all of him.

Flynn's cell phone ringing jarred me out of my lust-induced craze. Flynn tore his lips from mine and groaned at our interruption. Our gazes locked on one another, loaded with promises of passion yet to be unleashed.

If it hadn't been for the phone…

Cursing, Flynn took a step back and went to the coffee table to answer his cell. "Aye?" he gritted out. "Fine. We'll be there in an hour. Aye, an hour. She has to eat."

I watched him hang up. "Who was it?"

"Brad. Seems we have the guy who drugged you on camera."

My reality came crashing back to me. Desire fled, replaced by exhaustion and confusion. All I wanted to do was climb back into bed and sleep off my night. Was it too much to hope that Flynn would join me?

"That's good," I said, forcing bravado I didn't feel.

"It is," he said, reaching for the landline.

"Chelsea," I blurted out, remembering what I had wanted to tell him. The young cocktail waitress was responsible for selling drugs in Flynn's club and she'd disappeared. Only she hadn't.

He frowned. "What about Chelsea?"

"She found me in the park while I was running."

"What? When?"

"The day you left for your business trip."

"Why didn't you tell me? Why didn't you tell Brad?" he demanded.

"Because I wanted to tell you first, and it wasn't something I wanted to discuss over the phone."

He sighed. "Go on."

"She warned me away from you. She said I would get hurt if I stayed close to you."

"She threatened you?"

I shook my head and then winced when it hurt. "No. It wasn't a threat—it was a warning."

Flynn's face warred with concern and anger. "I'll call up for some food. You take a shower."

"I don't have any clothes."

"I'll have Lacey get you something to wear."

"Okay." I knew Flynn wasn't a man who asked for things —he just expected them to be done, so I nodded and headed toward the bedroom. I was so discombobulated that I wanted someone else to take control of the situation. At the moment, I was glad for Flynn's solicitous and arrogant behavior.

It meant I wasn't alone.

"Barrett?"

I turned.

"We're not finished. Not by a long shot."

My eyes widened at the promise I read in his face, in the tautness of his body.

I made sure my shower was cold.

While I was shampooing my hair, I remembered something from last night. Not about the guy from the club—Eric—who had been the culprit of my drugged drink. But about Flynn.

I was in bed, thrashing around, getting tangled up in sheets. I'd cried out, but someone had been there to soothe away my subconscious fears.

Closing my eyes, I doused my head under the magnificent spray. Another memory came to me. Flynn's lips on my forehead, his arms wrapped around me, saying soothing words in a lilting, hypnotic language.

I had no way of knowing if it was real or a figment of the drugs. I could ask him, but that would open up the gates of vulnerability, and I wasn't there just yet.

I turned off the water and reached for a towel. Wrapping myself in a robe, I went into the bedroom and found a pair of my jeans, a T-shirt, and a few comfortable undergarments. Flynn must've sent Lacey to my apartment. It didn't bother me if she'd been in my home without me there. The night she'd come to my place, and we'd downed martinis, had been a bonding experience. The people that Flynn kept close to him were steadfastly loyal and protective. It made me want to be part of his inner circle.

After I got dressed and pulled my wet hair into a ponytail, I headed into the living room. Plates of food graced the counter and kitchen table. I reached for a piece of dry toast, wondering where Flynn had gone. I saw a bottle of Aspirin on the counter and popped a few.

Flynn entered his penthouse suite from the private elevator, dressed in a pair of black slacks and a gray sweater. His hair was tousled, dark, and wet. He must've showered somewhere else. His large chest and shoulders made him look like he could take on the world and win.

"How are you feeling?" he asked.

"Still a little nauseous," I said. It was a challenge to stay awake—I was exhausted.

"Drink the OJ. It'll help," he commanded. "Aspirin is on the counter."

"I already took three."

"We'll make this as fast as we can. Then you'll take the rest of the day off. And don't even think about arguing with me."

"Okay." He looked like he could use a decent nap, too. "Have you been up all night?"

"Aye. I'm also suffering from jet lag."

"Jet lag?" I asked in surprise. "Where were you?"

He paused briefly before saying, "Scotland."

"Did you…" I trailed off, wondering why I was suddenly shy and nervous.

"Did I what?" he prodded.

"Never mind," I muttered, munching on a piece of toast.

Even though Flynn had been up all night, all that showed for it were the dark smudges beneath his eyes. I knew he wouldn't rest until this evening. I drank another cup of coffee before we headed down to the security room in the burlesque club.

Flynn stayed close to me, going as far as putting his arm on the back of my chair when we sat down. Brad wisely didn't comment on it, and I was too tired to care about Flynn's public show. It took all of my effort not to lean into him.

"We have the guy on camera," Brad said, fiddling with a few buttons on the computer keyboard. A photo of the hotel's front came into focus. It was a still of me collapsing against a man. I was blurry, but there was a clear shot of the guy's face.

"Alia said his name was Eric, but we haven't been able to confirm if that's his real name or not," Brad said. "Barrett, what do you remember about him?"

"Not a lot," I admitted, shame permeating my voice. I'd lived in New York for years and never had a problem. And now? One night in the place I should've been safe, and I wasn't.

"Hey," Flynn said softly. "Look at me." When I met his eyes, he went on, "This is not your fault. Women should be able to go to bars and clubs and not have to worry about this sort of thing. It's part of the reason I'm so adamant about keeping drugs out of my hotel."

I let out a breath and nodded. His words lightened my embarrassment. "The girls and I got off stage and mingled with the crowd. I'd tossed my pearls out into the audience and Eric was the one who returned them. He got me a drink because my champagne spilled." I shrugged. "We really didn't talk about anything serious. That's it."

"And then you went outside with him," Brad stated.

"I began to feel warm after I drank the glass of scotch Eric brought me. We got outside, and then I blacked out." I directed my apology to Brad. "I'm sorry, there's nothing really distinguishing about him. He was handsome but—"

"He was handsome?" Flynn asked.

I looked at him. "Really?"

Brad nodded. "Thanks, Barrett."

"I want more security. And for God's sake, tell the girls not to drink at the club. Not until we have all this resolved," Flynn commanded. "I think we're done for now."

Flynn stood and then held out a hand to me. He escorted me to the private elevator and once the doors closed giving us privacy, he pulled me into his side. I pressed my head against him, wanting to burrow into his warmth and steal a bit of his strength.

"Why didn't you tell him about Chelsea?" I asked.

"I'll tell him later. After I put you to bed."

"I feel like shit," I muttered.

He didn't reply. The doors opened, and we walked in silence into his suite. I kicked off my shoes and my eyes flitted closed even as I tried to keep them open.

"Bed." Flynn took my hand and led me to the bedroom. He pulled back the coverlet and gestured for me to get in. I unbuttoned my jeans and slid them off, nearly falling in the process.

Once my head hit the pillow, I struggled to stay awake. Flynn tugged up the covers and tucked me in. "You're not getting angry at me for being authoritative."

"You're being solicitous," I murmured. "And all women want to be taken care of, though a lot of them refuse to admit it."

"You're welcome," he whispered, kissing my cheek. "Sleep. You'll feel better when you wake up."

Chapter 16

My vibrating phone pulled me from a deep sleep. "Hello?" I croaked.

"Barrett?" Jack asked.

I cleared my throat. "It's me."

"You sound weird. You okay?"

"I have the flu." The lie peeled off my tongue easily. Too easily.

"Oh, sorry to hear that. Do you want me to come hang out with you? We can watch movies."

He was such a good guy. He was everything a brother should be. It made me resent my own brother that much more.

"No," I said. "Thanks for the offer."

"Want me to bring you something? Soup?"

"No, I'm good, really."

"Call when you're better and we'll go out to dinner."

"Will do," I said.

I hung up and momentarily took stock of my body. My headache was gone and though I felt a bit weak, I was no longer nauseous. My stomach rumbled. I reached for my discarded jeans as I glanced at the clock. I'd slept the entire day in Flynn Campbell's bed.

He was nowhere to be found. I was alone in his suite. I called his cell phone, but he didn't answer. Not thinking too much about it, I realized the only thing I really cared about was getting something to eat. The idea of going down to The Rex Hotel Bar and Restaurant didn't appeal to me, so I dialed room service.

While I waited for food, I couldn't help but think about everything that had happened the previous night. Flynn had taken care of me. He'd been by my side when it really mattered. Even if I didn't know all the pieces of him—I knew when he truly cared for people, he was there for them.

My reverie was interrupted by the arrival of food, brought to me by Lacey. "Hi," she said. "You up for a visitor?"

I smiled. "Sure."

"I won't stay long." The manager of the burlesque club came inside and set the tray of food down on the coffee table. "How are you feeling?"

"Hungry," I admitted with a laugh. "I slept most of the day."

"So I heard." When I looked at her questioningly, Lacey clarified. "Flynn. Kept me posted."

"Ah."

I uncovered the warm plate of food and began to eat. "Help yourself to anything."

"I'm good. I just wanted to make sure you were okay."

"Thanks." I paused. "Physically, I feel better. But mentally? I've never blacked out before."

"It's terrifying, isn't it?" Lacey asked quietly.

"Very. There's just a blank spot in my mind. I remember getting off stage, laughing with the girls, the guy and the drink and then—nothing."

"The girls all say to get well soon."

"Sweet of them."

"Well, finish up your food and get some more sleep. I'll see you later."

After Lacey left, I turned on the TV for some background noise and stretched out on the couch, my belly full. Though I'd slept most of the day, my eyes fluttered closed and I dozed.

"Barrett," a voice whispered.

"What," I mumbled into the couch pillow.

"Wake up."

"No."

There was a soft chuckle. "Please?"

With great effort, I opened my eyes and stared into Flynn's blue gaze. I stretched my arms over my head, feeling like a sleepy cat. "You're back."

"Aye."

"You've been gone all day."

"I checked in on you several times."

"You did?"

He grinned. "You were asleep—every time. How are you feeling?"

"Fine-ish."

He reached down to help me off the couch. I stood, peering up at him. He was so large. Large and looming, yet I wasn't afraid.

"I don't regret what happened between us this morning. I just wanted you to know that," I clarified.

His eyes narrowed and bore into me. I tried not to shiver. He hauled me up against him, his body hard, his hands settling on my hips as he gently maneuvered me so that my back hit a wall.

"Flynn—"

He closed his eyes like he was struggling for patience. "I'm tired of this. I want you. You want me."

"True."

"You're admitting it?"

"You take care of me."

"Not in the way you deserve. I didn't protect you." Flynn's jaw clenched with anger.

"I got drugged. You can't save me from everything."

"I'm not good at asking for what I want," he said, his mouth inching closer to mine.

"You don't seem like the kind of guy that has to ask for anything at all."

His smile was pure male arrogance. Cocky and knowing. "Exactly."

I looked up at him and waited. His fingers dipped just below the band of my jeans, skimming the skin of my hipbones. He pressed closer so that his chest grazed my breasts. His lips touched mine, fleetingly, making me want more. But he didn't oblige. He gently unsnapped my jeans, pulled them down, and toyed with the pink satin ribbons that graced my black lace panties.

"Jesus," he said. "Is this the kind of stuff you've been wearing all this time?"

"Maybe."

He tugged down the sexy contraption, baring me to him from the waist down. Flynn stared at me so long I almost begged him to do something—waiting for him to touch me, kiss me—was torture.

He glided his hands across my skin. "Spread your legs," he said, voice low.

I complied immediately, gasping in surprise when Flynn dropped to his knees. He looked up at me, his eyes greedy, voracious, before his tongue snaked out to graze the sensitive skin of my right inner thigh. My legs wobbled and Flynn's grip tightened, holding me in place.

"You're going to feel everything," he commanded, his voice gritty yet firm. "I'm going to make you come so hard you'll see galaxies."

I gazed down at him, running a thumb across his mouth. "You talk too much."

He grinned—and then he licked me, slowly, thoroughly. My hands sank into his hair as tingles began to move through me. He took me into his mouth, sucking gently, until a startled moan escaped my throat.

"Yes, Barrett," he murmured against my swollen, heated flesh.

"More," I demanded. "I want more."

His fingertips slid up and down my hips, my lower back. His tongue swirled and lathed until I trembled.

"You're close," he purred against me.

"Yes," I whimpered, not caring how I sounded.

His finger flitted across my mound as his mouth sucked me hard. I cried out, my back slamming against the wall. My orgasm washed through me, making me feel weak and powerful at the same time.

Flynn lifted his eyes to mine and deliberately licked his lips. He stood and his hands moved to take off my shirt. He unclasped my bra, his hands cupping my breasts.

I leaned into his touch, shuddering when my nipples pebbled. "How is it that I'm entirely naked and you've still got your clothes on?"

"I'm waiting for you to undress me."

I reached for his sweater and pulled it over his head. Next came his shirt. I took a moment to stare at his chest. Hard, muscular, covered in dark hair. I stroked a finger down the center of him, enjoying the sharp inhalation of his breath. I might have been nude, but I'd never felt more in control. His head dipped to kiss me when his pant pocket vibrated. He growled, even as he fished it out. He cursed and answered it.

"What?" He paused, his eyes lingering on my face. He sighed. "I'll be right down."

He hung up and kissed me briefly on the lips. "I'm sorry. There's a situation I've got to handle immediately." His eyes roamed the length of my exposed body. "I can't believe I finally have you naked and I have to go."

I reached out to touch the bulge straining through his pants. "Try to think about work," I teased.

"Not when I've got visions of you coming in my mind."

"Maybe you should try to wrap up everything quickly and then come back."

"Invitation?"

"Yes."

"So you'll stay tonight. In my suite?" He trailed a finger down my neck before circling a nipple. It tightened immediately.

"Yes, I'll stay."

Chapter 17

I woke up in the morning alone and dissatisfied. I blamed Flynn. He'd never come back to his suite. I waited up until about two but when it was apparent he wasn't coming, I sulked off to bed. Flynn's minimal but lavish attention had only inflamed my desire.

After I got dressed, I tossed my dead cell phone into my purse, ready to head home. I took the private elevator down to the lobby and on my way out, I left a message for Flynn with the concierge. I took a cab home, stopped at the corner bodega to get a weak cup of coffee, and then slowly trekked up my apartment stairs. When I got inside, I looked around, feeling like I'd been gone for days.

Plugging in my cell phone to let it recharge, I kicked off my shoes and then stripped on my way to the bedroom. I needed to go for a run. I was sluggish and tired, and it would help. I threw on some exercise clothes and then was out the door.

When I returned an hour later from my run to a fully charged phone, I saw that I had fifteen missed calls. As I scrolled through the missed messages, my cell rang.

Ash.

"Have you seen *The Post?*" she asked without preamble.

"No. I don't read the paper," I said.

She sighed. "You're in it."

"What do you mean I'm in it?"

"Just what I said. Get your computer."

I opened my laptop and navigated to *The Post's* website. I skimmed through the headlines, gasping when I saw my picture.

"What am I doing in the paper?" I asked, attempting to read the article while Ash babbled in my ear. "I'll call you back." I hung up on her so I could fully take in the story.

I was in the damn paper!

And the headline was less than flattering, *Hotel Mogul's New Girlfriend Seen Leaving With Unidentified Man.*

The article itself went on to speculate about the man and why I was slumped against him. There was a statement from Flynn saying it was a friend helping me to a cab because I had a bout of food poisoning.

It was a contrived excuse, yet he'd clearly been available to cover the truth, which meant he *knew* the story was going to hit.

And he hadn't warned me.

My phone rang again but this time it was Flynn. I answered on the first ring. "You've got a lot of fucking nerve," I hissed.

He paused. "You've seen *The Post.*"

"Yeah."

"Where did you go? You left my suite."

"Why would I have stayed?" I snapped. "You didn't come back—which now I know was because you were giving statements to *The Post!*"

"If you'll let me explain—"

I hung up on him.

My phone rang immediately.

I turned it on silent and then went to take a shower.

~

I got out of the shower, my anger slightly diffused. After pulling on some comfortable clothes, I headed toward the kitchen and let out a startled yelp when I saw someone sitting on the couch.

Flynn stood and turned.

"How the hell did you get in here?" I demanded.

"I made myself a set of keys."

"When?"

"Yesterday."

"You mean you made a set of keys while I slept the day away in your hotel suite?" I asked.

"Yes."

"You went into my purse and helped yourself to my keys. Anything else?"

He pretended to look affronted. "No. That would've been an invasion of privacy."

"Get out."

"No. You wouldn't let me explain about the article, so I came over here to do it. But before I do, you don't ever leave my hotel suite without texting or calling me to tell me you're leaving."

I crossed my arms over my chest and glared at him. "My phone was dead. I left a message with your hotel staff. And—go fuck yourself."

His jaw clenched in anger. "Did Chelsea accost you in the park?"

I blinked. "She did."

"She accosted you in the park to warn you away from me. Thank God that was all she did. I want you to tell me if you leave my suite purely for your own safety, not for any other reason."

"Oh," I said, deflating.

"As for the article—"

126

"Ash called to tell me. It should've been you."

"Agreed. And if you'd answered your phone, I would've been able to."

"I was out for a run," I explained. "Is that where you were last night? Tending to that?"

He nodded. "We have an 'in' at the paper. He gave us a heads up about the story going to print, so I was able to release a statement."

"And your statement was 'my girlfriend got food poisoning. Do you really think anyone will buy that?'"

"It's stopped all speculation, so, yes, Barrett, the press is no longer on my back trying to discover the truth."

"Why was I even in the paper?" I demanded. "I'm no one. I'm not your girlfriend."

"Is that why you're really angry? Do you want to be my girlfriend?"

"You patronizing bastard," I hissed.

"Okay, that's enough—"

"No, it's not enough! Did you call me your girlfriend because you needed a cover and couldn't tell the truth about what really happened in your club? Or are we suddenly in a relationship and you forgot to tell me?"

"I'm seriously asking if you want to be my girlfriend."

"No."

"No?"

"Yeah, I can tell by the disbelief in your voice that no one has ever said no to you. Well, there's a first time for everything. No. No. No. No."

He stared at me for a long moment and said, "It wasn't just a date rape drug in your system, Barrett. There was a tranq in there too."

"What does that mean?" I asked, my breath hitching.

"Someone wanted you incapacitated. For a long time. Don't you get it? It's not just people doing drugs in my club. Drugs are now being put in drinks, which means I can't guarantee my patrons' safety. This is serious shit we're dealing with. I couldn't have that in the press."

"Everyone is going to know," I murmured. "Alia and Shawna, everyone I work with. They're going to think I lied to them. Not to mention my cover's been blown."

"You don't need a cover anymore. We found out it was Chelsea bringing drugs into the club."

"Yeah, but we don't know who put her up to it."

He didn't reply, but he stared at me.

"You have an idea, don't you?"

"I know someone who might know."

"What does this mean for me? For us?"

His smile was slow. "Barrett? You're fired."

Chapter 18

"I'll give you the keys I had made," Flynn said, finally breaking the silence.

I shook my head. "Keep them."

"Okay."

"Are we doing this? Really? Out in the open, for real?"

His hand cupped my cheek. "We are, Barrett."

I sighed. "Then use the keys, okay? But maybe you could warn me before you come over?"

"I can do that." He pulled me close to him and pressed my face to his chest and wrapped an arm around me. "You don't trust me."

"I do."

"Really?"

"You took care of me the night I was drugged."

"You remember?"

"Bits and pieces," I admitted. "It's hazy. But you were there, and you held me while I thrashed around in your bed."

"It was the least I could do."

"You take care of things," I said suddenly. "People. That's what you do. I didn't realize…"

"Realize what?"

"Realize that whenever you do something and I find out about it later, it's because you want to take care of things. You want to take care of me."

His fingers ran through my wet strands. "I wonder…"

"Yeah?"

"I wonder if you're the only person who sees me."

I stared into his eyes. Lust brewed between us until it was ready to combust.

He claimed my mouth. Our tongues dueled, battled, engaged. My nails bit into his shoulders as I dragged him closer. He covered me with his body, bathing me with desire and yearning.

"Flynn," I whispered against his lips.

"Don't ask me to stop."

"Wasn't planning on it," I panted.

He pressed his forehead against mine. "Don't ask me to slow down."

"I don't want slow."

Flynn lifted himself off me and shook his head.

"What?" I asked, reaching out to stroke his jaw. My chest rose and fell in rapid breaths, my throat dry, my body aching for his. At the moment, I didn't care about anything except my desire for Flynn Campbell.

"You want this," he stated. "Me."

"Yes."

"You sure?"

"No."

He laughed. It was a rough, gritty sound, branding me with desire all over again. He swept me into his arms and carried me into the bedroom. "I had plans to come up here and ask if I could take you to dinner tonight. Out in the open."

"I was supposed to work at the club tonight," I stated as he set me down on the bed. "But it seems I'm out of a job."

He reached for the buttons of his white dress shirt and then tossed it aside. His undershirt followed.

My eyes dropped from his face to the skin at his throat, and then lower, to the tautness of his stomach. Thinking and speaking were becoming difficult. Resolve and resolution were far from my thoughts. He dropped his pants and my breath hitched.

He was glorious nude. All sinew, muscle, and strength. Swarthy skin. A devil in an angel's disguise. His erection was rigid, perfect. I reached out to touch him; the heat of him felt like it burned. Or maybe it was lust flaring in my veins.

I knew there was a risk being with him. I hated his secrets, hated that he kept a part of himself tucked away from me, yet when I was with him, I never felt more alive.

My lips closed over him and he inhaled sharply. My tongue twirled around the crown of his shaft. I licked, nibbled, tasted, drawing him deeper into my mouth. His hands came up to grasp my head.

"Enough," he said, his voice strained.

I looked at him, wanting him to see my need, my desire. "Afraid you won't be able to control yourself?"

"I haven't been able to control myself since I saw you in that French restaurant."

My brother had bartered me in lieu of his debt, and my life had never been the same. I hadn't realized that Flynn's life hadn't been the same either.

He tugged at my T-shirt and lifted it over my head. His gaze lingered on my skin, and when he went for the waistband of my leggings, he was a little rough.

I didn't complain.

He settled me onto the bed and then draped his body over mine. Bathing my collarbone in kisses, his tongue darted out to taste my fevered skin. He moved down with gentle care until he was at the heat of me and then his fingertips played with the tender skin on the inside of my thighs.

I quivered, wanting his tongue—him—inside me. I made an impatient sound.

He laughed, his breath shooting over me, but he didn't give in. Continuing his ministrations, he lapped and laved until I bucked beneath him, coming under his mouth.

Flynn grasped my hips and slid up my body, his erection pressing against me. "I'm clean."

"Me too. I'm on the pill."

"Thank God," he gritted.

I laughed, but it died on my lips as he eased into me.

"Look at me," he demanded.

We stared into each other's eyes as he sank into my depths, sheathing himself fully into my tight body. I cried out in pleasure when he began to move, rolling his pelvis and gripping my hips. My hands wove through his hair, and I tugged him closer. Our mouths collided, passion exploding between us.

Another orgasm began to shiver down my spine and then it ripped through me, wrenching a scream from my throat. I clung to Flynn as he thrust deeply a few more times before finding his own release.

I buried my face in his neck, content, sated, and not at all wishing to spoil it with talking.

"You leaving?" I asked when Flynn got up and sat on the side of the bed.

He looked over his bare shoulder at me and grinned. "You want me to go?"

I shrugged. "If you're so inclined."

He laughed. "I was going to order food."

"I thought you were going to take me out to dinner," I teased.

"I want you to stay naked," he said, his eyes drifting down my body. "I was going to pay for takeout. That okay?"

"Sweet. Very boyfriend of you."

"Are you calling me your boyfriend?"

"I think so."

"You think so?" he asked in amusement.

I tugged up the sheet to cover myself while enjoying the view of him without clothes. He looked relaxed yet powerful. "Nothing's really been resolved between us. I still want you to open up and you still seem inclined to keep things from me because that's your natural way."

"We'll order food and then you can ask me all the questions you want, and I'll try to answer them to your satisfaction. Okay?"

Recognizing his words for what they were, I nodded.

When he hung up, he went for his pants and then tossed me his button-down. I arched a brow but said nothing, donning his shirt and rolling up the sleeves. We moved into the living room, Flynn's chest still bare. It was a distracting sight. I sat on the couch and propped my legs up onto the coffee table.

"Your move," he said.

I nodded, trying to compose my thoughts but then decided to let it all out. "The casino and brothel…why do you really do it? It's not because of the danger. I know that was an excuse."

"It's complicated."

"Of course it is," I muttered. "Well, explain."

"I can't."

"And there it is." I got up off the couch.

"Hold on." He reached out to grasp my arm, tugging me down to sit. "Instead of you asking the questions, let me volunteer some information."

I crossed my arms over my chest and gave him a cold stare. "I'm listening."

"Have you heard of Giovanni Marino?"

"No."

"He owns The Dominus Hotel—the one on the Lower East Side."

"You want to talk about another hotel mogul?"

"Marino is head of the Italian Mob of New York."

"Mob? Wait. Are *you* in the mob?"

He paused. "There are certain powerful, wealthy men who run the city."

"Are you one of these men?" I demanded.

"Aye."

"So the casino and brothel allow you a certain form of power? Am I close?"

"Something like that. There are things I can't tell you—not because I don't want to but because I'm protecting you."

"Stuff about the brothel and casino?"

He paused and then, "Aye. Let's just say there are certain people who might use you to get to me. The less you know, the better off you'll be. Please trust me on that, okay?"

"Am I in danger?"

"There's always an element of danger—to anything."

"You're not doing a good job of reassuring me," I said.

"You were drugged. In my club. And you were almost put into a cab by a stranger. I don't need to tell you to be on your guard."

A shiver of fear raced down my back, and I rubbed my arms, suddenly cold.

Flynn's gaze was angry. "I should let you go."

"Go?" I murmured. "Go where? Back to my other life? I can't go back. Even if I wanted to. Which I don't."

"But your job—you loved your job. You can still go back to that. I made sure of it."

I glanced at him. "Yeah, my boss was pretty accommodating. Why?"

Flynn let out a small, self-satisfied laugh. "I made a huge donation to the department."

"Even back when you hardly knew me, you were trying to

take care of me," I whispered. "Keep your secrets for now, Flynn. I'll try to be more patient."

The intercom buzzed, and before I could get up to answer it, Flynn was there. He let in the Thai delivery guy and a few moments later, handed over some cash. We sat on the floor, eating out of containers, and using takeout chopsticks.

"There's a reason I mentioned Giovanni Marino," Flynn said, picking up the thread of our earlier conversation.

"Oh?" I'd completely forgotten about the leader of the Italian mob.

"He might have some knowledge about who drugged you."

"What makes you think so?"

Flynn went quiet.

"One of those don't ask don't tell things, huh?"

"Aye."

"Are there going to be a lot of those?" I grumbled.

"Probably," he said, reaching for a bite of my curry. "I'm going to pay him a little visit."

"And you think he'll just give up information?"

"Perhaps. You'll be coming with me."

"Why are you going to take me to a mob boss? What about protecting me and keeping me out of danger?"

"Bringing you will send a message," Flynn said.

"God damn, you're cryptic."

"A man doesn't go to Marino's turf without flaunting what he has," he attempted to explain.

"You don't 'have' me."

"No? I beg to differ."

"Girlfriend does not equate possession," I pointed out.

His eyes skimmed the length of my body, including my bare legs. "You're in my shirt."

"And that means what?"

He shrugged. "You'll see tomorrow night."

Chapter 19

The day after the article hit, I met with Lacey in the burlesque club's private office. She hadn't dressed for the evening yet, so she was still in her smart black dress and ridiculously high heels. She was one of those women that didn't care that she was tall—she loved heels and wore them anyway.

"Have you come to hand in your official resignation?" Lacey asked with a smile, taking a seat behind the desk.

I nodded and sat in my own chair.

"Kind of unnecessary. Flynn already did it for you."

"Shocking."

"Right? I told him if you still wanted to dance you had my blessing."

"Really?" I asked.

"Yeah. You're welcome to perform any time."

"Thanks, but I think my performing days are over."

"Hmmm. We'll see. Did you and Flynn work out what you're going to say to your former co-workers?" Lacey asked. "Even though you don't really owe them an explanation."

"They've become my friends," I stated. "I already feel crappy enough that I lied to them about why I started working here—"

"Which you still can't tell them."

"I'm aware." I peered at the manager of the club. "What did you tell them about Chelsea?"

"She took a leave of absence because of family problems."

"She went underground again, didn't she? How?" I demanded. "How can there be no trace of her?"

"He'll find her," Lacey said.

"How can you be sure?"

"Because Flynn always gets what he wants."

I trembled at the resolution in her voice. What did that mean for Chelsea when Flynn found her? Though Flynn took care of me and those he felt belonged to him, he wasn't the kind of man to take disloyalty lightly. And Chelsea had committed the ultimate betrayal—trying to take down part of his empire.

"Chelsea was a good actor," I stated.

"Too good," Lacey said flatly. "And there was nothing in her background check."

"Holy shit," I said in sudden realization. "You think she's FBI, don't you?"

"Not a lot of other explanations, Barrett. But don't go getting ahead of yourself trying to figure it out. We won't know for certain until we find her."

For some reason, her words comforted me. Flynn wasn't alone. He had people who had his back.

Was I one of them?

Lacey glanced at her watch and said, "The girls will be trickling in. Might as well go on out there."

"Thanks, Lacey."

"Sure. Can I ask you a question? Before you go?"

"Yeah."

"Are you going to go back to your old job? Research assistant in the history department?"

I frowned. "I don't know, why?"

She paused before saying, "I know your official job as

undercover cocktail waitress is over, but Flynn is still going to need you by his side."

"You mean as his girlfriend? It's a full-time job?" I teased.

Lacey didn't smile. "No, I mean as a *consigliere* of sorts."

"*Consigliere*? Really?"

"You know enough about his enterprises. He's let you in— more than anyone in the past ten years."

I raised my eyebrows. "Are you saying he trusts me?"

"To a degree," she said. "Flynn doesn't really trust anyone completely."

"Why?"

"You'll have to ask him that."

After I made peace with my former coworkers, who all demanded the story I wouldn't give them, I walked into the lobby and was immediately pounced on by Flynn. I tried not to falter, but the heat radiating off him was too much. The set of his jaw was hard and unyielding.

"Barrett," he greeted, his voice low and gravelly.

It instantly made me want to strip off all his clothes and devour him. One night with Flynn and I was an addict.

"Flynn," I answered, striving for casual.

"A word?"

I nodded, and he set his hand at the small of my back and ushered me to his private elevator. I refused to meet the gazes of the surprised employees that lingered in the lobby. Flynn pushed the elevator button with his free hand, his other tightening on me. When we were in the privacy of the elevator, Flynn pressed me against a plush wall and kissed me. His tongue sought mine, insistent, demanding.

"You left me sleeping in your bed this morning," he said, his hands threading their way through my ponytail, loosening

it. His mouth found my neck, and he gently bit my skin.
"Where did you go?"

"Out."

"Barrett," he growled.

"I went for a run."

I kissed him as if I'd die without his breath. My hands
were greedy for the feel of him, and I was insistent in wanting
to touch his bare skin. I yanked at his shirt.

The doors opened to the penthouse, and we stumbled into
the foyer, tearing at each other's clothes. He ripped at my
white blouse, buttons flying everywhere. His hands cupped my
breasts encased in a lacy white bra. He brought his mouth to a
nipple and laved it through the thin material.

I groaned, wanting to be naked as soon as possible. My
shirt was off, but everything else was still on. I made a move to
unclasp my bra, but Flynn's voice stopped me.

"Leave the rest on."

I nodded, lust filling my brain, zinging through my veins.
He pushed me toward the glass windows of the penthouse
and turned me around so that I was facing the tree line of
Central Park. Down below, I saw joggers and street traffic.

Flynn's hands traveled up my A-line black skirt, his thumb
grazing me through my underwear. I gasped when he exerted
a little more pressure. Placing my palms on the cool glass, I
needed something to steady me as Flynn tugged down my
panties. He cupped me, his hand warm and strong.

His breath was hot on my neck as he kissed his way across
sensitive skin. I shivered, a dull ache building inside of me. I
wanted him between my legs—tongue, fingers, everything. But
he was toying with me, playing, punishing.

"Please," I begged.

He gave in, slipping one finger inside my core. I tightened
and worked him against me. It wasn't enough, and the bastard
knew it. I pushed back, letting him know. We spoke the
language of lust; words were unnecessary. Flynn removed his

finger from inside me, and I gasped at the emptiness. But moments later, he was back, entering, filling me with his hard length.

The world was at my feet, and I felt powerful, unstoppable as I saw our dim reflection in the glass windows. He gripped my hips, ramming into me. My hand slipped up my skirt to play with myself while Flynn continued to assault my senses and body with his.

"Yes," I moaned, feeling the peak of release coming. "Harder."

He gave it to me. He claimed me, but I let him. Whatever I wanted, it was mine. I slammed a hand against the glass, the sound of it mingling with our cries of passion. I came with fierce abandon, bucking against him. He bit my skin where my shoulder met my neck, marking me before coming inside me.

We owned each other, completely.

$\sim$

We were on the carpeted floor of the suite, completely naked, clothes scattered about. I hitched a leg over Flynn's and snuggled into his embrace.

"Your bed is too small," Flynn said drowsily.

"You didn't sleep well last night?" I asked.

"Not really. My legs hang off your bed, and your mattress is—"

"Don't insult my mattress."

"Are you attached to your apartment?"

I didn't like where this conversation was going. "Yes, I'm attached to my apartment."

His fingers skated up my spine, and I closed my eyes while I waited for him to drop the bomb in his arsenal. I didn't have to wait long.

"You can have a bigger apartment."

"Can I? How?" I asked, feigning stupid, but he didn't buy it.

"You know how."

"No."

"No," he repeated flatly.

"No, I will not let you pay for a bigger apartment just so your legs don't hang off my bed."

"The bed isn't the only issue. All my clothes are here. I had to do the walk of shame in a wrinkled suit—and leave far earlier than I wanted to because I had no clothes at your apartment."

"So bring over a few suits."

"It's not just a few suits. It's shoes, and belts, and ties, and cuff links, and—"

"And I don't have the space. That's what you're really saying."

"Aye."

"There's another solution," I said.

"What's that?"

"When we spend the night together, we spend it in your suite. You get your bed, you get your suits, and you get your whole routine."

"And what do you get?"

"Besides the walk of shame through your hotel lobby?" I teased. "Nights with you. And maybe room service in the morning."

"I could give you a dresser drawer and some closet space. I have a lot of closet space."

"My walk of shame would be far more comfortable in clean underwear."

He laughed. "Does that mean you accept?"

"Yes, Flynn, I accept your dresser drawer and closet space."

Chapter 20

Flynn raised his eyebrows while he watched me fume. He had to know this was going to be an issue. Did he hope our sexual bout against his suite windows would lull me into doing his bidding? I was a woman in lust, but I was still me.

"I'm not wearing this," I said, holding up the diamond-encrusted collar. "And I'm definitely not wearing those." I pointed to his bed at the pair of diamond bracelets, one for each wrist. They resembled shackles. Diamond shackles were still shackles.

"Why?" he asked, trying to hide his smile and doing a terrible job.

"I knew I would have to pretend to be your chattel for the evening, but this is going too far. I wear these, then you really will think I'm your property."

"I would never think you were my property."

I snorted. "Yeah, right. Powerful men are collectors of things—and you are a collector of gorgeous women."

He finally gave into a full smile. "Jealous of Lana?"

"Thin ice, buddy."

Flynn laughed.

"You've already informed me that for tonight I'm to be seen but not heard."

He sighed. "What will it take for you to wear them? What do you want from me in return?"

"I want you to tell me about your family."

"No," Flynn stated, all traces of humor gone from his face.

"Why?"

"I never speak of my family."

I wondered if he'd ever tell me, if I would ever become a confidant, and not just his bed partner. I hated that he knew everything about my past and me. I hated that he knew how foul my brother truly was while I knew nothing of his family.

"You don't have to wear the jewelry," he said, turning away from me. "I'll wait for you to finish getting ready."

Twenty minutes later, Flynn escorted me to the private elevator. My auburn hair had been styled in loose waves, the black dress hugging every inch of me, showing a lot of leg, a lot of cleavage. Four-inch stilettos made my legs look even longer, and I'd painted my lips a dark red.

Flynn stared at my mouth and I grinned. "Wondering if I'll let you smear it?" I purred, hoping to torment him. I enjoyed the darkening of his gaze, but he remained silent.

We turned heads as we walked through the lobby. A bellman opened the door and said, "Good evening, Mr. Campbell, Ms. Schaefer."

Flynn's driver held open the door to the black Rolls waiting for us. I slid in and Flynn swooped in next to me, purposefully invading my space. I tried to move away, but he gripped my hand and hauled me onto his lap.

"What the hell!" I hissed as the door shut.

"You're supposed to be playing the role of devoted trophy."

I glowered. "You're pissing me off."

"I noticed."

He sifted a hand into my hair, and I couldn't stop my eyes from closing. I adjusted myself on his lap, so the heat of me pressed against him. I felt his arousal and wanted to grind myself on top of him.

"Not everything can be solved with sex," I gritted out.

"Barrett——"

I shoved his hands off me and tried to move away from him, but he wouldn't let me. "I don't want to do this."

"It's too late. And I need you."

"No, you don't. You can get anyone to do this with you. Hire someone—an actress who knows better than to ask you personal questions." Tears began to fall, unbidden. There had been no hope of holding back my emotions. Flynn continued to shut me out and I loathed it.

His hands framed my head, forcing me to look at him. His thumbs brushed under my eyes.

"My parents died when I was fifteen in a car accident outside of Edinburgh. I went wild."

I stopped fighting him, my body sinking against his and I waited. Waited for more.

"My godfather took me in, gave me a home, straightened me out and didn't give up on me. I——"

I kissed him, cutting him off, wanting him to know it was enough because he was trying. That's all I wanted—for him to try. His hands stroked along my curves as he paid homage to my neck, my arms.

His thumb gently brushed over the bite on my neck. "I shouldn't have done that to you. Marked you."

I sighed, finally giving him a piece of honesty. Maybe it would pave the way for something deeper. "I'm glad you did. I like looking in the mirror and seeing it. It reminds me that someone wants me."

"I want you," he said, his voice low. "I want you stretched out beneath me. That will happen later."

"I should reapply my lipstick."

"Don't," he commanded.

"Why?"

He took my hand and laced his fingers with mine. "When we go inside The Dominus, you need to remember one thing."

"What's that?"

"I'm not the man I'm pretending to be."

I looked at him, curious, but I nodded.

The car stopped and our driver opened the door. Flynn got out first, straightening his black tie, and buttoning his gray suit jacket. He looked like a man ready to sit in a library and smoke a cigar, drink some brandy, and talk about investments.

He helped me out of the Rolls, settled his hand on my hip, and guided me inside. The Dominus hotel was outfitted in modern décor. Gray and white furniture that didn't look at all comfortable, exposed steel beams, and industrial lighting. I preferred the old-world appeal of The Rex.

An attendant met us and escorted us through the stark lobby. "Mr. Marino is in the penthouse," the attendant said, holding the elevator open.

He didn't ride up with us, but Flynn and I still remained silent. The doors opened, and I tensed. The penthouse was filled with middle-aged men in suits and their beautiful, much younger companions. All of them wore tight revealing dresses and jewels.

"Oh," I said softly, finally understanding why Flynn had wanted me to wear the diamond shackles and collar.

Flynn turned his mouth to my ear and said, "Don't worry about it."

"Campbell!" a rotund man called.

"Marino," Flynn greeted.

Marino had a bulbous nose and his button-down shirt strained over his protruding stomach. The man clearly enjoyed food and drink. Marino had the lighter coloring of northern Italians as opposed to their darker Sicilian brethren.

"You're late," Marino said. "And you've got something on your mouth." He smirked, his gaze finally finding me. "Ah, I can see why."

Flynn tipped his head in acknowledgement. "Shall we get on with it? There are other things I'd rather be doing."

"I bet."

As if on cue, my hand came up to stroke Flynn's chest.

"Lucky devil," Marino muttered, waving us farther into the penthouse. "Get you a drink?"

"The lady will have champagne. I'll have nothing."

"Afraid I'll poison you?" Marino chuckled like he'd said something funny.

"Not at all. I know that's not your style. Drugging on the other hand…" Flynn shrugged, and I watched Marino's brown eyes cloud with anger.

"What are you saying, Campbell?"

"You know."

Marino held Flynn's gaze before lowering his eyes. "I'm not behind it."

"But you know who is."

Marino glanced at me. "We should discuss this in private."

"Agreed."

A server handed me a drink and Flynn released me. "Excuse me a moment, pet. I'll be right back."

I gave him a sultry little pout and even though it was for show, I knew he appreciated it. I could tell he didn't want to leave me alone, but men like Marino didn't discuss business in front of women. Women were pretty objects, nothing more.

The door to the library shut, and I wondered what knowledge I wasn't privy to.

~

An old goat grabbed my ass.

I nearly squeaked in surprise before anger overtook me. "Hands off," I spat.

The man leered, his gaze dropping to my breasts, his hand tightening on my behind. He acted as though he hadn't heard me. I didn't want to make a scene, knowing women were nothing more than commodities here. I knew how it felt to be traded like a possession. Even though I was a reflection of Flynn, I was not going to let myself be passed around.

"What do you say we head to a private suite?" he slurred, liquor fumes hitting me in the face. The man swayed, placing a kiss on my bare shoulder.

I grimaced, feeling violated and abused. "No!" I yelled, throwing my champagne in the man's face. He howled like a little boy who'd had his toy taken away.

"Bitch!" he fumed. "You'll fucking pay for that!"

Before I could register what was happening, the man harassing me went flying across the room. Flynn's angry face loomed in front of me, ready for a fight, his chest rising and falling rapidly.

The room was suddenly quiet as Marino strolled out of the library, looking around him. "What's going on in here?"

"Murphy was pawing Campbell's woman," a man with a gray goatee explained. Glad he'd noticed. The jerk could've helped me out. I shot him a glare.

Marino barked an order at a security agent who went to the fallen Murphy and escorted him out of the penthouse. Marino turned back to Flynn and said, "I apologize."

Flynn nodded his head, took my hand, and we left the suite.

"I—"

"Wait for the car," Flynn instructed as we made our way through the lobby.

We were both seething. I'd been handled like a prized filly at an auction—a man had put his hands on me. And Marino had apologized to *Flynn*. As if I was nothing more than an extension of him.

We didn't speak until we were on our way back to The Rex. The Rex, where things made a weird sort of sense to me. I felt like a pawn.

What had my life become?

"I'm so sorry, Barrett," Flynn gritted out. "I never would've left you alone if I thought for one moment you wouldn't be safe."

"They didn't do anything to stop him," I stated. "They let it happen. All the men and women just stood by and watched. Even the security guard. They made me feel worthless." Flynn tried to take me into his arms, but I pushed him away and scooted to the corner.

"I was an object tonight. And I didn't like it. I hated that I was in a place where I needed your protection." I closed my eyes like I was in pain.

Before I knew it, I was hauled into his side and forced to look at him. His eyes were dark in the night.

Predator and prey.

I'd deluded myself into thinking we could be equals. We weren't equals. Who was I kidding?

His mouth swooped in and covered mine. I wanted to shove him away but didn't. Instead, I yanked him closer. I was pissed at myself because I felt far too much for a man who could destroy me. He was nothing but danger and power and secrets. I was the quintessential lamb, offering my throat to the wolf.

When the Rolls came to a halt outside my apartment, my eyes fluttered open in confusion. I'd forgotten everything. Flynn did that to me. We broke apart. I was glad because I needed time to clear my head.

Flynn helped me out of the Rolls and followed me upstairs. Just when I thought I was going to have to explain to him that I wanted to be alone, Flynn said, "I need to speak with Brad about some things. Can we have dinner tomorrow night?"

I shook my head. "I need some time."

Flynn's face went blank, his eyes steely. "Fine. I'll call you later." He briefly kissed my cheek and then left.

After I showered off my evening, I crawled into bed, tugging up the covers to my chin, wondering why I—strong woman that I was—wanted Flynn's comfort.

Sometime in the middle of the night, I rolled over, encountering warm skin and a solid body. I snuggled close to him, put my hand on his chest, and went back to sleep.

Chapter 21

"You have violated the best friend code," Ash said, dumping more wine into my wineglass before settling back on her very expensive, very white couch.

"You mean hanging up on you while you tried to tell me I was in the newspaper?"

"That, and the fact that you're dating Flynn Campbell and I wasn't even the first person to know about it."

"Um. Ash. I wasn't even the first person to know about it."

She frowned. "I've had too much wine."

Though I still had to hide some things from Ash, I gave her the watered-down version of what had occurred. Her eyes widened in sheer disbelief. "You're kidding, right?"

"Nope. I'm officially in a relationship with Flynn Campbell. Privately as well as publicly."

Ash grimaced.

"What?"

"That's going to be new for you, having your name splashed across the society section."

"Why would my name be splashed across the society section?" I asked.

"Because you're dating Flynn who is one of the cities

more elusive playboys. People are going to be watching and waiting to see if he loses interest in you."

"Fantastic," I said with a shake of my head.

When I'd awoken this morning, there had been no sign that Flynn had slept in bed next to me except for his lingering smell on my pillow. He clearly hadn't liked the idea of spending the night apart, even though I'd wanted the space. But when I realized he was in bed next to me, I hadn't exactly kicked him out of it.

My phone buzzed, and I reached for it. A text from Flynn.

"What's got you frowning?" Ash asked.

"Nothing," I muttered as I opened the message. It was a picture of Flynn's closet—a section of it had been cleared for me. My frown melted into a smile.

"Now you're smiling."

I sighed and showed her the photo. "He's wants to share his closet with me."

She shook her head. "Never would've believed it. A man like Campbell making room for his *girlfriend's* clothes."

"I don't feel like his girlfriend."

"What do you feel like?"

"Not sure," I said. "He's intensely private and closed off. He doesn't trust, but…I don't know. I feel like we're really building something here. Is that stupid? Naïve? I mean, look at how we met."

"You have to get over that," she said gently. "That was Andrew's doing. And like you said, Flynn could've behaved differently. I think it's okay to trust yourself."

"I'm so limited in my experiences, Ash. But he doesn't make me feel that way."

"So, it's easy? Between you two?"

"I wouldn't say it's easy. I mean, we're two different people with different ways of doing things, but we always find a way to work it out, I guess. I don't know."

It was all so complicated, what I had with Flynn. "I think I shouldn't focus so much on our past. It doesn't do any good. I need to look to the future. Speaking of which…I think I'm going to go back to my old job."

"Yeah?"

I nodded. "But not until next semester. I'm going to take a few months off, let things settle. My life lately has been nothing but upheaval."

The money I'd made working in Flynn's club for the past few months would more than support me during my time off.

"That will be a big change for you," Ash said.

"I have a feeling it's not going to be the last big change I see."

I walked into The Rex with every intention of heading up to Flynn's penthouse suite to wait for him. I wanted to put the distance behind us and move forward. But Alia and Shawna waylaid me and before I could escape, they dragged me into the club and sat me down at a table.

"You're not quitting dancing," Shawna said, tossing long brown hair over her shoulder.

"I'm not?" I asked in confusion.

Alia shook her head, her dark almond-shaped eyes gleaming. "Nope. We won't let you."

"But—"

"We don't care that you're sleeping with the boss," Shawna said.

"I thought we went through all this the other day," I protested.

"We've had a meeting," Alia said, "With the other dancers and the cocktail waitresses. We like you. You're fun and you enjoy dancing. So no. I won't let you quit dancing. Quit waitressing if you want. That I get."

"Yeah, you're performing tonight," Shawna said. "So let's get you back to the dressing room and in costume."

They tugged me along, not giving me a chance to protest or fight. Not that I really wanted to. I enjoyed performing. It gave me something, fed a part of me I hadn't known was hungry.

When the club was in full swing, I took the stage. Blinded by the lights, I saw nothing, no one. I moved through my routine with assurance and pride. When I finished, the crowd whistled and cheered as I gathered my discarded costume pieces. I blew the audience a kiss and waltzed off stage and into the dressing room.

As I shimmied back into my blue satin dress and adjusted the straps, there was a knock on the dressing room door.

"Come in!"

"Barrett," came Flynn's gravelly voice. Tingly awareness shot down my spine when I turned to face him.

He stalked toward me, grasping my upper arms before his mouth collided with mine. Our tongues danced, tangled. The adrenaline from my performance was still humming in my veins, and it flared to life. I jumped into his arms, straddling him around the waist.

"I've never seen anything like it," Flynn muttered, his mouth moving to the column of my throat.

"What?"

"You on stage. You were incredible."

His words slammed into me, giving me something I didn't realize I needed. Power. Control. Dominance. Over him.

I slid down his body, my high-heeled feet hitting the floor, but I stayed in his arms. We hadn't been apart but two days, and yet I'd missed him.

"Flynn," I moaned into his ear.

"I love hearing you say my name." He smiled, but it was all teeth. He bent to nip my neck. "I've missed you."

He echoed exactly what was going on in my head.

I quivered. "Did you?"

"Not the same when I don't get to talk to you, feel you."

His hand skimmed up my dress, and his fingers toyed with the curve of my bottom, fingering the lace underwear I wore.

"Should I even bother asking about the conversation you had with Marino?"

"No."

I sighed, gently disengaged from his hands, and moved away. I already missed his heat. "I hate that you won't tell me."

"I know. But can you live with that?"

"I guess I have to. I don't really have a choice. Not if I want this to continue."

"Do you want this to continue?"

Pausing for a moment, I cocked my head to the side and bit my lip. I nodded and heard Flynn's slow exhale.

"Were you really worried I'd walk away?"

He paused and studied me. "I always wonder what it will be that inevitably pushes you away. Because something will."

"Don't be so fatalistic," I commanded.

"It's in my nature."

Not wishing to get into something heavy after a night of performing, I changed the subject. "Can you stay down here for another performance?"

"Will you watch with me?"

I moved close to him again, wrapping my arms around him, pleased that he let me. I rubbed my nose against his jaw line. "I've got something planned…but I need time to set it up."

"What is it?"

"A surprise."

"Will I like it?"

I grinned. Naughty. Just a bit dirty. "Oh, yeah. You'll like it."

When I was sure that Flynn was settled in his booth with a drink, I slipped up to his hotel suite. He'd left the diamond collar and bracelets in his bedside drawer. I'd refused to wear them the other night when we'd gone to Marino's, not realizing they would've helped me play a role and given Flynn an edge. Tonight, I wore them for him. Because I trusted Flynn, and I wanted him to know it.

I sat on my haunches in the middle of the bed, wearing a matching black lace bra and underwear set, the diamond collar at my neck, and the bracelets on my wrists.

For some reason, I was nervous. Submitting to him—in all the ways I wasn't accustomed to—frightened me. And I didn't do frightened very well.

I heard the elevator doors open and Flynn called out, "Barrett?"

"In here!" I was glad my voice didn't shake.

Flynn came into the bedroom and halted. His gaze rested on the collar before dropping lower. His eyes gleamed wickedly. "Nice underwear. Take it off."

I was unpacking my clothes in my newly acquired drawer of Flynn's dresser when the elevator doors chimed. It was Lacey, holding a tray of brownies.

"You made those?" I asked in surprise.

Lacey gave me a full, red-lipped smile and shook her head, sending expensively dyed caramel waves over her shoulder. "Do I look like the baking type?"

"Not at all."

"How's the moving in?" she asked.

"I'm not moving in."

"Right. Okay."

"I'm not. He gave me a drawer and part of his closet."

"In his private penthouse suite. That's not normal Flynn Campbell behavior."

"What *is* normal Flynn Campbell behavior?" I demanded.

"Since you showed up? I have absolutely no idea."

We had a laugh and then she cut into the tray of brownies, handing me one. She glanced around the living room and said, "He never decorated."

"Ah, I guess he didn't."

"It looks like every other one of his hotel suites. You should make it homey."

"It's not my home, though. It's Flynn's home, and I don't want to go about changing stuff."

"Honey, you've already changed stuff."

I tried to beat down the emotions that threatened to come up and choke me.

Lacey reached for a brownie as she glanced at my untouched one. "Don't like brownies?"

"Don't like chocolate," I explained.

"You're crazy," she said, polishing off the brownie in a few bites. "I have an amazing black and white photography series I think you'd like. I can donate it to the cause of making this place look more lived-in."

"Really?"

"Yeah. I'll bring them by."

"Thanks."

"Okay. Grab your phone and let's go," she said.

"Go? Go where?"

"We're going shopping."

"Shopping? Why?"

"Because Flynn asked me to take you. You need a formal dress. And shoes. And jewelry."

"Why do I need a formal dress?"

"You and Flynn are going to a charity event later this week." She peered at me. "He didn't tell you."

"Does he tell me anything?" I asked with a roll of my eyes.

"Probably not nearly as much as you want."

"That's the truth." I shook my head. "A charity event, huh?"

Lacey grinned. "Leave your purse. You won't need it."

Chapter 22

I should've had a difficult time adjusting to Flynn paying for obscenely expensive gowns, but it was one of the ways he showed his affection for me—another way for him to prove he wanted to take care of me. So I let him and didn't worry so much about it.

"I'm thinking purple," Lacey said as she opened the door to an upscale boutique.

"Purple? I don't want to look like a grape."

Lacey grinned. "Not grape purple. Amethyst purple. It will look great against your skin and hair."

"I trust you. After all, you're the one that's in charge of costumes at the club."

"I'm also in charge of the wardrobe choices for the other young ladies at The Rex. Those that work on The Fifteenth Floor."

The Fifteenth Floor was the brothel.

"Really?"

She nodded.

"What's it like?" I asked.

She glanced at me in amusement. "You should come by

one night and see for yourself. Whatever it is you imagine, it won't compare to the real thing."

Intriguing, to say the least. And I was definitely going to check it out.

I gazed around the boutique once again feeling entirely out of my element. In my old life, I never went to charity events or owned clothes that cost more than a down payment on a car.

Lacey knew her stuff, so I let her and the assistant discuss what I should wear. They were in good company. While they planned how to dress me, I walked around the boutique, studying the jewelry. I slid to the next jewelry case and bumped into someone.

"Oh, I'm sorry!" I said, finally looking up from all the shiny trinkets.

Ash's ex-fiancé smiled absently, and then his eyes registered it was me and not a stranger. "Barrett," he said. "Hello."

"Um. Hi. What are you doing here?"

His brown eyes darted away from mine before returning. "Birthday present shopping. For my sister. I thought…" He gestured to the jewelry we'd been appraising.

"Right."

"What are you doing here?"

John had been with Ash three years, and we'd gotten to know one another. Well, gotten to know each other in the sense that we understood what the other was about. We'd had Ash in common, but we weren't friends independently of her.

"My boyfriend and I are attending a charity event later this week. I need a dress."

"Boyfriend?" John asked. "New relationship?"

Guess he hadn't seen *The Post*. "Relatively."

"Well, I'm happy for you."

By mutual agreement we steered clear of the subject of Ash, but we'd run out of small talk. Awkward silence fell between us.

"Barrett," Lacey called out, her attention on me again.

"Coming," I called back, feeling relieved. I gave John a brief hug. "Take care."

"You too."

I watched John leave and then went to Lacey.

"Who was that?" Lacey asked as she guided me to the dressing room.

"Someone from my past," I answered with a shake of my head. Poor bastard. He looked completely broken and devastated. "Okay, show me what monstrosity you want me to wear."

Shopping with Lacey was relatively painless, unlike shopping with Ash who had no trouble trying on pair after pair of shoes, debating for hours over what to buy. Ash was a marathon shopper—Lacey was a sprint shopper. Once she saw me in the dress she deemed perfect, that was it. Next came the shoes, which weren't too high or too painful.

"You'll probably end up dancing," she said, when she handed over a corporate credit card to the store attendant.

"Dancing?"

"Ballroom," she clarified.

"I don't ballroom dance."

"That's okay, neither does Flynn."

"But—"

"You'll be fine. Trust me." Lacey turned to the boutique attendant. "Please have these delivered to The Rex Hotel. Mr. Campbell's suite. Thank you." Lacey took back her credit card and stuck it in her shoulder bag.

When we stepped out onto the sidewalk she said, "Now onto jewelry."

"But that place had jewelry. Why didn't we buy it there?"

Lacey shot me an amused look. "You are too adorable for

words."

"Don't patronize me," I said.

"Sorry. We're headed to Tiffany's."

"Veto."

"Why?"

"I detest Tiffany's."

A gleam of approval showed in Lacey's eyes. "All right then. I have another store in mind."

I sat in the lobby of The Rex, and though the couch was comfortable, irritation made me unable to sit still, I waited for Flynn, whose back was to me, his tall, suit-clad form making me sigh in feminine appreciation. Flynn said something to the man with him, making him laugh. When Flynn turned, his eyes caught mine, and he smiled.

"Mitch Armstrong," Flynn introduced when they were standing in front of me, "I'd like you to meet my girlfriend, Barrett Schaefer."

I stood up, held out my hand, and attempted to slap a smile on my face. "Nice to meet you."

"Mitch is the architect who is going to design the glass lounge on the roof."

"I love projects like these," Mitch confided. "Flynn is one hell of a businessman."

"Yes, he is," I agreed.

"I'll call you later this week," Mitch said to Flynn. "Barrett, great to meet you." With one final shake of hands, Mitch Armstrong strode out of the hotel.

Flynn's astute gaze was back on my face. "You're upset about something."

"Shrewd observer."

"Would you like to speak in private?"

"Here's fine. I won't make a scene."

"You look angry with me—and there are people watching. I won't have an out-and-out fight with you in public."

I lowered my voice when I said, "Oh, you want to have an out-and-out fight in private and then try to make up with me?"

"I prefer to think about that pleasurable hour rather than what's about to occur. Come on." He held out his hand to me and I took it. He used it as an excuse to bring me closer. "I missed you today."

I raised my eyebrows. "Did you?"

Not caring that guests milled about in the lobby, along with hotel employees, he lowered his head. "I've been thinking about your lips. All day. Through every meeting."

"Just my lips?" I taunted, with a hint of bite in my tone.

He grazed his mouth across my cheek, and I couldn't stop the slight shudder that rolled through me.

"I know I'm not supposed to like you angry, but you're an incredible sight when you are. Powerful. Like a hurricane."

"Don't try to flatter me," I snapped.

He continued to hold my hand as he led me to the private elevator. After the door closed, he refused to let go even though I was attempting to tug my hand from his firm grasp. Instead, he hauled me into his side, but I was as unyielding as an iron poker.

When we walked into his suite, I whirled on him, bristling with anger. "I can't do this, Flynn."

"You're not breaking up with me. I won't allow it."

I blinked and then shook my head. "I wasn't going to break up with you."

"Then what are you talking about?"

I ran a frustrated hand through my hair. "Lacey and I went shopping today."

"I'm aware."

"There was a man following us and when I confronted him about it, he claimed to be my bodyguard."

"You're angry because I'm seeing to your protection?"

"Well, no, not exactly..."

"Then what?"

"You didn't tell me, Flynn. I just turned around and there he was."

"You weren't supposed to see him at all."

"Okay, that doesn't make me feel any better. I don't need a bodyguard."

"You do," he insisted. "Look what happened the other night at Marino's. Look what happened in my club."

I lost some of my anger when I realized he was just doing what he always did—looking out for my benefit.

"They're isolated, unrelated incidents. And besides, what happened at Marino's couldn't really have been avoided. As for the drugging of my drink"—I shrugged—"a glass of water could've been drugged. What am I supposed to do? Never leave my home?"

Though I softened my stance, I continued on, "There's more I'm upset about."

"Okay, I'm still listening."

"You didn't ask me to this charity event. You just had Lacey take me shopping."

"I'm sorry, I—"

"I no longer feel like I have any sort of control over my own life. Ever since I met you, I..."

"You what?" Flynn asked quietly.

"I find out about things after the fact. And we bought jewelry that cost as much as a house. I don't want to be a kept woman. And now I have a bodyguard? It's too much. Don't you get that?"

"You shouldn't feel like a kept woman just because I want to buy you nice things and take care of you. I know you can do all that on your own."

"Let's not do the feminist debate, okay? That's not what this is about."

"Then what is it about?"

"Stop doing crap without consulting me first. It's that simple."

"I was just trying to—"

"I get it, Flynn. When we went to Marino's, I should've worn the jewelry because it was a place with different rules. But out here, in the real world, I don't want to be coddled and dressed like a decoration."

"*You* don't get it," Flynn snapped, his own irritation rising. "You're straddling the line. Either you're in or you're out."

"What are you talking about?"

"With me. You're either all in and you accept what you know and forget about the things you don't, or you leave. I'm calling your bluff because I'm tired of you happy with things one moment and then you're off-the-wall the next."

"I don't know you," I said. "Not the way I want to."

"I'm trying, Barrett."

"It's not enough," I whispered, feeling all my anger drain out of me. Would I ever be able to live in the dark?

He reached for me, but I went willingly into his arms and buried my face against his chest. He crooned into my hair before saying, "I have enemies, Barrett."

"I know."

"Are you going to stop picking fights with me because you're scared, and you don't know everything?"

I growled and pinched his arm. He laughed.

"You in or out?" he asked.

"Depends. Will you call off the bodyguard?"

"If I give on this—"

"It's called a compromise. Give me some of my normal back."

He sighed. "It goes against everything in me, but all right. See? I can bend."

I stood on my toes, so I could reach his lips.

He claimed me and I let him.

Chapter 23

"When you were shopping, did you buy anything other than the dress and jewelry?" Flynn asked, his lips grazing my naked shoulder. Our legs were tangled together as we lazed in his large bed.

"Yes."

"Yeah?" he asked seductively. "What did you buy?"

"Heels."

He chuckled. "No lingerie?"

"No."

"Why not?"

"I was mad at you by then," I explained and he laughed. "I wasn't feeling very charitable in wanting to buy things that you would also enjoy."

His teeth nipped lower, gently covering my nipple. "I'll have to rectify that."

"You should," I purred.

His tongue skated across the smooth skin in between my breasts. "So you found a ball gown for the charity event?"

"Yeees." I was a bit distracted due to Flynn's wandering hands and tongue. If I moved my hip just a little to the left... ah, there he was.

"Thanks for telling me about it," I teased.

"Barrett, we have a charity event to go to."

I laughed.

Some time later, I resurfaced from my haze of lust. My skin was flushed but cooling as I rested my cheek on Flynn's warm chest. "Is now the time to tell you I'm going to make your suite homier?" I heard the rumble of his laughter under my ear.

"What's wrong with my suite?" he wondered.

"It's gorgeous, but a bit…sterile."

"Never use that word when referring to me," he warned, mock sternly.

Giggling, I slid out of his arms.

"Where are you going?" he asked.

"Nowhere." I pulled back the covers so I could look at his amazing, impeccable legs. I leaned over and gently bit his thigh.

"Do you wear kilts?" I blurted out.

Flynn cocked his head to one side. "What, do you mean to my business meetings?"

I looked away but couldn't hide my smile. "What will it take to get you into a kilt?"

"Ah, a woman with kilt fantasies, aye?"

His brogue had thickened, and it was completely sexy. "Damn right I've got fantasies. Do you know your brogue gets thicker when…"

"When?"

I smiled and finally turned my eyes back to his. "When you're inside me, whispering things in my ear." I watched him still. He was beautiful, like a wild animal I'd never get close to.

"What do I say—when I'm inside you?" he asked.

My cheeks flamed. "You want me to repeat the words?"

"Aye."

"I can't."

"Why not?"

"Because some things are better left in the moment."

He peered at me like I was the only thing he saw. "Stay with me tonight."

"Why?"

"I like having you here."

I opened my mouth to reply, but I realized there was no real answer. I liked being there as much as he liked having me.

"We could have some dinner," he suggested. "And then watch a movie."

"Watch a movie? Flynn Campbell watches a movie?"

"I can be an average guy."

"Doubtful."

He grinned. "Or we could catch the burlesque show downstairs. We can sit in my booth."

"And show all of my old co-workers that we're officially together? Alia will never let me live it down."

"You made some good friends, didn't you?"

"I did."

I briefly thought of Chelsea. Though I'd been undercover to find out who had been selling drugs in Flynn's club, I'd believed Chelsea had been my friend. She'd disappeared and then came back to warn me away from Flynn. Only friends did that.

Should I have listened to her and stayed away from him? It would've made my life easier. I looked at the man next to me and felt my heart begin to race. I couldn't have stayed away even if I'd tried.

Flynn's phone rang at six the next morning. I groaned, even as Flynn reached to answer it. We'd had a late whisky-filled night, laughing and watching movies. But Flynn was boss, and he was on call all the time. What I wouldn't give for a few more hours of sleep.

"Campbell," Flynn answered. I heard rapid fire talk on the other end of the line. "I'll be right there." He clicked off and got out of bed.

"What happened?" I asked through a sleepy voice.

"One of the girls has been drugged. Lacey is with her now and called the doctor we have on retainer."

"A dancer was drugged?"

"No, one of the girls in the brothel," he explained.

"Fuck," I muttered.

I watched him rummage around for clothes—jeans and a sweater.

"Should I come with you?" I threw my legs over the side of the bed.

He shook his head. "No. I'll fill you in later."

I tried to shove away the sudden unwarranted feelings of dejection when I said, "Okay."

Flynn came to my side, leaned down, and kissed my lips. "I know what you're thinking. It's not that—there's a mess to clean up. The fewer people involved at this stage, the better."

"Go," I said. "And let me know if you end up needing my help."

He smiled, but it didn't reach his eyes. "Stay here. Order room service. Don't go home."

He kissed me again and then left. I climbed out of his bed, even though I wanted to linger and go back to sleep, but I was worried about the girl who had been drugged—and worried for Flynn. The stress of managing a hotel empire was an exhausting job. Sleep for me would be nonexistent, so I decided to run myself into the ground until I was tired enough to nap.

I did an hour of yoga, and by the end, I still hadn't heard from Flynn. As I cooled down and grabbed a bottle of water from the refrigerator, my cell phone rang.

"Hello?" I answered.

"You bitch," Ash said.

"What did I do now?"

"You didn't tell me you were going to The Houston Charity Gala."

"I didn't know it was The Houston Charity Gala," I explained. "How did you find out I was going?"

"I'm on the committee, hello. Your name is next to Flynn's on the guest list."

"You and your committees."

"I'm wealthy and well-bred. What else am I supposed to do but be on committees?" she joked. "You go shopping for a dress? Because no offense, you don't have those kinds of clothes."

I wasn't offended because it was true. "Lacey took me shopping, and I bought a killer dress."

"Ah, becoming the perfect society trophy, huh?"

"You annoy me."

"So tell me about the dress. I'm excited to see you in formal attire."

"Purple. Elegant. Whatever," I said. "I ran into John."

"Oh?"

"It was awkward."

"I bet."

I gave my friend a moment to tell me why she'd cheated on her fiancé, but Ash didn't volunteer any information. The secrecy was killing me.

My phone beeped. "Ash, I've got to go. I've got another call."

"Okay. I'll see you Friday at the charity event."

"Maybe before then." I hung up and switched over to my other call. "Flynn?"

"Barrett, can you meet me in Brad's security office?"

"Sure."

I rode down in the private elevator, walked across the lobby, and knocked on the security office door before entering. Brad and Lacey were the only other occupants besides Flynn in the room. Lacey's face was pinched with tension, Brad's mouth was grim, and Flynn—well, Flynn looked like he was ready to kill someone.

"How is…?" I asked Lacey.

"Bridget," Lacey supplied. "She's resting. Doctor says she'll be okay."

My gaze found Flynn's. I refused to shrink away when I saw his rage. He was in control of it and himself. That was Flynn.

"How did this happen? Could it have been a client?" I asked.

"Our clients are vetted and screened, so our ladies are protected. Everyone who comes to The Fifteenth Floor is put into our computer system. We went through our visitors last night, and they were all regulars. Nothing out of the ordinary," Lacey said.

"Maybe it was one of the girls. Maybe Chelsea gave one of them the drugs," I suggested.

"Long shot, but it's an idea," Flynn said. "I want the girls followed. See if any of them meet with someone in Dolinsky's crew."

"Dolinsky?" I asked with a frown. I'd never heard that name mentioned before. "Who's he?"

Flynn's voice was harsh. "The bastard trying to destroy me."

Chapter 24

"Igor Dolinsky is the leader of the Russian mob in New York," Flynn said.

"He's a dangerous, vicious bastard," Brad supplied. Flynn glared at him, but Brad just shrugged. "You can't keep her in the dark on this one. She needs to know."

"Know what?" I said.

"That Dolinsky is a dangerous, vicious bastard," Flynn repeated. "Let's leave it at that."

Flynn had a mob boss for an enemy? How the hell was I going to reconcile that?

"I'm supposed to trust you, right?" I raised my eyebrows.

Flynn's body was tight with tension, his mouth firm and unyielding. He didn't say anything more about Dolinsky and it pissed me off. I looked to Lacey and Brad—both of them wore blank masks. They took their cues from their leader. It reminded me they were a well-oiled trifecta, and I was just Flynn's bed partner.

Not wanting to get into it with Flynn in front of his colleagues, I did the respectable thing and left the office. I wondered if Brad and Lacey would berate Flynn for not bringing me into their confidences. I understood he wanted to protect me, but at what point was it dangerous to leave me out?

I headed back up to Flynn's suite to take a short nap. After setting the alarm clock, I turned my phone on silent. I had rehearsal in a few hours, and I needed to be alert and awake. Just as I was about to fall asleep, I heard the elevator doors.

"You were asleep," he stated, entering the bedroom.

"Almost." I grabbed a pillow and snuggled it against my chest as I rolled over onto my side. "I can't function on four hours of sleep. And I have rehearsal tonight."

"No, you don't."

"I don't?"

"My godfather is coming in from Scotland."

"That's nice. What does that have to do with me? And interfering with my nap?"

Flynn's lips twitched. "Malcolm was supposed to come after the charity event. He's decided he doesn't want to wait. He'll be here tonight."

"Still not getting it." I blinked, feeling stupid. Damn exhaustion. It really screwed with intelligence.

"He wants to meet my girlfriend."

"But—"

"Don't fight me on it, okay? Just say you'll meet my godfather."

"Fine," I said, my eyes closing, wanting to go back to sleep.

"Do you have dress clothes here?"

"No, I'll have to go home and change."

"Nap here, then I'll have my driver take you home. Oh, and Barrett? Try not to look too sexy."

"How do I look?" I asked as I slowly turned for Flynn's inspection. When I met his gaze, his eyes were dark, his jaw tense.

"I told you not to look too sexy."

"I don't," I protested.

"You do," he insisted. "Can't you put a sweater on or something?"

I took a deep breath. "My hemline is to my knee. The skirt of the dress flares out and doesn't even hug my ass."

"It hugs your other assets," he growled.

"I have breasts, Flynn."

"I know you have breasts."

"You enjoy them quite a lot if I'm not mistaken." I smiled suddenly. "You're nervous!"

"I'm not."

"Oh God, this is great, Flynn Campbell, powerful, assured hotel mogul is nervous." I reached out to run my hands up his crisp shirt, loving the look of him in a gray suit and black tie.

"Barrett," he clipped. "Let's go, we're going to be late."

Smiling, I took his arm and let him escort me out of my apartment down to his waiting Rolls. I was feeling restored and fresh, and I was eager to meet the man that could ruffle Flynn's feathers.

"So you want to give me a brief rundown of this man you're parading me in front of?" I demanded when we were on our way to The Rex.

"Malcolm Buchanan was my father's best friend. When my parents died, Malcolm took care of me. I was fifteen at the time and a complete terror."

"That doesn't surprise me at all. You're still a complete terror," I teased.

We arrived at The Rex, and Flynn guided me into the bar and restaurant. We ordered drinks and waited for his godfather to arrive.

A tall, robust man in his sixties stalked into the room, his eyebrows bushy and gray. He looked like he was nothing short of stoic and unapproachable. Flynn's face broke into a handsome smile when he spotted the man. And despite Malcolm's countenance, he embraced Flynn like a son.

When the two men pulled back, Flynn turned to me and said, "Malcolm, let me introduce you to Barrett Schaefer, my girlfriend."

I flashed what I hoped was a winning smile at the gruff man, but Malcolm didn't thaw. "So nice to meet you," I said.

Malcolm said something to Flynn in a thick garbled tone. Gaelic. *The man actually spoke Gaelic.*

Flynn answered in the same language, shooting me a meaningful look. Perhaps Flynn was attempting to remind Malcolm of his manners.

Flynn's godfather stared at me for a long moment, his dark gray eyes surveying me. Even though this man was important to Flynn, I was tired of the bored insolent look he was giving me. I glared back at him and then moved into Flynn's side. Suddenly, Malcolm smiled, and I didn't understand why.

He slapped Flynn on the back. "I'm ready for a drink," he said, switching to English, heavy on the Scottish brogue.

"Let's sit," Flynn said.

He signaled the maître d', and a moment later the three of us were nestled into a private dark booth. I reached for the menu, just to have something to do, still trying to understand Malcolm's sudden change of heart.

"The usual, Malcolm?" Flynn asked. Malcolm nodded. "And for you, Barrett?"

I smiled but didn't take my eyes off Malcolm. "I'll have what he's having."

"Lass, I'm going to be drinking single malt scotch. Are you sure you don't want something a bit more…subdued?"

"If it's good enough for you, it's good enough for me."

The craggy face of the old Highlander cracked into humor, and he let out a booming laugh. "I think you might give me a run for my money."

During the meal, conversation was easy, bouncing around

from one topic to the next. Our glasses were never empty. As dessert was being cleared from the table, the men enjoyed an after-dinner brandy. I was certifiably drunk. I'd insisted on attempting to keep up with Malcolm, if only to prove to him that I wasn't some wilting flower he could tread all over. It was stupid since the man was more than twice my size. I couldn't help myself from leaning against Flynn's suit-clad arm. He smelled so good, felt so warm.

"I think I'm ready for bed," I admitted, my eyes closing.

"I'll help you upstairs," Flynn said, rising from his seat so I could scoot out of the booth.

"No, you don't have to—"

He pretended like he didn't hear me when he said to Malcolm, "I'll be back in a few minutes."

Malcolm got out of the booth and pulled me into a tight hug. "Thank you for making this the most enjoyable meal I've had in a long time, lass."

I kissed him like I would my own grandfather. "It was my pleasure. I'll see you soon."

Flynn held my hand as he escorted me to the private elevator, but as soon as the doors closed, he pulled me into his side.

"Malcolm likes you," he said.

"Does he? I couldn't be sure."

"He's a hard sell."

"I didn't know you spoke Gaelic," I murmured into his chest.

The doors opened, and he helped me into his suite. I kicked off my shoes on the way to the bedroom while Flynn explained, "Malcolm lives in the Highlands—it's where I grew up. There are still pockets of places that speak only Gaelic, and the street signs are written in Gaelic and English."

"It's hot, you know," I said, turning around, struggling out of my dress.

"Yeah?"

I could hear the smile in his voice. He pulled back the covers of the bed and I slipped into it, moaning at the feel of cool satin against my scotched skin.

I was being tugged into unconsciousness. Flynn kissed my forehead and then was gone.

Chapter 25

"This has to stop happening," I muttered, throwing an arm over my eyes.

"What?"

"Me waking up in your bed feeling crappy." I heard Flynn's rumble of laughter beside me. Removing my arm, I squinted at him, wondering how he looked perfect after a night of drinking scotch—I felt like I'd swallowed rocks, moss, and tree bark.

"You're about half Malcolm's size, Barrett. What did you think would happen?"

"At least I didn't throw up," I said. "Right?"

He sighed.

"Shit. I threw up? I don't even remember it."

"It's better that you don't. Here," he said, reaching for the glass of water on the bedside table. He handed it to me and I drank greedily.

"Thanks," I said, setting it aside and then leaning back against the pillows. "So, what did you and Malcolm talk about after I left?"

Flynn rubbed his stubbly jaw. "You."

"Me?"

He nodded. "We also talked about business—opening another hotel in London."

"There's not a Rex Hotel in London?" I asked in surprise.

"Not yet."

"Huh."

"Would you go?"

"Go?" I threw my legs over the side of the bed and skimmed my tongue along my teeth. I was in desperate need of a toothbrush. And Advil.

"To London. With me?"

I'd made it to the doorway of the bathroom. I turned slowly, gripping the wall to steady myself, not knowing if it was my hangover or his question that had me wobbly.

"Say again?" I asked.

"Would you come to London with me while I opened the new hotel?"

"When? When would this happen?" I asked.

"Next spring."

"But my job—I was thinking of going back to work next semester."

He stared at me. "There are a few prestigious English universities that I'm sure would be glad to have you and your skills."

I thought of Oxford and Cambridge. I was American; it would be difficult to get a job right away at one of those universities. But then I thought of what Flynn had done for me, ensuring that my job at Columbia was waiting for me if I wanted to go back. Would it be wrong to ask him to pull some strings again? To live and work in London, a place steeped in history!

And I'd be with Flynn.

I knew my answer.

My heart thudded in my ears. "Yes. I'll go with you."

He smiled and climbed out of bed, sauntering toward me,

all arrogance and happiness. He wrapped his arms around me before gently coercing me in the direction of the bathroom.

"What do you say to a shower?" he asked.

"Is this because you want to see me naked? Or because I reek of scotch?"

"A little of both."

After we showered, Flynn stayed for a quick cup of coffee, but he had a morning meeting. He had a lot of fires to put out what with having another woman in his employ drugged and a mob boss for an enemy. I didn't know why Dolinsky wanted to destroy Flynn, but I guessed it had something to do with a power struggle. I tried not to think too much about it, because when I did, I tended to freak out. I'd gone from sheltered academic world to—well—the exact opposite.

Parading around in my bathrobe, I nursed a second cup of coffee and ordered room service. I had grown exceptionally lazy, and I needed to put a stop to it. After I ate, I got dressed, found a pair of dark sunglasses, and left the hotel.

Pulling out my phone, I called Ash. "You busy?"

"Not particularly."

"Want to run errands with me?"

"Not particularly."

I laughed. "I'm walking to your place. I'll be there in a few."

Twenty minutes later I was on the sidewalk outside Ash's building, still waiting for her to make an appearance. Just when I thought I'd have to call her again to hurry her along, she exited her building. She was in full makeup, her blond hair was perfectly styled, and she was wearing high-heeled boots.

"You do realize we're walking, right?" I asked.

"Let's take my driver."

"If I wanted a driver, I would've taken Flynn's. I need to remember I used to do things for myself all the time."

"Why?" she wondered.

"Why?" I repeated.

"Yeah. I mean, so what if it makes your life easier—using a driver and…"

"And ordering room service on the mornings I stay at Flynn's and having a bodyguard."

"You have a bodyguard?"

"I did. For a minute." I sighed. "I got Flynn to call him off."

"Why did you have a bodyguard in the first place?"

"Flynn's paranoid. Wanted to ensure my safety," I said evasively.

"That's sweet. In a smothering sort of way."

I bit my lip. "He asked me to go to London with him. When he opens his new hotel."

"Wow," she said. "That's big."

"Yeah."

"Do you love him?"

I needed to change the subject and fast. "Did you know The Rex is thinking about starting an amateur burlesque night? I think it's a great idea. You should perform."

Ash snorted. "Nice deflection."

"You do it, too," I pointed out. "Whenever you don't want to talk about John."

"How about I don't ask you about your feelings for Flynn and you don't ask me about John?"

"Deal."

By early afternoon, I was back in the lobby of The Rex, my hands full of grocery bags. I was determined to make Flynn's suite more of a home and home meant cooking. I waved away an insistent bellman who wanted to help me and headed up to Flynn's suite. Stepping into the living room, I noticed all the hotel wall art had been taken down. Lacey was in the process of unwrapping a large black picture frame.

She turned to me and smiled. "Hi."

"Hi."

"Hope you don't mind. Flynn let me in," Lacey explained. "I needed a project to keep my mind off of Dolinsky and Bridget."

"Right. How is Bridget?"

"Recovering. She's taking some time off."

I hadn't asked any more questions about Dolinsky—I was waiting, attempting patience when it came to Flynn and his secrets. He wanted me to go to London with him. That meant something. Didn't it?

"I heard you met Malcolm last night," she said with a large smile.

"Did you also hear that I was wrecked this morning?"

"There might have been some talk about it."

I shook my head. "I liked Malcolm. For all his gruffness. There's real affection between him and Flynn. It was...nice to see."

She smiled slowly. "See what? That someone besides you loves him?"

Was I so blatantly transparent?

"You tell him yet?" she pressed.

I remained silent.

"Not going to answer me, are you?"

"Nope." I walked toward the picture frame leaning against the wall, a black-and-white photo of a faceless man and woman wrapped around each other. Sensual. Beautiful. Bare.

"I love this," I breathed.

"Knew you would," Lacey said with a smile. "These are the art pieces I mentioned."

"Who's the artist?" I asked, moving around the room and looking at the four other pieces in the series.

"Me."

"You're kidding?"

"I took a photography class. Once," Lacey said, shrugging. "A lifetime ago."

I skirted past the regret I heard in her voice. What could we have been if life hadn't gotten in the way?

"It's all just a series of choices, isn't it? What leads us to here?"

"You're too young to be so philosophical," Lacey admonished.

"And you're too young to be talking like *that*," I said. "Why didn't you ever pursue photography?"

"Photography," Lacey snorted. "Art doesn't pay very well. Life costs money. Or haven't you heard?"

"Oh, I heard. Listen, my best friend used to work in the galleries. I have an in. You should think about having a show."

"I haven't taken photos in years."

I frowned in thought. "Why don't you photograph the burlesque show? Get some practice. Who knows, you might discover it's like riding a bike."

"I'll take some photos of the performances, but I think I'd like to photograph you, Barrett."

"Me? Why?" I asked in shock.

"Because you have this way about you. Especially when you're performing. I'd like to see if I can capture that on film."

"Anything, if it means helping you." I looked at the framed photograph again. It was truly remarkable.

After Lacey left and my groceries were put away, I made a quick lunch. Flynn texted, asking me to meet him and Malcolm on the roof of The Rex. Though the sun was shining, it was chilly. I wrapped my arms around myself since the light sweater I was wearing wasn't doing much to keep me warm. The view was unbelievable and Flynn's glass lounge would make good use of the skyline.

"Barrett," Malcolm greeted warmly, embracing me. "Are you cold?"

"Just a bit."

Before I could protest, Malcolm shrugged out of his wool sweater and handed it to me. "Wool from Highland sheep. You'll never be cold again." He winked.

I took the sweater with a smile. "I don't think you'll be getting this sweater back," I teased, rolling up the sleeves so I could see my hands.

"Consider it a gift."

"Quit flirting with her," Flynn growled, putting his arm around my shoulders and tucking me into his side.

Malcolm's rumbly laughter was infectious, and I chuckled along with him. "How are you feeling this morning, lass?"

"Still a bit of scotch head."

Malcolm grinned, his bushy eyebrows rising. "We were just heading down for lunch. Would you care to join us?"

"Oh, I just ate, but thank you for the offer."

"Come and keep us company," Flynn urged.

"Okay, then."

Malcolm offered his arm to me and I took it. I shot Flynn a look. I was developing a soft spot for Flynn's godfather. Once we were settled in a booth in the restaurant, Malcolm asked me, "Have you been to London?"

"Yes, a long time ago."

"Like it?" Malcolm pressed.

"From what I remember."

"Flynn is opening a hotel in London."

"Malcolm," Flynn warned. "I've already asked Barrett to go with me. And she said yes. So stop trying to make trouble, you old goat."

I laughed. Malcolm watched us with a warm glint in his eyes, looking relaxed and happy because Flynn had found someone. I wondered what Flynn had been like as an angry teenager, alone after the deaths of his parents. It was a sobering thought.

"You all right, lass?" Malcolm asked.

"Fine," I said, putting a smile on my face and placing a hand on Flynn's leg, wanting to be as close to him as possible. As if sensing my need, he pulled me closer, resting his hand on the curve of my hip.

"The lad," Malcolm said, with a chin nod at Flynn, "mentioned you sometimes perform in the club."

"I do."

"Excellent. Are you performing tonight?"

"Yes."

"Good, I'll be in the audience."

I squirmed. It would be like stripping in front of my own grandfather. "I'd rather you not."

"I'm told I can't miss it."

"Tell him," I said to Flynn. "Tell him he can't watch me perform."

"You don't tell Malcolm anything," Flynn answered pointedly. "He does what he likes."

"It's quite provocative," I said. "I'm not sure I'm okay with my boyfriend's godfather witnessing me parade around in lingerie."

"You're not aiding your cause," Flynn stage-whispered in my ear. I elbowed him in his side, causing him to chuckle.

"Tell you what," Malcolm relented. "You let me escort you to this charity event, and I'll refrain from watching you perform."

"Thought you were flying home tomorrow," Flynn said.

"Change of plans," Malcolm said easily.

"I'd be honored if you'd escort me."

"You're going to make me go stag?" Flynn demanded.

"I have two arms, Flynn."

"Then I'd be honored to be the trophy on your other arm," Flynn said dryly.

Chapter 26

Lacey sat next to me on the couch, tension in every muscle of her body as she waited for me to flick through the pictures she'd uploaded onto my computer. Last night, she'd been in the audience of the burlesque club with her new camera, snapping away for hours. She had taken at least a hundred photos and not just of the dancers, but of the audience members as well.

"Say something," she said almost desperately. "You've been quiet for ten minutes and I'm scared to death."

"You're insanely talented."

"You're just saying that."

"I'm not," I insisted. "You have a knack for capturing emotion and fleeting moments. Look at this photo!" Alia was standing in the middle of the stage, a little smile playing about her lips. Her long black hair was down, covering one eye, and her hip was cocked. The red sequined flapper gown stood out in stark contrast to her coloring.

"I like that one," Lacey admitted. "But I *really* like this one." Lacey hit the forward arrow and settled on a photo of me.

"Jesus Christ! You have to delete that!"

"Absolutely not! Look at you!"

In the photo, my head was thrown back in rapture, my hand on my thigh, the lights illuminating me from behind. "I look like I'm having an orgasm on stage."

"That's exactly what Flynn said when I showed it to him." Lacey smirked.

My eyes widened. "You showed it to Flynn?"

"Of course. He wants it framed immediately."

"And where does he plan on putting this intimate piece?"

"Hell if I know. So you see, I can't delete it."

I got up from my seat on the couch, went to the refrigerator, and grabbed myself a beer. "Is that really how I look on stage?"

Lacey nodded. "It was weird—not the pose, I mean, just what I realized. The other girls are good. Don't get me wrong. They're good burlesque dancers, but you're a natural."

I took a sip of my beer, trying to wrap my mind around what it was that people saw when I was on stage. I performed because it was fun to pretend to be someone else. But I had no idea that was how I looked.

"I'm thinking this was a bad idea," Lacey said, gathering up her camera and purse. "It might have been better to leave you in the dark. Now you'll go on stage totally aware. There's something about watching you on stage. It's effortless. I hope I didn't ruin that for you."

"Doesn't feel that way," I insisted, completely humbled by Lacey's words. Though I enjoyed the praise, something about it made me uncomfortable, and I was conflicted about it.

"And now you're frowning." Lacey sighed. "It's okay to be sexy. It's okay to have others see you that way."

"I just always thought it would be my mind that would get me noticed. Not my looks."

"What does it matter if people think you're beautiful?"

"I'm okay with people thinking I'm beautiful, I just don't want that to be the only thing they see."

"First and foremost, looks matter. At the end of the day, if that's all you have then it's not worth a lot. Flynn wanted you because you were beautiful. He loves you because you're smart."

"I don't think it's as simple as that," I protested.

"Of course it's not that simple."

"And love? No. Like, sure, but love? I don't think so."

Lacey looked at me and shook her head, a wry smile on her lips. "Why are you scared of love?"

"I'm not."

"You are. You think not admitting it means you don't feel it. But you do. And so does Flynn."

"And he's told you this?"

"No."

"Then—"

"I know him. But there are some things Flynn doesn't even talk to *me* about."

Surprise lit my face. "I thought Flynn told you and Brad everything."

She put her hand on mine. "You shouldn't feel bad, Barrett. Flynn is…closed off. Not as much since he met you, though."

"Is it because he lost his parents as a teen?"

"Partly, I'm sure. But Flynn is Flynn."

"You keep saying that. What does that even mean?"

"When you think of him, what words do you use to describe him?"

"Powerful. Protective. Generous. Sexy as hell."

We laughed.

"Yeah, he is that," Lacey agreed. "But why is he sexy as hell? His physical appearance?"

"Partly. I wouldn't call him beautiful, though. His face is too rugged, his jaw a touch too square. But somehow, he conveys this…this…"

"Innate Flynn-ness?" Lacey supplied.

"Exactly. You can't help but look at him, but it's the energy, the body, the whole package. The night I first met him and I had no idea who he was or the deal he made with my brother, I wanted him, like I'd never wanted anything in my life. He made me forget everything around me, and I wanted to soak him up. That sounds weird and makes no sense, right?"

"No, it does," she said. "You've got that look."

"What look is that?"

"The love look."

"Then I need to do a better job of hiding it."

"Barrett?" Flynn called out.

"In here!" I answered from the direction of the bedroom. Flynn came to the doorway and stopped.

I'd lit his bedroom with dozens of candles, casting sensual shadows on the walls. I was wearing a white satin negligee, fiddling with a digital SLR on a tripod.

"What are you doing?" he asked, removing his coat and tie and throwing them across the plush chair in the corner. It was a casual gesture, almost like we lived together.

I looked at him and smiled, my hands dropping from the camera. "Lacey told me you're getting a certain photograph framed."

"Did she?" He sauntered toward me to take me into his arms. I went willingly.

"It's a very personal photo, Flynn."

"That's why I love it. You—frozen—in a pose that is very similar to the way you look when I make you come."

His words were like a sinful caress; they made me shiver and ache.

He glanced at the camera. "Is this a tit-for-tat situation?"

"Perhaps." I began to unbutton his shirt, pressing my mouth to naked skin.

"Is it recording?"

"The camera does that?"

Flynn chuckled. "It does."

"Hmm. Something to revisit. Later."

I captured his mouth. Desire shot through my veins, dulling everything except Flynn. The smell of his skin, the taste of his lips, the feel of his hard, warm body against mine. I quickly forgot the camera as Flynn and I shed our clothing and collapsed onto the bed. My hands sank into his hair, tugging, greedy, wanting.

His mouth left mine to trail his tongue down my body. "You want me?" he asked huskily, drawing the flesh of my neck into his mouth, sucking just enough to leave a small mark.

"Yes."

"Where?"

I grasped him, trying to pull him into me, but he wouldn't give in. "Evil."

"Where?" he demanded.

"Inside me."

He grinned, kissing my lips, finally thrusting into me— hard and effortlessly. I screamed his name and colors exploded behind my eyes.

"When was the last time we slept apart?" I asked sleepily, running my fingers down his warm chest.

"I can't remember," he admitted.

"What are we going to do when we're in London? We can't live in a hotel that's not built yet."

My eyes were closing, and I was sated, being lulled to sleep by Flynn's heated body and smell.

"We'd get a place. Together."

"Live together?"

"Don't most couples do that at some point?" he teased.

"Guess so."

"What do you think?"

"I like that idea," I admitted.

"We should live together before then," Flynn said. "Here."

"Here? In this suite?" I asked.

"Sure, why not?"

"Or," I said slowly. "We could get an apartment together in the city."

Flynn's arm around me tightened, and I wondered if he realized it. "Dolinsky," he stated. "We should stay here where there are cameras and security. I can take precautions here."

I sat up and turned to him. "If we moved, then maybe the risk would diminish—"

"We're done with this conversation."

"No, we aren't!" I shot back, getting up out of bed. "Why are you being like this?"

"Like what?" he demanded, following me.

"Like you won't even listen to the validity of my point."

"Because I don't like the idea that I'm wrong, okay? I don't like the idea that I can't protect you."

"And moving out of your hotel proves that? You can't protect me from the world. Flynn. I don't think I like the idea of living in your hotel. I don't want my every move monitored. I will feel like a prisoner if we lived here."

"This has been my life for years. I don't know anything else."

"Won't you think about getting an apartment together?" I asked softly, pressing my hands to his chest, pleading with him.

He linked his fingers with mine and gazed into my eyes. "Jesus, when you look at me like that it's hard to deny you anything."

"Please? I'll let you keep that blatantly pornographic photo of me. We can hang it in our bedroom."

He laughed. "I'll think about it—the apartment, I mean. Now I need something from you. I need you to promise me that you'll be on your guard. I mean it, Barrett. No unnecessary risks. I called off the bodyguard even though I didn't want to. Take my driver if you have to run errands."

"You're really worried about Dolinsky, aren't you?"

"I'm worried about you. I'm a betting man. Never bet more than you can stand to lose—and I can't lose you. Promise me, you'll be careful."

I snuggled into his arms. "I promise."

Chapter 27

It was the night of the Houston Charity Gala, and I'd spent the better part of the day in The Rex Spa. I'd been treated to the works: waxing, massage, mani, pedi, and I'd even gotten my hair done. My auburn locks were twirled up into an elegant bun with wispy tendrils at my neck and temples. My makeup was demure, almost like I wasn't wearing any. The amethyst floor length dress had a modest neckline, but the back was open, showing inches of my skin. I wore antique amethyst drop earrings set in platinum the size of quarters and a matching cuff bracelet.

"You look absolutely stunning," Malcolm said to me as I strolled across the lobby toward him.

Malcolm was dressed in a classic tuxedo jacket, but he was wearing a kilt in what I assumed were the Buchanan colors. I couldn't help but smile. He was tall and impressive, his bushy eyebrows behaving.

"You're looking dapper," I said.

"Thank you, lass."

"Where's Flynn?" I asked. I'd gotten ready with Lacey's help in another suite, wanting to surprise Flynn with my appearance. I'd expected him to meet me there to escort me, but he'd called saying he would meet us in the lobby.

"Not here yet."

I laughed. "Obviously."

"I haven't worn a tuxedo in years," Malcolm said, fiddling with his tie.

I reached out to stop his hands from his nervous gesture. "Well, you look wonderful, so you shouldn't worry."

"I'm not good at these sorts of events," Malcolm admitted. "I'm a simple man."

"Then why did you insist on coming?" I demanded.

"Damned if I know," he answered gruffly.

"I have an idea," I whispered in a conspiratorial tone. "You love your godson and don't see him nearly enough. You're proud of him—and you want to see him in his element."

"You're a very astute young lady."

"I try to be."

"Have you ever been to the Highlands?"

"Yes, once, when I was studying for my masters. I loved it."

Malcolm's eyes glimmered with approval. "You have an open invitation to visit. See if you can drag Flynn away from work long enough to come for a vacation."

"Doesn't he like the Highlands?"

Malcolm paused, weighing his words. "It reminds him of his beginnings. And the death of his parents. For him the Highlands are bittersweet."

We chatted for a few more minutes, but I grew increasingly restless. Where was Flynn?

Finally, the elevator doors chimed open and the absent man made his appearance.

My mouth gaped when I saw him.

Flynn was wearing a kilt—and a devilish grin.

"You did this on purpose!" I accused.

"I wanted it to be a surprise. You're beautiful." Flynn dropped a kiss on my cheek and then shook Malcolm's hand.

I took in his appearance; his broad shoulders had been fit into an elegant tuxedo jacket, a tie at his neck. But his legs… damn those legs. They were a sight to behold in the Campbell tartan that consisted of blue, green, and black threads.

"You look incredible," I murmured.

He grinned. "Shall we?" Flynn asked, gesturing to the front door.

The three of us climbed into the waiting limo. "Isn't this overkill? We're only going a few blocks," I pointed out. The Met was on 5th and 82nd. The Rex was on 5th and 79th.

Flynn raised an eyebrow. "You thought we'd walk?"

"I don't know what I thought," I admitted. "Won't we spend more time in traffic than if we just walked?"

"Appearances," Flynn said.

"Right. Should've known," I said.

"I'll need this then?" Malcolm speculated, taking the glass of scotch Flynn had poured for him.

"You were the one that decided to come," Flynn reminded him. "You could be at home sitting in front of a fire, the hounds at your feet."

"Hounds? You have hounds?" I asked Malcolm.

"Aye. Three of them."

Sometimes I felt like I was living in a parallel universe. My eyes fell onto Flynn's bare calves, and I remembered the other night with the camera. I hadn't looked at the photos yet. Maybe I was afraid of what I'd see—a woman I didn't recognize and a man I was losing myself to.

Shoving all those thoughts away, I focused on the moment with Flynn and Malcolm. I couldn't believe I was about to attend a charity event. I didn't belong to the echelon that frequented these sorts of things—I wasn't a Rhodes. Ash was used to all this; she'd been a debutante, a socialite, and came from old money.

"What's this event for?" I asked.

Flynn gave a wry smile. "Funding for after school art programs."

"You believe in the children," I teased.

"They are our future."

"So I've been told."

We pulled up to the Met, and Flynn helped me out of the car. There were photographers standing on the steps, and they snapped some photos of me on Flynn's arm. He shielded me with his body as best he could and quickly ushered me inside, Malcolm trailing behind us.

The Great Hall of the museum was decorated in red and gold brocade. Private, elite events were nothing new at the Met, but it was new to me. Ever since I met Flynn, I was privy to a world I'd never had access to.

I wondered if I'd ever get used to Flynn's power and money. At some point, did he just expect things a certain way and only noticed when they weren't in the state he wanted them? Money had to change people. Looking around at women who wore jewels that belonged in protected vaults and men who controlled billion-dollar companies, I knew these people expected the best of the best.

With Flynn by my side, I was learning to enjoy the finer things in life. Every experience I had because of him, I wanted to relish. My smile was bright and genuine as Flynn escorted me around the room.

"I need a real drink," Malcolm said after meeting a deluge of Flynn's acquaintances.

I placed a hand on his arm. "Are you okay?"

He nodded. "I'm not used to these sorts of things."

"There's a bar nearby. But if you go that way"—I pointed in the opposite direction—"and you wander through there, you'll eventually get to the Arms and Armor collection."

"You're a lovely lass," he said, kissing my cheek in an unusual show of affection.

Flynn was lost in conversation about some sort of investment plan with an affable middle-aged man, so he didn't see his godfather leave. Flynn shook hands with the man and then turned his attention back to me. "Have we lost Malcolm?"

"I think so."

Flynn grinned. "He lasted longer than I expected."

"You're not worried about him?"

"No. He'll be fine. If I know Malcolm, then he'll find a way to sneak out."

"He's proud of you."

Flynn gave me a lopsided grin. "It's strange, you know? I'm an adult. I own a luxury hotel empire that I'm expanding, and yet, knowing Malcolm's proud of me…"

I nodded in complete understanding.

"Ready for another drink?" Flynn asked.

"I'm fine. I need some food first."

"Good call, but I—"

"Flynn," a woman's voice purred.

"Lana," Flynn greeted, all the warmth in his voice evaporating.

Lana's cold blue eyes devoured him, reminding me of a piranha. She was beautiful and blond, statuesque in a stunning green gown that clung to her curves.

The woman's eyes never left Flynn's face. "How are you?"

"Well," he clipped. "Lana Struthers, I'd like to introduce you to my girlfriend, Barrett Schaefer."

Lana's gaze finally turned away from Flynn to rest on me as if I were a lowly, pesky insect. "We've met."

"We have," I agreed.

"So, you're dating a cocktail waitress who works for you?" Lana sneered at Flynn.

"Barrett no longer works for me. Call it a conflict of interest," he said.

I possessively stole a hand across Flynn's back and molded

myself against him. "You seem surprised that we're dating. It was mentioned in *The Post* not too long ago."

Lana's face went white with unmistakable fury before she attempted to ignore me. To Flynn she said, "I thought you didn't believe in girlfriends."

"Not those who attempt to trap me," Flynn said, his voice controlled.

Lana glowered at him and then left in an angry flurry of silk.

"Well, she was something," I retorted.

"Aye."

"Not very bright, though. Everyone knows that if you want to trap a man you poke holes in your diaphragm—not his condoms."

He let out a loud laugh, causing other guests to look at us. I bit my lip, drawing his gaze to my mouth.

"What?" he asked.

"Did you ever…"

"Yes?"

"Think you were going to marry Lana? If she hadn't been so conniving, would you have eventually proposed?"

"No."

"Are you afraid that I'll want that from you?"

He stared down at me, his hand coming up to cradle my cheek. "Do you? Want that?"

"You offering?" I teased, knowing he couldn't possibly be serious. Moving to London with him was one thing. Marriage was another.

His eyes were open and so blue. "What if I am?"

Chapter 28

"It's too soon to be talking like that," I evaded, not knowing how to respond to him. I wasn't ready to put my heart out there—not all the way.

"I'll take that second drink now," I said.

Flynn leaned down and brushed his lips against mine. I pressed into him, giving him permission to kiss me again.

"Stop," he commanded. "Or we might have to find a coatroom."

"You're wearing a kilt," I said. "Easy access."

He sighed. "Pure trouble."

"Thank you."

"Champagne?"

"I'd prefer something stronger."

"Right. You don't like champagne. Don't move from this spot. It will be impossible to find you otherwise."

"If you can't find me, I'll be in the coatroom. Hide and seek."

His eyes burned with desire, but he didn't say anything. Instead, he turned and went in search of drinks for us. I was lost in thought, fantasizing about a coatroom sexcapade when I caught sight of Ash's blond, elegantly coiffed head moving through the crowd. My best friend saw me and waved.

"Hello, gorgeous," Ash said.

"Back at you. Love this." I gestured to Ash's dress, an aquamarine blue that highlighted her strawberries and cream complexion. "Did you bring a date?"

"Sort of," Ash said. I looked behind her at the man approaching us. Her brother looked handsome in his tux, his face lit with a smile.

"Hey, stranger," Jack greeted, throwing his arms around me in an exuberant hug. His lips brushed my cheek, and I could smell the liquor on his breath.

"Looks like you started the party early," I said in a light tone.

"These things are so dull," he said.

"Shhh," Ash said, trying to quiet her brother. She looked at me and rolled her eyes.

"I've been trying to get a hold of you," Jack said, filching four mini salmon tartlets from a passing waiter. "But you've been busy with your boyfriend. Where is Campbell?"

"At the bar," I said.

"That's where I'm headed. Can I get you two ladies anything?"

"I'm good," Ash said. "I think you are, too."

Jack ignored her comment and said to me, "Did you know he threatened me?"

My brows snapped together. "What are you talking about?"

"Your boyfriend," he spat, his voice rising, "threatened me. Told me to stay away from you. And to keep my mouth shut about what I found in his background check."

People were starting to look since Jack was making a scene. I didn't care at the moment what he was spewing about Flynn. Grabbing his arm, I tugged him out of the main room. We walked away from the event to the empty Greek and Roman art wing so we could chat in private. Marble statues were our only companions as we turned to face each other.

"Do you believe me?" Glassy eyed, Jack smiled at me, but it wasn't pleasant.

"Yes."

"Are you angry at him? For threatening me?"

"He must've had a reason for it. I shouldn't have asked you to delve deeper into his past," I replied.

"So you no longer want to know what he's keeping from you?"

Of course I was curious, but I thought trusting Flynn was more important. "No. I don't want to know."

He stepped back in disbelief. "What the hell happened to you? You're not the Barrett I know. Blindly trusting a man because you're fucking him."

I reached out and slapped him across the face. Friend or no friend, he couldn't talk to me that way. Jack slowly turned back to me, his hand going to his cheek.

"You love him."

I said nothing as I stared at him.

"Barrett," Ash called, striding toward us. "Are you guys okay?"

"Yes. Jack was just leaving."

With one look back at me, Jack left, shaking his head as he went. Ash sat down on a bench and peered at me from beneath the sweep of long blond lashes. "What's going on?"

"What has Jack told you?" I asked.

"Oh no, don't do that. Level with me."

I sighed, taking a seat next to her. "Okay. Let me think a minute."

"So you can make up a lie?"

My mouth dropped open. "You think I'd lie to you?"

"I think ever since you met Flynn, things have been different—you have been different."

"I am different," I admitted. "I'm performing burlesque,

and I'm involved with a man who's not an open book. That's weird for me, but I'm trying to accept it."

"What just happened between you and Jack?"

"Jack said Flynn threatened him."

"Why would Flynn do that?"

"A while back, I asked Jack to do a background check on Flynn. Nothing came up. It's like he doesn't exist. So Jack volunteered to dig deeper. And apparently he found something."

"What did he find?"

"Don't know, don't want to know. Not from Jack. I'll wait until Flynn tells me."

"And if he doesn't tell you?"

"Then I'll deal with that. But for now, I'll wait and be patient."

"So Flynn threatened Jack about what he found? And that doesn't bother you?"

"Of course it bothers me," I protested. "But I'm not sure what I'm supposed to do with that."

"You're in love with him."

"Yeah," I sighed. "Love."

"You don't sound happy about it."

"I'm not sure I want to be in love with him."

"I know what that's like." She frowned. "I don't like that Flynn threatened my brother."

"I don't either."

"He must be hiding something really terrible."

I sighed. "Yeah. He must be."

We sat in silence for a moment and then she said, "I didn't cheat on John just one time. I was having an affair."

I looked at her. "Oh."

"John caught us. In Monaco."

"That doesn't make sense to me," I said with a frown. "You were having an affair with someone who just happened to be in Monaco at the same time you were there with John?"

"It was his father," she admitted softly. "I had an affair with John's father."

Had. Past tense.

"It's over?" I asked quietly.

She nodded.

It was bad enough that Ash had cheated on her fiancé, but to have an affair with her fiancé's father, who was still very much married to his wife?

"Yeah, that's how I thought you'd react," she said when she saw my face.

"Why?" I asked through a tight throat. "Why did you do it?"

"Because I wanted to," she said simply. "Because I'm a terrible person."

I didn't know what to say, so I grabbed her hand and held it in mine. Ash was finally ready to talk, and I would be her ear.

"It started last summer," she began. "The night of our engagement party."

I remembered the night because I'd been there. The party had been in the Hamptons at John's parent's estate, a sit-down dinner outside under a large white tent. I recalled thinking that Ash looked happy.

"John's mother was playing hostess, flitting around like the perfect society wife while her husband laughed too loud at his friends' jokes that weren't funny. And then I looked at my parents. They stood together but could barely tolerate one another. I had this thought, like I was witnessing what my future was going to look like with John."

"You really believed that?" I ventured to ask. "About you and John?"

"Whenever we'd have a fight, he wouldn't get mad, he'd just get quiet and cold. Yeah, I believed our future was going to be the same as our parents."

"So what did you do?" I asked, completely enraptured by her story.

"When John, Sr. left the party to take a walk on the beach, I slipped away too. It was so easy. Too easy. He wasn't even surprised when I came up next to him on the beach. We watched the surf for a few moments and without taking his eyes off the waves he said, 'I think about you.' I turned to him and let him kiss me. When we were back in the city, he called to ask me to lunch. We went to a beautiful hotel, and I fucked my fiancé's father on three-hundred-thread-count sheets."

Ash's eyes got a dreamy, faraway look as she remembered. "I thought I'd feel shameful and dirty. But I didn't. I felt powerful and alive. We met every day that we could, all the while I was planning my wedding to his son. It was sick. But I wouldn't stop. Couldn't stop. Then we all went to Monaco to visit Mrs. Witherington's parents. On a day we were supposed to go sightseeing, I claimed to have a headache and John, Sr. said he needed to make some business calls. After we were together, he told me he was going to leave his wife. For me. I didn't want that. I told him it was the end, it had to be the end. I wanted to sever ties with the entire family, break off my engagement. I had plans to do it when I got back home.

"I tried to get out of bed, but he grabbed me and kissed me, not in a way that I was at all worried for my safety, but in passionate desperation. John came back early, found us in bed together, and then I got on a plane home. John, Sr. called nonstop for those first few weeks I was back. I blocked his number. And then he went back to his wife."

My heart beat in a rapid staccato, and my palms had started to sweat. I dropped her hand but made no move to stand. She didn't look at all upset after unburdening herself. In fact, she looked strangely free.

"I shouldn't have told you," she said

"No, you should have," I protested. "I'm glad you did. I'm just having a hard time——"

"Do you hate me?"

"Of course not."

"But you don't understand me."

"No," I admitted. "I don't."

"That's okay. I don't understand me either," she said with a pained smile.

I hugged her, lending her my support. "You're still my best friend, through and through. Good people do bad things. Doesn't mean you're a horrible person."

She let out a huff of air. "I needed to hear that."

"And I need to find the restroom," I said. "Meet you back in there?"

She nodded. "I'll tell Flynn where you went."

"Thanks."

I searched for the restroom, wanting a quiet moment to myself to think about all that had occurred in the last hour. I sat down on a white couch and closed my eyes.

Hearing the rustle of fabric, my eyes flipped open. Lana Struthers loomed before me, looking like a beautiful, avenging harpy.

Chapter 29

Lana's cold gaze raked over me before she turned to the mirror to gauge her appearance. She reapplied her already perfect red lipstick. After tucking the tube into her tiny clutch, she smoothed down her nonexistent, errant hairs.

She was the kind of woman who applied a full face of makeup before going to meet with her personal trainer. I wondered how she looked in the morning and if she ever let her lovers see her less than perfect. Had Flynn seen her that way? Had they ever spent a full night together? Did she know how it felt to sleep in his arms?

Jealousy—an emotion I rarely felt—blasted through me like a tornado.

I met her eyes in the mirror, and a little smirk appeared on her lacquered lips. She'd read me well; the expression on my face was obvious.

Sizing her up, my gaze drifted down her tall, slender form. I wouldn't underestimate her to say nasty things to me. She was a vindictive, spurned female who hadn't gotten what she wanted.

I sauntered to the sink next to her, washed my hands, and dried them on a laundered linen towel. Tossing it in the basket, I then took a step back and surveyed her, wanting to throw gasoline on the fire.

"Flynn's opening a hotel in London next year. He asked me to go with him."

"How lovely for you," she spat. "But he won't marry you."

I smiled, showing a lot of teeth.

"Flynn Campbell is not the marrying kind," she insisted.

"He just didn't want to marry you."

Lana sneered, an ugly expression marring her beautiful face. She reached out and grasped me by the wrist, squeezing the bones until I felt them grind. I couldn't even hold in a grimace. The woman had a death grip on me. My eyes met calculating blue ones.

"He'll get sick of you. He'll discard you without any thought, without any care. You'll be devastated, broken-hearted, and never the same again. A man like Flynn will burrow so deep into your heart, you'll never get him out." She flung my wrist away from her as if the feel of my skin suddenly disgusted her.

"Why are you sharing all this with me?" I wondered aloud, rubbing my wrist, not even attempting to hide the hurt Lana had inflicted.

"You deserve to know what you're in for."

"Thank you for being the one to enlighten me," I said. "But what makes you think I'd listen to anything you have to say?"

Lana's eyes blazed with anger. "Suit yourself. I just thought I was doing you a favor. The man can't open up. He won't trust you with any of his secrets."

"He already does." So I stretched the truth a bit. He was trying, which I hoped meant something.

"You're delusional."

"Not as delusional as you."

I attempted to move past her, but her hand shot out and she grabbed my hair, causing me to cry out and tears to leak from my eyes. Lana laughed, enjoying my pain. I clawed at the hand that held me, but she was relentless.

"You're a flavor of the month. You're stupid if you think you're anything else." She thrust me away from her and let go. With one last glare, she turned and stomped out of the bathroom.

"Women are crazy," I muttered, wincing when I looked in the mirror. My hair was completely askew and coming down from its bun. I touched my sensitive scalp and winced. Lana's fingernails had dug into my skin. My wrist throbbed, and I was suddenly exhausted from all the interludes I'd had that evening.

I took my hair down and ran my fingers through the hair-sprayed waves, hoping it did something to the slight headache that had begun to form. I was ready to find Flynn and leave. Unfortunately, by the time I found my way back to the party, people had begun the speeches, and there was no way to find Flynn in the crowd. Flynn had my phone in his tuxedo jacket, so I couldn't text him. I stayed by the doorway and gestured to a waiting attendant. The young blond man came over to me, looking sharp in a crisp waiter uniform.

"Yes, ma'am?" he asked. "Can I get you something? A drink?"

I shook my head with a smile. "No, thank you. I need a favor. Do you know who Flynn Campbell is?" When he nodded, I went on. "Would you find him and tell him Barrett has gone back to the hotel?"

"Of course," the man said eagerly. "It will be my pleasure."

I smiled. "Is there another exit around here? I don't want to disrupt the speeches." I also didn't want to alert the media that Flynn and I were leaving separately.

He gave me directions to the elevator that would take me out through the parking garage. After saying a quick thank you, I scurried toward the elevator even as I heard the applause signaling the end of the speech.

The parking garage was quiet and a blend of gray concrete with rows and rows of cars. I looked for the street exit, picking up the skirt of my dress. I was rushing to find my way out, not paying attention when I stepped in a little divot and my left heel snapped off. My ankle twisted, and I cursed, feeling a twinge shoot through my leg.

Fuck.

I wobbled a few steps on my broken heel before stopping. Even though it was a few short blocks to the hotel, I refused to take off my ruined shoe and walk barefoot on the streets of New York. It was not an option. I had no choice but return to the gala, find Flynn and demand he come to my shoe's rescue.

I felt the hair on the back of my neck rise.

"Barrett," a voice whispered.

I whirled.

Chelsea stepped out of the shadows, looking completely different since the last time I'd seen her. Her long blond hair had been dyed a deep chestnut and cut into a pixie style. She wore a long-sleeved black thermal shirt, cargo pants, and army boots.

"What are you doing here?" I demanded.

She strode closer. Her boots and my heels put us at eye level. "Dolinsky wants a word with you."

"Dolinsky?" I asked in confusion.

"Igor Dolinsky," she clarified. "You've heard of him, right?"

"I—yes. You're working for him?"

"I tried to warn you, but you wouldn't listen. Now you have no one to blame but yourself."

Her hand whipped out to lock around my tender wrist in an attempt to keep me in place as her other hand shot up to reveal a syringe.

I'd taken a self-defense class in college, but I'd never had to put it into real life practice. Until now.

My right foot came down to land on her shoe, but the dainty heel was no match for her heavy boot. I twisted my arm, forcing her to let go of my wrist. She hadn't expected me to fight. Though she let out a startled sound of surprise, she didn't waste any time coming after me again, the syringe in her grasp. I was at a disadvantage in my formal wear and there was no hope of outrunning her unless I took her out.

Now or never.

With a great deal of force, I upward thrust my palm into Chelsea's nose. She cried out in pain as she dropped the syringe, her hands flying to her face.

I kicked off my shoes, hiked up my dress, and ran.

Chapter 30

Fear and adrenaline pulsed through my veins as I flung open the stairwell door. I took the stairs two at a time. My ankle throbbed, but I pushed forward, hoping I moved fast enough to lose my attacker.

Chelsea.

The woman who I'd once thought of as a friend.

She worked for Igor Dolinsky, head of the Russian mob, the man determined to take down Flynn. Dolinsky wanted to speak with me. About what? It didn't matter—I was officially a target and on Dolinsky's radar.

Out of breath and completely light-headed, I finally made it to the main floor where the Houston Charity Gala was being held. The speeches were over, and the silent auction had commenced. Barefoot and bedraggled, I elbowed my way through the throng of people. I found Flynn chatting with an elderly, white-haired couple.

Flynn laughed, and he took a sip of his drink. His eyes wandered to collide with mine. A look of confusion washed over his face—and then his gaze swept down my body and his confusion turned into a scowl. He approached me even as I rushed to him.

"What happened?" His Scottish brogue was gravelly, thicker now because he was moved by deep emotion. His hand latched onto mine, and he dragged me away from the main floor, away from the eyes that were starting to look at me.

"Chelsea," I said. "Tried to grab me in the parking lot."

Flynn's hands moved up to grip my shoulders.

"She works for Dolinsky," I rushed on. "Said he wanted to talk to me. She had a syringe, Flynn."

His eyes went glacial. "How did you get——"

"I fought like hell and broke her nose," I said, striving for levity. It was either lighten the mood or start screaming. I began to shake.

He pulled me into the large, solid wall of his chest and wrapped an arm around me. With his free hand, he reached in his tuxedo jacket pocket and took out his cell.

"Meet me at the side entrance in three minutes," he commanded to our driver before hanging up. "What were you doing in the parking lot, Barrett?"

"I ran into Lana in the bathroom," I explained. "We had an…interlude, if you will, and I just wasn't up to returning to the party. I found a waiter—he was supposed to tell you that I was headed back to the hotel. I wanted to leave discreetly, so the paparazzi didn't——"

"I never got the message," he interrupted, his jaw tight. "Did Lana hurt you?"

The bitch had pulled my hair and squeezed my wrist until bones crunched. "Uh… Well, sort of." I gestured to my free locks. "I did come to the party with my hair up."

He shook his head. "Why did you go to the parking lot alone? I told you to be careful and on your guard."

I didn't like his tone. My ankle and wrist hurt, I'd been damn near kidnapped, and Flynn was lecturing me?

Hell. No.

"Can we do this later? I feel awful."

His mouth softened just a bit, apology tingeing his gaze, but he was silent as he guided me toward the side exit. Our limo was idling at the curb, and Flynn didn't bother waiting for our driver to get out. He opened the door, letting me slide in first before he got in next to me. He swallowed space, invaded mine, but I found it comforting. Flynn wrapped his arm around me, and I leaned into him, wanting his support, not even ashamed I wanted him to make this go away.

But I didn't think he could. Nowhere was safe.

"To The Dominus," he snapped to his driver.

"What's happening, Flynn?" I demanded.

"I need to pay Marino a visit." He whipped his cell phone out and shot off a text—no doubt to the man we were calling on.

I didn't know if Marino was Flynn's ally, but the Italian mob boss had knowledge of things going on in the city. I assumed he was the one who had given Flynn the head's up that Dolinsky was out to destroy him. Then again, Flynn edited what he shared with me, so it was all speculation on my part.

"Why is Dolinsky going after you?" I asked. I'd never considered the question before—and Flynn wasn't one to keep me in his confidence, though he claimed it was for my protection. "Why not target Marino?"

Flynn cracked his knuckles and stared out the window. He weighed his words but finally admitted, "Dolinsky considers me his equal and a threat. If he can get rid of me, he will have a monopoly on the sex trade."

I shook my head. "Sex trade? Does he own a brothel, too?"

"No. He sells women against their will, Barrett."

I shivered. *Evil man.*

Traffic was fairly light considering it was a Friday night, and it took very little time getting from the Upper East Side all the way down to the Lower East Side. We pulled into the underground garage of The Dominus Hotel. We climbed out of the limo and Marino was waiting for us. He was a middle-aged man with a round belly and a bulbous nose, but that didn't detract from his shrewd, calculating gaze. He never once glanced my way—he believed women were nothing more than beautiful trophies.

Reaching into his pocket, he pulled out a set of keys and tossed them at Flynn. "Last spot on the top floor," he said. "You owe me. For the risk of helping you."

"You'll get your reward."

The promise sounded ominous. I wondered if Marino noticed it, too. He was in the middle of two powerful men vying for the title of king. At some point, he had to pick his stallion and hope it won.

Flynn and I found the black Mercedes with tinted windows, got in, and headed for who knew where.

"Barrett," Flynn whispered. "Wake up, hen. We're here."

I didn't know if it was the endearment or the gentle insistence that finally had me opening my eyes.

"Where are we?" I asked, looking at Flynn. He sat in the driver's side of the car, looking exhausted. It was dark outside, the car was off and there was no light pollution which meant we were somewhere outside the city. I could actually see the glow of the moon.

"Quogue—the Hamptons," he clarified.

I glanced out the window and saw the house. Cottage. Modest. Flynn got out of the car, and I fumbled with the door. My limbs were tired, my brain numb. Though my wrist and ankle were no longer outright throbbing, my entire body ached. A soak in the tub would be amazing.

"Who owns this place?" I asked as I scrambled from the car.

"I do." He opened the front door and ushered me inside before locking up. Flynn flipped on the light switch. A soft glow bathed hardwood floors and light gray walls.

"You?" I was surprised. The house wasn't at all imposing or decorated in stark masculine decor and colors. It wasn't Flynn at all.

"I wanted to make it as close as possible to the house I grew up in. This is my mother's style. Was," he corrected.

Flynn's parents had passed away years ago when he was a teen. I didn't know anything more than that because he refused to talk about them.

"I've never brought a woman here," he said, looking at me, cobalt eyes tired but gleaming.

I looked around and my breath caught in my throat. "It's beautiful."

The hard line of his mouth softened, and he reached out to touch my cheek. "There are three rooms up here," he explained as we climbed the stairs. "Two for guests, and then the master bedroom." He gestured for me to enter first.

The master bedroom contained a huge bed and a vase of fresh flowers sat on the oak bedside table. I turned to look at him and raised an eyebrow.

"It's ready for whenever I want to use it," he explained. "Bathroom is through there. You want a bath?"

I sighed with tiredness. "Better make it a shower."

He smiled. "Come on." The bathroom was white tile and blue walls with a large claw-foot bathtub and a separate glass shower. He opened the linen closet and pulled out two towels and hung them on the rack. While Flynn turned on the water and adjusted the temperature, I took a moment to examine my body. Dirty feet, chipped toenail polish, torn gala dress.

I refused to look in the mirror, afraid of what I'd see.

I removed my amethyst drop earrings and matching cuff and set them aside. Flynn helped me out of my ruined dress and then went for his own clothes. The formal jacket and crisp white shirt went first. And then the kilt dropped. I couldn't stop a snort of laughter. Flynn grinned at me.

"It's true what they say. What a Scotsman wears under his kilt. Or doesn't," I said.

Flynn nodded and then urged me into the steaming shower. He stepped in behind me, and I leaned back into the cradle of his body. He was hard and ready and through my tiredness, I wanted him. I needed him. I tried to turn around to reach for him, but he stopped me.

"No," he said.

"Why?"

Flynn went for the bar of soap, made a lather, and ran his hands up and down my back. He was not attempting to seduce, but to take care, comfort. This felt different from any other time Flynn had touched me.

"I'm a selfish bastard," he said, his hands continuing to roam my body, washing off all traces of the night. "I wanted you. From the moment I saw you in that French restaurant, I wanted you. I was willing to do anything to have you." A shiver raced up and down my spine.

He paused, obviously weighing his words. "But I never expected you to come to mean something to me. And now you do—and I've dragged you into all of this. And I just—"

"You're breaking up with me, aren't you?" I tried to push his hands away, but his fingers tightened on my hips. "You don't want me to go to London with you anymore."

"Did you not hear me when I said I was a selfish bastard?" he demanded, his breath hot on my ear. "I should've let you go while you still had a chance, but you're in this now. Whether you want to be or not. Dolinsky went after you to get to me. Because he knows."

"Knows what?"

"Knows that you're mine." He maneuvered me to face him. He gently touched my chin, and his mouth came down on mine, hungry, unstoppable.

I kissed him back, grasping at him, wanting him closer, wanting to feel him inside me. Needing it. Needing *him.*

"If I'm yours," I panted against his mouth, "then you're mine."

"Aye," he agreed roughly.

"I'm not going anywhere." Before I knew what was happening, Flynn turned me away from him. The water beat down on us, warm droplets coating my skin.

His erection stroked the crease of me, and Flynn bit down on the skin where my shoulder met my neck. I pressed my hands against the glass wall of the shower. Flynn's fingers teased my opening, fluttering against my swollen flesh.

Without a word, he sank into me, one arm around me, the other braced against the wall. We stood like that for a moment, neither one of us moving. Joined.

I squirmed against him, needing relief. He bent me over and fucked me. Fucked me with raw abandon, branding me.

"Say it," he demanded.

"You're mine."

His fingers tormented me, driving me wilder, crazier.

"Say it."

"I'm yours!" I cried. Faster and faster he pounded into me, his fingers merciless. I slammed my hands against the glass and shouted when I came. He pulled me to him, and with a guttural shout of his own, found his release.

He eased out of me but kept close. I straightened my back and turned to look at him over my shoulder. "You didn't speak of love."

"Neither did you," he pointed out.

I grinned and reached for the soap. "All right then."

He nodded. "All right then."

Chapter 31

I woke up with Flynn's head between my legs. It took me a moment to realize it wasn't a vivid dream. He growled like a hungry animal as he continued to lick me.

"Flynn," I rasped.

He lifted his head and grinned. "Morning, hen." And then he went back to tending to me.

As I came back to awareness, Flynn scooted up my body, pinning my arms above my head. His eyes were clear and earnest.

"Are you sore?" he asked.

"From last night in the shower?"

He nodded.

"A twinge here and there, but I'm okay. I'm sturdy."

"So you don't want me to stop?" He pressed his erection into my cleft.

I wrapped my legs around him, hooking him closer. "Stop and I'll kill you."

After, he placed his head against my chest. "What are we going to do about Dolinsky?" I asked, stroking his scalp.

"I don't know."

I gripped his hair and forced him to look at me. "You don't know? You know everything."

He smiled tenderly. "I'm glad you have such faith in me."

"I'm scared," I admitted.

His arms tightened around me. "You're staying out of the city until this is resolved."

We stared at each other; I could see he was expecting me to fight him. "Okay," I agreed, giving in easily. I didn't want to be in the city. I didn't want to worry about looking over my shoulder every moment, wondering if there was some bad guy waiting to kidnap and torture me just to get to Flynn.

I brushed the hair away from his forehead and asked, "You can't stay here with me, can you?"

"I wish I could, love."

"You'll be careful?"

"Aye. You will, too." That came out as an order. "I gave it a shot your way. But you need protection now. If it had been a man coming after you instead of Chelsea..." He shook his head. "I've reinstated Jason as your bodyguard. He was in the Marines. He'll keep you company."

"Yeah, keep me company. With his gun," I mumbled. "This doesn't feel real."

"This is serious, Barrett. Even though this house is in my mother's name and not directly linked to me, I don't want to take any chances. Which is why I brought you here. I needed to get you out of Manhattan."

I sighed. "We have a sort of problem."

"Oh?"

"I don't have any clothes here."

His smile was soft despite the lingering intensity. "I don't find that to be a problem."

"You wouldn't," I said, getting up from the bed and strolling naked across the carpet.

"Brad and Jason should be here shortly. They're bringing you a bag."

I raised an eyebrow. "You had your head of security root around in my underwear drawer?"

"I had Lacey root around in your underwear drawer."

"That's better. It's not as embarrassing if she found my battery-operated device."

"I'm having her throw it out," he stated. He got up from the bed and walked to the dresser. He pulled open a drawer and yanked out a pair of boxer briefs. "That device offends me."

"You're much better," I teased. "And I haven't used it since I started using you. Much."

"You'd destroy a lesser man's ego."

"What happens when you're not here every night? I'm going to get bored, restless." I stalked toward him, watching his eyes heat as he looked over my naked body. I placed a hand on his bare chest and gazed up at him.

He smiled. It was slow and full of promise. "I'll be calling you at night, Barrett. Just to make sure you remember me." His hand slid down the length of my body, and though I was sated, I felt desire begin to pulse through me.

"There's a robe in the bathroom," he said with a lamenting sigh. "You can wear that until your clothes arrive."

"When might that be?" I asked, my hand dropping from his warm skin. There was no time for lazing away in bed, sadly.

The doorbell rang and Flynn smiled. "Now, I imagine."

I sat at the cozy kitchen table, sipping on a cup of coffee, dressed in my own jeans and a cream-colored sweater. Jason and Brad hadn't just brought my clothes—they'd unloaded groceries. From the looks of it, I'd be here a while. I hated the idea of sitting around and waiting for news. Then again, being in the city wasn't very appealing either.

Staring out the window, I saw trees in brilliant shades of orange and yellow. Though most of the leaves still remained on branches, there were some that had fallen to the ground. Autumn had arrived in full force.

Flynn rose from his chair. "I need to head back into the city. Malcolm is leaving today."

"Please tell him goodbye for me," I said.

"I will." Flynn leaned over and kissed me quickly. "Try to relax. Pretend it's a vacation."

I rolled my eyes. "This is not my idea of a vacation. A real vacation involves fruity alcoholic drinks, white sand, and the ocean."

"We'll discuss that when this is over."

"Promise?" I asked. I needed something to look forward to.

"Promise. While you're here, you can't contact anyone, Barrett. Even Ash."

"She's going to wonder where I am. I did just disappear from the gala," I reminded him.

"I'll handle it."

"Of course you will," I muttered.

With one final kiss, he said, "I'll talk to you later."

Brad and Flynn left, and I was stuck with my bodyguard who didn't look at all like the type that played cards.

Two days later, I was ready to beat my head against a wall. I slept a lot, tried to read, but there were only so many hours in the day I could sit idly by and stew. My bodyguard was a stoic ex-Marine who was doing nothing to ease the quiet.

"Do you have any siblings?" I asked Jason.

"Younger sister."

I tapped my fingers on the kitchen table. "That's it? That's all I get? Entertain me."

Jason didn't smile. "I'm not here to entertain you, I'm here to ensure your safety."

"That's nice. But can't we be a bit friendly?"

"No."

I glared at him. "Okay. You want to play that game? How about I tell Flynn that you saw me naked this morning? Think he'll take kindly to that?"

"It was an accident," he stated. "I knocked on your bedroom door. You didn't answer."

I bit my tongue; it wasn't worth getting into an argument. Luckily, I wasn't the type that embarrassed easily.

His phone pinged. Jason unlocked the screen and frowned. "One of the security camera's feed is out."

"That's odd. Do you think it's something to be concerned about?" I asked.

He shook his head. "No. It was probably a squirrel or another animal chewing on the wires. I'm going to go check it out."

"Are you sure that's a good idea?"

"Hey," he said, his gaze softening. "I'll be right out front." He bent over and lifted his pant leg and removed his backup pistol.

"This is a Glock 42. Keep your finger off the trigger unless you're willing to shoot it. Okay?"

"Okay," I said faintly.

He handed it to me. "Hold it. Get a feel for it. Good. Now raise it and point it at the wall. Nothing is going to happen. You're not going to have to use it, Barrett. This is just to make you feel better about the fact that I'm not in the house with you for five minutes."

He went out front and the door clicked shut. I got up from the table and went upstairs to grab a sweater, taking the weapon with me. Jason still hadn't returned by the time I came back downstairs. I set the Glock on the kitchen table and went to the fridge. I was rummaging through drawers when an arm wrapped around my waist and another clamped over my mouth. I tried to fight and kick my assailant, but it was no use.

"Stop," the voice hissed. "I'm not going to hurt you."

That only made me renew my efforts to struggle, but a palm covered my nose, and I had trouble breathing. Spots danced before my eyes, and my vision went in and out. I sagged against the body holding me.

"If I remove my hand, will you promise not to scream?"

I tried to nod my head. Apparently, it was sufficient because he lifted his hand from my mouth and released the other holding my body. I breathed in a few deep breaths while my assaulter came to stand in front of me. His dark hair was buzzed short in a traditional military style and his brown eyes were clear and calm.

"I don't have a lot of time," he said. "Your bodyguard is going to be back soon."

"How did you—"

He shook his head. "My name is Fred Winters and I'm with the FBI."

I blinked. Shit. The FBI? My palms grew sweaty and my mouth went dry, but I kept silent. Mostly because I was stunned stupid.

"We need your help bringing in Flynn Campbell."

Was this about the brothel? The casino?

I shook my head in disbelief. "Why?"

"We have reason to believe that he has ties to the SINS."

I frowned. "The SINS? What's that?"

"Sons of Independent Nationalists for Scotland. They're the Scottish version of the IRA. They want to secede from England, and they'll do it any way they can," he said impatiently. "Flynn Campbell is funneling money to aid their cause."

"I don't understand—"

"You don't think Campbell only dabbles in prostitution and gambling, do you? He uses his position, power, and money to aid a cause close to his heart. Only his cause is making a lot of problems for us. Illegal arms are coming into this country."

"And you think Flynn is...what? Selling them? Distributing them?"

"Both. But I need proof."

"I don't know anything," I said. It was the truth, and I was suddenly grateful that Flynn kept me in the dark.

"So you say."

I had to remind myself to stay calm, keep cool, and not to lose focus. Hysteria would not go over well. "I don't know anything. I swear."

"But you can find out."

"How?"

"Campbell has an inner circle, and you have become a part of it."

"I haven't," I insisted.

"You have. Campbell doesn't have girlfriends. You're different. You can get him to trust you."

I felt sick that Winters had been watching and gathering information. And I didn't like where this was headed.

"You have to work with us," he stated.

"To do what? Trap Flynn? Get him to admit to being a part of this organization?"

"You've met Malcolm Buchanan." He waited for confirmation, which I didn't give. He went on. "We want Buchanan."

I frowned in confusion and then understanding dawned. Winters nodded when he saw my look. "He's the leader, and he calls the shots."

Sweet, craggy, stoic Malcolm was the leader of the SINS? Winters said the SINS were committed to freeing Scotland by any means necessary. That meant violence.

"You really think Flynn is going to give up his godfather?"

Flynn Campbell was all about loyalty, and even if his

moral code didn't point due north, he was honorable. He would never betray family.

Winters's eyes were hard and flinty. "It's going to be your job to get him to do it."

"My job?"

"You're going to help us," he repeated.

I crossed my arms over my chest, hearing the unspoken "or else."

With a final stare down, he broke eye contact and then moved toward the back door. "I'll be in touch in a few days."

The door closed, and I let out a whoosh of air. Icy fear raced up my spine. The FBI wanted me to bring down Flynn and Malcolm—all because they belonged to the SINS, an organization I knew nothing about. I didn't know for sure if they were violent, but I assumed they were. I didn't know if they targeted innocents.

And illegal guns? I was dating an arms dealer? Was it really that black and white? Was I supposed to judge Flynn? Love him less? Flynn had warned me; so had Brad. What I thought I knew…

Shit.

"Barrett?"

I jumped, shooting a startled glance at Jason. I hadn't even heard him return.

"Are you okay?" he asked, coming toward me, concern on his usually impassive face.

Winters had discovered my whereabouts when I was supposed to be under the radar. All of a sudden, my mind started working again.

"Give me your phone," I demanded.

"What? Why?"

"Give it to me," I said again.

Jason frowned but reluctantly handed me his phone. I dropped it on the ground and then stomped on it. "Hey! What the hell!"

I took my phone and did the same. Then I scooped them up, put them in a pot of water, and boiled them.

"You need to explain what the hell is going on. Right. Now."

"In a minute." When I was sure both devices were destroyed, I looked at him. "We need to go. Now."

"I'm not—"

"Either you drive me back to Manhattan or I'll go by myself."

He took in my face and something about my expression must've convinced him I was serious. Because boiling our phones hadn't been serious enough.

Chapter 32

"What the fuck is going on in here?" Flynn demanded, glaring at the two-hundred-and-fifty-pound bodyguard who was currently on top of me. To be fair, Jason was restraining me in pure self-defense.

"Get off me," I said to Jason. "Or he might kill you."

Jason gently released my wrists. I sat up on Flynn's couch and then turned my attention to my very angry boyfriend. His scowl had transferred to me, so I wasted no time trying to explain. "Jason wanted to call room service, but I wouldn't let him. And when he reached for the hotel phone, I attacked him."

"It was self-defense," Jason stated.

"We'll get to that in a moment." Flynn's eyes blazed with ire. "Why are you back in the city? You're supposed to be hiding out in the Hamptons." To Jason he said in a low raspy tone, "How could you bring her here?"

"It's not his fault," I said. "He went on faith. I needed to come here. Something happened…"

Flynn came to the couch and loomed over me, waiting for me to tell him why I'd risked my life by coming back to the city. I shook my head and looked at Jason.

Jason sighed. "I'll be in the bar and restaurant getting something to eat."

When we were alone, Flynn opened his mouth to say something, but I cut him off. "Give me your cell phone."

"In a minute." He grabbed me and hoisted me toward him. "I haven't kissed you hello." His mouth covered mine. All the worry and concern about being in over my head melted away. Reluctantly, I pulled back. If I let him continue kissing me, I would forget why I was here, why I'd disobeyed common sense and placed myself in danger. Again.

"Flynn," I protested.

Sighing, he released me. "Start talking, Barrett."

"I will after you give me your cell phone."

Without hesitation he handed it over. I stood up, dropped the phone, and stomped on it.

"Barrett!"

"Hold on, I'm not done." I went around the entire suite and shut down electronic devices and unplugged phones. When I got back to the living room, he tried to speak, but I shook my head. I turned on music and then I walked to Flynn and kept my voice quiet when I said, "Your hotel room might be bugged. We should sit." I gestured to the couch. "And I'll explain."

"On a scale of one to Dolinsky, how bad?"

"FBI."

Flynn cursed.

I told him everything that had happened with the FBI agent, and I didn't leave anything out. Flynn's face remained passive, and he watched me with cool blue eyes.

"Is it true?" I asked. "Are you part of the SINS?"

"If I am?"

"I came here to tell you, didn't I?" I got up off the couch. I needed to move, pace, clear my head. "The casino and the brothel…that was one thing. Guns? Really?"

He nodded slowly.

"It's all in the name of this political cause, isn't it?"

"Aye," he said. "Now that you know, what will you do? Work with the feds? Turn me in? Bring down Malcolm?" His body was tight with tension as if he genuinely didn't know which way I was leaning.

I whirled and stared at him. "Fuck him. He doesn't touch what's mine."

Flynn's eyes gleamed with pride.

"I'm on your side, Flynn. I'll always be on your side. You asked me to trust you and I do. I'm not sure how to reconcile everything I know, but I'm with you, Flynn. I promise."

He stood up and stalked toward me. Reaching out, he cupped my face in his hands. He didn't say anything. He just kissed me before pulling back. "I got this."

"How?" I whispered. "There are so many—"

"Do you have faith in me?" he cut me off.

"Yes."

"Do you have faith in you?"

My brow furrowed. "Yes."

He smiled. "Then have faith we'll figure this out. All of it. Together."

Jason and Brad did a sweep of Flynn's suite and came up empty. No bugs. Once it was deemed that we had privacy, I reiterated all that had occurred with Fred Winters, barely pausing to even take a breath. Brad's jaw clenched in fury— his reaction made me strangely relieved because it meant Flynn had a man at his back. Jason was quiet, but I could still make out the anger in his eyes. Someone had gotten to me, and he blamed himself.

So many players in this game, and I had gone from measly pawn to a more powerful rook. Two men wanted to bring down Flynn—for entirely different reasons. I couldn't let either of them succeed.

Brad and Flynn talked in low tones, but I wasn't paying attention, lost in my own head. "Have the jet readied," Flynn said to Brad, jarring me from my silence.

I raised my eyebrows. "We're taking that vacation early, huh?"

Flynn grinned but shook his head.

"So why are you readying the jet?"

Brad and Flynn exchanged a look and then Brad said, "Come on, Jason. We've got a few things to do." Brad and Jason left the penthouse, and Flynn and I were alone.

"You're not going to take me somewhere and make me hide out in a bunker, are you? Because hiding won't solve anything," I said, gearing up for a debate.

"I agree," he said calmly.

"Then—"

"Las Vegas."

I frowned. "Vegas? You're taking me to Vegas?"

He nodded slowly.

"So we *are* taking a vacation."

"Guess again."

"There's nothing in Vegas except casinos and wedding chapels. What? Are we going to gamble and then get married?"

"No, of course not."

"Thank God."

"We're going to get married and *then* gamble."

My jaw dropped open. "Excuse me? Married?"

He nodded like it was the most logical thing in the world.

"Care to share your thought process with me?"

"Later," he stated. "When we're on the plane. Come on, you should probably pack the clothes you have here. We can buy you what you need when we're in Las Vegas."

"Wait just a minute," I seethed. "You can't just tell me

we're getting married and expect me to—you didn't even ask me!"

"Barrett, will you marry me?"

"Um. No."

"Why not? I'd make a good husband."

I started to laugh, hard enough that I felt it in my ribs and stomach. I laughed harder when he looked offended.

"You're doing everything bass ackwards."

"Bass ackwards?" he questioned.

"Ass backwards," I clarified. "You've never heard that?"

He shook his head. "Doesn't matter, we're getting away from the marriage discussion."

"There is no marriage discussion," I stated.

"Why?" He asked it calmly, like he was genuinely confused about why I was refusing his proposal. "Do you love me, Barrett?"

I swallowed. We hadn't spoken of love. "It's too fast."

"Do. You. Love. Me?"

"Yes."

"And I love you."

"You do?" I asked, feeling something inside of me softening.

"I do."

"There's more to this, isn't there? This isn't just about love?"

He sighed. "I wish it was. I wish the FBI wasn't on my tail or trying to intimidate you into helping them, but these are the facts. But this is also a fact: they don't know of your loyalty or your love for me. They expect you to flip. And I'm protecting you the only way I know how."

"By marrying me?"

"If, for some reason, I'm indicted, you would be protected from testifying against me."

I blinked. "Oh."

"It's not romantic, I know."

"Romance takes a back seat when the FBI is after you. Not to mention that little matter of a mob boss trying to take you out."

Flynn took me into his arms. "I wish I could give you romance and the proposal you deserve, but I can't. Not at the moment. I would still want to marry you—even if we weren't in this situation. Do you believe me?"

I smiled. "I do."

"You don't like flying?" Flynn asked, his hand covering my white-knuckled hand gripping the seat rest.

My eyes were tightly shut, and I focused on my breathing. "Just take off and landing. I usually pop something."

"We haven't even begun moving."

"I'm anticipating," I said.

"I have champagne chilling so we can toast. But I can have them serve it now."

"I don't like champagne."

"You have to toast an impending marriage with champagne. It's bad luck otherwise."

"Let's wait for thirty-thousand feet."

I opened my eyes just a tiny bit, enough to see Flynn. Jason and Brad were seated in the rear of the plane, close enough to hear us if we talked at a normal volume. I didn't want them to eavesdrop, so I kept my voice low when I asked, "We didn't talk about what happens when all this is over." The plane began to roll away from the gate and I swallowed, my throat dry.

"You really want to discuss this now?" he asked.

I nodded. "It will help distract me. I'm okay with signing a prenup. I have nothing and you have everything."

"How business-minded of you." He smiled. "You're not so great with the romance either, you know."

"I'll woo you later," I joked. "Should we talk about divorce?"

"Why?" he wondered.

"Because when all this is over, I won't need to be protected anymore."

"You think this marriage is a means to protect you for a finite time?"

"Isn't it?"

"Woman, you are intent on driving me insane, aren't you?"

"I'm just trying to give you an out," I attempted to explain.

"I don't want an out. I already told you I loved you. I already told you I wanted to marry you."

"So? Love and marriage don't always have to go hand in hand."

"It does for us. Or it would've. Eventually."

"You mean that?"

"I do."

"We haven't talked about marriage and what a life together will look like," I said.

"Is that what's worrying you?" He had the audacity to laugh and I would've smacked him, but I didn't want to remove my hands from my death grip on the seat rest.

"Let's talk about it now," he suggested. He pulled out a pen from his suit breast pocket and retrieved a pad of paper from his briefcase. He looked at me, waiting for me to speak.

"I have to go first?"

"This was your idea."

I glared at him. "You think you're hilarious."

"Not at all. I'm listening, Barrett, go ahead."

"Prenup. I'd like a prenup."

"We'll deal with a post-nup when we get back. Next."

"Children. Do you want them?"

"I hadn't thought much about it. I assumed...eventually. Aye. Do you?"

My gaze dropped to my lap when I shook my head.

"You don't want children? Or you don't want *my* children?"

"I don't want children in general," I stated, forcing myself to look at him. "Oh God, I couldn't bear it if you thought I didn't want your children."

He let out a breath. "Can I ask...why? Why don't you want them?"

"I just don't. I never saw my life with them in it. I don't want to be a parent." I bit my lip in worry. "Does that change —do you still want to marry me?"

His smile was gentle and sweet. "There are a lot of amazing things in life that don't include children. Aye, Barrett, I still want to marry you." He leaned over to kiss my lips. "You ready for that champagne? We made it to thirty-thousand feet."

Chapter 33

"You're drunk," Flynn said.

I snuggled against him, running my hand up and down his chest. "Yes."

"I like you drunk."

My hands continued to wander. Flynn's lips grazed my ear, and he whispered, "Save it for when we're alone."

"What's the point of a private plane if I can't grope you in it?"

"You make a strange sort of sense," Flynn said but gripped my hands to stop their wandering.

I harrumphed, causing him to laugh. "Where are we staying?"

"The Bellagio."

"Fancy."

When we landed, it was dark, and I was coming down from the champagne. I slid into the waiting limo and Flynn climbed in next to me. Jason closed the door before sitting up front with Brad who was driving.

I curled into Flynn, enjoying the hard warmth of him. We had a bit more privacy than we had on the plane and I quickly made use of our drive. I pulled his head down to mine and captured his lips. I hungrily tasted him, yearning for our connection to blaze between us, driving away all the fear and unknowns in my life.

His fingers plowed through my hair as he strained toward me, eager, wanting. I didn't even register when the limo stopped.

"Barrett," Flynn panted against my mouth.

"What? Don't stop."

"We have to. We're here."

The door to the limo opened and I got out, Flynn right behind me. He placed a hand at the small of my back and guided me into the lobby. I couldn't stop myself from gazing at the domed ceiling like a tourist. It took no time at all to check in and before I knew it, I was being ushered toward the decadent elevators. We weren't in the penthouse thirty seconds before Flynn was stripping out of his clothes and stalking toward me.

"What are you doing? The bellman will be here any minute to drop off our luggage."

Flynn's eyes glittered with suppressed desire. He whipped off his tie and cast it aside. "I told them we'd call down when we were ready for our luggage to be brought up."

"In that case…" I reached for my sweater and tugged it up over my head. I got out of my clothes in record time, needing to feel his strong, warm body against mine. I reached for him, wanting him naked. He obliged. I dropped to my knees and let out a deep sigh.

"I love seeing you like this," I said, my hands grazing up his thighs. "Hard and ready for me." I took him into my mouth, feeling him swell even more. I wanted all of him, every last bit, but Flynn wouldn't let me. He tugged me up from my knees, and I moaned in aggravation, but only until his lips took my nipple into his mouth. His fingers explored downward, finding me wet and eager.

We fell to the luxurious carpeted floor of the living room.

"I can't wait anymore," I stated. His ministrations were driving me wild, and I wanted him inside me.

"Thank God," he muttered against my mouth as he guided his length into my body.

I gasped, placing my hands on his lower back and lifting my legs to take him deeper.

"Fuck, that's the best thing I've ever felt." He growled.

His lips found mine again as he started thrusting. I pulled and pushed, took and gave. He placed an arm underneath me, lifting me up. The new angle had me screaming in pleasure, my nails scoring his back.

Flynn thrust faster, not slowing down for an instant. I came hard, clamping down around him. With one final thrust, he emptied himself inside of me. I sighed into his shoulder, placing my lips against his heated skin.

"That was fast," he said, rearing up to look at me. "And it was on the floor."

"I'm not complaining." I smiled.

"One of the many things I love about you."

We took our time cleaning up in the suite's enormous glass shower. When we were drying off, I asked, "So, man with a plan. What's next?"

He smiled. "More of this."

"Can we get our bags and food first?" I asked, my stomach rumbling.

He laughed. "Another thing I love about you." He helped me into a robe, his hands lingering on the sash. He slipped into the other one and then went to a hotel phone and called down for our luggage while I looked at the room service menu. I wanted one of everything.

"Decide on dinner?" Flynn asked.

"No. I can't make up my mind. It all looks so good."

He chuckled, dialed room service, and said, "Yes. I'd like an order for room service, please. One of everything. Honeymoon suite. Thank you." He hung up and grinned at me, looking carefree and boyish.

"My, my, aren't we generous," I teased.

After our bags were dropped off, we settled onto the couch to wait for our food to arrive. "So can I show you something?" he asked.

"Please," I said.

He got up off the couch and went to his discarded suit trouser pants and pulled out a velvet ring box. He came back and handed it to me.

I took it and stared at it for a moment before opening it. It wasn't what I expected. It wasn't what I expected at all. My eyes filled with tears as I stared at the most beautiful, delicate filigree wedding band I had ever seen.

"It was my mother's," he explained.

I looked up. His face was filled with emotion.

"It's perfect."

"Really?"

I nodded. "I thought…for some reason, you'd want to give me something…"

"Gaudy and ostentatious?"

"Something like that," I admitted with a sheepish smile.

He touched my cheek. "I thought this would mean more to you."

I brought my hand to cover his. "It means everything."

I smoothed the skirt of the gorgeous A-line white dress. It had a demure sweetheart neckline and straps that tied behind my back. Red kitten heels completed the outfit that I'd found in one of the hotel's boutiques. I'd managed to style my hair in a classic pin-up 'do, with big sweeping curls that brushed my shoulders. My makeup was simple, my lips a bright cherry red. In my haste to pack, I'd forgotten jewelry.

"Barrett?" Flynn asked, knocking on the dressing room door. "You okay?"

"Fine," I called.

"I don't believe you."

"I'm fine," I insisted.

"Open up. Let me in."

I didn't know if he meant the dressing room or something else. I sighed and flipped the lock. He closed the door and leaned against it, looking at me in my wedding dress.

"You're perfect," he said simply.

I took him in—he was dressed in a pressed three-piece gray suit with a skinny black tie. He looked incredible, his shoulders broad, his dark hair combed off his forehead. I wanted to lay my head against his broad chest and let him ease the wave of sadness that surged up inside me.

"What is it, hen?"

I raised my eyebrows. "Why do you call me 'hen'?"

"You don't like it?"

"I love it."

He smiled and it made my pulse race. "I'm Scottish, aye?"

"Aye," I agreed.

"Tell me what's wrong," he said.

"No one's here," I stated. "Ash or Malcolm. Those we care about…" I had no family to walk me down the aisle—not after I'd cut off my brother. My wedding day was making me sad and lonely, and that wasn't what a wedding day was supposed to be.

He cradled my cheeks in his hands. "I hate that I'm marrying you like this. I wanted to give you a real wedding with friends and family but…"

I put my hand over his mouth to stop him. "I'm marrying you, Flynn. Here, now. Maybe, one day, we can have a reception and invite all our loved ones to celebrate with us. Because that's what it should be—a celebration."

He smiled softly. "You really do love me, don't you?"

"I do," I said.

"Save it for Elvis."

I laughed and so did he. "Looks like you forgot earrings," he said, pushing my hair over my shoulder to see my naked ears.

"I did."

"Well, it's a good thing your future husband comes prepared." He reached into his pocket and pulled out a jewelry box.

"Sir," I teased in a flirtatious, over-done Southern belle drawl. "You are spoiling me."

"That's the hope."

I took the jewelry box and opened it, revealing diamond stud earrings at least two carats in size. I sighed. "You're too good at this," I stated, as I put them in my ears.

He took my hand and said, "Ready?"

"Ready."

Chapter 34

"Feel any different?" Flynn asked later when we were in bed.

"Very," I said, gazing down at my newly adorned ring finger.

"Really?"

I nodded. "Doesn't feel real. We just started dating. If you could even call it that. And now we're married."

"Hmmm," he murmured. His lips grazed my collarbone and I gripped his hair, enjoying him and the pleasant sensations he created.

"Flynn," I murmured. "What are we going to do about the FBI?"

His hand wandered down my body, urging my legs to part. He teased me with his fingers while his tongue invaded my mouth, battling with mine. I knew if I let him overwhelm me and make me forget, it would be hard to come back to myself.

"Please," I whispered against him. "I need some reassurance."

"I'm trying to give it to you."

"No. You're trying to distract me."

He sighed and his fingers stopped their love play. Flynn got up off me, and though his face reflected his frustration at being thwarted, he took a deep breath and didn't lose his patience. "You said Winters was going to get in contact with you in a few days. He threatened you, said that you needed to give him information that would lead to my take down. So that's what we're going to do."

"Give him information that could hurt you? I won't do it, I'll—"

He silenced me with a kiss before pulling back. "Do you really think I'd let that happen?"

"I'm usually pretty smart, but I'm not getting this."

He cupped my cheek and smiled at me with tenderness. "You'll be giving him information, but it will be false."

"False," I repeated.

"With just enough truth so he doesn't suspect anything, giving me time to finish the rest of the plan."

"And what plan is that?" I asked.

"That's enough for now."

"But—"

No longer in a placating mood, Flynn took me to bed.

"You're kidding, right?" Ash asked, her eyes widening. "You eloped?"

I nodded. "Yep."

"But why? You guys just started dating."

I was cooped up in Flynn's penthouse suite while he was off setting things up, things he wasn't sharing with me yet, and I was left to face my best friend. Alone.

"Because we love each other," I stated. "And we didn't want to wait."

"You guys don't even live together."

"We're rectifying that," I said. The rest of my clothes were in the process of finding drawers and closet space.

"You moved into Flynn's hotel?"

"Just until we find an apartment," I said. Flynn and I weren't going to leave the hotel until Dolinsky was no longer a threat. Flynn felt my safety could be better managed in his hotel due to the number of security cameras and a suite that could only be accessed by a private elevator and key card.

"You're happy," she stated, her face still wearing a picture of shock.

Aside from a known mob boss at large and the FBI on my tail, yes, I was happy. "Very much."

"This is the craziest thing you've ever done. Did you tell him? About the kid thing?"

I nodded. "He was okay with it."

"For now, maybe. What if he changes his mind?"

"It's one of my biggest fears—that Flynn is going to wake up one day and think about his lack of legacy and his mortality and decide he wants children. For now, he gets it, gets that kids aren't for everyone and that they're not for me. I hope he loves me enough not to resent me."

Ash shook her head, striving to lighten the mood. "Enough with the serious talk. You just got married! Tell me everything. Don't leave anything out."

I faithfully recounted the details of my wedding, showing her my wedding band and the earrings Flynn had given me. She oohed and aahed like any woman who liked shiny, sparkly things. "I can't believe you got married by Elvis. When the announcement hits the tabloids, they're going to have a field day."

I frowned. I hadn't thought about that. Flynn was high-profile and in the limelight, and the fact that we'd eloped was probably more news than if we'd had a perfect society wedding.

My thoughts were disrupted by the arrival of my new husband. I didn't think I'd ever get tired of him. I smiled as he came over to kiss me on the forehead.

Ash jumped up from her chair and came over to Flynn and hugged him. "I could kill you."

Flynn gazed at her with a slight smile on his face. "Oh. Why?"

"Because I was supposed to be maid of honor at your wedding. You have denied me."

"I am eternally in your debt. How can I repay it?"

"I get to help plan your wedding reception," she said.

"We weren't going to have a wedding reception," I said before Flynn could say anything.

"We weren't?" Flynn asked with a look in my direction. "I thought you wanted one."

"Yeah, when things calm down," I whispered. "Not now——"

"Of course you have to have a wedding reception." Ash interrupted. "You married Flynn Campbell—and you did it in secret. It will be the party of the year."

"You society people," I muttered.

"As Flynn's wife *you're* a society person now," Ash pointed out.

I stifled a lot of curses, but said to Flynn, "We might have to have a party. You are an important person, aren't you?"

"Very," he admitted with a roguish smile. "You can hire as many assistants as you need and with Ash's help, I'm sure it will be the most beautiful party I've ever seen."

With a squeal of excitement, Ash hugged us both. "I'm leaving now. Barrett looks like she's about to explode with tension and I've already got a million ideas." With a wave, she left.

"You'll wish you never made such a promise," I stated.

He shrugged. "Frankly, we have bigger things to worry about at the moment than our wedding reception."

He pulled out two phones from his pocket. One was a new iPhone, and the other was a cheap black flip phone. He held up the cheap black phone. "This is a burner. This is for when you need to get a hold of Brad, Jason, or me for any reason relating to the FBI. As soon as you use it, throw it away and we'll get you a new one. This"—he held up the iPhone—"is your 'regular' phone. Use it as normal. This phone can be tracked by anyone. Me included. I have it set up that way. The FBI has to be able to find you, but that means Dolinsky could too. We're playing a dangerous game, Barrett. A lot of moving parts."

I took a deep breath. "I don't even recognize my life anymore."

"I know."

Shaking off the somber feeling that I might not recognize myself when all this was done, I looked Flynn in the eye. "So, what information am I feeding to Winters?"

I sat in a busy coffee shop, trying to appear normal as I sipped my decaf latte. Jason lounged in the corner pretending to read a book. He was being discreet and doing a decent job of blending in. He wore jeans and a bulky sweater to hide his muscled form and the concealed weapon.

"Barrett," Fred Winters greeted. "Sorry, I'm late. Have you been waiting long?"

I looked up and forced a smile. "Just got here." I rose and hugged him. For public appearances, we looked like two old friends catching up over a cup of coffee.

Winters scanned the cafe as we took our seats. "You've been out of touch for a week."

I showed him the wedding band on my left ring finger. "I was in Vegas getting married."

The FBI agent couldn't hide his surprise. "Really? Interesting."

"Very," I said. "Flynn fell hard and fast for me. When he suggested eloping, I went with it."

"You must have some very unique skills to get a man like him to commit to one woman."

"We aren't here to discuss my assets. It's all true. Everything you told me."

Winters leaned back in his chair, evaluating me. "When we last spoke, you seemed hesitant to help us. Why the change of heart?"

I shrugged, feigning discomfort. "He's not the man I thought he was, and I have no desire to get bogged down in some political agenda that I have no loyalty to. I'm American; my loyalty is to the United States first."

"Good, I'm glad you said that." Winters nodded eagerly. "You married him. Will testifying against him be a problem for you?"

"No."

"What can you tell me?"

I repeated word for word what Flynn had made me memorize, watching Winters's reaction. He gave nothing away, and all I could do was hope he believed me.

"How did you find this out?"

"I overheard him on the phone," I lied. "With Malcolm."

"Good. Is your husband aware that you're onto him?"

I shook my head. "No clue."

Winters stood. "I'll be in touch."

I finished my coffee and then left. Jason followed me at a tactful distance until we got to The Rex Hotel. I popped into the burlesque club, waving to a few of my old co-workers, giving Jason time to catch up with me. The dancers were teaching a beginner's burlesque class, and I watched from the corner for a few minutes, enjoying the eclectic turn out. A lot were young women in their twenties and thirties, but there were a few middle-aged women and some even older. They all were laughing and having a blast.

"Should we find Mr. Campbell?" Jason asked, sidling up next to me.

"We should," I said, heading back out to the lobby, running into Lacey.

The burlesque club manager hugged me to her and said, "Hot damn, girl."

"What?"

"Mrs. Campbell," she said with a smirk and I laughed. "Is it too early for a celebratory martini?"

"Never," I said. "But I'm actually trying to locate Flynn. Have you seen him?"

She paused. "When did you see him last?"

"This morning. Why?"

"Ah, no reason."

"What do you know," I demanded.

"I shouldn't—you should wait for him."

"Lacey—"

"I can't, Barrett."

We stared each other down. "I can't just sit around and wait."

Lacey put a sympathetic hand on my arm. "You have to."

Chapter 35

Flynn didn't answer when I called his phone. He didn't answer when I made Jason call either. I spent the rest of the day in the penthouse suite, unpacking, rearranging, and trying to make it look like a home instead of a hotel room. I ate dinner by myself, refused all calls that came through, and waited.

And waited.

By midnight, I was exhausted from stewing. I was in deeper, married to a hotel mogul who wasn't at all what he appeared to be, and I still felt left out. I fell into a fitful sleep sometime around one.

I woke up when Flynn crawled into bed next to me, wrapping himself around my body. He kissed my temple, and I settled back against him.

"You still have secrets," I muttered.

"For now."

"Don't like it."

"I know, hen, I know." His mouth found mine, and I gave into him.

"Do you need me, Flynn?" I whispered against his lips, our skin heating, our breaths tangling.

He kissed me with fervor as if he was afraid I was slipping

away from him. He slid into me, scorching me with love and desire.

"I need you," he gritted out, his body taut and looming over mine. His hands framed my face, keeping our eyes locked on one another. In the faint moonlight streaming through the curtains, I could see his intensity.

I opened my legs wider so he could move deeper. His hands held mine over my head. Tears gathered in my eyes as wave after wave of pleasure hit me. With one final thrust, we both came. He collapsed into my arms, bathing my tear-streaked cheeks with his lips.

"Aye. I need you," he repeated in a whisper. "I need you because you're home, and you do anything—anything—to protect your home."

I sighed, caressing his face, feeling his words deep in my heart. He held me for a bit longer, his fingers stroking up and down my spine.

"Why does Lacey know where you were today?" I ventured to ask.

"You're the most important thing in the world to me, and I'd never forgive myself if something happened to you," he said, not answering the question.

"More than the SINS?" I lifted myself up, so I could look him in the eyes.

"More than the SINS," he admitted. "Which is why I can't tell you where—which is why you can't—"

I put a hand over his mouth to stop him from apologizing. He kissed my palm and then placed it on his heart. "We're warriors, Barrett. Our mission for a free Scotland is supposed to come first before anything. Before our own wants, needs, or the women we love and the families and lives we build with them. But it's easy to promise that Scotland comes first when you don't have anyone or anything to lose. I could lose you. Dolinsky could…"

Placing my lips on his mouth, I kissed him and said nothing. Whatever I said would sound paltry after my husband just admitted that I was his everything.

Over the next few weeks, I fed Fred Winters information. A piece here, a piece there. Everything on the Dolinsky front was quiet. It was like the man had simply vanished. But Jason continued to shadow me, and I was grateful for his presence. Flynn spent many nights away from home, not returning until early morning.

I didn't ask where he went, and he didn't volunteer information.

One late autumn afternoon, the city was gray and rainy, and I was cooped up with Ash looking at bridal magazines. I was going stir crazy and I hated it. I tossed aside another magazine and said, "Okay, enough."

"Enough what?" Ash asked, not looking up from a copy of *Vogue*.

"Enough of this planning nonsense. Let's get dressed up and go watch the burlesque show."

"That doesn't happen for a few more hours," she pointed out.

"So what. Let's eat dinner and then go over there."

Ash smiled. "I'm down." She got up, and we headed into the bedroom. She walked into my closet and began sifting for something she could wear. Ash was a good few inches taller than me, so whatever she wore of mine would be short on her.

"I'm glad we're doing this," Ash said, finding a classic black dress with a tight bodice and a flared skirt. "I've missed you."

I stopped looking at my dresses and gazed at her. "I've been kind of MIA, haven't I?"

She shrugged but nodded. "I get it. I mean I was in

Monaco when you started this thing with Flynn, and then I had to deal with John, but I just feel…"

"What?"

"I don't know. Like you're not telling me everything. And I get it, I do, because I didn't tell you what had happened with John right away, so you're entitled to your own secrets."

My heart began to pound, but I had to force myself to stay calm. "What wouldn't I tell you?"

"I don't know. My brother is different, too. And all this started when you met Flynn Campbell. Don't get me wrong, I like him, and I love how he treats you. But, I don't know—"

"There are things I can't tell you, Ash, no matter how much I may want to." There were things I didn't even know myself.

"So you're admitting there are things you're keeping from me."

"Yes."

She took a breath. "Okay."

"Okay? That's it?"

"You're my best friend, and I know you'd tell me if you could. I appreciate you being honest about not being able to tell me things."

"What does Jack say?"

"Not much. He's buried himself in his work." She bit her lip in worry. "He's just been acting really funny."

Jack's weirdness had something to do with Flynn, about what he had wanted to tell me the night of the charity gala. Shaking off the tense conversation, I hugged Ash to me.

"Crap," Ash said when she was dressed, her hairstyle and makeup perfect.

"What?"

"I won't fit into your shoes. The dress is a little shorter than I normally would like, but it'll be okay for tonight."

"Ah, I've got a solution." I picked up the suite phone and

called Lacey. Twenty minutes later, the woman herself came by with two pairs.

"Take your pick, honey," Lacey said holding them out for Ash's inspection. Ash settled on the red, pointy-toed torture machines. "Excellent choice."

"Thank you," Ash said, admiring them.

"Have you guys met yet?" I wondered, looking between them both.

"We haven't," Lacey said, holding out her hand for Ash to shake.

"Would you like to join us for dinner?" Ash extended the invite.

Lacey looked pleased and then regretful. "I'm sorry, but I have things to do this evening. Another time?"

"Absolutely."

I hugged Lacey goodbye, and then Ash and I set off for the bar and restaurant. "We'll see her at the club later," I said.

"Good evening, Mrs. Campbell," Robert, the host said. "Are you joining Mr. Campbell and his guest?"

"Flynn is here?" I blurted out before I could stop myself.

Robert nodded. "Yes, ma'am. At his usual table. Should I escort you—"

"No need, I know the way." I threw Robert a smile.

"You didn't know he was here?" Ash whispered. I shook my head as we strode through the restaurant and stopped at the table in the corner. Flynn was sitting with a handsome man I didn't recognize. They were in deep discussion and didn't see us approach.

"Well, hello stranger," I said.

Flynn looked up in surprise before he stood and kissed me on the cheek. "What are you doing here?"

"Ash and I wanted to have dinner at your table, but you had the same idea."

Flynn wrapped an arm around me and gestured to the

dark-haired man he was dining with who couldn't seem to take his eyes off Ash. "This is Malcolm's oldest son, Duncan."

Duncan rose from his seat, his silver gaze sliding to me.

I smiled. "I'm a fan of your father."

"My father is a big fan of yours. He speaks very highly of you," he said with a wide, roguish grin. His brogue was as thick as clotted cream and just as decadent.

"Flynn didn't tell me you were coming for a visit."

"Spur of the moment," Flynn interjected with a quick glance at me. I knew what that glance meant—he'd tell me later. Maybe.

"And who is this beautiful woman?" Duncan asked, turning his body ever so slightly toward Ash. That line, coming from any other man, would've been cheesy. But Duncan Buchanan was a sexy, burly Scotsman. He towered over Ash, despite the fact that my best friend was close to five feet nine.

"Ashby Rhodes." Ash held out her hand and Duncan took it and refused to let it go. She didn't seem to mind. I watched them size each other up.

"Join us for dinner," Duncan commanded. It was directed at Ash.

Ash smiled and I swore I could see Duncan's eyes dilate. "Love to."

I looked to Flynn and he nodded, gesturing for me to take a seat. He slid in next to me, coming close. After we ordered drinks, Ash asked Duncan, "What are you doing in the States? Here for a visit?"

"Business," Duncan answered vaguely. "And to catch up with this lad." He tossed a smile in Flynn's direction.

"Have you ever been to New York before?" Ash went on.

"I have not."

"Need a tour guide?" She flashed a flirty smile at him.

"Do you even think they know we're here?" I whispered at Flynn.

"No."

Duncan and Ash were laughing and teasing one another, and I highly doubted I would get a night out with my best friend. It seemed she was ready to move on from her disastrous broken engagement.

"This means you're stuck talking to me," I said to Flynn.

"Oh, I wonder how I'll ever get over it." He grinned. "There's a certain pleasure knowing we get to spend the night in bed together."

"Don't make promises you can't keep," I warned.

Flynn looked across the table at Duncan who was leaning close enough to Ash so her blond waves touched his face.

"Come on," he said, scooting out of the booth.

"We can't ditch them."

"Duncan, we're leaving you and Ash alone."

Ash and Duncan went on talking—they hadn't even heard Flynn. Flynn looked at me and raised an eyebrow.

I nodded. "Okay, let's ditch 'em."

Chapter 36

I collapsed on the bed, breathing hard. My skin was flushed and slick, and I briefly closed my eyes.

"You alive?"

I heard the amusement in Flynn's voice.

"Barely. You?" I replied.

"Barely."

I chuckled, feminine power surging through me. "Are you going to tell me why Duncan's here?"

"You wouldn't buy the excuse of a family visit, would you?"

"No." I turned my head so I could look into my husband's eyes.

"He's a tracker," Flynn explained slowly. "For the SINS."

"A tracker?"

Flynn nodded. "Whenever we have an enemy, Duncan is the one to ferret him out."

"Dolinsky. You asked him to come here and help you with Dolinsky, didn't you?"

"Aye."

"Because you're having trouble locating him. That's where

you've been the last few weeks. At night, I mean. Hunting him."

"Aye," he said again.

I shivered.

"But he's gone so far underground even Marino hasn't heard a whisper."

"And you think Duncan will be able to flush him out?"

"He's never failed. If anyone can do it, Duncan can."

I didn't have to ask what would happen when they finally found Dolinsky. Flynn would take down every enemy that tried to topple him from his position.

"Where did you go just now?" Flynn asked, reaching out to touch my cheek.

"Just thinking about what happens when you find him."

"Does it bother you? What I'll do? What I'll have to do?"

"No."

"No? Really?"

I sat up, not at all concerned about my nudity. Sometimes, it wasn't skin that made you bare. "It must be hard for you to believe me, but if there's anything you taught me it's that life isn't black and white. This man wants to destroy you—and to do it, he will go after everything you value. I love you. I trust you."

Flynn's hand reached out for mine, taking it in his firm grip. "Dolinsky and I...we're not so different, Barrett. I will destroy everything he has, burn it to the ground, burn it all so that nothing can rise from the ashes."

"You think I don't know that?" I wondered. "That the man I love is capable of such things? It's not everything you are, Flynn. There's more to you. A lot more. I think about the moments when you hold me to you and whisper beautiful things to me, and I know I love you. All of you. All the parts of you."

"It was a lot to hope for," Flynn admitted. "I didn't think

I'd ever find a woman that would be able to make peace with who I really was. I didn't look for it."

"Hard to know what to look for when you're not sure it exists," I said honestly. "You took me by surprise too, Flynn."

He grinned at me as he got out of bed. Making his way to the bathroom, he said, "So, should I have a discussion with Duncan?"

"Why would you do that?" I wondered as I followed him.

"Because I know Duncan, and he's a bit of a lad."

"What's that mean?"

"He likes the ladies."

I chuckled but then sobered. "I think you should speak with Duncan and warn him away from Ash. She'll break his heart."

"*His* heart? I was going to warn him not to break hers." He drew a bath and then settled into the gargantuan tub first. I steadied myself and then eased down into the steaming water, releasing a sigh as I leaned back against the wall of his muscled chest.

"You don't know Ash like I know Ash," I said, tracing his leg under the water.

"Meaning?"

I debated on whether or not to tell him what I knew. Then again, if there was any man capable of withholding judgment, it was Flynn. "She cheated on her fiancé," I said slowly.

"Didn't want to marry him, huh?"

"Not that simple. She was having an affair," I said. Flynn didn't need to know it was with her fiancé's father. Not all information was necessary—so I was learning.

He sighed. "Maybe I should caution Duncan."

"It's all your fault, really."

"My fault? Why?"

"Ash and I were supposed to hang out tonight, just us girls, and watch the burlesque show. And now she's probably in bed with a hot Scot, ruining him for the rest of his life."

"Hot? You think Duncan is hot?"

"Not as hot as you, darling."

"I should hope not," Flynn huffed.

I smiled.

I invited the burlesque dancers up to the suite where we'd had our slumber party for a major catch up session. So much had happened since that night it felt like I was living another life.

"So what's it like being married to Flynn Campbell?" Alia asked as she reached for another Oreo.

"Pretty good," I said with a smile.

"That's it? That's all we get?" Alia demanded.

"I'm not giving you sex details," I stated. "Because I know that's what you're really after."

"You know me well." Alia grinned.

"You married a wealthy, successful, sexy Scot," Shawna said. "Yeah, I bet being married to him is just 'pretty good.' Let me tell you about the last guy I went on a date with…"

"He can't be worse than the guy I dated before I met my husband," Renee chimed in.

I listened as the ladies recounted their horror stories of dating in Manhattan while we ate junk food. It made me exceptionally grateful that I'd once been too caught up in the academic life to date. There were some real duds out there.

"Why are you so quiet, Jamie?" Alia asked the petite, shy brunette. She was the new cocktail waitress who also danced that had been hired to replace me. And Chelsea.

Chelsea. That bitch had tried to stick me with a syringe.

Jamie blushed. "Oh, you know…"

"We don't know," Renee said. "Which is why we're asking."

"I met someone," she admitted. "He's wonderful."

All conversation and direction turned to Jamie who was

bright red and gushing over her boyfriend. "He's so sweet and wonderful and…" she babbled on and on about the man she was seeing. "But he doesn't like that I'm a dancer."

"It's not his choice," Alia said. "It's yours."

"I really like him," Jamie admitted. "What do I do?"

I reached over and took her hand. "If he really cares for you, he won't make you give up what you love to do." I knew she wouldn't hear me. When you were wrapped up in someone, you never heard what others were trying to tell you. Jamie might fall head over heels in love with this guy, and she might quit dancing. I hoped that didn't happen, but we all had to make our own mistakes.

"Just don't do anything drastic," Renee said.

"Yeah, like marrying him after only knowing him for a few months," Alia teased with a look in my direction.

"Have you seen Flynn Campbell? A man like that asks you to marry him and you say 'yes!'" I said with a loopy grin.

"Actually, you say 'hell yes!'" Shawna laughed.

"And to think—when you first started working at the club, you pretended there was nothing between you guys," Alia reminded us all.

I wondered what they'd think of him if they knew about his political affiliations and the danger surrounding him. It would probably make them hotter for him. There was something taming a bad boy.

"Have you guys talked about kids?" Renee asked. She had a three-year-old daughter who was always caught on video doing really cute and funny things.

I nodded, feeling uncomfortable. They all looked at me expectantly as they waited for me to share.

"I don't want to talk about it," I said quietly.

Thankfully, they read the cues, and Alia changed the subject. "Who was that hot guy your best friend was with?" Alia asked.

I frowned. "When?"

"Last night. Ash was sitting in Mr. Campbell's booth with a very handsome man," Shawna said.

Oh, so they'd made it to the show after all. "An old family friend of Flynn's," I said. "Here for a visit."

"He is hot," Alia said, fanning herself. "Ashby Rhodes is one lucky woman."

"You've got your own hot guy," Shawna stated, referring to Alia's fiancé who tended bar in the club.

"Are we done with the catching up?" Renee asked. "Can we go down to the spa now? I'm in need of a massage. Sophia likes to play 'Ride the Horsie.' My shoulders are killing me."

"She's too cute for words," Jamie said.

Renee smiled. "Thanks."

"I need a pedicure," Alia said. "I've got some caveman toenails going on."

"Not to mention wildebeest legs. You might want a wax, too," Shawna teased. Alia tugged Shawna's ponytail in a friendly manner.

They were all becoming friends outside of work, and I was really glad for them. "Let's roll," I said getting up off the floor.

A cell phone rang, and we instantly all checked ours. It was Jamie's. "Boyfriend," she said, holding up the phone. She stared at it a moment as if debating whether or not to answer it. Alia did it for her.

"Hello, Jamie's phone, Alia speaking." She listened for a minute. "Jamie is unable to come to the phone right now because she's about to get a massage." Alia hung up and then handed Jamie's phone back to her.

"What did you just do?" Jamie asked in horror.

"Showing him who's boss. Now, who's boss?" Alia demanded.

"Uh, you?" Jamie asked meekly.

"No. You are!" Alia said with force. "Just because he calls doesn't mean you go runnin'. Got me?"

"Got you," Jamie answered.

"Good, now let's go."

Arm in arm, Jamie and Alia left the suite followed by the rest of us. We crowded into the elevator, and I hit the Spa button. Moments later, we spilled out of the elevator, and the girls followed me to the smiling receptionist who greeted me.

"Good afternoon, Mrs. Campbell."

I didn't think I'd ever get tired of hearing my married name. Call it old fashioned and antiquated, I didn't care. I loved it. "Good afternoon, Charlotte. Are you guys ready for us?"

Charlotte laughed. "We are. Where would you guys like to start?"

"Mimosas and pedicures and then massages." I looked at the girls for confirmation and they nodded. We were ushered through the spa to a row of pedicure chairs. I settled in and closed my eyes as everyone chattered around me.

"A toast," Alia said, when we had our flutes. "To the new Mrs. Campbell."

There was a chorus of cheers, and we all threw it back. Feeling wonderful and full of champagne bubbles, I sighed when the spa technician began to rub my feet.

"What color are you getting?" Jamie asked me.

"Harlot Red," I stated.

"That's not really a color, is it?" Jaime looked disbelieving, and I handed her the bottle of nail polish. She looked at the bottom. "Well, what do you know? Okay, I want that color, too!"

I worried that Jamie would always be a follower, but not everyone could be a leader.

My phone buzzed in my pocket, and I pulled it out; it was a text from Winters wanting to have coffee. I held in a sigh. I'd been feeding him information for weeks, and he'd only grown more adamant about finding something to pin on Flynn.

"Why are you frowning?" Alia asked me.

"Nothing. Wedding reception stuff," I lied. "It's all a pain in the ass." That much was true.

"Well, at least it's not a full-blown wedding," Alia said with a look of commiseration.

"Might as well be. I imagine Flynn's wedding was supposed to be the party of the season."

"Party of the season?" Renee smiled. "Really? Is this the 1800s, and he's some duke getting married?"

"Just be glad it's not *your* best friend who's obsessed with this stuff. Ash has some pretty grand plans."

I wanted a quiet place to relax and have someone work on the knots that had taken up residence in my shoulders. "I'm ready for my massage," I said to the technician who was cleaning up my pedicure station.

"Of course," the young woman said with a smile.

"What's your name?" I asked her.

"Annabelle."

"Annabelle, thank you for taking care of me."

She looked surprised and a little bashful. "You're welcome. Let me just go tell your masseur you're ready." A few minutes later, Annabelle came back and escorted me down a long white hallway and pointed at the last door on the left.

"Go ahead and get comfortable and Sean will be with you in a few minutes." She closed the door, and I breathed in the tea tree oil permeating the room. The walls were a soft green and faint sounds of Native American flutes drifted through the speakers. I began to relax as I shed my clothes, leaving on my underwear, and climbing beneath the sheet. Putting my face in the hole, I closed my eyes and waited.

The door opened and closed. The masseur padded closer. He stopped at the table and placed a large hand on my shoulder blade, letting it rest there a moment, letting me get comfortable with his touch. Slowly, he stroked a finger down my spine.

The hair on the back of my neck rose.

I felt the prick of something sharp in the side of my neck and warm breath near my ear when he said in a thick Russian accent, "Sleep."

Chapter 37

I turned my head and retched onto the floor. There was very little in my stomach, mostly champagne and bile. As I trembled from the effort, it took me a moment to realize I was wrapped in a sheet, and I was on a bed. And not a grungy, sweaty mattress in some dank warehouse. No, I was in a beautiful room with white walls and gold accents. The massive four-poster bed would've been downright comfortable had I not had a ball of fear in my stomach.

Scrambling out of bed, I wrapped the sheet more securely around me. I tried the door, finding it locked. It didn't matter; it wasn't like I was going to get very far in a sheet and no shoes.

Panic surged through me, and I began to tremble. I had to stay calm, so I shoved the terror down and thought about what I could control.

Thirst. I was parched. I headed for the bathroom. Sticking my head under the sink faucet, I drank greedily. When my thirst was satiated, I began opening drawers, but found nothing of use. Anger and fear pulsed in my veins, but it wouldn't help me to lose my cool. I had to keep a calm, rational frame of mind. Locked in a room with no escape, I could do nothing but wait, so I went back into the bedroom and collapsed onto the bed.

I had no idea of the time, but I was hungry. My stomach rumbled as I looked around for a clock. No luck.

The sound of a key in a lock and the bedroom doorknob turning had me leaping off the bed—to go where? I forced myself to stand my ground, knowing the best I could do was watch and wait.

A handsome man of an undistinguishable age stood in the doorway. He had chiseled cheekbones and a firm jaw, brown eyes a shade or two darker than the styled hair on his head. Regal and powerful, I knew this man was behind my kidnapping.

"You are awake," he said in heavily accented English. "Good." His gaze dropped to the sheet covering me, lips quirking in amusement.

My hands gripped the sheet tighter.

"You know who I am." It wasn't a question but a statement.

"Yes." My throat was tight with fear.

He stared at me for a long moment and then strolled to the heavy wooden armoire along the far wall, flung it open, and grabbed a long black sheath dress from a hanger. He walked over to me and presented it like a gift. "Put this on," he commanded. "And we will dine together."

I swallowed and took the gown which was much more suited for a date to a gala. As my hand clutched the hanger, the man's fingers wrapped around my wrist, exerting just enough pressure to let me know he could hurt me if he desired.

"Do not think to escape," he said, his voice low. "No harm will come to you if you listen to me." His brown eyes bore into mine, waiting for my answer. I nodded. He released me. I exhaled slowly.

What was his game?

"I will give you ten minutes to make yourself ready and then I will come for you." He left the room, closing the door, making sure to lock it.

I didn't waste any time putting on the dress and even went as far as searching for shoes in the armoire. There were none. When I glanced at myself in the mirror, I nearly blanched. I looked like I was wearing lingerie. The material stopped at my ankles, but the skirt was sheer with a long slit down the left leg. The bodice was form fitting, almost corset-like.

I felt like a whore, a kept woman, a trophy for a man who won all the trophies.

Fear morphed into terror as I waited for Igor Dolinsky to come back for me.

Dolinsky returned, and if I had a stopwatch, I would've bet it had been ten minutes exactly. His eyes raked over me in appreciation, but while I expected it to be lewd, it wasn't. That surprised me.

He offered me his arm in a gentlemanly fashion and waited for me to take it. It would go a long way to humoring this powerful, unpredictable man.

Dolinsky led me out of the bedroom and down a hallway. Under different circumstances, I would've taken time to notice the opulent wealth and decor, but I was too caught up in my own head.

Why was Igor Dolinsky treating me like a welcomed houseguest?

We walked down a long, wide wooden staircase, and I had to stop myself from gaping. I was in a ballroom. An old-world Russian ballroom, like something in the time of Nicholas II, Czar of Russia.

"Beautiful, isn't it?" Dolinsky asked gruffly.

"It is."

He smiled like I'd pleased him with my answer. Guiding me across the ballroom, he took me through a set of ornate wooden doors and into a dining room. A long table that could seat a state dinner was set with silver candelabras, two white china place settings, and a blood red tablecloth.

If I could get my hand around one of the candelabras, would I have the strength to bludgeon him with it? Or was it foolish to attempt such a thing? Even if I did manage to wound him, there was no way I'd escape from his home—surely he had security lurking in the shadows to prevent me from fleeing.

No, better to watch and wait. Keep my eyes and ears open and take my shot when I had a better chance of success.

Dolinsky escorted me to the seat next to the head of the table. He held out my chair for me and waited. I sat down slowly and automatically reached for the napkin. Dolinsky took his place.

For a long moment, Dolinsky stared at me, and I had to stop myself from fidgeting. "You must be curious as to why you're here," he said politely, still playing the gallant host and gentleman.

"A little."

He smiled. "Most women would be crying and demanding to know what was in store for them. They'd beg and plead and cower."

"I'm not most women."

"No, you're not," he murmured as if to himself.

He reached for the little brass bell near his empty crystal wine glass, picked it up, and rang it. Two women entered the room, and Dolinsky spoke to them in Russian before dismissing them.

"Why are you treating me like an honored guest?" I asked.

He leaned back in his chair to study me. "A beautiful woman should be cherished."

"For how long?"

He smiled, but for once it wasn't charming—it was predatory and terrifying. "Until she is no longer useful."

The two women came back. One carried a platter and put it down in front of us while the other poured us two glasses of red wine. They departed the dining room and went back into the kitchen.

Dolinsky lifted his glass of wine to signal a toast. With no choice, I did the same, wondering when all of this would hit me and my panic would come back.

"To partnerships."

He kept his eyes on me as he took a sip. I took a small drink and then set my glass aside. I needed to keep my wits. The food could be drugged, but there wasn't much I could do about that.

"Do you like beets?" he asked, reaching for the serving spoon. Before I could answer, he plopped a spoonful onto my plate and then served himself. I picked up the correct fork and took a bite.

"Delicious," I said.

He hummed with pleasure as he sampled the food. "You have not asked where you are."

The man wanted to play, did he? I arched an eyebrow. "Where am I?"

Setting down his fork, he leaned close to me, and with too much familiarity, gently pushed a strand of hair behind my ear. "Your new cage."

Chapter 38

All through the six-course dinner, Dolinsky chatted amiably and explained each dish that was served. If I hadn't been his prisoner, I would have seriously considered him charming. To hell with that, he *was* charming. He didn't ask me one question about Flynn or our personal relationship, and I had no way of knowing if Dolinsky realized we were married. After all, it still wasn't technically public knowledge, and the subtle wedding ring I had on my finger could easily be explained as just another piece of jewelry.

By the end of the meal, I still had no inkling of Dolinsky's master plan for me. If I didn't know any better, I would've assumed he was attempting to seduce me. Not sexually—that would've been a byproduct. No, Dolinsky was trying to seduce me with his charm, wealth, and power. What was his angle? Was he hoping I'd change allegiances just because he was being kind to me?

Flynn had told me Dolinsky was a killer, ruthless and hard. That wasn't the persona he was showing me now. He was acting the part of doting playboy.

"I'm curious," I said when we were lingering over coffee and dessert. "Were you the one who took me from the spa?"

"No," Dolinsky said. "I sent one of my most trusted men to get you."

"How did he kidnap me without anyone noticing? There were security cameras and I was in The Rex Hotel, surrounded by people who knew me by name."

Dolinsky chucked me under the chin like a child. "Nothing is foolproof. There's always a way."

I stifled the urge to rub my skin. I noted that he hadn't actually given me an answer, but had evaded my question.

"Any other inquiries?"

I took a deep breath and asked the question that had been plaguing me. "Do you plan on torturing me? Raping me?"

He frowned. "Why would I do such heinous things? You think because I am your husband's enemy that I abuse women just because I can?"

Ah, so he knew who I was to Flynn. No matter what he said, I couldn't trust him, no matter how fascinating and debonair he could be.

"I have but one goal," he went on, "and that is to topple Flynn Campbell from his lofty throne—and burn his empire to the ground. That is no great secret."

"I'm part of that empire, am I not?" I pushed, feeling bold.

His eyes were speculative. "Are you having his child?"

"No."

"Then I see no reason for you to burn with Campbell."

"What makes you think you're safe from me?" I wondered. "I could take this dessert fork and stab you in the throat."

"Try," he said in amusement.

"You don't think I'm a worthy adversary." For some reason that deeply offended me.

"Oh, *moya krasotka*, I wish I could explain it all to you, but it is too soon."

"What do you mean?"

"It means that for now there are no more questions and

dinner is over." He rose from his seat and came around to help me. Before he pulled out my chair, he leaned over, and I felt his warm breath on my bare skin.

"Make yourself at home, Barrett."

Dolinsky caressed the back of my neck and then was gone.

Make yourself at home.

The words churned in my mind as I stared at the ceiling of the lavish bedroom. After Dolinsky had left me in the dining room, I hadn't had the energy to test his words, so I'd gone upstairs to the bedroom I'd woken up in. The sheets had been changed and the room had been aired out. There was no sign at all that I'd been sick to my stomach. I closed the door, removed the sheath dress, and then took a bath. No longer forced to put on a brave face, I cried.

All the adrenaline I'd been running on leaked out of my body, leaving me exhausted. I'd found a pair of light pink silk pajamas in a chest of drawers. Because there wasn't a clock, I had no idea of the time, so I climbed into bed. I tossed and turned, missing Flynn, worrying for him.

I wondered why I wasn't afraid of Dolinsky. Was that part of his plan? Capture the bird, stick it in a cage but feed it, stroke it, take care of it, so it will forget it was once free?

I was forced to play a game, and I didn't know the rules. How long was Dolinsky going to keep me here? And where was *here?* Was I still in the United States? For all I knew, while I was drugged, I could've been on a plane bound for Russia.

Sleep continued to elude me, so I threw off the covers and climbed out of bed. I put on the terrycloth robe hanging on the bathroom hook. I tried the bedroom doorknob, surprised to find that it turned easily. It hadn't been locked.

Discovering a smaller, less for show staircase, I walked down it. I held onto the carved wood rail and found myself in a long hallway with many doors. I heard the faint sounds of a viola and I hesitated. The only other souls I'd seen in Dolinsky's massive mansion had been the two Russian women who had served us dinner. No guards, no cronies. Not that I doubted he had security lurking about, but this was Dolinsky's haven—I realized—his home.

I walked toward the mournful sounds of the instrument, approaching cautiously. I didn't know Dolinsky—only what he chose to show me—and I had to remember it was all a facade. The man wanted to destroy Flynn. In destroying Flynn, it would destroy me.

I came to the doorway of what looked like a music room. The light from the chandelier was on but dim, casting the room in a romantic glow. Dolinsky was turned slightly away from me, but I could see enough of his face to realize his eyes were closed as he expertly elicited despondent notes from the viola. When he was finished, he paused a moment before opening his eyes. He breathed deeply, like he was letting go of a memory and returning to the present. He glanced at me, not at all surprised that I was there.

"You could not sleep," he stated, shattering the quiet.

"No."

"You miss your husband." It was a statement, not a question.

Dolinsky set his instrument in its case, gently, like a child, before looking at me. I saw puzzlement on his face and a deep yearning. For what, I wondered.

"Are you married, Mr. Dolinsky?"

"Igor," he corrected. "My name is Igor."

"Igor," I repeated. "Are you married?"

"I was. Once." He turned away to stare out the window. His hand reached out to touch the glass. It took me a moment to realize it was snowing thick, fat flakes. It was winter, wherever we were.

"Why am I here?" I asked.

"Why do you think you're here?" He looked over his shoulder at me, and I was struck by the man's beauty in the moonlight. Soft beams illuminated his carved cheekbones, and I found myself wanting to know his story. I quickly shut down that thought. To know him would make him human. I could not empathize.

"I'm here because I belong to Flynn. And you want to destroy Flynn. So, in destroying me, you destroy him." I hated making myself sound like a possession, but for all intents and purposes, I was Flynn's. My last name was Campbell, and I belonged with him.

Dolinsky's sculpted mouth curved into a rueful smile. "When Chelsea first told me of you, I thought you were nothing more than a distraction for Campbell. When she failed to kidnap you in the parking garage at the Met, I was furious that she let you slip through her fingers. Chelsea underestimated you." He shook his head.

"What happened to her?"

"The same thing that happens to anyone who fails me."

I shivered at the coldness in his voice.

Dolinsky watched me with aloof brown eyes, his voice lowering. "At first I was irate, and then I realized what good fortune it was."

"Why?" Blood was rushing through my ears, and I strained to listen to Dolinsky.

"You don't destroy magnificence, Barrett," he said.

"Stop speaking in riddles! What the hell do you want from me?" I cried in desperation.

He stared at me a long moment before his gaze returned to look out the window. He said nothing. In a blaze of anger, I stomped from the music room, wondering what the hell my life had become.

Chapter 39

Coffee.

Opening tired eyes, I let out a surprised squeak. One of the women who had served dinner last night was setting down a breakfast tray on my bedside table. She pushed down the lever on the French press, and I slowly sat up. She was young, blond, and didn't say anything as she orchestrated my breakfast in bed.

"Thank you." Dolinsky had spoken to her in Russian so I had no way of knowing if she understood me. "*Spasibo,*" I said suddenly, remembering the word from a long-ago episode of *Sex in the City* when Carrie dated the Russian artist.

The woman nodded her head but didn't smile, or say anything, and then she left. A wave of loneliness washed over me. I was isolated with no one to speak to, no one except Dolinsky.

I missed Flynn. Everything about him. He must have been out of his mind with worry.

There was no technology in my gorgeous prison—no computer or phone. I was truly cut off from the world. As I ate breakfast and sipped my coffee, I thought about my options. I could try to find something to use as a weapon and take Dolinsky out, but he was expecting me to do that. Even if I was successful, or at least managed to wound him, I doubted I'd get far—I still had no idea of my location. The cold snap of winter brought snowfall, and I wasn't foolish enough to leave the comfort of a warm place and take my chances in the elements. Besides, even though I didn't see anyone besides Dolinsky, I didn't believe we were truly alone. A man like Dolinsky planned. I assumed I was well guarded even if I didn't see anyone. No point in being foolhardy, and so far, my captor hadn't shown me an ounce of violence.

I would continue to be wary and watchful, but for now, there was nothing to do except wait. Wait for Flynn to find me.

I finished my coffee and then headed for the shower. After, I padded over to the chest of drawers and found a pair of jeans and a white angora sweater. They fit me perfectly. I pulled on wool socks and then peeked out of my bedroom. All was quiet.

Instead of heading toward the familiarity of the music room, I turned the opposite direction and discovered the most incredible library. Dark wood, comfortable leather reading chairs, and a narrow staircase that led to a second tier. Shelf after shelf of books. More books than I could ever read in a lifetime.

"Good morning, *moya krasotka.*"

I started at the sound of his voice, not having heard his approach. I turned to look at him. Dolinsky stood behind me, his eyes watchful.

"Good morning," I murmured and then focused on the gorgeous room. I felt like Belle in *Beauty and the Beast*. The irony wasn't lost on me.

"You did not sleep well." He came to stand by my side, his fingers reaching out to clasp my jaw in a gentle grip.

I tried not to flinch from his overly familiar touch. "No, I didn't." No point in lying. He could see the dark shadows underneath my eyes.

His hand lingered on my skin, and I held his gaze. Almost reluctantly, he dropped his hand and then gestured to the room. "What do you think?"

"Incredible," I answered truthfully.

"Yes," he murmured, though his eyes were still on me and not the library. He took my hand and led me to one of the brown leather chairs and gestured for me to sit. I rested my feet on the matching ottoman while Dolinsky went to a nearby shelf and picked up a book.

He walked over and handed it to me. I expected it to be a book by a Russian author but again, Dolinsky surprised me by giving me a leather-bound copy of the *Aeneid*.

"*Audaces fortuna iuvat*,'" he quoted.

"'Fortune favors the bold,'" I translated.

"Yes," he said, obviously pleased. "My favorite quote in all the *Aeneid*."

"It's how you live your life—it's how Flynn lives his life, too."

"Men like us… It's the only way to live."

I wondered how long we were going to do this dance, but I was tired of asking questions and receiving no answers. I could tell he wanted me to ask why I was here, what his plans were for me, beg him to take me back to the city, but I wasn't going to give him the satisfaction.

Let the dance continue.

"Can I ask you something?"

"You may," he said, his tone hopeful.

"Might I get an alarm clock in my room?"

"Why?"

"Because I'd like to keep track of the time."

"What's my name?" he asked.

"Dolinsky."

He looked disappointed. "No, you may not have an alarm

clock." He strode from the library, leaving me with a room of leather-bound books and my swirling thoughts.

Over the course of the next week, I carved out a routine. Every morning I woke up to a breakfast tray and coffee. I ate and then showered before putting on clothes that magically found their way into the armoire, closet, and dresser. I'd discovered an expensive pen in the library, and I'd taken it with me to my bedroom. In the far back part of the closet, I pushed aside the rack of evening gowns and made a tally of my days in Dolinsky's home. I still had no alarm clock.

During the days, I spent my time in the library, attempting to read. I rarely got more than one paragraph in before my mind began to wander, and I thought about Flynn. I worried for him, much more so than I ever considered worrying for myself. I wondered how he was explaining my absence to my best friend, but more importantly, I wondered why he hadn't found me yet. Had my trail gone cold?

I'd found an English/Russian dictionary and somehow managed to absorb a few words. It was the only thing that seemed to occupy my mind.

Dolinsky left me to my own devices during the daylight hours, but every evening, we dined together in the spacious, elegant dining room. He insisted I dress for the occasion, and he was complimentary. He always wore evening attire, looking fashionable and handsome.

I hated that I noticed his appearance, but more so, I hated that he treated me like an equal and asked my opinion on many subjects. He genuinely seemed interested in what I had to say, and he wouldn't let me give him one-word answers.

On night eight, I let my guard down just enough to be lulled into a peaceful state. Dolinsky and I were in the middle of a debate and forgetting myself, I yelled at him for playing devil's advocate. We laughed.

Together.

Horror registered across my face, and I shoved away from the table, running to the illusionary privacy of my room. Throwing myself onto the bed, I cried for all the confusion I felt. Dolinsky was my enemy, my captor, and I had been enjoying his company.

There was a knock on my door. I sat up quickly and jumped off the bed. I hastily ran my fingers under my eyes. "Come in," I mumbled.

Dolinsky stood in the doorway. "Are you all right?"

"Fine," I lied, refusing to meet his gaze. "Just a little too much wine."

"You never have more than a glass." He took a step toward me, and I held up my hand to thwart him.

"Please, don't. I don't have the energy for this. Not tonight."

"Energy for what?"

"For games. How long are you going to keep me here, pretending I'm a houseguest and not a prisoner? Even though you're here with me, your men are out there, hunting down my husband."

Dolinsky stalked toward me with a determined look on his face. I couldn't stop the quiver of fear that dashed down my spine. I backed up until I hit a wall, Dolinsky pressing close to me. I grabbed the lapels of his suit jacket and demanded, "What the hell do you want from me?"

I saw the tick in his jaw as he looked down at me, but he remained silent.

"Answer me, damn it!"

"What's my name?" he asked quietly.

I'd been vacillating from fear to calm constantly. I was tired of this waiting game. It needed to end, now. "Fuck you," I lashed.

"What's. My. Name?"

"Dolinsky!"

Dolinsky placed his hands on mine and gently removed them from his lapels. "Good night, Barrett." He left my room and closed the door on his way out.

Taking off one of my high heels, I chucked it after him and then ripped the beautiful gown from my body.

Chapter 40

I woke up with a headache from crying most of the night. There was no breakfast tray next to my bed, and that threw me into a bout of uncertainty. It had been something I could count on, but no longer, apparently. After getting up, I splashed some cold water on my face, feeling marginally restored but listless. I refused to put on a good show, so I headed for the dining room still in my two-piece silk button up pajamas.

Dolinsky sat at his customary seat at the head of the table, a newspaper open, a half-finished plate of breakfast in front of him. He rose when I entered, ever the gallant gentleman. It pissed me off.

"Don't bother," I said waspishly when he attempted to help me with my chair. He didn't listen and did it anyway. I sank into it, itching for caffeine. Dolinsky rang the little brass bell. Nothing I did seemed to faze the man. He had the patience of a saint and the charm of a prince. It was difficult to remember he was an evil man who sold and bartered women, who wanted to take down Flynn, who'd had me kidnapped.

"I thought after breakfast you might like to see the grounds," he said conversationally, as if all the emotion that had transpired between us the evening before never happened. "It snowed last night. It's quite beautiful."

Fresh air. The idea appealed to me since I'd been cooped up inside for days. A prison, no matter how large and beautiful, was still a prison.

"I'd like to see the grounds," I answered amiably. My coffee and breakfast arrived, and even though I stared at my plate while I ate, I could feel his eyes on me.

"I am not without compassion," he said.

"Then take me home."

"I can't."

"You mean you won't." My voice wasn't angry, just dispassionate.

He inclined his head in agreement. "I wish for us to be friends."

"We can't be friends."

"You mean 'won't,' correct?" His smile was winsome and painted with sadness.

"You are my husband's enemy. How can we be friends?"

"But I am not *your* enemy. If we were enemies, do you think I would have brought you here, to my home, treated you like the treasure you are?"

I closed my eyes, so I didn't have to see the pleading in his gaze. He tugged emotion from me, and I didn't like it. Exhaustion made it harder to piece everything together.

"You plan to kill my husband, the man I love—"

Dolinsky's hand shot out and swiped the delicate china teacup off the table. It hit the floor and shattered into pieces. His face was red with rage. "You will not speak of him with love."

"Doesn't change anything," I said, too stupid, too tired to care. I hoped he hit me, and then I could hit him back. But

Dolinsky refused to engage. He stood with composure, as if he hadn't lost his temper.

"Be ready in thirty minutes. Dress warmly. It's cold out."

I closed my eyes and breathed in the clear air. It hurt my lungs—and it felt amazing. Turning my face up to the sky, I sought the sporadic rays of sun that kept dodging behind thick gray clouds. It looked like snow was in our forecast. Again.

Tromping in snow boots that I'd found in my bedroom closet, I tried to forget about the man walking next to me. Dolinsky was dressed in a heavy red parka and what looked like a Russian hunting hat.

He had a good deal of property—secluded—and it went on for acres. In the distance I could see pine trees bathed in white, but there was a nice clearing around the mansion. I didn't bother asking him where we were—he wouldn't tell, not until he was good and ready.

He told me of his penchant for horticulture. Spring would bring a wealth of colorful flowers and a manicured garden, Dolinsky explained.

We didn't speak much after that as we continued to walk around the grounds. Soon, I got lost in my own thoughts. I wondered if the city had seen any snow yet. What would Flynn and I have done if we were together? Stayed inside and enjoyed the sight from our room or ventured out to Central Park to build a snowman?

My longing for him grew worse and suddenly, the only thing I wanted to do was build a snowman and pretend Flynn was next to me. "Can we stop a moment?" I asked, halting.

"Of course." Dolinsky thrust his hands into his parka pockets. "Are you tired?"

"No." Without saying more, I crouched to the ground and

began assembling the body of a snowman. I was increasingly thankful for my waterproof mittens as well as my snow pants. Dolinsky didn't attempt to help me, not that I would've let him. This was for me. I stopped building when the mound of snow reached about four feet. I looked around for branches, but there were none. I settled for taking off my scarf and wrapping it around the snowman's neck, but I kept my hat. The temperature was dropping, and the clouds were growing darker.

"Maybe we should head back," I said, looking at the sky. Without saying anything, he took off his hat and placed it on the snowman's head. We trekked toward the house, Dolinsky's ears beginning to turn red.

He never complained.

I was curled up on the couch in the living room with a wool blanket covering my legs. A fire blazed in the gas fireplace, the flames licking the synthetic wood logs. I held up a mug of steaming tea close to my face as I watched the snow fall. Nothing but snow for three days.

"Do you get to spend a lot of time here?" I asked.

Dolinsky looked up from the book he was reading. He had taken to seeking me out in the afternoons, not exchanging a lot of words, just wanting to be in the same room as me. I was surprisingly grateful for his presence because even though he was the reason I was alone, he was still a comfort in the large house.

"No," he answered. "I'm usually in the city."

"A shame," I said. "It's beautiful here. Peaceful."

"It is. Unfortunately, it's hard to monitor things from this remote location. I am going into the city for a few days."

I instantly perked up.

"You will remain here."

I glared at him and all he did was smile. "And who will you have watching me? You can't leave me unguarded."

"No, I cannot," he agreed, going back to his reading.

"Hey," I demanded.

"Yes?"

"Talk to me."

"About what?"

"About whose presence I'm going to have to endure while you're away."

"Are you going to miss me?" he teased.

"Miss you? Miss *you*. This is bullshit, Igor!" With a huff, I threw off the blanket and stood. In a rage, I hurled my full tea mug at the wall, enjoying the dribble of liquid running down the light gray paint. I turned to Dolinsky, expecting to be reprimanded for my outburst and childish behavior.

I was not expecting the grin.

"Don't smirk at me," I commanded.

His grin widened as he stood. "How many days have you been here?"

"I don't know."

"Yes, you do. You keep track."

"How did you—" I clamped my mouth shut.

"How many days have you been here?"

"Eighteen."

"Who am I?"

"Stop asking me that!"

"What is my name?" he whispered. "What. Is. My. Name? Say it."

I licked my lips, wondering why my throat had gone suddenly dry, wondering why I now understood the question that he'd been asking me for days. I understood the rules to the game we'd been playing.

Finally.

"Igor," I murmured. "Your name is Igor."

"Say it again."

"Igor."

"Who am I?" he asked.

"Not my enemy."

His smile was triumphant.

"Igor? Who am *I*?"

Dolinsky strolled toward me with purpose. He took my hand and kissed it. "My queen."

Chapter 41

The next morning, I woke up to a breakfast tray and French press coffee. We were back to that, apparently.

I'd gone to bed with my head reeling, wondering how I was supposed to play this game. Even though Dolinsky told me what I was doing in his home, he still didn't trust me. Not yet.

I knew about Stockholm syndrome. After all, one of my favorite Disney movies was about Stockholm syndrome. *Beauty and the Beast.* In exchange for her father's life, Belle stays with the Beast, and then he gives her a library and learns to cow his temper. My situation with Dolinsky could easily have been explained away, but to say I was conflicted was a drastic understatement.

Reaching for my coffee, I mulled over the thoughts rushing through my mind. I nibbled on a piece of toast, and my eye caught the white envelope resting on the tray. I opened it, marveling at the elegant handwriting.

Moya Krasotka, My Beauty,

. . .

I left early this morning, knowing you were sound asleep in my home. I cannot tell you how joyful I am that you know the truth about why I have brought you here.

I realize how difficult it must be for you to reconcile, but I believe, in time, you will come to feel about me the way I feel about you.

You are not only beautiful but also strong and courageous.

Vlad and Sasha, my two most trusted men, will keep you company while I am away. They are instructed to treat you as the queen you will one day become.

I should be gone no more than four days. Be well, *Moya Zvezda.*

Yours,

Igor

I read the letter again, more confused about my feelings than ever. As much as I wanted to sit alone and dwell on circumstances I couldn't change, it wouldn't do me any good. I needed to leave the sanctuary of my room and meet the two men Dolinsky had deemed my keepers.

After a quick shower, I headed downstairs toward the living room, hearing them immediately. There was yelling in Russian and my heart tripped with anxiety.

It was all for nothing; I found the two men sitting at the antique backgammon table by a large window. They looked like they were in the middle of a heated argument, but then the blond cracked a smile and laughed. His friend, the dark-haired giant, shook his head and then rolled the dice.

"Good morning," I greeted.

The blond shot up from his chair, his good humor remaining. "Good morning, *moya koroleva.* My name is Sasha." His Russian accent was barely detectable.

The dark-haired giant didn't smile as he slowly stood up from his chair. Something about him…his eyes…they were as cold as Sasha's were warm. "Vlad," he clipped, his accent much thicker.

"Barrett," I introduced.

"We can't call you by your given name, *moya koroleva*," Sasha explained. "It would be disrespectful."

I felt like I'd been transported into old world European aristocracy. "Please, don't stop on my account." I waved them back to their game of backgammon. "Have you both eaten?"

"Yes," Sasha said. "Galina and Katrina fed us."

Ah, the two women had names. I'd never thought to ask, and Dolinsky had never volunteered their names. I was a selfish, self-involved bitch, too caught up in my own issues to remember there were human beings who cooked and cleaned for me.

Vlad snapped something in Russian to Sasha and Sasha nodded. Vlad looked at me and spat, "Patrol." He stalked from the room and I let out the breath I'd been holding.

"I don't think Vlad likes me," I said to Sasha.

"Vlad doesn't like anyone." Sasha smiled and I found myself smiling back. "Do you play?" He began to reset the monstrous backgammon pieces.

"I do."

"Do you want to play me?"

"Sure." I took Vlad's empty seat and picked up my dice. "Why doesn't Igor have a television or computer here?"

"He thinks they're distractions," Sasha explained. "And when he comes here, this is his sanctuary, and he wants it to remain…what's the word…unsullied."

"It's very beautiful. He has exquisite taste. The library alone…"

Sasha grinned. "That's his pride and joy."

We each rolled one die to see who would go first. I got a four and Sasha a two. I kept the roll and moved my pieces.

"What did you call me?" I asked. "When you said you couldn't call me by my given name?"

"*Moya koroleva.* Means 'my queen.'"

Sasha ran a thumb down his jaw, clearly in thought. His eyes were blue, but light like aquamarines, not at all like Flynn's dark cobalt.

"He plans to kill your husband."

The idea of Flynn dead left me feeling sick to my stomach, and like someone had carved out my insides, leaving me hollow. "I'm aware."

"You don't sound upset by it. Do you not love your husband?"

"I thought I did. But I hardly know him," I lied.

"Then why did you marry him?"

"Security. Wealth. Authority. As the wife of a powerful man, I have power in my own right."

"Are you going to exchange one formidable man for another?"

"Igor involves me, talks to me, takes me into his confidence. He values me in a way that Flynn doesn't and never has. To Flynn, I'm nothing but my appearance. To Igor, I'm more. I can be more. Together, we can have more."

He was silent a moment and then, "It's your turn."

I picked up the die and rolled.

Chapter 42

Vlad didn't like me, and he made his feelings clear. He took his keeper duties seriously, but he was the one who always volunteered to do patrol, leaving me with Sasha. Vlad didn't say a lot and when he did, it was clipped, and he usually spoke Russian. He was trying to ostracize me. I had to put him in his place—instinctively I knew that. I couldn't let him get away with his insubordination and attitude. I had to show strength.

On the second morning of Dolinsky's absence, Vlad was testing my patience with his snarling, broodiness. The three of us were having lunch at the dining room table. Sasha, with his good humor, kept trying to pull me into conversation, but I was more interested in keeping my eyes on Vlad who was frowning into his plate. He detested my presence and resented his duty.

"Don't you like your borsht?" Sasha asked.

"It's wonderful," I said. "I will pass along my compliments to Galina."

"Then why aren't you eating?" Vlad nearly snapped.

"I want another hard-boiled egg in it."

"I'll tell Galina," Sasha said, setting aside his napkin.

Before he stood, I said, "I don't want Galina to make me the egg. I want Vlad to do it." I stared at the hulking angry giant, whose jaw had gone even tighter, his dark eyes colder.

"I am not your cook."

"Are you my humble *pekhotinets*?" I threw out the Russian word for foot soldier, enjoying the widening of Vlad's eyes.

Vlad shot up from his chair, looking like he wanted to do me bodily harm. Our battle of wills was tense. The man could snap my neck, but I had to show no fear. If there was any hope of proving to Dolinsky that I was commanding in my own right, that I could be trusted as his queen, then I had to go head to head with Vlad.

Without another word, Vlad turned and stalked toward the kitchen. When he was gone, Sasha let out a chuckle.

"Think he'll poison my food?" I asked him.

"Not if he knows what's good for him."

"He started it," I pointed out.

"Yes. And you finished it. I'm impressed."

Smiling, I picked up my spoon. "This borsht really is delicious."

Sasha let out a deep belly laugh. By the time Vlad came back with my peeled hard-boiled egg and an even more ferocious scowl, I was finished with lunch. "I don't want it anymore." Rising from the table, I inclined my head and swept from the room.

Later that afternoon, while Vlad was on patrol and Sasha and I were in the library reading, Sasha's cell phone rang. I'd been devoid of communication and had already forgotten what it was like to be constantly tethered. Sasha answered the phone, and a moment later he passed his cell to me.

"Hello?"

"Hello, *moya krasotka*," came Dolinsky's baritone rumble.

"Igor," I said, purposefully using his name. Somehow I'd become a mastermind, a queen on the chessboard of power. I got up from my comfortable leather chair and walked to the library stairs that took me to the second floor. Settling down in the corner, far away from Sasha and his ears, I made myself comfortable.

"Do you miss me?" Dolinsky asked.

"If I did, I'd never tell you," I teased, making my voice sensual and husky.

His warm laughter echoed in my ear. "How are my men treating you?"

"Sasha is delightful."

"And Vlad?"

"We had a battle of wills, but I won. He doesn't like me."

"He will. I'll see to it."

"No," I stated, "I'll see to it."

"Yes, I believe you will."

"How's the city?"

"The city or do you mean your husband?"

"Have you seen him?" I demanded. I made sure to sound cold and careless.

Dolinsky paused. "The city is gray and disgusting."

I buried my disappointment when Dolinsky didn't discuss Flynn, but I knew he was waiting for me to push, so I didn't. "Then hurry home," I said. "Everything is pristine and white. Hurry home. To me." I didn't even choke on my words.

"You want me?"

"Yes."

"I'll see you soon, *moya koroleva*."

Check.

If there was one thing I believed about Flynn Campbell, it was that I knew he could take care of himself. He was protected, insulated. He had Brad and Lacey, Duncan and Malcolm—he had people who would ensure his survival.

The only person I could rely on, at the moment, was myself.

Dolinsky had left me alone with two men, men I didn't trust because they were loyal to him.

After I ended my phone call with Dolinsky, I headed back down to the main sitting room of the library. Sasha pretended to be engrossed in his book, but it was an act. "Think fast," I said. He looked up and I tossed the phone at him. He stared at it a long moment, pressed a few buttons, and then nodded.

"You expected me to call someone, didn't you?"

"Yes."

"Did Igor?"

"Probably. He's not a stupid man. Stupid men don't stay in power long."

"No, they don't."

"I don't trust you."

"I know," I said with a sardonic smile. "And I don't trust you."

"You should trust me. I'm loyal."

"To Igor, not to me. And if he and I have our way, it will mean the same thing."

He looked surprised. "You want him?"

"Flynn Campbell thought of me as nothing more than a beautiful possession. As his wife, I was to sit on the sidelines, build up his fragile ego, and live in the shadows. With Igor"— I licked my lips, enjoying that Sasha's gaze followed my movement—"with Igor, I am ready to step out of the shadows and be a queen worthy of him."

"How should we take down Campbell?"

"I'll discuss it with Igor and no one else. Teach me to speak Russian," I commanded. Though I'd memorized a few words, it wasn't enough.

"I can't without his permission," he said.

I raised an eyebrow and smirked. "Ah, just another foot

soldier, I see. Fine, then teach me some terms of endearment."

"You want to learn terms of endearment?"

Leaning closer, I lowered my voice so that I could speak in a sensual rasp. "When he fucks me and my nails dig into his back, I want to whisper them in his ear."

Sasha's eyes narrowed with lust and spots of color appeared on his high cheekbones.

Check mate.

I dined with my two keepers, purposefully dressing for the occasion. There were more than enough gowns in my armoire —Dolinsky had seen to that. I wore an off-the-shoulder red frock that showed an expanse of creamy flesh and just the hint of cleavage. Sasha's face was habitually pink, but Vlad—oh, Vlad. I enjoyed toying with him.

When he thought I wasn't paying attention, his gaze roved over me hungrily, like a man who hadn't eaten for days. He barely touched his food. I made sure to draw attention to my mouth as I ate, closing my eyes like a woman in the throes of lust, drawing my tongue across my lips, which were painted with bright red lipstick.

Halfway through the meal, Vlad stood up, and with a mumbled excuse, left the table. Turning my attention to Sasha, I teased and joked with him but never flirted. I had a plan, and Vlad was the one in my clutches.

I went to sleep that night with a smile on my face and my door locked.

The next morning, I strolled downstairs, done up for the day. Tight skinny leg jeans, supple black leather boots and a V-neck gray T-shirt, sans bra. I greeted my wardens and sat down to breakfast, throwing all of my attention at Sasha and ignoring Vlad. Instead of asking Vlad to pass the jam, I made sure to reach for it, giving him a nice shot of what I wasn't wearing underneath my shirt.

I swore I could hear his jaw clench.

"I'm tired of being cooped up in the house," I pouted in Sasha's direction. "There's only so many times I can beat you at backgammon."

"I let you win," Sasha complained.

Letting out a throaty chuckle, I looked at Vlad. "Is he letting me win, Vlad?"

"How should I know?" he clipped.

"You're grumpy. Did you sleep well?" I let my eyes travel down the length of his body, watching his jaw tighten even more. "I was out cold. My bed is so comfortable—and huge."

Galina came into the dining room and said something in Russian. Sasha stood up and then helped me with my chair. "Something came for you."

"Me? Where is it?"

"Front room," Sasha said.

I didn't wait for him as I excitedly traipsed to the front room and then squealed in delight when I saw the old fashioned wooden red sled. Plucking off the small envelope that was taped to the sled, I ripped it open and read, *The first of many gifts.*

I looked at Vlad. "The note says you have to pull me."

"It does not say that," Vlad insisted, reaching for the note.

I reared back so he couldn't snatch the paper from my hands and deliberately shoved it into my back pocket. "Does too."

"Vlad doesn't have a sense of humor. I'm going to go change for outside," Sasha said and left.

My eyes trailed down Vlad's body, a smirk lighting my mouth. I licked my lips. "You don't need a sense of humor."

"What are you doing?" he asked, his voice low and gruff. His hands were clenched into fists, resting by his sides.

"Nothing," I said.

"All it would take is one phone call to Igor to let him know about your behavior."

I shrugged, letting the sleeve of my T-shirt fall, showing off a naked shoulder. "My word against yours. And who do you think he'll believe?"

Vlad unclenched his fists and stalked away. He was on simmer. Time to crank him up to a boil.

Chapter 43

The afternoon sun was bright, but the air was still cold and bordering on frigid. Sasha stood guard, sadly unable to engage in snow play.

"Faster!" I yelled, laughing as Vlad tromped through the snow, pulling me on the sled. I heard him mutter in Russian, but damn if he didn't start jogging.

After a few minutes, I called out, "Stop!" Like a good pack animal, Vlad listened, but glared at me over his shoulder. I nimbly hopped up off the sled and began packing a snowball.

"What are you—"

I fired, catching Vlad in the face. His look of surprised outrage had me laughing and running away. I ducked behind a tree and made another snowball. When he was in my sight, I hit him again before he could react or retaliate. I ran and launched myself at him, so that he had no choice but to catch me. We fell back into the snow, Vlad underneath me. He was breathing hard, his eyes dark. I leaned in close so that our mouths were almost touching.

"What are you going to do, Vlad?" I whispered, letting my breath tease his skin. "Are you going to tell on me?"

I felt his hands tighten at my waist before he lifted me off him. I got up and brushed the snow from my pants. "I'm tired, I'm ready to head back."

With a firm nod, he led us toward Sasha, the mansion, safety. I enjoyed watching lust tighten him like a coil. I had to make him snap.

"Who wants hot chocolate?" I said when we were back in the house, removing our outerwear and struggling out of our boots.

"I do," Sasha said.

"And you, Vlad? Would you like some hot chocolate? With marshmallows?" I kept my tone and face innocent.

Vlad's cell phone rang, and he pulled it out of his pocket and answered it. With a gruff, "Here," he handed it over to me.

Ah, my daily Dolinsky call.

I took the phone with a smile and said, "*Moy korol.* Thank you for the sled."

He chuckled. "You're quite welcome. Someone has been learning Russian?"

"Sasha has taught me a few choice phrases."

"What else have you learned?"

"You'll just have to wait and see." I flirted.

He sighed. "Yes, I will. I have to stay in town a few more days."

"No." I moaned. "Why?"

Dolinsky paused, and I knew he was weighing what to tell me. "We've had some trouble with Campbell."

"Oh? Are you hurt?"

"Your care for me warms my heart," he drawled. Almost like he didn't buy that I was concerned for him. He was smart, though. Not to trust me.

"No, I am unharmed," he went on.

I let out a slow, contrived breath. "Thank God."

"The same cannot be said for your husband." He paused, like he was finally waiting for me to admit that my allegiance hadn't changed.

"Is he dead?" I asked, sure that Dolinsky could hear the thundering of my heart, the lie in my voice.

"No. You are not a widow. Yet."

"When you come home, I want the story."

"You will have it," he promised.

We said our goodbyes and I hung up, handing Vlad back his phone. "You look pale," he commented.

"Igor could've been hurt," I managed, trying to cover all the emotions I was feeling. Flynn was alive, but he was injured. And I wasn't there for him. I no longer had the luxury of time—I needed to shift my plan into high gear.

"I say we skip hot chocolate and go straight for the vodka," I stated.

Sasha shook his head. "I don't think that's a good idea—"

"Vodka."

Sasha let out a lamenting sigh as he glanced at Vlad.

My voice went cold. "Find me a bottle of vodka so that we can toast our good fortune that Igor is alive."

Vlad and Sasha exchanged another look and then finally Sasha went to the kitchen. Without waiting for his return, I headed into the living room. After switching on the gas fireplace, I wrapped my arms around myself while I stared into the flames.

"I found the vodka," Sasha said from behind me.

Nodding, I turned around. "I'm not drinking alone."

"We can't drink on duty," Vlad stated.

"One of you can," I said. "And I vote for Vlad. Maybe some vodka will do something for your disposition."

"No," he stated. "You drink, you drink alone."

"Fine," I said, taking the bottle from Sasha's hands. I took a swig right from the bottle. "How am I doing?"

"If you keep drinking like that, you'll need to eat. I'll tell Galina to fix a plate," Sasha stated before leaving again.

I collapsed onto the carpeted floor and spread out in front

of the fire. I let the alcohol mellow me and run through my body. I tried not to think of Flynn. Thinking of Flynn would make me weep and I needed fortitude.

Vlad had settled into a chair across from me, and when I sat up and met his eyes, I saw his dark hunger. "Do you ever feel lonely, Vlad? Or are foot soldiers not allowed to feel?" A muscle in his jaw twitched, but he said nothing as he rested his hands on the arms of the chair.

"I'm lonely. Alone," I whispered. "And I hate it."

I took another swig of vodka, careful not to overdo it. I had to come across as a lightweight, not in control, needy. I discreetly covered my mouth, pretending that I'd had too much. "Maybe this wasn't such a good idea." I put the bottle on the coffee table as Sasha walked back into the room, carrying a plate of smoked salmon and white fish. He set it in front of me.

"Eat," he commanded.

I did. After I finished, I pushed it away and got to my feet, pretending to stumble. "I'm going to go sleep this off. Please, whatever you do, don't tell Igor that I got drunk. I don't think he would like that." When I got to the doorway, I turned my head ever so slightly, cast a yearning look at Vlad, and then disappeared.

There was a knock on my bedroom door. I set aside the book I was trying to read and called out, "Come in."

Sasha stood in the doorway. "How are you feeling?"

"Fine. I didn't have that much vodka."

"I wasn't referring to the vodka."

"I can't talk to you about this," I stated.

"Why not?"

"Because we aren't friends."

"We could be," Sasha said.

I smiled sadly. "You belong to Igor."

"And you."

"By extension. I don't trust your loyalty. Whatever I say, how do I know you won't go blabbing to Igor?"

His eyes were calm as they assessed me. "You don't."

"The only person I can trust is myself," I said.

"You and Igor are similar in that regard, that's for sure."

"If you trust the wrong person, you're dead." I looked at him. "You're not laughing."

"It wasn't funny."

I sighed. "But it was the truth."

"Yes."

"I miss my life," I said.

"Your old life, you mean? With Campbell?"

"I mean, my life before him. Everything used to be so… uncomplicated, so black and white."

"Was it fulfilling?"

"It was—in its own right. But I hadn't known what I was missing," I explained. "Life changes on the flip of a coin. And there's no use worrying about what I can't control."

"Do you want to be alone?" he asked.

"Yeah, I do," I said with a nod. "Thanks, Sasha."

He looked surprised. "For what?"

I shrugged. "For not being what you seem."

Not knowing what to say to that, he nodded a few times and then shut my door, leaving me alone.

It was time to plan my strategy.

Chapter 44

After a fitful night's sleep and a breakfast tray alone in my room, I was gifted with another surprise from Dolinsky. Four Scandinavian women arrived at the mansion prepared to give me a spa day. I couldn't help but be reminded of the day I'd been kidnapped from The Rex Hotel and Spa a little over a month ago.

Had it already been that long?

The women flitted around me like a gaggle of geese, touching my hair and face and saying things in a language I didn't understand. They pulled out their grooming devices and hairbrushes, and before I knew it, I was lathered and slathered. My hair needed a good cut, and my nails were rough and jagged. I nearly moaned in delight when I discovered I was getting a full-blown massage, too.

I hadn't seen my two keepers since the ladies had arrived, but I figured they were out of the house, patrolling, and wanting to stay far away from girl-land.

The massage table was set up in my room, along with candles and soft, soothing music. I had a brief moment of panic when I undressed and crawled underneath the sheet. It made the day of my kidnapping vivid. Remembering the fear,

I tried to take deep, even breaths while I waited for the masseuse. In the midst of my almost freak-out, the door opened.

The masseuse asked, "Would you like deep tissue?"

I recognized the Swedish accent, and all of my worry dissipated. This would not be like last time. "Please."

The woman got down to business, using strong hands to work on my muscles. At some point, her touch lightened and because I felt safe and relaxed, I fell asleep. Unsure of what startled me awake, I turned my head and opened my eyes.

The Swedish masseuse was gone, and Vlad was standing over me, his finger lightly tracing the outline of my naked shoulder blade, as if he had all the right in the world to it. His eyes swam with dark, dangerous intensity.

"What are you doing here?" I asked throatily. His gaze dipped to the bare swatches of skin that weren't concealed by the sheet.

His hand dropped to his side. "I don't know. I feel…" His tongue traced his bottom lip. "What are you doing to me?" His question came out a whisper, yearning. "I can't stay away from you."

I smelled the vodka on his breath and noted the glassiness of his eyes. Words like "tortured" and "entranced" raced through my mind. The strong and mighty Vlad was crumbling before my eyes.

"I don't sleep, I don't eat. To be in this house and see you but not be able to touch you. What is it? What's your power?" he demanded, his eyes hardening. Vlad was drunk, drunker than I'd thought.

I rolled over under the sheet so that I was on my back. Vlad closed his eyes, like he warred with himself. He went on. Rambling, "Campbell, Igor, me. What do you do to us?" His face came close, his lips were a breath away from mine and everything froze.

Could I do this? Carry out my plan? Was I cruel enough? Cold enough?

"I don't do anything," I said, my heart picking up speed as Vlad's mouth grazed my cheek before dipping to the hollow of my neck and staying there. His lips were soft, his breath warm.

"You make me powerless…helpless." His voice was low, and I felt his teeth against my skin. My pulse pounded in my temples.

"Helpless…wanting you. You're Igor's."

"I'm no one's," I stated calmly. My hand reached up to touch his dark hair, stroking the silky mass of it. "We could be together. No one would have to know. Igor wouldn't have to know."

He lifted his face from my neck to look into my eyes. His lips descended toward mine, but instead of kissing me, he wrapped a large strong hand around my throat.

A shot of terror flared through my body as he began to squeeze, slowly cutting off my air supply.

"You won't be the reason this dynasty falls. You won't be the reason Igor makes decisions with his *khuy*—dick."

I struggled against the vice around my neck, clawing at the hands choking the life out of me. Black spots danced before my eyes as I continued to flail, attempting to kick my legs. This wasn't how my plan was supposed to go. Seduction, lust, pleasure—that was how I was going to bring Vlad down.

But the joke really was on me. I had trusted the wrong person, and now I was going to die.

I'd trusted myself, and I shouldn't have.

Chapter 45

I was dead.

I had to be. Why else would I be in so much pain? My head was pounding and my throat felt tight.

My lids fluttered opened, and I took in a deep breath, and struggled to swallow.

My hand went to my neck, but before I could touch what I knew was swollen flesh, a hand grasped mine.

"You're here," I croaked.

Dolinsky's brown eyes were hard, emotion lurking in their depths. "I came as soon as Sasha called."

"Sasha," I murmured.

"He's the reason you're not—that Vlad didn't—he came to check on you and he's the only reason why you're still here."

A rush of gratitude enveloped me. I struggled to sit up and Dolinsky helped me, puffing up pillows behind my back. I noticed I was wearing a silky pajama top and wondered who had dressed me. At the moment I didn't care.

If Vlad had succeeded, they would've found my corpse, naked and pale. For some reason, it felt like I'd dodged a great indecency. I shook my head, trying to clear it, but it only made it throb.

"The doctor's here," Dolinsky said, moving toward the door. "Will you let him examine you?"

"Doctor?" I asked in surprise.

"He's one of us," he explained.

I nodded. "What happened to Vlad?"

"Nothing," Dolinsky clipped. "Yet."

"You're going to kill him?"

"*Da*—yes."

"When?"

Dolinsky's eyes narrowed. "Why?"

"I want to be there. I deserve to be there. I want to watch." I saw his surprise; he hadn't expected me to be blood-thirsty. I wasn't a wilting flower, I couldn't be. I needed him to see me as more than a pet.

"I promise you'll be there." He slipped through the door, and I was left alone. I leaned back my head but didn't close my eyes. If I did, Vlad's angry face would loom before me.

I had no idea he'd been so conflicted. I thought he'd hated me because he hated wanting me. If I had known the depth of Vlad's true rage, I never would have taken such a risk trying to break him just to prove that I could—just to prove I was capable of being Dolinsky's queen and commanding his men.

Dolinsky came back with the doctor, a middle-aged-man with dark hair streaked with gray at the temples. I was quiet while he examined me, his touch gentle, especially at my throat.

"You will have bruises," he said in a gruff voice. He, too, had a Russian accent. Was I the only non-Russian?

"But," the doctor went on, "you will have no lasting damage. You will heal."

On the outside, maybe. At night, when sleep came for me,

what nightmares would lurk in the shadows of my subconscious?

"Thank you," I croaked.

The doctor nodded and left us alone.

Dolinsky stood next to my bed and said, "I have Galina preparing a tray for you. Broth. You should rest." He leaned over and kissed my forehead. Before he could leave, I wrapped my arms around him, pressing my face to his strong chest. It was as much for show as anything else. I needed the comfort.

"This is my fault," he whispered into my hair as he stroked it.

"You couldn't have known. He was one of your trusted few."

"I can't trust anyone. Not when it comes to your safety." He pulled away from me so that he could stare into my eyes. His mouth descended toward mine and he pressed a soft kiss to my lips. I gently cupped his cheeks and kissed him back, shoving the guilt deep into my belly.

"I want you," he said against my mouth.

"I want you, too."

His jaw hardened. "Not as long as you are bound to Flynn Campbell. I will not have you as my mistress. I will have you when you are a no longer his wife."

I forced my voice to be completely detached when I said, "The only way to do that is to kill him."

"Yes."

"Take me back to the city with you," I pleaded. "Do not separate us. We're stronger together."

He kissed me quickly before scooting off the bed. "Get some rest."

A slight tap on my bedroom door roused me from a doze. Sasha stood in the doorway, carrying my dinner tray. His face was devoid of all emotion, and I couldn't tell what he was thinking or feeling.

He set the tray on my bedside table and sat in the chair Dolinsky had occupied. "How are you feeling?" His gaze strayed to my throat. I hadn't looked in a mirror, so I had no way of knowing how ugly and terrible the bruises were.

"I'm okay," I whispered. It was painful to speak, but I pushed through the ache anyway. "Apparently, I have you to thank for my life."

Color splashed across Sasha's high cheeks in what I assumed was embarrassment. "How could he? I thought I knew him."

I was wrong. It was anger.

"We all have our breaking points."

"How can you be so calm? You almost died. I'm used to this life, the death, but you…"

"I'm not so delicate," I assured him. I moved closer to the edge of the bed so that I could grip his hand. "Sasha, I cannot thank you enough for saving my life, for protecting me, for choosing me over Vlad who you have known a lot longer and at some point trusted. Today, you didn't just become my savior —you became my friend."

He squeezed my hand. "I asked Igor if I could be your main bodyguard."

"I would like that very much." I dropped his hand and reached for my bowl of broth. "Can I ask you a question?"

"Yes."

"How do you feel knowing Vlad is going to die?"

Sasha rubbed a finger down his stubbly jaw. "You're blunt."

I shrugged and took a sip of broth. It was delicious and soothing to my battered throat.

"Vlad proved he is unstable. Unstable means untrustworthy."

"Didn't answer my question."

He sighed. "No point being upset about what's going to happen. It won't change anything."

"Again, you didn't answer my question." I bit my lip. "Did he…confess why he tried to kill me?"

"No. He hasn't said anything since I pulled him off you."

"Where is he?" I demanded.

"Handcuffed in the garden shed behind the mansion."

I set aside my near empty bowl of broth and threw back the covers. My pajama top covered me to the middle of my thighs.

"What are you doing?" he demanded, keeping his eyes on my face.

"Getting dressed."

"Why?"

I didn't answer as I headed to my walk-in closet. I found a pair of black jeans and a black V-neck sweater. After sliding on a pair of black suede boots that molded to my calves, I looked over my shoulder at him.

"Will you please get Igor?"

Closing his eyes for a moment before opening them, looking at a loss, he finally nodded. He left and I headed into the bathroom. I stared at myself a moment, taking in the necklace of bruises. They were dark, purplish, and I had no intention of hiding them. I brushed my teeth and washed my face, and just as I was dabbing my cheeks dry with a hand towel, Dolinsky appeared in the doorway of the bathroom.

"What are you doing out of bed?" he asked, his gaze trained on my neck.

I swirled my hair up into a bun, out of my way. "I want to see Vlad."

His eyes narrowed. "Why?"

"We have some unfinished business. Will you take me to him?"

Dolinsky looked thoughtful before grasping my hand, leading me out of my bedroom and down the stairs. We took a moment to bundle up before we exited the back of the mansion, tromping across old snow in dying afternoon light to get to the garden shed.

It was a substantial one-room building, cluttered with garden tools, seed, and other gardening odds and ends. Vlad was handcuffed to a thick metal pipe and didn't look up when we entered. There was a space heater far enough away that he couldn't get to it, but close enough, so that he wouldn't freeze to death. Dolinsky clearly wanted to mete out justice on his own terms.

I felt the controlled tension in Dolinsky's body as he stood next to me. He gazed at the man he had trusted to protect me, not ever realizing Vlad would have turned. I glanced at Dolinsky, silently asking a question. He nodded, giving me his permission.

I faced Vlad. "Look at me," I demanded, my voice calm, intractable. Vlad glanced up slowly, his face blank except for his eyes. They burned with hatred, desolation, lust.

"Get on with it," he spat coldly.

"Look at what you tried to do." I gestured to the violent ring around my neck. "Look what you failed to do."

Vlad's jaw tightened and without taking his eyes off me, he addressed Dolinsky. "She will be the death of you, and you don't even see it."

Dolinsky opened his coat, extracting a gun. He held it in his hand, effortlessly, like it was a part of him. He pointed it at Vlad.

"Wait," I said to Dolinsky.

He didn't lower the gun when he looked at me.

"Do you trust me?" I asked.

Dolinsky paused for a long moment. My pulse throbbed in my temples, and I nearly grew lightheaded as I waited for his answer.

Finally, he said, "Yes. I trust you."

I held out my hand to him, palm flat. Dolinsky lowered his

arm and gently placed the gun in my hand. The metal was warm against my skin.

Vlad began to laugh.

Gripping the gun, I raised it and aimed for Vlad's chest. I heard Dolinsky's breath catch in his throat and still Vlad continued to laugh, a hysterical maniacal sound.

"You don't have it in you to be a killer," Vlad choked.

My breathing slowed; my vision narrowed.

I pulled the trigger.

Chapter 46

Bright lights lit up the gray darkness of the Manhattan skyline, even as winter kept a firm hold on the city. From my vantage point on the balcony of the Battery Park penthouse, I felt like I was living up in the clouds, far away from the world. I shivered as the wind whipped past me.

Arms encircled me and lips that did not belong to my husband grazed my ear. "Why are you out here?"

"Couldn't sleep," I admitted, refusing to lean back into the granite-like chest behind me.

"Nightmares?" His Russian accent was thick but cultured.

I shrugged.

Igor Dolinsky sighed. It was a knowing sigh, a sigh that commiserated, and his arms tightened. "You should not lose sleep over something so inconsequential."

He referred to the incident that had occurred three days ago—when I shot one of his trusted few in the heart for attempting to strangle me to death. The only reason I was still alive was because of Dolinsky's other man, Sasha.

"He deserved to die," I heard myself say. "It was either him or me, and I choose me. Always."

Dolinsky chuckled at my back, his arms sliding down so

that his hands gripped my sides. His fingers dug into the bones of my hips in a show of lust. But Dolinsky had told me that he valued the sanctity of marriage and wedding vows. He would not sleep with me as long as I was another man's wife.

It had been a little over a month since I'd been kidnapped from The Rex's spa. After I'd killed Vlad and proven my loyalty to Dolinsky's legacy, he'd brought me back to the city. When he finally told me I'd been kept at his secluded mansion in Vermont, it made me feel foolish that I hadn't tried harder to escape.

He brushed a tender kiss along my jaw. "I'm growing impatient."

"I know." Without looking at him, I reached up to touch his face, attempting to reassure him that soon I would be all his.

With a kiss to the top of my head, he let me go and stepped away. "Don't stay too long out here. You'll freeze." The sliding glass door opened, then shut, and I was alone.

I'd lied to Dolinsky.

I didn't have nightmares about killing Vlad. I had nightmares that I didn't, and he got his way—finishing what he'd started when he attempted to strangle me.

When I closed my eyes and slipped into sleep, I saw my own death.

Dolinsky and I had breakfast together the next morning, each of us reading a section of the newspaper like any other couple.

Couple.

We weren't a couple. Not really. We slept in separate rooms on purpose. Dolinsky was strangely old fashioned when it came to courting, and court me he did. Though he'd had me kidnapped, Dolinsky hadn't tortured or raped me—he treated me like a valuable, beautiful pet, one he was trying to win over to his side. He attempted to seduce me with gifts, luxury, decadent meals, his attention, and seclusion from the rest of the world.

He believed I wouldn't ever truly be his until I was no longer Flynn Campbell's wife.

"More coffee?" I asked Dolinsky, rising.

"Hmmm," he murmured as I strolled by him, sliding a hand across his shoulders. "What was that, *moya krasotka?*"

My beauty, he called me.

Flynn called me hen.

I shoved thoughts of him away, needing to focus, remain cool and calm. "Coffee, *lapochka.*"

He put down the paper and smiled at me. "I like that you are learning Russian."

"Sasha is a good teacher."

"Is that all he's teaching you?" Dolinsky's eyes darkened with jealousy.

I touched his cheek and leaned down to place a kiss on his lips. "That's all he's teaching me. Promise."

Dolinsky huffed and turned his attention back to the paper. A man in lust was dangerous, unpredictable. I'd learned that from Vlad. I had thought I could control the outcome of his demise by enticing him, flirting with him. His desire had turned into a wild inferno, blazing out of control and almost killing me.

I snatched the paper out of Dolinsky's hand and threw it to the floor. He looked up at me in surprise. I perched on his lap and threw my arms around him. "Am I not more interesting than your paper?" I purred. His hands skimmed up my sides as I traced his mouth with my fingers. He nipped playfully at them, smiling.

"Far more interesting than my paper."

"The longer we leave Campbell to his own devices, the longer we are apart." I took his earlobe between my teeth and sucked gently. Dolinsky groaned. "Let's talk about the plan."

"You want to know the plan to take down your husband and his empire?"

I ran my fingers through his hair and leaned back so I could look at him. "I do."

"You."

"Me?"

Dolinsky smiled. "You are his weakness, and you will be his downfall."

"No doubt," I murmured, a shot of fear running through me. "When?"

"Soon."

"When the time comes, I want to be the one who pulls the trigger," I stated, staring into his brown eyes. I needed him to promise me, and though he was a criminal, he was strangely a man of his word, a man who had his own code of honor.

"I would love to see that. Yes, *moya krasotka*. You will pull the trigger."

Chapter 47

I sat at the vanity in the guest room of Dolinsky's penthouse, trying to lock my nerves away. They had no place here. Running a brush through my sleek auburn waves, I stared at my reflection. The fluttering beat of my pulse at my neck betrayed me. The black negligee I wore was made of French lace, expensive, classy, and perfumed with lavender.

Setting the brush aside, I adjusted the straps of the lingerie, tightening them ever so slightly so my breasts didn't spill from the top. A hand swept the hair off my neck and remained there. I looked in the mirror and met Dolinsky's warm brown eyes.

"You're afraid," he stated.

"A bit," I admitted.

"It's to be expected," he said soothingly.

He placed a kiss on my bare shoulder, trying to reassure me. Dolinsky held out his hand and helped me from my chair. I let him lead me down the hall until he stopped at his bedroom door. "If we go in, there's no turning back."

"I know."

Pushing open the door, he gestured for me to enter. His

bed was king-sized, elegant with black covers. The walls were robin-egg blue. Soft. Welcoming. Strange.

As I took in the wood furniture and thought about what was about to happen, Dolinsky went to the bedside table where a bottle of vodka and two glasses rested. He poured two shots and brought one to me, holding the other in his hand.

"It will steady your nerves," he said.

Nodding, I put the glass to my lips and took a sip. My hand shook, so I threw it back quickly, hoping I went numb. Dolinsky watched me with banked desire in his eyes, but he kept his hands to himself.

"Another?" he asked. I shook my head. He took the glass from me and set it aside along with his now empty glass. He came back to me and placed his hands on my hips, bringing me toward his body.

He trailed a finger down the lace negligee and sighed. It was a tortured sound. "I hate that I have to do this."

I lifted my arms up to wrap around his neck. "I know."

"Are you ready?"

"No."

He didn't smile. "I'll make it up to you."

"How?"

Dolinsky pressed a kiss to my jaw. "A gift. Every day. For a year."

"Will you buy me a pony?" I teased.

"*Da.*"

"A castle?"

"*Da.*"

"A dynasty?"

"*Da,*" he whispered.

"Then let's do this."

Dolinsky released me, and I went over to the bed to sit on the edge. He pulled out his cell phone from his trouser pocket and quickly dialed Sasha.

"We're ready." He hung up and set the phone aside.

Removing his jacket, he tossed it onto a wooden chair. He unfastened the top few buttons of his crisp, white dress shirt and rolled up the sleeves. Despite his casual appearance, there was a strained ferocity in his body, a coiled tension.

He dimmed the lights, giving the room a romantic, sensual glow. My pulse flickered with a different level of fear. I didn't know what to expect; I couldn't predict the outcome.

"I'm here," Sasha said from the doorway of the bedroom.

"Good," Dolinsky said.

Sasha's blue eyes, dark in the low light, looked at me. To his credit, his gaze remained on my face instead of scrolling down my body. I was showing a good amount of skin, but I wasn't at all embarrassed by it. Performing burlesque had taught me to shove my real persona away and don a new one. This would just be another performance.

"Barrett," Dolinsky said, "get in the middle of the bed. Sit on your haunches. Sasha, set up the camera on the tripod."

I moved and got myself situated while Sasha did as Dolinsky orchestrated. Dolinsky came around to stand in front of me, rearranging my hair so it fell down my back, exposing my cleavage. His eyes lingered on my face for a moment before returning to himself. He kissed me gently, tenderly, and then he climbed onto the bed. Glancing behind me, I saw he was on his knees, looming tall and in a position of power.

"Wait," I said to Sasha who was getting ready to turn on the camera.

"Yes?" Dolinsky asked.

"I think I need another shot. Don't bother with the glass," I said.

Sasha went to get me the bottle of vodka. I took a few more swallows, hoping it numbed me enough, fortified me enough.

"Easy," Sasha said, taking the bottle away from me so I couldn't drink myself into oblivion.

My tongue swiped the droplets of vodka from my lips, and

I watched Sasha's face tighten before he turned away from me. He set the bottle aside and returned to his spot behind the camera.

"Okay, I'm ready," I said, glad my voice didn't waver.

With a press of the button, Sasha nodded letting us know the camera was recording. For a long moment, nothing happened. And then Dolinsky reached out to stroke my hair, like a man would stroke his lover. The air in the bedroom thickened with tension.

I kept my eyes on Sasha. For some reason I trusted him, trusted him to get me through this. His eyes remained locked on mine, and ever so slightly he inclined his head.

Dolinsky's hands gripped my hair and pulled me up into his hard body. Pain shot through my scalp and tears gathered in my eyes. He was deliberately rough as he bent to expose my neck. He ran his nose along the skin below my ear, his tongue delving out to trace my shoulder. He murmured something in Russian as he continued to tongue my flesh. To my ever-loving horror, my nipples tightened.

The hand holding my hair eased just a bit, but Dolinsky didn't let go. His free hand skimmed down my body, over the curve of a breast. He cupped it, his thumb grazing my nipple through the lace. He played with it until it hardened.

Lust and vodka swirled in my blood, and I let out a moan.

Dolinsky released my hair, and I almost sagged against him. I felt his erection pressing into my back, and I nearly wiggled against it.

"Do you like that?" he asked, his tone low and guttural. When I didn't answer, he pulled down the lace that shielded my breasts and exposed them to the camera. I kept my eyes open and locked on Sasha. His face was devoid of emotion, and it was exactly what I needed.

Fingers roamed over my breasts, kneading flesh, eliciting goosebumps from my skin. Dolinsky tweaked my nipples before he placed a hand at my hip, the other worming its way under the lace negligee. I let out a whimper as he found the place between my legs wet and wanting.

His finger skated across my bare skin before he slipped it inside of me. He held me to him as he pleasured me for the camera, his labored breathing harsh in my ear. My body was primed and needy. I wanted an orgasm as much as I knew I shouldn't. But Dolinsky played my body like an expert. My skin flushed and tingled. The camera on me heightened the intensity of my enjoyment. Before I knew it, I was coming on his hand.

Dolinsky withdrew his fingers and moved next to me. He reached out to grasp my chin and forced me to look at him. His face was harsh, his mouth taut. My breasts were still free, but his gaze didn't stray from my face until he went to pick up my left hand. He roved a finger over the wedding band and then guided it off my knuckle.

"This is just the beginning of what I can do to you. Did you like it?"

"Yes."

"You're beautiful," he said, right before he broke my ring finger.

Chapter 48

"I'm sorry," Dolinsky said again. His gaze was compassionate; something about him appeared completely devastated. Like it truly hurt him to hurt me.

My throbbing, splinted ring finger rested in my lap. It looked pathetic and naked without my wedding ring. Dolinsky had taken it, the ring that had belonged to Flynn's mother, and placed it in his pocket for safekeeping.

"It doesn't hurt. Much," I said, lifting a glass of vodka to my lips. The doctor who wrapped my finger had urged me to take a heavy pain med, but I refused. I preferred the vodka.

"Do you really think he'll show?" I asked.

"I do."

At the end of the video, after I'd stopped screaming from the shock and pain of Dolinsky breaking my finger, he'd turned to the camera and instructed Flynn to meet him at a warehouse in Queens tomorrow at eleven. Flynn was to come alone and unarmed—or Dolinsky had promised to do worse to me and make sure Flynn saw it all.

"Campbell will come because he wants to ensure he gets you back—all in one piece. He'll do anything to protect you."

I wasn't so sure. Not anymore. Dolinsky had made me

come on camera. I hadn't faked it—my belly burned with shame and remorse.

We sat in the living room of the penthouse suite, a gas fire burning in the hearth. It was far too normal for what had transpired between us a few hours ago. Sasha had been the one to dispatch the video, so he was gone. It was just us in this still place, filled with feelings and things I didn't want to deal with.

"You're quiet," Dolinsky noted.

"Just thinking."

"About?"

"Tomorrow. I can't wait until this is all over," I said. For once, I wasn't lying.

"After it's done, how should we celebrate?" he asked.

"We will climb back into bed and spend the day there."

"Is that a promise?" he asked, his voice husky.

Men. So easy. Letting women lead them around by their cocks.

I forced a smile. "Promise." Standing up, I set my unfinished vodka on the coffee table. "I think I'll head to bed now." I brushed a kiss on Dolinsky's cheek and whispered, "Don't lose sleep over what happened tonight."

His gaze slid to my broken finger and his nostrils flared. "I hate myself. For hurting you."

"I know."

"I loved touching you."

"I know that, too."

Once I was in the privacy of my own room, the weight of what I'd done smothered me. I'd been pleasured by another man's hand. I'd enjoyed having Dolinsky touch me. My body had overruled my head.

I hated myself.

And it wasn't only my finger that was broken.

The next morning was cold and gray. After I dressed in all black, I stood in my bedroom, staring out the window. There was a knock on the door before Dolinsky appeared in the doorway holding a long mink coat.

"Apology gift?" I asked with a slight smile. My finger hurt, but it was my spirit that was truly battered.

"Furs fit for a queen," he said, helping me into the coat, mindful of my injury. His hands lingered on my shoulders, his lips close to my ear.

I turned around. "When this is over, I will come to you wearing this mink and nothing beneath it."

His eyes darkened with banked lust, and I smiled despite the heaviness weighing on me.

"You did not sleep," he stated.

"Neither did you." I noted the circles under his eyes.

"Perhaps, tonight, we will finally sleep soundly."

I grinned. "Perhaps."

When we were seated in Dolinsky's black town car driving toward the Queens warehouse he said, "You did not touch your breakfast."

"I don't like to kill on a full stomach," I quipped.

Dolinsky barked out a laugh.

"I'll eat an entire celebratory meal when this is over."

Dolinsky clasped my uninjured hand in his, and we fell into silence. Thirty minutes later, we turned down a near abandoned street in north Queens. Blocks and blocks of warehouses stretched across the neighborhood. There were a few large trucks parked, but no people. It was unnaturally quiet.

The town car pulled to a stop and Dolinsky looked at me. "Ready?"

I nodded and climbed out. My breath formed a cloud in front of my face, and my ears were bitten with cold since I'd pulled back my hair and refused to wear a hat.

Dolinsky's phone rang, and he answered it, speaking in Russian. I assumed it was Sasha. Dolinsky confirmed it when he said, "Sasha has done a sweep of the surrounding area and warehouse. No one has arrived yet."

"Good." We walked into the designated warehouse and Dolinsky looked around, surveying the room even though he knew we were alone. We were early on purpose, and everything was ready to go. He kissed me briefly and then ducked behind a large stack of crates.

And then I waited.

Eleven a.m. on the dot, Flynn walked inside. My heart stuttered in my chest and then started beating in rapid staccato. God, he was so...*Flynn*. Too much time had passed since I'd last seen him. His cobalt blue eyes were intense, his jaw angular and sharp. He looked dangerous and swarthy.

His gaze landed on me and he halted, his eyes betraying his surprise at my presence. "Why are you here? Where's Dolinsky?"

I wanted nothing more than to take him into my arms, beg his forgiveness for the things I'd done. But the torture wasn't over yet. For either of us.

I reached into the lining of my mink coat and pulled out a gun. "Sit down, Flynn."

"Barrett, what are you—"

"Sit. Down."

Cold acceptance washed over his face as he realized I was colluding with Dolinsky. He lowered himself onto a nearby crate.

"Igor," I called. "Will you come out here, please?" I didn't take my eyes off Flynn while I waited for Dolinsky to come to my side. When he did, he wrapped an arm around my waist in a show of possession.

"I'm sorry," I said to Flynn. He watched me with eyes so dark and blue I wanted to drown in them.

Flynn said nothing. No pleading or begging.

Stepping away from the shelter of Dolinsky's arm, I turned to him. I kissed him softly on the lips before pulling back. Raising the gun, I pointed it at Flynn whose eyes burned with hatred and loathing.

"You can do this, *moya krasotka*," Dolinsky said.

"Yes, I can." I turned my head and grinned, all teeth.

"The city is ours," Dolinsky stated. "As soon as you finish this."

"The city is ours," I repeated.

I whirled and pulled the trigger.

Dolinsky's face registered shock, even as he sputtered, blood gurgling from his mouth. My captor dropped to his knees, and I watched the life bleed out of him. This man had kidnapped me, thinking he could mold me into his queen. He thought me weak, malleable, his.

I was no one's.

Chapter 49

"Barrett," Flynn called.

I looked up from the still form of Igor Dolinsky and into the face of the man who owned my heart and soul. The man I willingly killed for. The man who I had to let think…

Flynn had come toward me, but he hadn't touched me. I was cold. So cold.

"I love you. I never stopped loving you or doing everything I possibly could to get back to you."

"Shhh," he said. He reached into his pant pocket and pulled out his cell phone. He called Brad and commanded him to find a discreet cleanup crew.

The persona I'd been wearing for the past six weeks crumbled in the wake of Dolinsky's death. Adrenaline and fear had been warring inside of me, and now it all zoomed out of my body, leaving me to stand on shaky legs.

"Come on," Flynn said. "Let's get out of here."

"Hold on," I said. "I have to call—"

"Later."

"No," I stated, tugging my hand out of his.

"Who do you have to call?" Flynn demanded.

Ignoring him, I pulled out my own cell phone and dialed

Sasha who had been commanded by Dolinsky to remain outside the warehouse—hidden.

He answered immediately. "Are you safe?" he demanded.

"Yes, I'm with Flynn." I cast a glance at my husband, wondering what he was thinking as he watched me with cool, calm eyes.

"It went off without a hitch?"

"Yes. Dolinsky never suspected a thing."

He sighed. "You sure you want to do this?"

"Yes. I'll be in touch and we'll figure out how best to proceed." I hung up and looked at Flynn.

"Who was that?"

I paused. "Dolinsky's right-hand man."

"And he knows——"

"I'll explain everything, I promise." I turned away from Flynn to head back toward Dolinsky's body. Flynn reached out and grabbed my injured hand.

Pain shot through my broken finger, and I let out an involuntary yell. He let me go like he'd touched fire, a look of horror crossing his face.

"Oh God," he said.

I shook my head, bringing my injured hand to my chest, tears leaking out of the corners of my eyes. "He has something of mine," I gasped through the throbbing pain.

I knelt by Dolinsky's corpse and fished around in his coat pocket, pulling out my wedding ring. For the time being, I put it on my right ring finger, wondering if I'd ever get the chance to put it back where it belonged.

"Barrett, we need to go."

I got up off the floor and followed Flynn outside. We briskly walked a few blocks before we reached his car. He unlocked it and went to open the passenger door for me. After climbing in, he started the transmission, blasting the heat. I put my hands in front of the heater, feeling some of the coldness leave my fingers.

"Flynn—"

"Not right now, Barrett." His grip on the wheel tightened as he drove through the Queens neighborhood.

I fell silent and looked out the window. There was so much distance between us. And time. Would we ever be "us" again? Could he forgive me for the things I'd done?

Could I forgive myself?

We drove in silence for three hours—I was stewing and brooding—and I assumed Flynn was doing the same. Every now and again, I would glance at him and catch him looking at me with an indiscernible look on his face. I'd been storing up things I wanted to say. It was all there between us, like a living entity.

Finally, we pulled into the driveway of a two-story wood cabin in the Poconos. Flynn cut the engine, and we sat for a moment in the car. I didn't want to go into the house. When we went in there, we'd have to talk. We'd have to talk about our time apart—we'd have to talk about the video of me with Dolinsky's hands on my body. We'd have to talk about the pleasure I'd found with another man.

"You ready?" Flynn asked. His voice was tight, like he had to force the words from his throat.

"No."

"Not much choice, is there?"

I sighed. "No."

We got out of the car and headed to the front porch of the cabin. Flynn unlocked the door, and I was greeted by wood, brown leather, and mountain lodge decor, complete with large windows that showed off the landscape. Flynn shrugged out of his coat and then helped me with the mink.

"He bought you this," Flynn stated, though it was completely unnecessary.

"Yeah. He bought me all of this." I gestured to the black cashmere turtleneck dress and black suede boots that fit me perfectly.

"Take them off," he commanded. His brogue thickened when he felt deep emotion, and his anger was evident and palpable.

I struggled out of my dress, trying to be mindful of my injured hand. Flynn watched me with an unwavering gaze and didn't offer to help me. He stood, with his legs braced, his arms by his side.

Kicking aside my discarded clothes, I forced myself to stand before him completely naked and unashamed. His gaze slowly traveled down my body, lust warring with anger. Sighing, he walked over to the couch and picked up the plaid blanket and held it out to me.

He wanted me to cover up, but I didn't want to. I was tired of concealing myself. I took the blanket anyway and wrapped it around me.

Flynn turned away and built a fire. Only when the wood was crackling and heat blasted from the fireplace did he look at me again.

"I don't know where to start," he said.

"Me either," I admitted.

"Glass of scotch? Might make this easier." Flynn walked to the bar at the other end of the living room. I sank down onto the couch, attempting to get comfortable. Flynn returned and handed me a glass. Instead of sitting down next to me, he moved to stand by the fireplace.

I threw back the drink in one long swallow. It burned my still tender throat, causing me to cough.

"That was supposed to be savored," Flynn admonished.

Silence descended again.

"To hell with this." Flynn growled. "Did you sleep with him?"

"No. That video—"

"Christ, that video. Did you know he was going to do that?"

Shame coated my cheeks. "I didn't know exactly what to expect, but yes, I knew he was going to touch me. I didn't know he was going to break my finger."

"Did you know you were going to like it?"

The shame intensified and a ball of regret settled in my stomach. I dropped my gaze to my lap.

"Barrett? Answer me."

"No," I whispered. "I swear I didn't know I'd like it."

Flynn was quiet for so long I finally dared to look at him. There was an undistinguishable look on his face, and I hated that I couldn't read him.

"Do you—do you want a divorce?" I forced the words out, hating the ugliness of them.

"Nothing has been resolved with the FBI. Ever since your disappearance, it's been nothing but a waiting game."

"You didn't answer my question." I dreaded his response. In doing everything I could to get back to Flynn, I might have lost him.

"Tell me what happened," he commanded.

"When?"

"When you were with Dolinsky."

"Why didn't you come after me?" I fired back instead.

He frowned. "Come after you?" He raised his voice. "There was no way to find you! Even Duncan couldn't find your trail."

"You're telling me," I asked in disbelief, "the man you call The Tracker, couldn't find me?"

"Aye. We never stopped looking for you, but Dolinsky had you tucked away so thoroughly that we—"

"You didn't think I was dead?"

Flynn paused. "Dolinsky sent...word."

"He did?"

"Chelsea, he—I'll spare you the gruesome details—but he

said he could do to you what he did to her if we didn't back off."

I swallowed the bile that threatened to surge up my throat.

"He sent other messages." The haunted look returned to Flynn's eyes. "Little notes. Like how you looked when you slept. What your laugh did to him."

Nausea continued to churn in my stomach.

"He wanted to torment me."

"He wanted…" My voice was weak and strained, so I cleared my throat. "He wanted me to fall in love with him. He wanted to tell you I was truly his because he wanted you completely broken before he killed you."

Flynn looked away, staring at the flames in the hearth.

"Everything I did, I did it so I could come back to you," I stated. I needed Flynn to believe me. Maybe then I'd believe myself. Dolinsky had reached a part of me I hadn't known existed, pulling it out into the open.

"You let him touch you. You went along with it."

"Yes."

"You didn't fight him. You didn't try to get away—"

"I had no idea where I was!" It was my turn to become angry. He had no idea what I'd been through the last six weeks. I killed Vlad. I let myself be touched and tortured on camera while Sasha had watched.

"No," I said. "You don't get to do this."

"Do what?" he huffed.

"Blame me for all the things I've done, all the things I didn't do—to survive."

"I saw you 'surviving'," he spat in an awful voice as he stalked toward me.

I stood up and went face to face with him. Before I knew it, our anger erupted into lust. I tore at his clothes while he ripped the blanket off me. We were rabid, teeth and lips, bruising.

Pain.

It was what I deserved, and I welcomed it.

Flynn punished me because I'd found pleasure in another man's arms. I punished Flynn back because he hadn't been able to keep me safe from Dolinsky.

We collapsed onto the rug, panting hard. He reached for my hand, and we didn't say anything more about our time apart and the people we'd become. We were here, now, because we chose to be.

And hopefully that was stronger than love.

Chapter 50

I examined Flynn's bullet graze. It was still red, but it was minor, a flesh wound. "Dolinsky shot you?" I asked.

Flynn nodded.

"Does it still hurt?"

"No."

I sighed.

"We should get your finger looked at," Flynn said.

"It's fine," I dismissed.

"Barrett—"

"It's been seen to, okay?" I whispered, wanting him to drop it.

He nodded, still looking a bit troubled.

"Can I borrow some of your clothes?"

Flynn reached out and grasped my chin, pulling me to him for a kiss. "Aye."

We got up off the floor, and I followed Flynn to the master bedroom, enjoying the view of him. He opened a dresser drawer and pulled out sweats and a T-shirt for me.

"You need to call Brad," I said as I stuck my head through the neck hole.

"Why?"

"Because there needs to be a ceasefire."

"There isn't a war going on," Flynn said in exasperation.

"Isn't there? The Russians don't want a war. They don't want blood on the streets. They want an alliance. With you."

"You know this how?"

"Sasha."

"Sasha Petrovich, Dolinsky's right-hand man? That Sasha?"

I nibbled on my lip, pleased that Flynn's gaze strayed there. I hoped we might find a way back to each other, and if lust was the answer, then so be it.

"He's now the head of the Russian mob."

He blinked. "You both staged a coup, didn't you? How did this happen? How did you even discuss this without Dolinsky discovering what was going on right underneath his nose?"

"Sasha became my bodyguard while I was with Dolinsky. He was the one who broached the subject."

"Risky, don't you think?"

"Yes."

"So Petrovich didn't believe you'd really switched allegiances, did he?"

"No. He didn't." I frowned. "He wanted something different than what Dolinsky was giving them. Sasha wasn't the only one tired of the violence and cleaning up messes. He knew that if Dolinsky was successful in bringing you down, then it meant more bloodshed."

"They want to go legitimate," Flynn realized.

I nodded.

"And they want an alliance? With me? I don't trust it."

"Sasha is my friend," I stated. "You can trust him."

"Trust a man who took out his own leader so he could rule? I don't think so, Barrett. That doesn't lend itself to trustworthiness. Besides, what's the point of an alliance?" he wondered. "Dolinsky is out of the picture, so why wouldn't I just absorb their jurisdiction?"

"Because you need them," I said. "And I promised Sasha."

"Promised what, exactly?"

"Your cooperation. If you back Sasha, so will others, and he won't have to spend valuable time fighting to maintain control."

"I don't trust him."

"You've made your point clear. Do you trust me, Flynn?" I inquired.

He went silent and I waited, afraid of his answer. Finally, he nodded.

"We have a chance here. To do things differently," I said.

"How?"

"The FBI wants you, so we make a deal with them. We tell them Dolinsky and his dynasty has been dismantled. I'm sure he was on their radar. We'll tell Winters it's a show of good faith. In the meantime, you quit funneling money to the SINS. We'll direct money to the SINS through Russian enterprises. Legitimate Russian enterprises."

He rubbed his jaw. "That's what you said by needing Petrovich."

I nodded.

"Do you think that will work?"

"You got any other bright ideas?"

"No. I guess it's the best we have."

"Thanks for your vote of confidence," I quipped.

Flynn chuckled and shook his head while looking at me in amazement. "I do have confidence in you. Why would Petrovich do this for you?"

"Because he watched what I went through to get back to you," I said quietly.

Would Dolinsky always be between us? Would his ghost linger? Would his touch on my skin fade? I wondered if Flynn and I would ever be able to move past all that had occurred. I was different now. We might be able to forgive, but we'd never be able to forget.

Though our foundation had once been solid, it was now full of cracks and shifting ground. I hoped we could rebuild it, make it stronger than it was before.

"Okay, Barrett. We'll work with the Russians." He took my hand and brought it to his lips. "Let's get back to the city. Let's deal with this once and for all."

And just like that, I knew where we stood. We were partners, now and forever.

We arrived at The Rex around midnight, entering through the back entrance, not wanting to draw attention that I'd returned. Everyone would know soon enough. Getting ready for bed, I tried not to think about the fact that I didn't feel safe in the hotel. I'd been kidnapped from a massage table in The Rex Spa, when I was supposed to be enjoying a luxurious day laughing and kicking back with the girls from the burlesque club. Even when Flynn took me into his arms, my heart beat like a jackhammer.

By two, it was clear I wasn't going to be able to fall asleep. I moved to get out of bed, but Flynn's hand on my thigh stopped me. "You're awake," I said quietly.

"Hard to sleep with you tossing and turning."

"Sorry." I settled back against the pillows.

"Talk to me," he commanded.

"I can't live here. It's not a home, Flynn."

"You don't feel safe," he stated astutely.

"No, I don't. Even when I did feel safe, it never felt like home. You know that."

"I know," he said. "We'll start looking for a place."

"Promise?"

"Promise. Dolinsky's no longer a threat, so we can find a real home. For us."

He leaned over to kiss me, his mouth discovering mine. I

sank into him, loving the feel of his hard body and warm skin. Soon, I was too caught up in Flynn to worry about anything. Exhausted and sated, I fell asleep.

The next morning, we ate breakfast in the hotel restaurant and halfway through, Duncan joined us.

"You're still here?" I asked in amazement, standing up to hug him.

"Wanted to make sure you came back safe and sound," he said. "Glad you're here with us, lass."

"I'm happy to be back. Will you join us for a cup of coffee?" I asked.

He sat down and began to regale me with tales from his childhood, no doubt picking up the uneasiness between Flynn and me and wanting to distract us from it.

After we finished eating, I said, "I need to call Sasha."

Flynn's jaw hardened, but he nodded. We headed to the security office and met up with Brad who looked through me. Clearly, he had judged what he thought he knew. He would not sentence me—he had no idea what I'd lived through.

Brad handed me a burner phone, and I immediately dialed Sasha. Before I'd ditched the cell Dolinsky had given me, I'd memorized Sasha's number.

He answered immediately. "We've got a problem," he said by way of greeting.

"What now?" I demanded.

He explained and a stream of curses went off in my head. "All right," I said when he was finished. "Can you meet me in an hour?" I hung up and then looked at Flynn. "Sasha seems to be having a little problem with a certain FBI agent."

"Winters," Flynn clipped and I nodded. "That bastard has been relentless."

"Great, something else to contend with." Brad glared at me.

"What's your problem?" I demanded.

"I don't have a problem."

"Liar. You've been nothing but cold to me since I walked in here. Out with it, already. I have enough to deal with. I don't need you adding to it."

"I don't trust you," he said.

"Brad," Flynn warned.

I touched Flynn's arm, and leaned to whisper in his ear, "Did he see the video?"

Flynn shook his head.

I breathed a sigh of relief and then focused on Brad. "Why don't you trust me?"

"You were with Dolinsky for six weeks and then you killed him. Now you want the Russians to be our allies. How do we know that you haven't switched loyalties?"

"How would I switch loyalties? As you pointed out, I killed Dolinsky—which I did to get back to Flynn."

"Yeah, you killed Dolinsky. Convenient. How do I know you and Petrovich haven't concocted a plan to take out Flynn?"

"And why would I want to take out Flynn?" I demanded. "Sorry to tell you this, Brad, but I have no drive to rule any of these illegal enterprises."

"You're out of line," Flynn said to his head of security.

"I know she's your wife," Brad stated with quiet reserve, "but ever since she came into your life, you haven't acted like yourself. You haven't acted like the man I've been friends with for the last ten years."

"Be very careful how you proceed," Flynn said, his voice tight with anger. "We have history, but don't think I won't bury you. Find a way to make peace with Barrett. I trust her so that should be enough for you."

"Well, it isn't," Brad stated.

"If you two are finished discussing me like I'm not here, maybe we could get back to the Winters situation." Both men looked at me, Brad's countenance still unyielding.

I smiled grimly. "I think I have an idea."

The Dominus Hotel was cold, austere lines, postmodern architecture and design. Gray chrome and white were part of the minimal color scheme, and I was the only splash of color in the room. My dress was Jessica Rabbit red and clung to my figure. My auburn hair was styled in big, loose waves, and I'd gone heavy on the eye makeup. A glass of expensive vodka sat within my reach, but I didn't touch it.

I perched on a stool next to the head of the Italian Mob at his hotel bar. Giovanni Marino was as unctuous as he was misogynistic.

Marino swiveled on his bar stool, his foot grazing my leg in a non-subtle gesture of desire as he gripped his glass of an Italian apéritif.

"Why am I having a meeting with you? Where's Campbell?" Marino demanded.

"Flynn's a wee bit tied up at the moment," I said. "He sends his regards, though."

"So he sent in a woman to do a man's job?"

"No," I said coldly. "He sent his wife."

"Wife?" Marino's eyes widened.

"Wife," I confirmed.

"It seems congratulations are in order then," he stated, his gaze sweeping down my form. "It's no secret that Flynn Campbell isn't the marrying kind."

I almost rolled my eyes but held it in check. "We're not here to discuss my marriage."

"We're not," he agreed.

"Have you heard?" I asked.

"Heard what?"

"Someone killed Dolinsky."

Marino, bull that he was, wasn't able to conceal his shock and disbelief. "I haven't heard anything like that—"

"Well, of course you wouldn't. It was cleaned up."

Quietly."

Marino peered at me. "You know who killed him."

I shrugged. "It's not important."

"Not important?" Marino nearly hissed. "The head of the Russian mob is dead and you don't think who killed him is important? Was it one of his own men?"

I ignored his question when I asked, "Have you heard of Sasha Petrovich, the former right-hand man to Dolinsky?"

"Former?"

"He's taken over the Russian mob."

Marino scoffed. "I'll believe that when I see it."

I held my grin in check as I reached for my cell phone on the bar. Pressing speed dial number two, I waited a brief moment and then spoke to Sasha.

"He'll be along in just a moment," I said to Marino, whose mouth was agape.

"First you married Campbell and now you have a Russian mob boss on speed dial?" Marino's eyes gleamed with desire as he leaned forward, his hand reaching out to touch my cheek. "I'm impressed."

I slapped him across his face, my palm stinging from the force.

"Be careful," he warned, voice low and full of rage.

"I'm not here for that. Sasha and Flynn have an alliance and Sasha would like to discuss something with you."

I looked at the entrance of the hotel bar to see Sasha strolling toward us, dressed in an elegant suit that concealed the weapons beneath. He shot me a smile, and his boyish face and bright blue eyes lit up. I hugged him to me. "Sasha Petrovich, Giovanni Marino. I'll leave you gentleman to it."

Hopping off the stool, I lifted my glass of expensive vodka and threw it back in one long swallow.

With a smile at Marino I said, "This is no place for a woman."

I stalked from the hotel, the plan set in motion.

Chapter 51

"You're really okay?" my best friend asked with a hug.

"Yes," I rubbed her back in a gesture of comfort, even though I wasn't okay. Not even close.

"You just disappeared. If Flynn hadn't told me…" Ash pulled back and looked me over, taking stock of the changes. Were they visible like scars?

"Flynn told you? That I was with…"

She nodded. "It's not like he could've said you were visiting your nonexistent family. And you were gone six weeks… God, I've been so worried." Her gaze dropped to my broken finger and she gasped. "What happened?"

I cradled my hand protectively against my chest. "One of those things I'd rather not talk about."

"I don't even know how we're supposed to have a normal conversation anymore," she muttered as I gestured for her to take a seat on the couch. I poured Ash a cup of coffee and then went to the penthouse windows to stare out at the park.

"I need you, Ash. I need your help. I wish I didn't, because I really don't want to involve you, but I can't do this without you."

"My help?" she asked, her voice full of wonder. "What could I possibly do for you?"

"Before I got kidnapped, I was feeding information to an FBI agent trying to take down Flynn."

"Of course you were. What kind of information? Stuff about his brothel and casino?"

"There's more to it," I said slowly.

"More? How much more?"

"Have you heard of the SINS?"

An hour later, my best friend was gone and I sat alone, contemplating the person I'd become. The transition had begun when I met Flynn, but when I ended Vlad's life, I'd become a liar, a murderer. I'd done it all in the name of love, but that didn't matter. There was supposed to be a clear right and a wrong, black and white, only I no longer believed it. Somewhere along the way, I'd decided that I could live in the gray.

Was I no different from Dolinsky? Or Flynn, for that matter?

"What are you doing?" Flynn asked, jarring me from my reverie.

"I didn't hear you come in," I said, startled.

Flynn went to pour himself a drink. "Want one?" he asked, gesturing to his glass. I shook my head.

"Do you want to talk about it?" He came to the couch and took a seat next to me, but I didn't lean into him.

"Just trying to work through things," I evaded.

"That doesn't happen overnight."

"No. But I wonder…"

"Go on," he said when I fell silent.

"I wonder if I'm dealing with it at all. Everything is happening so fast I don't know if I have time to think. I barely have time to breathe."

He stared into his glass. "How did your talk with Ash go?"

"Exactly like I thought." I ran a hand through my hair.

"She looks at me like she doesn't even know who I am. Can't say that I blame her."

"You offered her a pass," he reminded me. "When she told you she cheated on her fiancé, you didn't make her feel bad about it."

"Killing a person isn't the same as cheating and you know it."

"You told her you killed Dolinsky?" he asked in shock.

"Of course not. I refused to explain what happened to my finger. But she's my best friend and can tell when things are off with me."

"I don't know what to say to comfort you."

"There's nothing you *can* say." I sighed. "You met with him?"

Flynn nodded. "I met with Marino."

I couldn't stop the grin from spreading across my face. "How much does he hate me?" I'd told Flynn everything from my meeting with Marino, including the slap.

Flynn laughed. "He somehow had the amazing ability to keep his loathing to himself. But he is quite happy with the deal he and Sasha worked out."

"He should be." I shook my head in disgust. "I hate that we couldn't shut down the human trafficking completely."

"Stages," Flynn said. "We've got our guys recording everything and where the women are going. Just a few more days and then that part of the operation will shut down for good." He went for the hotel room phone. "What do you say we have dinner and then look at some apartment listings?"

"The king and queen of crime lords look at apartments. That seems way too normal."

I sat at a corner table in the Upper East Side dive bar, an untouched bottle of beer in front of me. Sasha was at the bar, looking inconspicuous even as he monitored everything in the room. When Fred Winters, FBI agent and colossal pain in my ass, walked in, I stood and greeted him. He took the seat next to me, his body coiled and tense, waiting for any lurking danger.

"I have to say, I'm shocked that you called," he said.

I raised my eyebrows in surprise. "Seriously?"

"Well, when you disappear without a trace..." he shrugged. "Thought you went underground, so you didn't have to work with us."

"Ah, and here I thought you might actually be concerned about me."

"Where were you?"

"Igor Dolinsky kidnapped me."

Winters's eyes widened in surprise.

"So you've heard of him," I asked.

"Head of the Russian mob? Yeah, I've heard of him. Impossible bastard to nail. How did you get away from him? Did Campbell ransom you back?"

"Something like that." I finally reached for my beer and took a sip, letting the cool liquid slide down my suddenly parched throat. "Someone killed Dolinsky."

"Someone took out Dolinsky? Who?"

I shrugged. "No idea."

"Really?" he drawled, clearly not believing me.

"I didn't call you to discuss Dolinsky's death. I called you to discuss the repercussions."

"I'm not following."

"Dolinsky's empire is in chaos without a leader and while the Russians are scrambling to find someone to take Dolinsky's place, Giovanni Marino has swooped in and taken over the docks. Marino. Italian Mob boss. You've heard of him, too, right?"

Winters's jaw clenched and he nodded. "Why are you giving me this information?"

"Call it a show a good faith," I said.

"What do you want?"

"I know the date of the next shipment of illegal contraband coming into the city. You can make a bust, and it will make your career. In exchange, you'll leave Flynn alone. You'll forget you know anything about the SINS."

"Marino would be a big feather in my cap," he said slowly.

I nodded. "Especially when you find out that the illegal contraband is women. Human trafficking." Winters cursed, but I wasn't done speaking. "I can also guarantee that Dolinsky's empire never regains its footing."

"How can you guarantee that?" he wondered.

"That's for me to deal with. Do we have an agreement? You quit trying to nail Flynn to the wall, and I'll give you Marino."

He held out his hand for me to shake. "Done."

Our business attended to, Winters got up and left. I sat by myself for five minutes until Sasha came over to join me.

"He gave in too easily," I said to him.

"Yeah, that took a lot less time than I expected."

I pushed my beer toward him. "What do you think?"

"I think he's not going to uphold his end of the bargain."

"You think he'll get Marino and still come after Flynn?" Sasha nodded and I said, "I think you're right."

He took my beer and drank from it.

I sighed. "I really don't want to have to kill him." Sasha choked on the beer and I started to laugh. "I was kidding."

"Were you?" Sasha asked, peering at me with consideration.

"I don't know anymore," I said softly. There was something about Sasha; he had seen what Dolinsky did to me. Something had passed between us that night, a bond had formed. And he'd saved me more than once.

"Have you talked to your husband?"

"About?"

He gave me a knowing look.

"Some. Not all," I admitted. "Not about Vlad. Not about you. There are ugly parts in me."

"There are ugly parts in all of us," he pointed out. "I'm sure there are things in Campbell's past that you've had to get over."

"But this stuff with Dolinsky, what I did to Vlad, happened in our present. It's who I'm becoming."

Sasha gripped the bottle while he stared at me. "Do you know it was my job to watch you?" he asked suddenly.

"It was?" I asked in surprise.

"Yes. When Chelsea came to him about you, he set me on your trail. I watched you. And—" his thumb fiddled with the beer label, "and I used to see nothing but a beautiful woman. Smart, yes. But I didn't understand what Igor and Campbell saw in you. They knew you were special. It took me longer to see it, but once I did… I'm grateful you're my friend. And you shouldn't be afraid of who you are, who you're becoming."

I reached out and squeezed his hand. "Thank you."

He squeezed back. "Do you not trust that he'll accept you for who you are?"

"Not that," I said quietly, finally admitting to the deepest horror in my soul. "I'm worried that I won't be able to accept myself."

Chapter 52

My lips trailed down Flynn's body, tracing the sculpted contours of his chest and belly.

"Barrett," he whispered in rapture. His hands sank into my hair as my tongue found the source of his desire. He groaned and I became voracious, refusing to stop until he was coming.

"I love you," he panted, trying to recover his breath.

A powerful man like Flynn Campbell whispering words from his heart had me shaking. "I love you, too."

He brought me up to his side and cuddled me against him. My hair spilled across his chest, dark in the moonlight. Flynn sighed, his breath teasing my skin, my heart thudding in cadence with his.

"Has Brad stopped hating me?"

"You want to talk about Brad while we're in bed together?"

"It's a serious concern," I stated. "He's been with you for the better part of a decade, and ever since I came into your life, things have changed. I understand why he's acting the way he is."

"I understand too, but it doesn't mean I like it. I don't like that he's questioning my judgment and your loyalty."

"Some people are afraid of change."

"Aye."

"You've impressed Sasha," I said, switching the conversation. "He likes how you handle things."

"That guy is adaptable," Flynn said, his voice filled with reluctant admiration. "I'll give him that."

"You'll never trust him, will you?"

"He was Dolinsky's right-hand man for years. And now he's the head of the Russian mob and is steadfastly loyal to you. Just strange."

"Some people are afraid of change," I repeated to him.

He smiled faintly. "If he helps pull this off with Winters, then I won't question him ever again."

"Hopefully, it will all be over in two days, and then we can focus on expanding our empire."

"You're thinking of expansion. Already?" he asked in amusement.

"Think about it. With us in league with the Russians, and Marino about to be the sacrificial lamb, we can swoop in and take over the rest of the city. I think we should have a plan."

"We?"

"I support you, Flynn, whatever you want to do. And I know things now… It would be difficult going back."

"I'm glad you know things."

"Yeah?"

"I don't have to hide anything from you now."

"I like that there's nothing between us." As soon as I said it, I realized it wasn't really true. For the first time in our relationship, I was the one with secrets. I had a new respect for the burden that Flynn had once carried. But sharing secrets didn't always mean absolution. It could taint us, what I'd done to Vlad. Taint us further, anyway.

"You're sure Marino has no idea what's about to happen?"

"He's none the wiser," Flynn assured.

"So much could go wrong. What if—"

He cut me off with his lips, and I let him distract me. When I was sated and relaxed, I let my mind wander while his hands slid down my body in a lazy caress. I wanted to sleep, but I hated what waited for me there. I was unraveling. I suddenly had a vision of myself, sitting in a shrink's office, feeling very much like Robert De Niro in *Analyze This.* The idea had me chuckling.

"What's funny?" Flynn asked, his voice drowsy.

"Nothing." I didn't think Flynn would find it amusing.

"Hmmm," he murmured, before sinking in to sleep.

I didn't even bother attempting to get comfortable knowing I would just toss and turn for hours. Throwing back the covers, I got up out of bed and headed to the living room. I didn't want to sit around and worry, so I put on some clothes and called down to the club, asking for Lacey. She wasn't in.

I hadn't seen her since I'd returned to The Rex. Perhaps I could unload on her. She was good at giving advice, having shared Flynn's confidence for the better part of a decade.

Perhaps she was on The Fifteenth Floor.

I'd wanted to check out the brothel for a while, but there had always been something else to do. Flynn's private elevator had access to all the hidden parts of the hotel.

The elevator doors opened to reveal a floor unlike the rest of the hotel. Decorated in dark wood, red velvet brocade and gold accents, it could very well have been tacky, but due to Flynn's style and eye, it all blended together to give an old-style saloon feel.

Beautiful women clad in silk dresses, not at all revealing, but somehow still provocative, walked around the room engaging men in conversation and laughter. There was a mixer of some sort going on. Champagne flowed and wallets opened. Out of the corner of my eye, I saw a man lean toward an escort's ear and whisper something. She smiled widely, took his hand, and led him away, no doubt to a more private setting.

"You're lovely," a voice said next to me. I turned, taking in the man. Suit, graying dark hair at the temples, brown eyes.

"Thank you," I said absently.

"Can I get you a drink?"

"No." My gaze searched the room, looking for Lacey, but I didn't see her. Not through the haze of cigar smoke.

The man took two flutes of champagne from a maneuvering waiter and attempted to hand me one. "I'm good, really," I said.

"And here I thought all the ladies at The Rex Hotel were the same." There was a hint of a smile on his mouth.

I was not in the mood to be charming or flirtatious. "Excuse me, I'm looking for someone."

"Aren't we all," he said, raising his flute to me in a silent toast. It took all of my effort not to roll my eyes. As I moved away from him in search of Lacey, I watched him turn to the nearest woman and offer her the extra champagne glass.

I snorted. Why bother with a challenge when a sure thing was a few feet away?

Leaving the main room, I went down the hallway. Even through the closed doors, I heard the sounds of fucking. I'd never call it love making, even if the men held the women after. I didn't care what they did, how women earned their money, or how the men spent theirs. That wasn't for me to judge.

Another hallway intersected the main one, and I wondered if I'd find Lacey down that way.

"I'll fucking take what I want," I heard a voice growl. Familiar.

Brad.

"Do you want me to do that?" he asked.

A woman whimpered, not in pain, but in complete and total arousal. "Please," she begged.

Lacey.

Lacey and Brad!

From the shadows, I could see he had her pushed up against the wall, one of her legs wrapped around him. One of his hands held both of hers hoisted above her head, the other was skating down her body, coming to rest between them. She threw her head back, the sound of her skull smacking against the wall.

I jumped and then scurried back the way I'd come like a twitchy little rodent. What the hell was going on?

As I waited for the elevator car, I pulled out my phone and pressed speed dial two. He answered on the first ring.

"Want to go for a walk?" I asked.

Chapter 53

Sasha and I strolled around a snow-covered Central Park, talking about everything and nothing. I told him about how I'd met Flynn, about my estranged brother offering me in lieu of his monetary debt.

For some reason, I could speak to Sasha in a way that I couldn't speak to anyone, like I didn't have to guard my words or pretend to be anyone other than who I was. He let me be the fractured parts of myself, the made-up puzzle of pieces that didn't yet all fit together. And he didn't expect me to reconcile anything. And he never acted as though I was defiled or broken because of what had occurred with Dolinsky.

An hour before dawn, I crawled into bed next to Flynn and woke him up by sliding my naked body on top of his. I took from him what I needed, but he didn't complain, and because he was Flynn, he gave it to me.

Falling into an exhausted sleep, I awakened a few hours later, bleary-eyed and in need of coffee. Flynn was gone from our suite and while I waited for the coffee to brew, I called Ash.

"What happened between you and Duncan?" I demanded.

"Good morning to you, too."

"Seriously."

"Why are you asking?" Ash evaded.

"Because I remembered the night you guys met. You couldn't take your eyes off each other, and I never got the chance to ask about it."

Ash paused before she said, "Something did happen between us, but I stopped it."

"Why?"

"I needed a break from all that man stuff. My judgment's been off. I wanted to clear my head."

"I understand."

"You do?"

"Of course I do," I said.

"Thanks for not judging me."

"You're my best friend—and nothing is going to change that. Not on my end."

She breathed a sigh and I could hear the relief. "Not on my end, either."

"Thanks, Ash," I said, meaning it. "You have no idea—these last few months, I've felt so…"

"Yeah, I can only imagine."

"I'm disappearing," I nearly whispered.

"You're not," she insisted. "The Barrett I know and love is in there. There's just other parts of you now, too."

"I'm not sleeping," I admitted.

"You know what you need?"

"What?"

"A girls' vacation. Somewhere tropical."

"I wish," I said mournfully. "Maybe when all this calms down."

"It might never calm down."

"Don't say that. I can't handle that idea."

"But it's a strong possibility, isn't it?"

"Yes, unfortunately. For now, can we settle for eating a meal together?"

"Sure, I'd like that."

"Soon," I promised.

We hung up, and I got ready, slugging down more coffee. The caffeine just wasn't doing it. I had a busy day of looking at apartments, so I fought through the tiredness. I left the hotel and took the town car to the first place, a luxury building that I didn't even enter because I didn't like the look of it from the outside.

Yeah, house hunting was going to be an involved process. My phone rang.

"How's the apartment hunting going?" Flynn asked.

"I just started, but I rejected the first place based on the exterior of the building."

"What was wrong with it?"

"I don't know. I just had a feeling. I didn't like it."

"Whatever makes you happy. I mean that."

I went all warm and gooey. "Thanks. I won't buy without your approval though."

He chuckled. "I didn't really call to discuss apartments."

The car pulled to a stop, but I didn't make a move to get out. "Why did you call?"

Flynn paused. "Jack Rhodes is refusing to back down."

"What do you mean?"

"He's talking to people. The wrong kind of people—about me and my affiliations."

I went on high alert. "Are you serious?"

"Yes."

"And you haven't done anything about it," I stated.

"Yet."

"Why? Jack running his mouth is dangerous and he needs to be stopped."

"I agree. I was hoping you might be the one to speak to him," Flynn said. "Before I do."

Flynn's method of speaking would be a bit more violent.

"You think he'll listen to me?" I asked.

"I think there's a better shot of getting him to keep his mouth shut if you remind him of your history."

"He could've remembered that at any moment," I pointed out. "He still talked."

"Barrett." He growled. "Silence him."

Or I will.

The words went unspoken, but I knew they were there.

"All right, I'll talk to him."

We hung up, and I stared at my cell phone for a moment before telling the driver, "Change of plans."

With a cool nod, I walked past Jack Rhodes's receptionist who sputtered in indignation. Not bothering to knock, I pushed his office door open. Luckily, he was alone.

"Barrett!"

"Hello, Jack." I loomed in front of his desk.

"I'm sorry, sir," Jack's peeved secretary said. "I couldn't—"

"It's fine, Anna. Thank you."

Anna shut the door on her way out and I was alone with Jack.

"What brings you here?" Jack asked, rising slowly.

"We've been friends a long time, yes?"

"Yes."

"Your sister is my best friend, yes?"

"Yes."

"Then listen to me very carefully," I said. "Stop what you're doing."

"What in the hell are you talking about?" he blustered.

"You know what. Stop talking to people you shouldn't be talking to. Leave it alone, Jack, or you won't like the consequences."

"You came here to threaten me? I thought that was your husband's job."

My eyes narrowed, and anger simmered just below the surface of my skin, but I held it in. I held it all in. "He respects you only because of my history with you. If you were anyone else, I wouldn't be here. Flynn would be here."

I once trusted Jack, but he was clearly ruled by emotions. People ruled by emotions were dangerous, irrational. I'd learned that the hard way and almost died. Jack could get in the way of all Flynn and I were trying to accomplish, and I couldn't risk it.

"Remember your loyalties," I said quietly. Spinning on my heel, I left. My driver was waiting for me at the curb, and I climbed into the car. Emotion drained out of me, leaving me exhausted. I must have dozed in the car because when we came to a stop, I realized we were out front of The Rex.

When I got back upstairs to the penthouse suite, I was barely able to strip out of my clothes before I tumbled into bed. I slept until the sound of a door opening woke me up. Rolling over, I glanced at the clock and saw that it was close to seven in the evening. I sat up and ran a hand across my face.

"Barrett?" Flynn asked from the doorway of the bedroom. "Were you sleeping?"

"Yeah." I threw my legs over the side of the bed, feeling woozy.

"Are you okay?"

"I think I'm coming down with something."

"Sorry to hear that. How did your talk with Jack go?" he asked.

"Oh, I forgot to call you to tell you about it, didn't I? Sorry. I was so tired after our confrontation that I came back here and crashed."

Flynn came to my side and helped me stand. "Maybe you shouldn't go out walking in the park with Sasha late at night."

I flinched when I heard the coldness in his voice. "Excuse me?"

"That's where you went last night, after I fell asleep. Don't bother denying it. The cameras caught you leaving and your phone—"

"My phone what?" My eyes widened. "Are you checking my phone?" I shook off his hands, not wanting him near me, not with that look in his eyes.

"You don't trust me," I spat, hating my tone, hating his, and feeling like I woke up from a nightmare into another one.

"Are you having an affair?"

"Are you kidding me?"

"No. Are you?"

"Fuck you."

He reached out and grasped my arms, almost like he wanted to shake me, but held me steady instead. "Answer me."

"You forgave me for Dolinsky, but you wouldn't forgive me for Sasha, is that it? What kind of code is that?"

Flynn's jaw clenched. "Love. We're talking about love."

"Are we?" My voice had come out breathless, and I wasn't even aware that my hands had reached up to grip his suit lapels.

"Barrett," he whispered, his breath teasing my face. "I don't know what I'd do if you told me you were in love with another man."

I watched him carefully; tension filled every line of his face. "I don't sleep at night, Flynn. I have nightmares."

His brow furrowed. "Nightmares? About what?"

"About the person I'm becoming. I'm scared."

Flynn all but yanked me into his arms, pressing me against his hard body. "Why didn't you tell me?"

"We don't talk about my time with Dolinsky. And I know it's because of what's on that video. It's still between us, Flynn. Don't deny it."

"I won't. But I thought by you talking about it, you'd be reliving it. I didn't want you to have to relive it."

"Me? Or you?" I pressed. He didn't answer and I told him, "Dolinsky wasn't the first man I killed. There was another." I finally told him about Vlad, about what I'd done.

"Fuck," Flynn rasped. "You've been holding all this in?"

I shrugged.

"Sasha," Flynn realized. "You can talk to Sasha."

"Because he was there. He knows. He's the one that stopped Vlad from killing me. He's the one who…"

"What? Tell me, Barrett. No more secrets."

"He filmed the video," I confessed.

I felt the tension in Flynn's body, hating it, hating that I'd put it there. But I couldn't keep it all to myself anymore. It was too much.

I cried against him, pouring out my fear and anguish and all that I'd kept bottled up inside of me. He stroked my hair and held me, even went as far as to kiss my tear-stained cheeks. I tugged at his clothes, but he stopped me.

"Barrett. No."

"What?"

"We have to talk," he insisted. "If not, you'll just lose yourself in me, and I'll let you."

"I don't want to talk," I muttered.

"You have no problem talking to Sasha," he pointed out. His voice was no longer cold, just hurt.

My hands dropped, and I took a step away from him. My stomach rumbled, breaking some of the tension. "I'll talk," I said, "but can we eat first?"

Flynn smiled. "Yes."

An hour later, I was pushing away an empty plate and drinking mineral water, feeling content and full. Flynn sat across from me, holding my hand and stroking my knuckles. "Never be afraid to tell me things."

"I don't want to hurt you," I said.

"You only hurt me by keeping things from me. Hurt us."

I shook my head in disbelief.

"What?"

"No one would believe me if I told them how sensitive you really are."

He chuckled. "How are you feeling?"

"Better," I admitted. "I needed to eat."

"And talk to me."

"And talk to you," I agreed. "I'm still feeling really tired, though. If I can't shake this bug, I'm going to the doctor."

He looked at me for a long moment.

"What?" I asked.

"Nothing." He rose and held out his hand to me. I took it and stood, wrapping myself around him. "You know what you need, hen?"

"What?"

"A bath," he said, leading me toward the bathroom. "With me in it."

"I'll never say no to that."

Chapter 54

"I hate this," I stated.

"I know," Flynn said, shrugging into his coat, "but I'll feel better knowing you're here."

"I want to come. I can sit quietly on the roof and watch everything go down. You won't even know I'm there."

He sighed. "Barrett—"

"Flynn."

"You'll be a distraction," he cut me off. "I'll worry about you every moment. If you stay here, I'll know you're safe. Safe and warm. It's cold out there."

"At least it's not snowing." I dropped my arms to my sides, losing some of my resentment. "You'll be careful."

"Of course."

"And if Marino looks like he's going to try something funny..."

"I've got a weapon. Sasha, Brad, and Duncan are carrying, too. I'm going with a well-armed entourage."

"Call me the minute it's over and Winters has Marino. Okay?"

"Okay."

"Promise me," I commanded.

"I promise," he said with a smile. Leaning over, he kissed me on the lips—a quick brush and then it was over. "Call Ash. Have her come over and distract you."

"It was a really good idea letting her in to our little circle."

"I did that for you," he said. "You needed someone to talk to."

I smiled. "You have good ideas sometimes."

"That I do. I love you."

"I love you. Now leave, before I have half a mind into distracting you into staying."

With one last smile, he was out the door, and I was left to contemplate how the showdown was going to play out. So many things could go wrong. Try as I might, I couldn't stop thinking about Flynn lying in a pool of his own blood. The idea had me running to the bathroom, and I puked up the light supper I'd eaten only a few hours earlier.

Weak and drained, I washed my mouth out and then dabbed my face with a hand towel. I couldn't shake the bug I'd gotten a week ago. One minute it was gone, the next it came back with a raging force. Just as I was getting ready to hit the light of the bathroom, I stopped.

I hadn't been taking my birth-control pills.

Not since Dolinsky kidnapped me. And with all the stuff going on that I'd had to deal with on my return, I'd completely forgotten.

"No," I whispered in denial. "No, no, no."

It couldn't be.

I ran for my cell phone and dialed my best friend. "I need you."

"I'm on my way," she said without pause.

"Good. But can you stop at the Rite Aid and get me something?"

Thirty minutes later, the elevator doors to the penthouse suite opened and Ash came inside.

"Did you get it?" I demanded.

She rummaged through her large brown shoulder Fendi and handed me the Rite Aid plastic shopping bag. Pulling out the box of pregnancy tests, I stared at it.

"Are you going to go take that test, or make us both wait?"

"I think it's a bit of a formality at this point. I've been pukey and tired."

I gripped the box and marched my way toward the bathroom, determined to at least know one answer in my life. Ash sat with me on the edge of the bathtub while we waited for the results. When Ash's phone alarm beeped, she turned it off.

"You look for me," I said. "I can't."

Ash let go of my hand and got up to go to the counter. She glanced down at the test. "Well, you're pregnant."

"Oh God," I muttered, putting a hand to my head. "I think I might faint."

"Take a deep breath. There ya go. Again."

I did as commanded, but I wasn't feeling any better about having confirmation. If anything, I felt worse.

"I didn't want this," I whispered.

"I know."

"I never wanted to be in this position—to have to… Shit, I've always been so careful. Until now."

Ash knew I didn't want kids, so she was being pragmatic when she asked, "Are you going to—"

"I don't know."

"You don't know? You always knew what you were going to do if you—"

"I know. I know what I planned to do *before*. Before hormones got in the way. Before all rationality fled. And before—"

"Before you found Flynn," she said gently.

"Before I found Flynn," I agreed.

"Come on," she said. "We're going to hang out on the couch, order up some dessert, and watch some fun movies."

We settled in and Ash found something on Netflix, but I

hardly paid attention. I kept glancing at my phone, waiting for Flynn to call. When I wasn't thinking about Flynn, I thought about my situation. I still didn't want children. But how could I…

"He's fine," Ash said, not taking her eyes off Jennifer Beals dancing on screen.

"How do you know?" I asked, feeling relieved that she was hell-bent on distracting me.

"Because he's armed, and he's got how many bodyguards with him?"

"You make a valid point."

I sat up and reached for a bite of chocolate torte left over on the table when the elevator doors slid open. "Did we order something else?"

"No," Ash said with a shake of her head.

It was Lacey, holding a bottle of vodka. "Hi," I said.

"Hi. I thought I'd stop by and we could catch up and wait for Flynn to finish…" she trailed off when she saw Ash. "Oh, sorry. I didn't know you had company."

"Join us," Ash said generously.

"Thanks," Lacey said, setting the vodka down on the kitchen table. She made herself at home by opening the cabinets and pulling out three shot glasses.

"Ash knows all about Flynn," I said to Lacey. "So you don't have to worry about what you say in front of her."

"Wow, okay," Lacey said. "I didn't think Flynn would've told you." She looked at Ash.

"Well, when your best friend disappears for six weeks, you know something's up."

"Flynn told her about Dolinsky," I said. "But I told her about the SINS."

Lacey handed us shots, and I stared at mine for a minute. Ash wasted no time throwing hers back, but I had no idea what I was supposed to do.

"Ah, I'm not in the mood to drink," I said, setting my shot aside.

"Trust me, you'll want to," Lacey insisted before downing hers. "Waiting for men to come back from these sorts of things will drive you insane. Drinking helps."

"You've done this before?" Ash asked.

"Oh yeah. I've worked for Flynn for a decade. It's part of the territory."

"I'll do another shot," Ash said.

They did another round and then Lacey set the vodka aside. I sat back down on the couch with Ash next to me and Lacey took the chair. "Want some food?" I asked, gesturing to the half-eaten desserts on the coffee table.

Lacey grabbed a fork and said, "Yeah, I think I'll go for that blueberry pie. Did you guys order every dessert on the menu?"

"Yep," Ash said.

"I approve." She stuck a bite into her mouth and nearly moaned. "This is so good."

"I know," I said, picking up the plate with the rest of the chocolate torte and digging in.

"So weird you're eating that," Ash said.

Lacey frowned. "Right. You refused to eat the brownies I brought you, but you're devouring that chocolate torte like it's the last thing you'll ever eat."

I sighed.

"Wait a second," Lacey said, gesturing at me with her fork. "You also aren't drinking. What's going on?"

"Nothing," I said quickly. Too quickly.

Lacey's eyes narrowed and then she broke out into a smile. "You're pregnant."

"No!" I denied.

"You're a terrible liar!" Lacey said, jumping up in excitement. "You're pregnant! Does Flynn know?"

No use lying anymore. "No."

Lacey embraced me and said, "Why aren't you happier?"

"I'm still in shock," I said truthfully. "And I never wanted kids."

"Oh," Lacey said in sudden understanding. Amazing woman that she was, she didn't focus on it and ask me a bunch of questions.

My cell phone rang. I jumped up, pouncing on it, eager to hear my husband's voice.

"Flynn?"

"It's Sasha."

"Why are you on Flynn's phone?"

"There's been an accident."

I felt all the blood rush from my head. Forcing myself to take deep, calming breaths, I kept the phone to my ear. "What happened?"

"Flynn was shot," Sasha went on, "in the shoulder. He's with the doctor now."

"Where are you?" He gave me the address. "I'll be right there." I hung up and then grabbed my purse and searched for my shoes.

"What's going on?" Lacey asked.

"Flynn was shot. I've got to go."

"Wait, I'll go with you," Ash said, getting up.

"No. I'm good. I've got this." All my nerves had somehow disappeared, and I was able to think clearly.

Because I was a queen.

Chapter 55

I met Sasha outside a warehouse by the docks. "Tell me every-thing," I said in lieu of a greeting.

"Marino's dead," he said flatly. "Winters botched the timing. Marino got trigger-happy and scared. He let off a shot, and it caught Flynn. Winters took out Marino and here we are."

"Where's Winters now?" I asked as Sasha led me into the warehouse, down a long hallway lit with garish overhead fluo-rescent lights.

"Cleaning up his mess."

"And while that was going on, you were able to get Flynn out of there." We arrived at the end of the hallway and Sasha gestured for me to go into the room. Flynn was on a cot in the center of the room, moaning in pain as a man stood over him, doing something I couldn't see.

Brad and Duncan were in the corner, their faces lined with tension, their bodies rigid. I barely spared them a glance as I raced to Flynn's side, crouching down on the floor, my knees hitting cold cement.

"Flynn," I said, my hand going to his forehead. He was

sweating and pale and when he looked at me, his eyes were glassy with pain.

"Barrett."

Scotch fumes wafted toward me. I looked at the man who I assumed was the doctor. He was pressing a cloth to Flynn's left shoulder, a bloom of red marring the whiteness.

"I dug out the bullet. He still needs stitches," the doctor explained.

"I'll do this," I said, going for the cloth and putting my hand on top of it. The doctor took a step back and went for his medical bag, but I kept my gaze trained on my bleeding husband. "What did you do to yourself?"

"Got myself shot," he slurred, his brogue coming out due to pain and liquor.

"So I heard."

"You came."

"Of course I did."

"I love you," he muttered right before he passed out.

The doctor took a seat next to Flynn and put a needle and thread to his skin. He worked quickly and efficiently before Flynn woke up.

"Can we move him?" I asked, looking at the doctor who tied off the last stitch and backed away.

The doctor nodded and then gestured for Duncan and Brad to help him. I got to my feet and stood back and watched them struggle with Flynn's bulk. Once he was in a sitting position, the doctor was able to put Flynn's left arm into a makeshift sling. Flynn mumbled but didn't awaken as they carted him out of the warehouse, Sasha in front to make sure all was clear.

We piled into the waiting black Suburban. I sat next to Flynn, keeping him upright around the corners. Every now and again, the doctor, who had taken the middle seat all to himself, would check Flynn's arm to make sure the stitches held.

An hour later, Flynn was passed out in our hotel suite bed, and I was closing the bedroom door. Everyone was in the living room, including Lacey and Ash who had waited for us to return. Tiredness sank into my bones, but I refused to collapse in front of them. I wanted to remain strong, stoic, without giving away how terrified I felt.

"You should go," I said to both of my friends.

"I'll stay," Lacey volunteered, her eyes landing on me and then sliding to Brad. "I can help."

"Flynn's asleep for the foreseeable future," I said. "I don't need help."

"You can call me. Any time. Day or night." Lacey said it to me, but then her eyes went to Brad again.

"I'll go. I don't want to be in the way," Ash said, her voice tight, her face shell-shocked.

"I'll take you home," Duncan said to her.

She shook her head. "I'm sure Barrett needs you here."

My friends hugged me goodbye, and I was left with the men I trusted.

"We've got a problem," Brad said.

"Another one?" I nearly snapped. Pregnant, shot husband, what the hell was next?

"Marino is dead," Brad went on, like I hadn't interrupted him. "As you know."

"Yes."

"The deal didn't include ending Marino," Sasha said, picking up the thread of conversation. "Winters wanted to have someone in custody, turn him rat, so he'd give up others."

"He's going to take Flynn, isn't he?"

"It's a safe assumption," Duncan voiced. "Unless we get him out of the country."

"You want to move him? He's unconscious."

"What choice do we have?" Brad demanded. "We fly out

tonight. By the time Winters is done cleaning up the mess on the docks, it will be too late. Flynn will be safe."

"And what about me?" I asked. "I'm just supposed to leave the city?"

"You can't leave," Brad said. "You have to stay here."

"Why?"

"Because Winters needs to believe you're both still in the city. You can't flee," Brad explained.

"But Flynn," I said. "I need to—"

"I'll look after Flynn. Take him to my father's house," Duncan said.

I put a finger to my third eye and began to rub. A headache was looming. "I don't know," I murmured. "I need some time to—"

"There isn't time," Brad said. "You have to decide now."

Would Flynn leave my side if the situation were reversed? No, he would be with me. But I had to do what was best for both of us, and at the moment that meant being separated from him.

"Ready the plane," I said.

By dawn, Flynn was thirty thousand feet in the air and soaring closer and closer to Scotland, farther and farther away from me.

"You made the right choice," Brad said as the car returned us to the front of The Rex Hotel.

"Did I?" I wondered. I hadn't slept in eighteen hours, and I was delirious. Delirious and weepy and…pregnant. And still not at all sure how I felt about it.

"It was an impossible choice," Sasha said, "but you didn't make it about emotion. I respect that."

I sighed, knowing even though I was exhausted, I wouldn't sleep well until I was next to Flynn again. Sasha climbed out of the car first, followed by Brad. Too numb to pay attention to what was going on around me, I got out of the car and caught sight of Fred Winters and three of his men waiting out front of the hotel.

He looked a little worse for wear, lines etched at the corners of his eyes. Brad and Sasha immediately flanked me, but I gently urged them aside.

"You need to come with me," Winters demanded.

"I don't need to do anything," I stated.

"I just want to ask you some questions."

"No."

Winters's jaw clenched in annoyance.

"What did you expect?" I asked. "Accost me outside of my husband's hotel, and I'd be more inclined to do something for you? I did enough for you, and it got my husband shot."

Sasha put his hand on my shoulder, no doubt as a way to silence me. I listened and shut my mouth. I moved forward, wanting to get off the early morning Manhattan street. It was relatively quiet and devoid of traffic, but that would change. Trucks, people, and honking horns would soon be rampant.

Winters said nothing as I entered the lobby. I gave a sigh of relief. Sasha and Brad escorted me to the private elevator and rode all the way with me to the penthouse suite. I was beginning to hate the place.

"I'll stay," Sasha said. "On the couch."

I shook my head, looking at both of them. "Go home. I'll call if I need anything."

"Why don't I believe you?" Brad asked.

"Out."

I waved them both away and then collapsed into bed. Rolling over onto Flynn's side, I fell asleep. The phone ringing jarred me awake. I went to answer it and wet my dry lips. "Hello?" I croaked.

"Barrett."

"Flynn," I said in relief. "You're awake."

"Unfortunately," he groaned. "I feel like hell."

My eyes settled on the alarm clock. It was two in the afternoon, which meant it was evening in Scotland. "God, I miss you," I blurted out.

"I miss you," he said. "I wish you were here."

"Me too. I'm sorry I had to stay here. We thought it would be—"

"I know, hen," he crooned. "I know why you're there. If we were normal people, you'd be with me."

"If we were normal people, I doubt you would be in this position."

"Valid point."

"How is Duncan? And Malcolm?"

"Malcolm has been cursing at me in a Gaelic English mix, saying I was a damn fool to trust an FBI agent."

"Oh no," I said with a chuckle.

"He's called me a bloody eejit no less than five times. Somehow that man makes me feel like a teenager all over again."

"I don't want you to worry about a thing," I said. "Just get well, and I'll figure a way out of this mess with Winters."

He paused for a moment before asking, "Do you think there's really a way out of this? Winters is after my blood. He won't stop until he gets it."

"There's always a way," I said, believing it. "I just haven't figured it out yet."

"We," he corrected. "We haven't figured a way out of it. But we will."

"We will," I vowed.

Chapter 56

Two weeks passed, and everything with Winters was quiet. Flynn was on his way to a full recovery, and even though we talked and video chatted every day, it wasn't the same as being able to touch his face, love his body, or have him cradle me in his arms.

Everyone was still on guard—the bust with Winters had everyone tense and overly cautious. I didn't believe it was over. That just wasn't our lives. We had brief lulls and moments of calm, but usually, we were dealing with catastrophes, kidnappings, and gunshot wounds.

I went to the doctor who confirmed I was pregnant—and about six weeks along. The reality of it hadn't hit me yet, but I knew I needed to tell Flynn. I still wasn't sure how I felt about it, but I knew I was keeping it. There never seemed to be a good time to drop that kind of bomb on him, especially with an ocean separating us.

"Have you told Flynn you're pregnant?" Ash asked one day over lunch. We were at a French restaurant on the Upper East Side, close to The Rex.

"Have you told Duncan you have feelings for him?" I shot back.

Her fork stopped halfway to her mouth. "Why would I do that? He's in Scotland."

My eyes widened. "How did you—"

"He calls to check in on me."

"You want to sleep with him."

"Well, sure. Have you seen him?" Ash asked in amusement.

"You like him."

"Yes."

"Well that settles that," I said.

"What?"

I grinned. "We're going to Scotland. You should be with him."

"But what about all the stuff going on here? With you?"

"Things are stable enough here for the moment. I need to be with Flynn."

I zipped my suitcase closed and lifted it to the ground. Pulling on a comfortable sweater and boots, I looked around the bedroom one last time to make sure I had everything. I wheeled the suitcase to the pile of luggage already packed. Picking up my shoulder bag, I took a deep breath, trying to settle the nausea rolling through my belly. Flying would be interesting.

"Are you sure this is a good idea?" Sasha asked me as we followed the bellman through the lobby. We headed outside, and the bellman began stowing away my luggage into the waiting town car.

"It's not ideal," I said, "but you and Brad have a good handle on things. Your position is secure. It'll all be fine." Flynn had told me that everything was in place for the Russian empire to funnel money to the SINS and hopefully the FBI would no longer watch Flynn.

I also missed my husband and telling him about the baby was something I needed to do face to face.

I hugged Sasha, and he squeezed me back before releasing me. Just as I was about to climb into the waiting car that would take me to Ash's apartment and then to the airport, Fred Winters walked toward The Rex, jaw clenched, body tight. He moved with purpose. Two agents flanked his sides, and I knew this wasn't one of his tricks to come here and ruffle my feathers. Something was up. He'd been silent for two weeks, but I'd never been lulled into thinking he'd given up interest in all that had gone down with Marino.

"Barrett Campbell," he called out. "You're under arrest for the murder of Igor Dolinsky."

Everything seemed to freeze, including my breath. I said nothing even as Fred Winters turned my body so he could cuff my hands. My eyes found Sasha, but I remained silent. He nodded, his face lined with anger. Even when I was put into the back of a black car, I didn't say anything. Trick of the trade: keep your damn mouth shut.

There had been three of us in that warehouse: Flynn, Dolinsky, and me. No way a dead man could talk. Sasha knew what had gone down, but he would never betray me, I knew that in my bones. And Flynn was my husband.

Flynn had called Brad to clean up the mess, and Brad had had a team. I didn't know those men, so I couldn't vouch for them. Could one of them have squealed? Could it have been Brad?

Winters and the driver in the front seat were quiet too, except for when Winters got a call on his cell phone. He said a few words and then hung up—I was too caught up in my head to pay attention to what was being said. I didn't know how long we drove, but the car finally came to a stop outside a tall nondescript building. I peered at it through the window until the car door opened and Winters waited for me to scoot out.

He took me by the arm, my hands still cuffed behind me,

and led me up the front steps of the building. Did he really think I'd make a break for it?

We passed by two security officers seated in the lobby and headed toward the elevators. I raised my eyebrows in surprise when Winters pushed the button for the twelfth floor. Guess I wouldn't be taken to a basement and tortured. Well, not yet.

When the elevator doors opened, I saw rows and rows of desks and harried people in suits. No one looked up as Winters all but hauled me down the hallway to a private room. He opened the door and ushered me in. It was a cube with a table and two chairs. And it was completely private. Winters gestured for me to take a seat. Without much choice, I did as bid, wondering why I was here instead of in a holding cell. I was sure Winters would enlighten me. At some point.

I sat, but he remained standing, no doubt trying to intimidate me. It wouldn't work. I wasn't who I used to be. A surge of protective instincts overwhelmed me and it wasn't just for Flynn—it took all of my willpower not to place a hand on my belly. I had to give nothing away.

Winters quit pacing, pulled out the chair on the opposite side of the table from me, and sat. He stared at me. I smiled. His face darkened with anger.

He really needed a better poker face.

"Does nothing affect you?" he demanded.

I shrugged but said nothing.

"You're under arrest for murder—and you have nothing to say?"

"I'll say nothing without my lawyer present," I stated. "If you'll actually let me make a call. Because, let's face it, you're not really a man of your word." I leaned back in my chair, pretending I had all the time in the world, pretending that I wasn't terrified of rotting in a cell without a fair trial.

Winters glared at me one long moment before shoving back from the table, stalking out of the room, like I was some cancerous contagious entity.

I was alone.
Nothing to do but wait.

Chapter 57

My stomach growled and I was parched. I hadn't gotten up from my seat at the table, refusing to engage in this pissing contest with Winters. I knew I'd win—the bastard didn't have a trump card. But I did.

Eventually, I put my head on the table and dozed. When I came to, I was still alone. And with a full bladder. I needed to use the facilities and quickly or I was in danger of giving away my pregnancy.

I grinned, hoping the bastard could see me through the cameras he was no doubt watching. It was time to end this once and for all.

"You win," I said, lifting my head from the table. "I'll talk."

I counted to five. And then I counted to ten. Just when I thought I had misjudged the situation, the door opened and Winters strolled in, looking relaxed, as if all the anger he'd thrown at me before was gone.

"Hungry?" he asked, placing a wrapped sandwich in front of me along with a bottle of water.

I reached for it, but my hands were still shackled. Winters

released me. I went for the sandwich, unwrapping it and looking between the bread slices. Ham and Swiss. Not my favorite, but I'd make do. I chewed while watching Winters take a seat across from me. He politely waited for me to finish my meal. Discreetly wiping my mouth with a napkin, I set aside the plastic wrap, grabbed the water bottle, and took a drink. It took all of my willpower not to wet my pants, but damn if I was going to ask to use the bathroom.

"Thanks," I said, my hand staying around the water bottle.

He inclined his head and folded his hands and rested them on the table. "You said you were ready to talk."

I smiled. "I lied."

Winters sighed.

"You think you can keep me here for an extended period and I'll just become malleable? Laughable, really." I chuckled. "Tell me what you want, Winters. I gave you Marino and it wasn't enough. Apparently."

Winters's face didn't change, but I knew I could get him to show his anger. "Ah, let me take a stab at it then," I said, when he remained silent. "Marino *alive* would've been enough, but he's dead and it was your operation. Is your superior breathing down your neck? How am I doing?" I asked, twisting the verbal knife, holding in a grin. Winters's nostrils were flaring, his jaw was clenched, but still he said nothing.

"You don't really believe I killed Dolinsky, do you? Just a straw you're grasping at." Finally, I stood and moved to the door.

"What are you doing?" he demanded.

"Well, let's see. I've been held in this room for God knows how long, and I have to use the restroom."

He glared, but rose.

"How lovely, an escort."

We walked through the room of agents, dying sunlight

streaming through the large windows. I'd been in this place for most of the day. Winters had confiscated my phone, and I had no way of knowing if he dismantled my ability to be tracked. It didn't matter. Brad and Sasha had ways of hacking anything and could find Winters if they needed. I wasn't shocked that they hadn't shown up yet. Everything in its time.

Winters stopped in front of a wooden door with a woman icon on it. "Five minutes," he said. "Or I'm coming in after you. Don't lock the door."

I rolled my eyes. "You think I can find a way out through the airshaft in five minutes? Give me a break."

I did my business and then washed my hands, touching the cool water to my cheeks. Nausea was roiling through me, and I had no idea if it was due to the sandwich I'd eaten, the tamping down of extreme emotion, or morning sickness that was becoming afternoon sickness. A knock sounded on the door. My five minutes were up. Drying my hands, I opened the door, my FBI escort waiting with his arms crossed over his chest.

As we walked back toward the desks, I refused to give him the satisfaction of asking if I'd be staying the night in this luxurious place. Striding in silence, a slow smile spread across my face when I saw two men waiting for us.

"Took you long enough," I teased.

An appreciative grin spread across his face. "Good to see you too, love." My husband's blue gaze sharpened when he looked at Winters. "Allow me to introduce you to Barrett's lawyer, Allen Masterson, the best criminal defense attorney in the country."

"Criminal," Winters stated.

"Why has my client been detained for the past eight hours without so much as a phone call?"

"Let's go inside—" Winters gestured to the room I'd been held in, but Masterson cut him off.

"No need. My client is leaving the premises. No criminal charges have been filed."

"You know the FBI has its own jurisdiction," Winters spat.

Masterson was a tall man, who seemed to grow even taller. He looked at me, his brown eyes shrewd. "Sasha Petrovich informed me that you were roughly handled outside of The Rex Hotel. Tell me, Mrs. Campbell, how did Mr. Winters treat you?"

"Inhumanely," I said automatically. "I was fed once and had only one bathroom break."

"All in eight hours," Masterson said with a rueful shake of his head. "And he didn't let you make a phone call, did he?"

"No, he didn't," I said.

"You son of a bitch," Winters growled at Masterson.

Flynn finally reached out to me and pulled me into his side, but I refused to melt into him. Strength was the only character trait Winters responded to.

"You want to file those criminal charges, and we'll be having a different discussion. Until then." Masterson nodded at me. Flynn took my hand, and we headed toward the elevator.

I looked over my shoulder at Winters and smiled. "A pleasure. As always."

Flynn barked out a laugh. The elevator dinged, and then the doors opened. "Say nothing," Masterson said. Flynn's hand tightened on mine as my eyes took him in. He looked like he'd healed completely from the bullet to the shoulder, but I wouldn't know until I got his shirt off, and my hands all over him. We rode the elevator in complete silence to the lobby, and when we made it outside, I took in a breath, no longer breathing stale, circulated air. Our car was waiting for us, idling, and I could almost make out the form of our driver through tinted windows.

Flynn opened the door for me, but before I climbed in, I turned to Allen Masterson. He was no fool—you didn't get to be the best criminal defense attorney in the country by being stupid. "He won't stop."

"No," he agreed. "He won't. We need to have a meeting to discuss strategy and everything that went on while you were in that building. I need you to write it all down, okay?"

"Okay."

"We'll talk tomorrow," he promised, reaching out to shake my hand and then Flynn's.

"Can we drive you somewhere?" Flynn asked him.

"No, I have my own car waiting for me. Tomorrow," he said again before striding away, strong and confident.

"Car," Flynn ordered me gruffly.

I scooted inside and Flynn followed, sitting so close that our thighs touched. The car pulled away, and Flynn rolled up the partition so we had privacy.

"Barrett," he whispered.

My mouth met his, and I sank into him, greedily soaking up all the comfort he offered me. His hands wove through my hair, and his lips gentled, moved, and brushed across my cheek. "I think we've established we're stronger together than apart, aye?"

"Yes," I agreed. "I was on my way to Scotland. I missed you."

"I missed you."

"Winters accused me of killing Dolinsky. How would he know such a thing?"

I stared up at him, Flynn's hands still holding the sides of my face. "Because a man of ours who was on Brad's trusted team tipped him off."

"What?" I asked, my eyes widening. "But—"

"It was part of the plan."

"Plan? You mean, you wanted Winters to arrest me?"

Flynn's hands dropped, but only so he could grasp my shoulders. "Not you," he said curtly. "Me. We had our man tell Winters I was the one who killed Dolinsky."

"I don't understand," I said, shaking my head. Everything was so muddy. Layers and layers of deception. "When he picked me up, he said I was under arrest for Dolinsky's death."

"I would never, ever let you take the fall for that."

"But I did it," I whispered.

"Doesn't matter," he answered. "So we fed Winters fake information to see how he took it. I thought for sure he'd come after me, but he considers you weak. He thinks he can use you to get to me.

"He wanted to make a deal with you," Flynn went on, "and if he thought he had you backed into a corner for murder, you would give me and the SINS up. He never mentioned that?"

I shook my head. "He left me alone after I told him I wouldn't speak without a lawyer present. I finally said I would talk and that's when he came in, but I still wouldn't give an inch."

Flynn smiled. "Of course you wouldn't."

"Why didn't you tell me?" I asked, suddenly exhausted. "That you fed Winters fake information?"

"We just thought the fewer people that knew about it, the better we could control the spin."

"Who did you tell?"

"Excuse me?"

"Don't play dumb," I snapped. "Who knew?"

He sighed. "Brad."

"Who else? Did you tell Sasha?"

"No."

"So this was all you and Brad."

"Aye."

"Glad to know the bromance is alive and well." I moved away from him, turning my gaze to the window. We passed through Manhattan, but I wasn't seeing the city. I saw nothing except Flynn's betrayal and the fact that he still didn't trust me.

"Barrett—"

"No, Flynn. You don't get to do this. You don't get to dictate everything and then let me in on things when it's convenient for you. I thought we were past all this."

I closed my eyes and leaned my head against the glass, shutting him out. Shutting everything out.

Chapter 58

"Where are you going?" Flynn asked when he realized I hadn't pressed the PH elevator button.

"I'm going to stay in another suite. I need some time to process," I said. I was so defeated I wasn't even mad. Blindsided. Yet again.

I hadn't told him I was pregnant yet, but that could wait. I didn't want to tell him when this was between us.

"What about Masterson? You have to write down everything that happened today," Flynn pressed.

"I'll get it done."

"Barrett, please—"

Straightening my spine, I felt my resolve harden. The more he pleaded and begged, the more distance I wanted. "No. Not tonight. Tonight, it's all about me and what I need. Not you."

The doors opened, and I stepped out of the elevator. I turned. "Respect what I want. For once."

It was a low blow, but he absorbed it. His face went blank and he nodded. "Call if you need me."

The doors shut, leaving me alone with my thoughts. I went into the hotel suite and settled down onto the couch. I was hungry, but I didn't want to call down to the front desk and let them know I wasn't with Flynn. No one needed to be aware of our fight.

Picking up my cell phone, I called Sasha. "You hungry?"

"I could eat," he replied. "Heard you just got back, though. Don't you want to eat with Campbell?"

"You hungry?" I asked again.

He sighed. "What am I bringing?"

Twenty minutes later, I let Sasha in. He brought the bags of Chinese takeout and set them on the coffee table. "What's going on?" he asked. I shrugged and went for the beef Lo mein. "Is it Winters? Do I need to—"

"If you're about to suggest something illegal, please don't." He immediately closed his mouth. Glad I could read him so well.

"I trailed Winters's car when he picked you up and called Campbell immediately. He took his private plane out of Scotland as fast as he could."

I nodded distractedly as I began to eat, the knot in my belly slowly loosening. "I'm supposed to write down everything that happened today from the time Winters picked me up until Allen Masterson and Flynn came for me."

"What's going on?" he asked quietly, his Kung Pao chicken untouched.

Though Sasha and I were close, he was not a girlfriend, and I would not confide my marital troubles to him. There were some nails in the coffin that I wouldn't be hammering myself. Let outside forces do that, I thought morosely.

I swallowed before saying, "I think I have an idea of how to stop Winters once and for all."

He raised his eyebrows. "You do?"

I nodded. "I want to ask Masterson, but Flynn hired him, which means nothing I say is confidential."

"What can you possibly want to ask your lawyer that you

don't want your husband to know?" Sasha frowned. "Are you
—are you thinking of leaving Campbell?"

Leave Flynn? I loved him and he loved me, but what about
trust? I believed trust was one of those marital foundation
blocks. Without it, what did we have? Was I overreacting
about Flynn not letting me in on his and Brad's plan? I knew
he was trying to protect me, but—no. I wasn't overreacting.

But I wasn't leaving him either.

"Barrett?" Sasha whispered, his hand reaching out to
stroke my cheek.

"What are you doing, Sasha?"

His hand dropped. "I—I don't know." He got up and
moved away from me, pacing back and forth across the living
room carpet. "Campbell doesn't know what he has in you. If
you're questioning him, then he's severely tested your loyalty.
And you're the most loyal person I know." His bright blue eyes
delved into me, and for the first time, I saw the way he looked
at me. Either he'd kept it shielded from me all this time, or I'd
been too wrapped up in other things to see it.

Sasha was in love with me.

"I'm pregnant."

The love on his face evaporated, replaced by calm, blank
resolve.

"I need you, Sasha," I said quietly. "As my friend. But I
love Flynn. Even…"

"Even though he hurts you without trying."

I swallowed and looked away, not liking his bitter, truthful
tone. "I've hurt him, too."

"You hurt each other," he stated, shaking his head. "You
are the strongest, bravest woman I've ever met."

"Thank you," I whispered. "Sasha, I need a friend. More
than anything in the world. Can you be that for me? Please?"

"I'll be whatever you need me to be."

"Good. Now, sit down and let me tell you my idea."

Bleary eyed and confused, I rolled over and threw the alarm clock against the wall, snuggling back under the covers.

"A bit dramatic, don't you think?" Flynn asked from the doorway of the bedroom, sipping a cup of coffee.

"What are you doing here?" I growled.

"Making you coffee. Sasha almost didn't let me in—and he looked like he wanted to rip me apart. What did you tell him? And why was he here this morning?"

"He brought Chinese last night. And he let me talk. He crashed on the couch. Is he still here?"

"No. He's gone."

Throwing off the covers, I got up out of bed, intending to give him a verbal set down, but a bout of morning sickness decided to assert itself. I ran for the bathroom, unable to shut the door to give myself privacy while I emptied my belly. Pulling myself off of the floor, I went to the sink and cleaned up. I glanced out of the corner of my eye to see Flynn standing in the doorway. The coffee cup was gone, and his hands were at his sides, fists clenched.

"Something you want to tell me?" he asked quietly.

"I didn't think we had to tell each other everything. That's clearly how you choose to operate." I brushed my teeth while he continued to lurk, refusing to rise to the bait.

"How far along are you?"

"Almost eight weeks." I dried my mouth and looked at him. I couldn't read him, and I hated the distance between us. He'd put it there first. What was I doing? Keeping us apart out of spite? I purposefully went to him. He looked down at me but didn't touch me.

I swallowed. "When I was with Dolinsky, I ran out of birth control. And then I came back and we—there was so much—"

Flynn's arms shot out to hug me to him, pressing my face

to his chest. His hands were in my hair, and before I knew it, I was shaking with emotion, and tears leaked out of my eyes. He held me, whispering words in Gaelic into my hair before pulling back so he could stare into my eyes.

"I thought you didn't want children," he said.

"I didn't."

"And you do now?"

I shrugged. "I don't know," I said truthfully. "But when I found out, and thought about—" I swallowed, not even able to say it. "I couldn't do it. Couldn't go through with it." I looked up at him. "I'm sorry."

"For what?"

"For this unforeseen—"

"You have no idea how happy you've made me, hen."

His lips covered mine. I was losing myself in him, in my desire, but I managed to tear my mouth from his.

"I didn't do this on purpose. I didn't do this to trap you."

"Trap me?" He frowned. "Why would you think—oh. You think I'd stay with you out of obligation instead of love. You still don't think we're back to us, after Dolinsky."

"No, I don't. And after last night… Let's get one thing straight," I said, my voice soft but firm.

"I'm listening."

"You ever pull this kind of crap again, not involving me, I will leave you. I can't be with someone I can't trust."

His eyes darkened. "Never again," he stated, his thumbs sweeping across my cheeks.

"Promise me, Flynn. I need to hear you promise."

"I promise."

The rest of my anger dissolved when I saw his contrition and his sincerity. I stood on my toes wanting to kiss him, but he stopped me.

"Now it's your turn to promise me something," he said.

"What?" I asked warily.

"We'll never spend a night apart again—not because of anger, anyway."

"Promise."

"Missed you," he murmured, his head descending.

"We haven't even had a proper rendezvous. Two weeks apart and—"

Flynn scooped me up into his arms and carried me to the bedroom. Gently settling me down on the bed, his body blanketed mine. His mouth grazed my lips, my cheek, my neck as he worked my T-shirt off me. He quickly divested himself of his suit and he threw it to the floor. His fingertips glided down my body. Heat began to build inside of me as his hands cupped my breasts, his thumbs teasing my nipples. They were so tender. Growling, I arched into him. His mouth covered a nipple, taking it between his teeth, sucking lightly.

"God, Flynn," I moaned, my eyes rolling back into my head as I savored the sensations.

My hands sank into his hair, my legs falling open to cradle him against me. I was wet and wanting, needy, greedy and more than ready for him.

As he slid into me, I gasped in blissful agony. He took me gently, but no less eager. He wrapped a strong arm underneath me, bringing me closer to him.

"Legs. Around me," he said in a guttural tone.

I did as bid. He sank deeper, and together, we climbed higher and higher until we both came with a shattering release. He nearly collapsed on top of me and his breath fanned my skin. I hugged him to me, wanting his weight, but he refused to give it to me. Slowly, he disentangled from me, rolling onto the bed, propping himself up on his side. His hand came to rest on my belly before he leaned over to kiss it. I smiled.

"While that was very much needed, I'm afraid we can't lounge around. Allen Masterson is meeting us in the lobby in an hour."

Reluctantly, I got out of bed and headed back towar
bathroom. "I wanted to run an idea by you."

He followed me into the bathroom, and I turned on the
shower, waiting a few seconds for it to adjust before stepping
into the hot water. "It would be easier to talk to you if you
were in here with me," I purred.

"Don't tempt me more than I already am. Or we'll never
get to our meeting on time," he teased.

I shut the glass door of the shower and talked through it.
"You owe me one long honeymoon," I said. "Where we don't
have to get dressed if we don't want to."

"Barrett," he growled.

I laughed. "Okay, Flynn. I'll focus. I think I have an idea
of how to settle this thing with Winters. I want your opinion.
And if you like the idea, then we should run it by Masterson
and see what he says."

"I'm all ears."

Chapter 59

Flynn shook Masterson's hand and said, "Thanks for coming." He gestured for the high-profile attorney to sit at our designated table in The Rex Hotel Bar and Restaurant.

"Mrs. Campbell," Masterson greeted.

"Barrett, please," I corrected.

We sat down, my stomach growling. Flynn put a discreet hand to my belly and gestured for the waiter. He approached immediately. I ordered breakfast while the two gentlemen ordered lunch. I didn't think I could wait for food, so I asked for a breadbasket and then turned my attention back to Masterson, who sat across from us.

"Barrett had a great idea for how to get Winters off our back, but before we go ahead with it, we'd like your professional and legal council."

Masterson smiled, showing white teeth. The man didn't appear relaxed. Like most powerful men, he seemed to be at the ready for anything to jump out at him. His power was familiar, and I was glad for it. I quickly explained my idea, trying to gauge his reaction. He gave me nothing.

When I was finished, he took a sip of his mineral water and said, "It's risky, for sure. And I like risk. We don't know what kind of blowback to expect. However"—his dark eyes seemed to twinkle—"I think it's a great idea—and it will tie up Winters for a long time."

"That's what we're hoping for," Flynn said.

"I suggest you take care of it as soon as possible," Masterson said. "I wouldn't put it past Winters to get an arrest warrant."

I frowned. "Didn't he have one the other day when he questioned me? He said I was under arrest for the murder of Igor Dolinsky. I assumed he had a warrant. He isn't that stupid, is he?"

Masterson grinned, pure wolf in a suit. "The reason he held you so long and wouldn't let you call a lawyer was because he was waiting for a judge's signature."

"You mean he scooped me up before he had the power to?" I demanded, anger radiating through my body.

"Yes."

I looked at Flynn. "I'm going to destroy him."

"I like your wife," Masterson said as a waiter put down a dish in front of him.

"Makes two of us," Flynn answered.

"How did you know that? About detaining me while he got the signature?" I asked.

"I can't say," Masterson said.

Fair enough. We all had our secrets, we all had people in our pockets.

Lunch was a quick affair and after we said goodbye to Masterson, Flynn turned to me and asked, "You ready for this next part?"

"Ready for all this to be over with."

Did mob bosses get their happily ever afters? Guess I was about to find out.

～

"Well, isn't this a surprise," Adam Richards teased as he embraced me. "It's been how many years?"

"Two, I think," I said.

"And you called me because you want something."

"You'll want this just as much as me, I promise," I answered, pulling back. We were in the privacy of the penthouse suite with Sasha and Brad standing guard at our door. No one was getting past them. Contingency plan, considering I expected Fred Winters to show up randomly. He had a habit of doing that.

"Adam Richards," I introduced, "my husband, Flynn Campbell."

"Husband?" Adam asked, reaching out a hand toward Flynn. "Why didn't I hear anything about this?"

"It was quick," I said, waving my hand evasively.

"Is that why you called me? You want a wedding announcement in *The New York Times*? I have no jurisdiction over the wedding section."

"You think I care about that?" I demanded, putting my hands to my waist.

Adam and Flynn laughed. "Guess not," Adam said.

"Can I get you something to drink, Adam?" Flynn asked, heading toward the bar area.

"Sparkling water, thanks." He set down his messenger bag, pulling out his pen, paper, and iPhone to record the interview.

"Hen?" Flynn asked me.

"Sparkling water," I said with a small grin. "How have you been, Adam?"

"Good, busy," Adam said.

"Sheila?"

"All good. So tell me why you didn't go through with a society wedding," Adam asked me, taking his water from Flynn with a smile of thanks. Flynn handed me my glass and then sat next to me on the couch, his arm on top of the cushion, his fingers tickling my shoulder.

"Because it was expected," Flynn interjected. "So we did the opposite. And I don't believe in long engagements."

"He's a man that goes after what he wants," I said with a grin.

"How did you guys meet?" Adam asked.

"Another story for another day," I said, wanting to get on with why Adam was here.

"Okay, let's get started then." He reached for his iPhone to set up the recorder.

"One thing," I said. "This has to be anonymous. You can't reveal who we are."

Adam frowned. "Okay."

"Your word."

"My word. It's also my career and I'm not an idiot," he muttered.

"Well…" I teased.

"I see where this is going, so let me go ahead and put a stop to it. I'm turning on the recorder now, okay?"

"Okay." I looked at Flynn. "You ready for this?"

"Are you?"

"No turning back now." I leaned my head against him just for a moment. Taking a sip of water, I turned my attention back to my old college friend.

"We're recording," Adam said.

"Have you heard of Igor Dolinsky?" I began.

I made sure Flynn was completely asleep before I crawled out of bed. Closing the bedroom door, I crept into the living room and grabbed my phone. I dialed the number I knew by heart. He picked up on the second ring.

"Check fucking mate," I said before hanging up.

Smiling, I got back in bed, molded myself to Flynn's back, and fell asleep.

~

"Barrett."

I moaned.

"Barrett, come on, wake up," Flynn said.

"No. If I wake up, I'm going to have to puke, and I don't want to puke."

"I have *The New York Times*."

Somehow that did it. My eyes flew open, and just like clockwork, I hauled it to the bathroom and threw up. While I brushed my teeth, Flynn read the article to me. Adam had spelled out for his readers about Dolinsky and Marino, the illegal activities of the city, the power struggles, and how it ended in death for both of them. Adam wrote that someone close to Dolinsky had murdered him, wanting to usurp his place. Adam named Fred Winters as the cause for Giovanni Marino's death due to a botched take down. And finally, Adam blew the lid off Winters when he wrote that the FBI agent had made an arrest for Dolinsky's murder without a warrant.

No sooner had Flynn finished reading did his cell phone ring. He went to answer it, smiling into the phone and then handing it over to me.

"Hello?"

"Barrett, Allen Masterson."

"Hi, Allen."

"Just wanted to let you know all the charges against you have been dropped."

"Good news," I stated.

"Very. Read the article. Fred Winters's career is over. Enjoy the rest of your day."

We hung up and I handed Flynn's phone back to him. "I'm hungry. You hungry?"

He grinned, reaching for me. "Famished."

I went to him and jumped into his arms. Throwing my

head back, I shouted with laughter. I felt light, joyful, like all the weight of the world had been lifted from my shoulders. We were safe.

Everything was perfect.

Or so I thought—until his lips covered mine. Then I knew perfection.

Chapter 60

Flynn and I walked around the expansive three-thousand-square-foot penthouse apartment on 83rd and 5th, right across the street from Central Park. Large double pane glass windows let in the soft afternoon winter light and hit the dark wood floors.

I went into the kitchen, gliding my hand across the gray granite island. Passing steel appliances and custom designed wood cabinets, I headed for the sliding glass doors. Opening them, I stepped out onto the private balcony that wrapped around the corner of the building.

"What do you think?" Flynn asked, coming to stand next to me.

"The view is gorgeous," I admired.

"What about the rest of the apartment?"

"I don't know."

"What don't you know?" he asked.

"I'm having a hard time picturing it as a home. I went from my tiny, cluttered, prewar studio to a penthouse hotel suite. This"—I turned my back on the skyline to face the sliding doors of the apartment—"isn't either."

Flynn grasped my cold hand in his and pulled me inside.

We stood in the kitchen for a moment and he said, "Over there"—he pointed to the wall—"is where the kitchen table goes. Imagine Ash sitting there, drinking a glass of wine, telling you all the ways she's ruined Duncan for anyone else."

I chuckled, thinking about my best friend, who was currently in Scotland with a man who was nothing like her ex-fiancé.

Flynn led me out of the kitchen and back into the living room with a gas fireplace and the space for bookshelves along the walls, a gargantuan couch, and a baby grand piano. We walked down the hallway to the master bedroom with its own bathroom, including a state-of-the-art Jacuzzi tub, separate glass shower, and two sinks. "In here, we'll get a king-sized, canopy bed. At night, I'll hold you and rub your back when it gets sore."

"Go on," I whispered. "Paint me a picture."

He nodded and then guided me out of the master bedroom and opened the door next to it. "And this room will be the nursery," he stated. "With yellow giraffes and gray elephants. A mobile." His smile was slow. "A Campbell plaid."

My breath caught because I could see it. Everything he said.

"I don't just want a home with you, Barrett. I want a life."

"We can't start fresh," I said. "If that's what you're getting at."

"I know. I know there are things that I have to live with, but can't we move forward? I want to move forward."

Reaching up to caress his cheek, I took a deep breath. "Let's move forward. Let's make this place our home."

Fabric swatches and paint samples took up every available space of the living room. Redecorating wasn't complicated—not when all I had to do was make a choice. Flynn and I would hire people to paint and others to custom design our furniture.

The hotel phone rang and I answered it. It was the front desk, telling me that Jack Rhodes was here. I told them to send him up.

I hadn't seen or spoken to him since I stormed into his office and told him to keep quiet about Flynn and what he knew.

The elevator doors opened and I peered at Jack's face, trying to gauge his mood.

"Thanks for coming," I said.

"My secretary told me about your message." He came in and looked around the suite. "Redecorating?"

"We bought a place," I explained. "Would you like something to drink?"

"Can we cut the pleasantries?" Jack asked.

"If you want."

He nodded. "Why did you want to see me? You were pretty clear how you felt about me the last time we saw each other."

I sighed. "Jack—"

"And then you sent a message and expected me to come to you."

"I didn't think it was appropriate to come to your office."

"What do you want? I quit trying to bring down your husband. I stopped talking, okay?" He frowned. "I'm not like my sister, Barrett."

"How's that?"

"I have a hard time with the sliding scale of right and wrong."

"Life isn't black and white," I stated. "You know that. You've even been to Flynn's casino."

"That's different."

"It's illegal in the city. But still you've been. Still gambled.

Maybe you need to re-examine what you think is right and wrong."

Jack leaned forward and lowered his voice. "The SINS—"

"Enough," I cut him off. "I'm not discussing this with you. I love you, Jack. You're the brother Andrew always should've been. But we're not going to discuss this. Okay?"

"Fine. Should we talk about the fact that you threatened me," he stated coldly.

"Not outright."

"You are un-fucking-believable, do you know that? I don't even recognize the person you've become."

"Jack, I—" A wave of pain through my belly cut off whatever I'd been about to say. I placed my hand on the back of the couch to steady myself, my vision suddenly spotty.

"Barrett?" Jack's voice sounded far away.

"I'm pregnant," I said, swaying. "Something's wrong."

Jack's strong arms went around me, ushering me toward the elevator. I concentrated on breathing, but the nausea was debilitating.

"I've got you. You're going to be okay," he said, his words comforting in my ear.

And then I heard nothing.

The constant beeping brought me out of a doze. I looked around and realized I was in a hospital bed. Flynn jumped up from the chair next to me, his smile relieved.

"What happened?" I croaked, struggling to sit up.

"Easy," he stated, aiding me. Once I was settled back against the pillows, I looked up at him, waiting for him to explain. "Doctor said it was extreme stress. You have to remain calm." He set a gentle hand on my belly.

I sighed. "Stress. I was with Jack."

"I know. He brought you in. He's still in the waiting room."

"He hasn't left?"

Flynn shook his head. "I don't like him. But he took care of you. For that he'll always have my appreciation."

"I was trying to make amends," I explained. "I don't think it went over too well. He's angry."

"And hurt," Flynn said. "He thought he was protecting you."

"I'm not his to protect. But he is my friend and I hate that it all got so…"

"I know." He squeezed my arm. "Let me go tell a nurse you're awake."

I smoothed down the covers of the bed, resting a protective hand over my stomach. "I'm sorry," I whispered. It was my job to take care of the growing baby in my belly, and I hadn't even done that well. The baby had been a surprise, a shock. I hadn't wanted it, but I wanted it now.

Flynn returned, the doctor in tow. He was a middle-aged-man with a kind smile and tired brown eyes. Rotation must have gotten to him. "Mrs. Campbell, I'm Dr. Martin. How are you feeling?"

"Better."

"Good. You almost had a miscarriage, but we stopped it. Acute stress brought this on. I'd like to keep you here over night just to monitor you and the baby." He looked at Flynn. "Your job is to make sure she takes it easy."

"Done," Flynn said, shooting me a resolute look. "Bed rest it is. For the next month."

"That's a bit extreme," I protested. "Don't you think, Dr. Martin?"

"I agree with your husband. I think bed rest would be an excellent idea."

"You're all against me." Leaning my head back against the pillows, I sighed. "Thanks, Doctor."

"Glad you're feeling better." Dr. Martin nodded and then left.

"What am I going to do during a month on bed rest?" I demanded.

Flynn leaned over to kiss me on the forehead. "Let's see. You still have to choose the color schemes for the new apartment."

"Okay, that will be done in about five minutes."

"Doubtful. You can't even make up your mind."

I rolled my eyes.

"And you can finish planning our wedding reception."

"We're not still doing that, are we?"

"Why wouldn't we?"

"Because I'm pregnant."

"So?"

"So, I got pregnant like a minute and a half after we got married."

"And?"

I glowered. "I don't think I'd be able to enjoy it—and it would turn into a baby party instead of being what it's supposed to be."

He smiled. "Okay."

"Really?"

"Sure."

"What about your image? My image? As your wife?"

"When have I ever cared what people thought about me?"

"Point taken," I said. "I have an idea, though. Why don't we donate the money we would've spent on the reception? We'll pick a good charity."

He raised an eyebrow. "Anonymously?"

I shrugged and then closed my eyes. "I want to get some sleep."

"What about all your visitors?"

"How many are there?"

"Well, there's Jack, Sasha, Lacey, Brad, Alia, Shawna,

Renee, and someone else—young, scared of her own shadow."

"Jamie," I said. "The newest cocktail waitress and dancer."

"Ash keeps calling me to check up on you. I'm going to let her know you're okay."

"Tell everyone thanks for coming," I said, emotion constricting my throat. "But I'm not up for visitors."

Flynn kissed my forehead and then my lips. "I'll let them know. On my way, I'll ask a nurse for a cot so I can sleep in your room."

"I'd like that," I whispered, tired and drained. Flynn kissed me once more, turned out the light and then left.

The next morning, I woke up to a disheveled husband and hospital food. "Don't even think about eating that stuff," Flynn commanded.

I glanced at the lime green JELL-O. "Yeah, I was going to pass, anyway." I pushed the tray away from me. "Can we please get out of here? I want to go home."

Picking up his wrinkled gray suit jacket, he kissed me good morning and said, "I'll go see to your discharge."

I swung my legs over the side of the bed, hating the draft I felt in the hospital gown. Looking around, I saw a small suitcase underneath Flynn's cot, not at all surprised to find it. I leaned down to retrieve it when I heard a voice behind me say, "Should you be doing that?"

I turned, finding Sasha standing in the doorway. I smiled. "I think I can handle it. It's not heavy."

He came into the room and before I could pick up the suitcase, he did it for me, putting it on the hospital bed. "Thanks," I said, riffling through my things, feeling a bit embarrassed when I caught sight of the black lacy panties. I looked up and caught sight of Sasha's blush.

"Not this," I muttered. "Anything but this."

"What?" he demanded.

"Are things going to be awkward for us now?"

"I don't want them to be," he said with sincerity.

"I trust you," I said softly. "In ways that I never thought I could trust another person."

"I'm here for you. I'm not going anywhere."

"I don't question your devotion—never that. But how can I—we—I'm married. I'm having a baby."

His eyes were pained, tortured. I loved Sasha, but only as my friend. I could get past his sentiments, but I wasn't sure he could. "I don't think we should see each other for a little while."

"What?" he asked, startled.

"We should take some time apart. So you can—to come to terms with—"

"I don't need time," he protested.

"Sasha," I begged. "I am so grateful that you came into my life when you did. But I will not take you for granted. If you won't do this for you, then do it for me."

We stared at each other for a long moment, his blue eyes bright. Finally, he nodded. Without another word, he turned and left. And I didn't know if I'd ever see him again.

Chapter 61

Flynn reached over and took my hand as the car jerked to a stop halfway in between two lanes of Manhattan traffic. Horns honked and cab drivers yelled.

"You're quiet," he said.

I squeezed his fingers, loving their warmth, their strength, but it was Sasha who was on my mind. My heart was heavy, and I already felt his absence. Something had happened when Dolinsky had kidnapped me. Sasha and I had connected, in a way that was complete, but for me platonic. I trusted him, without a doubt, but never as a potential lover.

"Sasha is in love with me," I said.

"I know."

I looked at Flynn whose face wasn't masked in jealousy. He understood, I realized. "How did you know?"

He shrugged. "I saw him look at you with uncontrolled longing, and just as quickly, I saw him conceal it."

"Does he know? That you know, I mean?" I wondered.

"Aye."

"You guys ever talk about it."

"No."

"Typical," I muttered. "Why didn't you tell me?"

"I tried to."

"When?"

"When I accused you of having an affair with him."

"*That's* what that was about?" I demanded. "Jesus, Flynn."

"I wanted to know if you felt the way he did, but I also didn't really want the truth."

"Well, obviously," I said. "Who really wants to hear that?"

"No one," he stated.

"Nothing has ever happened between us. You have to believe me."

"I know that." His fingers skimmed my knuckles, and I felt my pulse steady.

"I gave him some time—to himself. To get over—if he can—"

Flynn was silent, turning to look out the window.

"Do you think he can? Get over his feelings for me?" I asked.

"I don't know, Barrett," he said honestly. "His love for you runs deep."

"I need him."

"What the fuck?" Flynn tried to pull his hand from mine, but I wouldn't let him.

"Let me explain, if I can," I said, holding tight. "When I was with Dolinsky, Sasha and I... I don't know, bonded. He's been nothing but loyal and there for me, even going as far as turning on his leader, his oldest friend."

"Because he loves you and he was trying to win you."

"No, I don't think that's it." I ran my tongue across my suddenly dry lips. "I think Sasha was looking for something to believe in. I think Dolinsky was breaking him, leaching him of hope. I don't know. What you and I, and Marino and Dolinsky do—did—it's all a matter of gray, right? But I think Sasha has a clear view of right and wrong, for him anyway. Maybe it's all bullshit, but I think I...inspired him? Showed him we can live in this world and still have some sort of moral code."

"That's convoluted."

"And just a theory. I also think a part of him was waiting for me to turn on you—for Dolinsky. And when I didn't or wouldn't, it was just another reason for Sasha to believe in me and offer me his unwavering friendship."

"I believe in you," Flynn said. "I believe in your strength and bravery, your intelligence."

"I know you believe in me. It's just—"

"Different."

We drove the rest of the way to The Rex in silence. When we pulled up to the curb, Flynn helped me out of the car and gestured to the bellman to come and grab my suitcase.

"Is that really necessary?" I asked. "It's tiny."

Flynn didn't listen to me and waved the bellman on. He lifted me into his arms and carried me across the lobby. Guests and employees of the hotel smiled and waved. I tried not to be embarrassed, but I hated looking helpless.

"What are you doing?" I asked Flynn quietly.

He maneuvered me so that I was able to press the button for our private elevator. "Taking care of you."

"This is absurd," I said as Flynn stepped into the elevator. "You know that, right?"

He said nothing as the elevator ascended. The doors opened, and I saw a welcome home sign. Ash and Lacey stood in the living room, smiling in excitement.

"What are you doing here?" I demanded at Ash. "You're supposed to be in Scotland."

"Your husband sent his private jet," she explained.

Flynn set me down onto the couch and pointed a finger at me. "Do not move."

"What if I have to pee?" I asked.

Flynn rolled his eyes and looked between Lacey and Ash.

"Don't let her move. I'm trusting you both to keep her sufficiently entertained while she rests."

Ash saluted. "Aye, aye captain."

"I'll be back in a few hours," Flynn said, leaning down to kiss me.

"Where are you going?"

"I'm giving you some girl time."

When we were alone, Ash said, "Your husband is something special."

"I think so."

"Want something to drink?" Lacey asked, heading to the refrigerator.

"Please. Sparkling water?"

"You got it."

"You didn't have to come back from Scotland," I said to Ash.

She smiled. "Yes, I did. Malcolm and Duncan send their regards."

"You've met Malcolm." I grinned.

"I love that craggy, grumpy old man."

"Me too," I said.

"My brother sends his regards, too."

I swallowed when I thought of Jack. Lacey returned with three glasses of water and handed me one, setting the other two on the coffee table. She took a seat in the chair next to the couch and crossed her ankles.

"How's Jack?" I asked. "Flynn told me he was in the hospital waiting room."

"He feels like shit," Ash said. "He thinks he's the reason you wound up in the hospital."

"He's not the reason. The doctor said I almost miscarried due to stress. I've been a bit frazzled lately."

"Understatement," Lacey said. "So, can I ask a question?"

"Yeah."

"A personal question," she clarified.

I squirmed but nodded.

"Flynn might've confided in me how you felt about children," Lacey began. "How did you go from not wanting kids to wanting kids?"

"Oh, that is personal," Ash said. "But I want to know the answer to that, too."

"Knowing what you're going to do when you're hypothetically pregnant isn't always the same as what you're going to do when you're *actually* pregnant," I said in an attempt to explain. "Besides, I don't want kids. I want *Flynn's* kids."

"Kids plural?"

"Shut up, Ash."

She grinned.

"Now, can I ask *you* a personal question?" I said with a glance at Lacey. "How long have you been sleeping with Brad?"

Lacey's eyes widened. "How did you——"

"I paid a visit to The Fifteenth Floor one night not too long ago."

"Did you tell Flynn?" she asked, the color high in her cheeks.

"No. It wasn't my secret to tell." I cocked my head to the side. "How long has it been going on?"

"Ah, it's been brewing for a while," Lacey admitted.

"Is it something serious or are you just scratching an itch?" I wondered. "I'm asking because Flynn counts on both of you, trusts both of you, and you've all worked together for years."

Lacey remained quiet and I nodded.

There were some things you wanted to keep to yourself.

I looked at Ash. "What about you? I want to hear everything that happened between you and Duncan. Start at the beginning."

"I'll tell you stuff," Ash said with a grin. "But I want a real drink while I do it."

~

Flynn's fingers slid along my belly as he shifted closer. Night had fallen and moonlight peeked through the curtains, allowing me to see in the dark. We were in bed and I was content having him next to me.

I ran a hand down his cheek, my thumb lingering on his lips.

"Did I wake you?" he asked.

"No, I was awake."

Flynn patted his chest and I moved into his arms, resting my head against his heart. I breathed in and sighed.

"You all right?"

"I am," I said. "Just thinking."

"About?"

"Are we still going to London in a few months? To open your new hotel?"

Flynn's hand stroked my hair, his fingers weaving in and out of the strands. "Yes."

"Why haven't you opened a hotel in London yet? It's one of the major cities of the world."

"Truth time?"

"Always."

"For a while, Malcolm hated the idea of having anything to do with the English. But then I pointed out that we could make money from them and use it to aid our cause."

"So in essence, funnel English money into freeing Scotland."

"Exactly."

I frowned. "How did Malcolm become the leader of the SINS?"

"His father. It's passed down, father to son."

"What happens if you don't agree with him and his edicts?"

"Me? Or the faction?"

"The faction. Are there coups?"

"There have been in the past. Why do you ask?"

"Just curious about how it all works. If there was a coup against Malcolm, would Duncan still take over?"

"Doubt it. Unless he planned the coup. Luckily, we don't have to think about it. Everyone is happy with Malcolm's leadership, and the SINS is growing, and we have a real chance at our goal."

"That's good."

"Very good," he agreed. "We bought an apartment, we're fixing up the nursery, we're happy, Barrett. We're so happy."

I breathed in a sigh of contentment, my eyes closing.

"Everything is perfect," I said.

For now.

Additional Works

Writing as Emma Slate

SINS Series:
Sins of a King (Book 1)
Birth of a Queen (Book 2)
Rise of a Dynasty (Book 3)
Dawn of an Empire (Book 4)
Ember (Book 5)
Burn (Book 6)
Ashes (Book 7)

The Spider Queen

Writing as Samantha Garman

The Sibby Series:
Queen of Klutz (Book 1)
Sibby Slicker (Book 2)
Mother Shucker (Book 3)

From Stardust to Stardust

About the Author

Emma Slate writes on the run. The dangerous alpha men she writes about aren't thrilled that she's sharing their stories for your enjoyment. So far, she's been able to evade them by jet setting around the world. She wears only black leather because it's bad ass...and hides blood.

Printed in Great Britain
by Amazon